# Never Less Than a Lady

**Center Point
Large Print**

Also by Mary Jo Putney
and available from Center Point Large Print:

The *Lost Lords* Series
*Loving a Lost Lord*

# Never Less Than a Lady

# MARY JO PUTNEY

CENTER POINT PUBLISHING
THORNDIKE, MAINE

This Center Point Large Print edition
is published in the year 2010 by arrangement with
Kensington Publishing Corp.

The text of this Large Print edition is unabridged.
In other aspects, this book may vary
from the original edition.
Printed in the United States of America.
Set in 16-point Times New Roman type.

ISBN: 978-1-60285-771-1

Library of Congress Cataloging-in-Publication Data

Putney, Mary Jo.
  Never less than a lady / Mary Jo Putney. — Center Point large print ed.
    p. cm.
  Originally published: New York, NY : Kensington Pub., 2010.
  ISBN 978-1-60285-771-1 (lib. bdg. : alk. paper)
  1. Large type books. I. Title.
  PS3566.U83N48 2010
  813'.54—dc22

                                                    2010003381

In memory of Rose Curtain,
who brightened any room she entered.

# ACKNOWLEDGMENTS

To my usual patient writing buddies, who know that listening to each other wail is part of the writing process.

Special thanks to Fiona McArthur, author and midwife, for help with technical information, such as the fact that speaking cheerfully to a woman in labor could be grounds for justifiable homicide!

Also, once again I thank ER nurse Laurie Kingery for her help in pursuing the best and most convincing ways to maul my hero.

As always, any errors are mine.

# Prologue

*Spain, 1812*

War was hell. Letters from relatives could be worse.

The day had been full of musket balls and skirmishing. Randall returned to his tent limping, dusty, and wanting to sleep for twelve hours.

Washing off the dust was easy. His highly competent batman, Gordon, had water waiting. Sleep was in shorter supply. Relief from his aching thigh was nonexistent.

Today Randall had lost one of his soldiers, a raw Irish recruit with an eager smile, which meant that a letter must be written to the boy's family. It was the worst part of being an officer, but every life deserved recognition, and every family deserved to know how one of their own was lost.

"The post from England, sir." Gordon handed Randall three sealed letters.

Randall thumbed through them. One from the Duke of Ashton. His old school friend was his best correspondent. Another from Kirkland, also a school friend and reliable. And the last . . .

He stared down at the arrogant signature that franked the letter. Daventry. The bane of his existence. Randall had been five when his parents died of fever. He'd been left in the guardianship of his uncle, the Earl of Daventry.

The years that followed were the worst of Randall's life. He had been brought to the Daventry seat, Turville Park, and put in the nursery with the heir, nine-year-old Lord Branford. Large for his age and with an arrogance that would have been impressive even in an adult, Branford had been a brute and a bully. Randall had learned to fight early.

Since the heir could do no wrong, Randall was packed off to school at a tender age. In fact, he'd been sent to several schools, some of England's finest. After being expelled from them in rapid succession, he'd ended up at the Westerfield Academy. As the school's owner and headmistress, Lady Agnes Westerfield, liked to say, it was for boys of good birth and bad behavior.

In the school that Daventry regarded as punishment, Randall had found kindness and friendship. He had endured holidays at Turville with stoicism and clenched fists. He hated Daventry and Branford, and they had despised him in turn. Fortunately he'd inherited a comfortable income. When Randall left school, he bought a pair of colors and joined the army, ignoring his grand connections as thoroughly as they ignored him.

Until now. Wondering what the devil Daventry had to say to him, Randall broke the wax seal and scanned the few lines written in the earl's bold hand.

*Your cousin Rupert Randall is dead. You are now heir presumptive to Daventry. You must sell your commission and return home. I will expect you to choose a wife and marry within the next year.*

Randall stared at the heavy paper, feeling the bitterness in the words. Branford had died years before in some kind of drunken accident, and Daventry's other son, a sickly child, had died young. But there were any number of cousins nearer to the title than Major Alexander Randall.

He thought about the family tree. Actually, the number wasn't that great—the Randalls didn't seem to be good breeders. The other heirs had mostly been older—Randall's father had been a much younger half brother to the current earl. Apparently the intervening cousins were all gone now and hadn't left any sons.

Randall frowned as he realized that there was no one after him. Otherwise, Daventry would probably have hoped that his despised nephew would die in battle or fever so that the next in line would become the heir presumptive. But there was no next in line, and Daventry was fiercely proud of the title. Even the prospect that the earldom would go to a man he loathed was better than knowing the title would disappear.

Randall's instant reaction to Daventry's order

was to refuse, as he always did when his uncle gave orders. But he was a grown man now, not a boy, and the idea of selling out was rather appealing. He was weary of war, weary of the ceaseless pain of a leg that had never fully recovered from a wound the year before. The army didn't need him. Though he was a good officer, there were others equally as good.

With a sigh, he folded up Daventry's letter. Returning to civilian life would be easy.

Finding a wife would be harder.

# Chapter 1

*London*

The grand sprawl of Ashton House was a welcome sight after Randall's long journey home from Spain. The mansion was the largest private residence in London, and Randall never entered without thinking how much more impressive it was than Daventry House, his uncle's London home.

Since the place was far too large for one man, the Duke of Ashton had given Randall his own set of rooms for use whenever he was in London. More than anywhere else, Ashton House was home. The place where he was always greeted with pleasure.

The butler, Holmes, almost smiled. "Major

Randall, welcome! I shall inform his grace that you've arrived."

Randall shook raindrops off his hat before handing it over. "The duke and duchess are in residence?"

"Very much so." Ash's familiar voice came from behind. Randall turned to see his friends entering the wide foyer.

Mariah, blond and beautiful and glowing with warmth, swept forward and hugged Randall. "What a lovely surprise! Will you be staying in London long?"

"Long enough for you to tire of me." Randall hugged her back, thinking what a lucky man Ash was.

"Take a few minutes to refresh yourself, then join us in the family dining room." Ash took his wife's arm. "We're dining informally so no need to change, but we have a guest you'll enjoy. We can hear everyone's news at once."

With such an appealing prospect, Randall took only a few minutes to wash up and produce a general look of respectability before heading downstairs. As he entered the family dining room, a familiar dark, compact figure set down his glass of wine and crossed the room to greet him. "Ballard!" Randall seized his old friend's hand. "I assumed you were in Portugal."

"And I thought you were in Spain." Justin Ballard shook hands with equal enthusiasm, his gray eyes bright in his tanned face. His family owned a famous port company, and he was in charge of Portuguese operations. "I had business in London and it was a good time to return. I like to remind myself that I'm British every year or two."

"The London weather will take care of that very quickly," Randall said as he accepted a claret from Ashton. He could feel his tension unwinding as the warm atmosphere embraced him. It was good to be home with friends, and the buoyant Ballard was a particular pleasure. It had been several years since they had last seen each other in Lisbon. "How are things in Oporto?"

"Much better now that you army laddies have moved the war into Spain." Ballard retrieved his wineglass and took a sip. "Are you home on leave now?"

Randall shook his head. "I've recently become the heir presumptive to Daventry, so it's time to return to civilian life."

"You're selling out?" Ashton asked, startled. "That's unexpected."

Randall shrugged. "Technically I'm not selling out, but giving the commission to a qualified captain without the means to pay the purchase price."

"That's generous," Ballard observed as they moved to the waiting dinner table.

"Not really. Seeing this particular captain take

over my duties means I can leave with a clear conscience."

Mariah studied him with wide brown eyes. "Will you miss the army?"

"There are people I'll miss," he said slowly. "But on the whole, I'm ready to leave. I've never been fond of army discipline. If there wasn't a war on, I would have been court-martialed for insubordination several times over." The others laughed, though it was more truth than joke.

Ashton said sympathetically, "As heir, I suppose now you'll be told it's your obligation to wed and produce another heir. I was subjected to such pressures for years." He glanced at his wife, his expression warm. "It's worth waiting for the right woman."

"I do not expect to be so fortunate as you." He raised his glass to the duchess in an informal toast. "There is only one Mariah."

"Flatterer," she scoffed. "When first we met, you thought I was a fortune hunter who had sunk my evil claws into Ash when he was helpless."

"True," he admitted, "but I was willing to admit my error."

"So very generous of you!" she said teasingly. "As to there being only one Mariah, remember that I have an identical twin sister. Sarah looks almost exactly like me, and having been raised normally, she's far better qualified to be a peeress."

"Having been raised normally makes her less interesting than you," he said instantly. Though the comment was lighthearted, it was also true. Mariah's unconventional upbringing had made her an intriguing woman. She had depths and resilience more "normal" misses lacked.

"You really are getting skilled at flattery. A useful talent if you're in the market for a wife." Mariah's gaze showed female calculation.

"Surely you're too fond of your sister to wish my bad temper on her!"

"There is that," she agreed, "but you'd make such a handsome couple. Think of the lovely blond children you'd have together!"

"If we're promoting the marriageability of sisters, my sister Kiri would be worth considering," Ashton said, only half-joking. "You'll only be an earl, of course, but since she's the daughter of a duke, it will be hard to marry up to her rank."

"I have a sister, too," Ballard interjected. "Granted, she's only fourteen, but she shows promise of being an excellent countess." He grinned. "She would prefer to become a princess, but I've explained there simply aren't enough princes to go around."

"All of your sisters are far too good for me," Randall said firmly. "I expect I'll look for a wife eventually, but I'm in no hurry. It would be deplorable if Daventry actually thought I was obeying him in this."

"Rushing to the altar would be foolish," Ashton agreed. "And your inheritance isn't guaranteed, since Daventry might still have a son."

"Possibly, but his wife is at that awkward age," Randall said. "Too old for childbearing, but young enough to probably outlive her husband."

Ash frowned. "Given his appalling behavior to you, might Daventry find a way to remove his present wife so he could acquire a younger one?"

"You mean would he push his countess down the stairs to be rid of her?" Randall shook his head. "Despite Daventry's occasional desire to see me dead, I doubt he's a murderer, and he's fond of his current wife. She's his third. He's had bad luck with wives and offspring, and a new wife wouldn't necessarily improve the situation."

"If I recall correctly, there aren't any other known heirs," Ballard commented. "Now he'll have to come to terms with you."

"I suppose, but not right away. I'll send Daventry a note that I'm out of the army, but rather than call on him now, I think I'll go to Scotland. Visit Kirkland. Enjoy fresh, cool air that doesn't have musket balls flying through it."

"That's sensible." Mariah's eyes twinkled. "If you're going to Scotland, you might want to stop by Hartley since it's not far out of your way. My sister may be more interesting than you remember."

"I shall consider it." Randall applied himself to his roast beef and Yorkshire pudding. Mariah was right about her sister. Sarah was exactly the kind of girl he should marry—attractive, sensible, capable of fulfilling the responsibilities of a countess when the time came. She would make someone an excellent wife.

But the only female to have caught Randall's interest in the last decade was a woman, not a girl. And she was certainly not a lady in the view of society. Mrs. Bancroft—Julia—was a widowed midwife and healer in Hartley, and a good friend of Mariah's. She was reserved to the point of invisibility, and she'd certainly shown no signs of interest in Randall. She was entirely unsuitable.

Yet she haunted him.

If he visited the Townsends, he could also see Julia. It was a foolish thought.

But irresistible.

# Chapter 2

"Mrs. Bancroft?" a light female voice called as the bells on the cottage door rang to indicate a visitor. "It's me, Ellie Flynn."

"Good afternoon, Ellie." Julia moved from the kitchen into her examining room, taking the young woman's toddler into her arms. "How is Master Alfred feeling today?"

"Much better, Mrs. Bancroft." The woman smiled fondly at her redheaded son, who was reaching for Julia's cat. "That horehound and honey tea you gave me helped his cough right smartly."

"The Duchess of Ashton's cough remedy." Julia looked the little boy over. He grinned back at her. "The name alone is halfway to being a cure."

The tea was a recipe she'd learned from her friend Mariah, who hadn't been a duchess then. Mariah had been raised by a grandmother who was a village healer not unlike Julia, but more knowledgeable about herbs. Julia had learned a few simple remedies from the mid-wife who had trained her, but Mariah knew many more, and her recipes had been a good addition to Julia's store of treatments.

She handed the little boy back to his mother. "He's flourishing. You're doing a fine job raising him, Ellie."

"I couldn't have done it without your help. When he was born, I hardly knew which end was which!" Ellie, also redheaded and no more than nineteen, shyly offered a worn canvas bag. "I've some nice fresh eggs for you, if you'd like them."

"Lovely! I've been wanting an egg for my tea." Julia accepted the bag and moved to the kitchen of her cottage, removing the eggs from their straw packing so she could return the bag. She never turned away a mother or child in need, so while many of her patients couldn't afford to pay in cash, Julia and her household ate well.

After Mrs. Flynn and her little boy left, Julia sat at her desk and wrote notes about patients she'd seen that day. Whiskers, her tabby cat, snoozed beside her. After finishing her notes, Julia sat back and petted the cat as she surveyed her kingdom.

Rose Cottage had two reception rooms at the front of the house. She used this one as an office for treating patients and storing remedies. The other front chamber was her sitting room. Kitchen, pantry, and a bedroom ran across the back of the cottage. A slant-roofed but spacious second bedroom was up the narrow stairs.

Behind the cottage was a stable for her placid pony, and a garden that produced herbs and vegetables. The flowers in front of the cottage were there simply because she believed that everyone needed flowers.

Rose Cottage was not what she'd been raised to, but that life had turned out very badly. This life was so much better. She had her own home, friends, and she provided a vital service for this remote community. With no physicians nearby, she had become more than a midwife. She set bones and treated wounds and minor illnesses. Some claimed she was better than the doctors in Carlisle. Certainly she was cheaper.

Though her trip to London several months earlier as Mariah's chaperone had left her restless, she was mostly content in Hartley. She would never have a child of her own, but she had many children in her life, as well as the respect of the community. She took pride in the fact that she'd built this life for herself with her own hard work.

The front door opened and a young woman bustled in, a toddler on one hip and a canvas bag slung over her shoulder. Julia smiled at the other two members of her household. "You're back early, Jenny. How are Mrs. Wolf and Annie?"

Jenny Watson beamed. "Happy and healthy. Since I delivered Annie myself, whenever I see her I'm as proud as if I'd invented babies."

Julia laughed. "I know the feeling. Helping a baby into the world is a joy."

Jenny reached into her bag. "Mr. Wolf sent along a nice bit of bacon."

"That will go well with Ellie Flynn's eggs."

"I'll fix us our tea then." Jenny headed into the kitchen and set her daughter in a cradle by the hearth. Molly, fourteen months old, yawned hugely and curled up for a nap.

Julia watched the child fondly. Jenny was not the first desperate pregnant girl who had shown up on Julia's doorstep, but she was the only one to become part of the household. Jenny had married a man against her family's wishes. Her family had turned their backs when he abandoned her, saying that she'd made her bed and must lie in it.

Near starvation, Jenny had offered to work as Julia's servant for no wages, only food and a roof over her head. The girl had proved to be clever and a hard worker, and after Molly's birth, she became Julia's apprentice. She was well on her way to becoming a fine midwife, and she and her child had become Julia's family.

Jenny had just called, "Our tea is ready!" when the string of bells that hung on the front door jangled.

Julia made a face. "I wish I had a shilling for every time I've been interrupted during a meal!"

She stood—then froze with horror at the sight of the three men who entered her home. Two were strangers, but the burly scar-faced leader was familiar. Joseph Crockett, the vilest man she'd ever known, had found her.

"Well, well, well. So Lady Julia really is alive," he said menacingly as he pulled a glittering knife from a sheath under his coat. "That can be fixed."

Whiskers hissed and dashed into the kitchen while Julia backed away from him, numb with panic.

After years of quiet hiding, she was a dead woman.

The pretty maid who answered the door of Hartley Manor bobbed a curtsy as she recognized the caller. "I'm sorry, Major Randall, but the

Townsends are away from home. A niece of Mrs. Townsend is getting married down south, so they decided to attend the wedding."

During Randall's pleasant fortnight in Scotland with his friend Kirkland, he toyed with the idea of visiting Mariah's family, but he hadn't made up his mind until he reached the road that followed the Cumberland coast west to Hartley. He liked the Townsends and there was no harm in calling on them, even if he wasn't interested in courting Sarah. And if he chanced to see Julia Bancroft—perhaps that would cure him of his unfortunate attraction.

Impulses didn't always work out well. He gave one of his cards to the maid. "Please let them know I called."

The girl frowned at the card. "It's getting late, sir. Mr. and Mrs. Townsend will be right unhappy with me if you don't spend the night here as a guest of the house."

Randall hesitated only a moment. There was a decent little inn down in the village, but he'd had a long day, his leg ached, and he was traveling alone since his servant and former batman, Gordon, was visiting his own family. Randall and his horses deserved a rest. "Does Mrs. Beckett still reign in the kitchen?"

The maid smiled impishly. "She does indeed, sir, and she'd be pleased to have a hungry man to feed."

"Then I accept your kind invitation most gratefully." He descended the stairs to take his light travel carriage and horses around to the stable. While he wouldn't be seeing Sarah Townsend, surely manners dictated that he pay a call on Mrs. Bancroft in the morning before resuming his journey south.

Useful things, manners.

Joseph Crockett stepped close and touched the tip of his knife to Julia's throat. As she stood rigid, wondering if she was going to die right here and now, he growled, "You're going to take a ride with us, your ladyship. You know who will be at the end of it." He applied enough pressure to pierce the skin. As a drop of blood oozed down her neck, he added, "Mind you behave, or I'll cut your throat. No one will blame me if I have to kill a murderess."

A horrified gasp sounded from the door of the kitchen as Jenny appeared, drawn by the voices. Crockett cursed and spun toward her, raising the knife.

"No!" Julia grabbed his wrist. "For the love of God, don't hurt her! Jenny can do you no harm."

"She might raise the alarm after I take you," he growled.

Molly wobbled into sight, her round face scrunched with worry as she grabbed her mother's skirt. Jenny scooped up the child and backed into the kitchen, her eyes terrified.

"Get her!" Crockett snapped.

The younger of the other two men moved after Jenny and took her arm so she could retreat no further. "Killing a mother and her babe would raise a hue and cry for sure," the man said. "I can tie the lass so she won't be able to escape till tomorrow. We'll be far away before anyone notices anything wrong."

After an agonizingly long pause, Crockett said grudgingly, "Very well, tie the chit up. We'll leave as soon as you're done."

Voice not quite steady, Julia said, "Since I'm not coming back, I'd like to write a note saying I leave the cottage and its contents to Jenny."

"Ever the lady bountiful," he said brusquely. "Be quick about it."

After she scrawled the two sentences that were her last will and testament, Crockett scanned the paper to see if she'd said anything about her fate. Satisfied, he dropped it on her worktable. "Get your shawl. There's a long journey ahead."

She did as he ordered, collecting her warm, shabby shawl and bonnet. Was there anything else she should take?

Dead women needed nothing. Ignoring Crockett, she went to the Windsor chair Jenny was tied to and gave the girl a hug. "I leave you my cottage and everything else." She bent and kissed Molly, who hid behind her mother's skirts. "You're a good midwife, Jenny. Don't worry about me. I . . . I've had more good years than I expected."

"What is all this about?" her friend whispered, tears on her cheeks.

"Justice," Crockett snapped.

"The less you know, the better. Goodbye, my dear." Julia wrapped her shawl around her shoulders and turned to the door.

Crockett raised several coils of chain. "Now, to make sure you can't run off, your ladyship." He snapped a manacle around her left wrist and jerked her toward him like a leashed animal.

The chain came near to breaking her. She would drop to her knees and beg for her life if she thought it would do any good. But Crockett would laugh at her weakness. Since death was inevitable, she'd face it with her head high and her dignity intact.

She had nothing else left.

Julia walked outside, chain clanking. A plain closed carriage waited, a driver on the box. Four villainous men to one undersized midwife. There would be no escape.

Crockett opened the door and pointed her to the corner seat on the far side from the door. Then he sat next to her, the chain firmly in his grasp. When Crockett and his minions were in place, the carriage set off.

Numbly she gazed out the window as they drove through Hartley. When the village fell behind them, she closed her eyes and suppressed her tears. She'd been happy here at the far edge of the world.

But it hadn't been far enough.

# Chapter 3

Randall was halfway through a plate of Mrs. Beckett's chops when he heard pounding at the door of Hartley Manor. The sound was so frantic that he considered answering the door himself, but the chops were excellent.

A few moments later, voices sounded from the front hall as the door was opened. Hearing the name "Mrs. Bancroft" yanked him from his chair and sent him striding to the front hall. Emma, the pretty maid who had invited him to stay earlier, looked shocked as she talked to a young woman with anxious eyes and bloody wrists. Something was very wrong. He snapped, "What has happened to Mrs. Bancroft?"

"Three men came and took her away!" The young woman wiped at her teary eyes. "I'm Jenny Watson, her apprentice. My baby and I live with her. The men who took her tied me up. When I managed to get free, I came here hoping for Mr. Townsend's help, but Emma says he's away. I don't know what else to do!"

Randall's fear kicked up higher. "Do you know why they took her?"

"The man called her Lady Julia, but that might just have been to be mean. He said they were taking her for justice." Jenny swallowed hard. "He said that . . . that she was a murderess. But that's impossible!"

Randall also had trouble imagining that, but no matter. His first consideration was to rescue Julia from her kidnappers. "What exactly was said?"

The girl took a deep breath, then recounted the conversation she'd overheard. "They're taking her on a long journey," she ended. "And . . . and she doesn't expect to come back alive. She wrote a note leaving her cottage and everything in it to me." The tears started again. "I don't want the house! I want Mrs. Bancroft back safe!"

"How long is it since they left?"

Jenny furrowed her brows. "Maybe an hour, or a little more."

He glanced at her bloodied wrists. "How did you escape your bonds so quickly? You dragged your hands out?"

"They didn't tie my Molly," Jenny explained. "She's only fourteen months so they left her free. After they left, I had her bring me a knife so I could cut myself loose."

"Clever girl," he said approvingly. "Were the accents English or Scottish?"

"English. Southern English."

"So they'll probably take the road east to Carlisle, then head south into England rather than north to Scotland." He turned to Emma. "Mr. Townsend had a fine blood bay, Grand Turk. Is the horse here?"

"Yes, sir."

"I'll take him then. Have the horse saddled."

"Be careful, sir," Jenny said. "They're dangerous men. I . . . I don't want to think what they'll do to Mrs. Bancroft."

"If they wanted her dead, they would have killed her when they found her. She is safe until they reach their destination, and I will find her before then. I promise you that." He spun on his heel and headed to his room while he thought about what he needed to take. Money and his hat and cloak, plus a pack with bread and cheese and ale so he wouldn't have to stop to eat.

Luckily, he always traveled well armed.

On his way through Hartley, Randall paused to talk to old Mrs. Morse, who was working in her garden and saw all the local comings and goings. After getting as many details as he could of the carriage's appearance, he headed east toward Carlisle. Grand Turk was as good a horse as Randall remembered, his long strides eating up the distance.

There were no posting houses on this road, so

the kidnappers would be unable to replace the horses tired by the drive to Hartley. With luck, he would catch up with them before they reached Carlisle. Once the devils reached a busier road, they would be harder to track.

They must know that pursuit was unlikely. Even if Charles Townsend, the most prominent man in the area, had been home, he wouldn't have been able to do much. Plus, the poor road would slow their pace. A pity that Randall's servant Gordon was visiting his family. Randall was quite capable of looking after himself on the trip to Scotland, and Gordon had certainly earned a holiday. But he was a good man in a fight, and his presence could be useful here.

No matter. Randall had surprise on his side. With luck, he could get Julia away with no one getting killed. Though if killing was necessary . . .

He settled into the horse's ground-eating trot. His leg ached like the devil and would get worse, but it would last for as long as necessary.

As he rode into the darkening sky, he wondered what Julia would do after he rescued her. Her kidnappers knew where she lived, so she would never be safe in Hartley again.

Another solution must be found.


Julia's captors rode steadily on as night fell. In the dampest, cloudiest corner of England, why did this particular night have to be clear?

There were no inns or posting houses, but a couple of hours along the road, the carriage stopped briefly and the youngest man, Haggerty, retrieved a sack of food and a jug of ale from the luggage area in back.

As the carriage started up again, a cold meat pie was thrust into Julia's hands. She tried to eat the dry pastry, but it was like clay in her mouth.

"Here, your ladyship." Crockett offered her the jug. She shook her head. Though she was thirsty, she didn't want to drink from the same jug he'd used.

Giving up on the meat pie, she stared out the window at the empty landscape. The rough, mostly bare hills were pale and uncanny. Though not yet full, the moon was bright enough to light the road as long as the pace was moderate.

How long would this journey take? A week, perhaps. She tried not to think of what awaited her at the end. A quick death, she hoped. Torture was unlikely—but not impossible. She had no faith in her enemy's restraint.

After another hour, she said, "I'd appreciate a stop, Mr. Crockett."

He laughed. "And here I thought ladies like you never needed to piss."

Hopelessness made it easy to keep her voice steady. "I am a woman like any other, Mr. Crockett."

"We're a good distance from that grubby village of yours, and the horses wouldn't mind a rest." He signaled the driver. They were rounding a hill, so the carriage rumbled to a halt after reaching the straightaway on the other side of the curve.

The men climbed out first. Haggerty headed to the back of the carriage to get more drink while Crockett jerked at Julia's chain. The manacle bit into her raw wrist, drawing blood. She stumbled outside, muscles stiff and shivering from the cold.

As she stretched, Crockett jerked at the chain again and said with calculated menace, "You should be more afraid, Lady Julia."

"Why?" she said coolly. "Fear is pointless when there is no hope."

Crockett laughed. "Death may be inevitable, but there are better and worse ways to go." He put his hands on her shoulders and drew her hard against him.

Revolted by his touch, she spat in his face.

"Bitch!" Crockett slapped her cheek so hard she fell to the ground.

Not, unfortunately, hard enough to break her neck.

Tracking the kidnappers was dead easy when there was only one road, and his quarry made no effort to be inconspicuous. Randall caught up with them when they halted for a rest. Luckily, his horse whickered when it sensed other horses so he could stop before he was on top of them.

He listened and heard casual voices. After tethering his mount in a copse, he pulled a battered wool scarf from his saddlebags. It was a relic of his army service, dark gray and smelling of horse, but useful on cold, windy roads. Tonight it would do for concealing his light hair and most of his face.

He pulled his carbine from its holster and checked that it was ready to shoot, then silently made his way around the bend in the road. These rugged hills were mostly sheep pasture, but there were enough trees and shrubs along the road to let him stay in shadow.

Moonlight made it easy to see the carriage, horses, and passengers who had climbed out. His heartbeat accelerated when he saw Julia Bancroft step down from the vehicle. The bastards had her leashed on a chain, like an animal. As he considered the best way to free her from her captors, one of the men made a taunting remark and dragged her into an embrace.

She spat in his face. The man bellowed, "Bitch!" and struck her.

*Damnation!* Randall's carbine was trained on the man's skull before Julia hit the ground. He barely managed to stop himself from shooting. In battle, he had always been cool, using his anger as a weapon, but seeing a man beating a woman half his size shattered his control.

He didn't doubt that he could take all four men, but a mass killing would be awkward to explain, and there was the risk that Julia would be injured. It would be best to extract her with a minimum of violence.

Not Julia. Mrs. Bancroft.

Narrowing his eyes, he weighed the possibilities.

# Chapter 4

Swearing, Crockett handed the chain to Haggerty. "Take her damned ladyship into the bushes before I strangle her."

He took a swig from the jug and passed it to one of the others as Julia struggled dizzily to her feet and followed Haggerty into the nearest clump of shrubs, a hundred yards or so from the carriage. At least the chain was long enough to allow her a measure of privacy, and her captor turned away as she went behind a bush.

When she emerged, the young man said awkwardly, "I'm sorry, my lady."

"Probably not sorry enough to set me free," she said dryly.

"No, ma'am," he said with regret. "Even if I did, you wouldn't get far."

He was right. The hills were mostly plain pasture, and the moonlight would make her easy to chase down.

Wishing she had worn her shawl, she was turning toward the carriage when she saw a dark shape loom up behind Haggerty. An instant later, the young man collapsed, Julia's chain rattling as it dropped to the ground.

Julia gasped. "Who . . . ?"

Her words were cut off as a hard hand clamped over her mouth. "Silence," the man breathed in her ear. "We must leave as fast and quietly as possible."

She froze, shocked. There was something familiar in that whispered voice. But the man whose name flashed through her mind couldn't possibly be here.

No matter. Any rescuer would do. She nodded and he released her. She saw he carried some sort of rifle.

After she wrapped the loose chain around her arm to silence it, he bent over, gesturing for her to do the same. His clothing was dark and his face covered, making him a shadow among shadows. Her own gown was also dark. They moved away from the cluster of bushes, heading parallel to the road and back the way she'd come.

Her rescuer was a master at taking advantage of any cover available. Luckily Crockett and his other two men were talking and laughing as they passed the jug around. She hoped they wouldn't notice how long her visit to the shrubbery was taking.

After they rounded the bend and had the hill and some trees between themselves and Crockett, her rescuer stopped and turned to her. His lean, broad-shouldered form still seemed familiar, but his identity was obscured by a dark scarf.

She caught her breath when he tugged off the concealing scarf. Cool moonlight slid over blond hair and the lethal elegance of his chiseled features. Impossibly, her rescuer was Major Randall, as beautiful and fearsome as hell's own angels.

Recognition was followed by a feeling of inevitability. She'd first met Randall at Hartley Manor, when he and two others had come in search of their missing friend, Ashton. They'd found him with Mariah Clarke, mistress of the manor at the time. Of Ashton's friends, Randall was the prickliest, the wariest.

For some reason, probably punishment for her sins, there was an itchy, powerful connection between them that was as undeniable as it was unwelcome. When the group made the long journey to London together, Randall wouldn't even ride in the same carriage with her. She'd been grateful for that.

Yet of all the men on earth, he was the one who had rescued her. "Why you, Major Randall?" she asked softly, her question more philosophical than practical.

He answered literally. "On the way back from Scotland, I decided to call on the Townsends." His voice was equally soft as he started off again at a brisk pace. Now that he had straightened up, his limp was visible and worse than she remembered.

She fell in beside him. "The Townsends are away."

"So I learned, but I was invited to spend the night. I was dining when your apprentice came to report that you'd been kidnapped."

"Jenny is all right?" she asked.

"Yes. She got her little girl to fetch a knife so she could cut herself free."

"Thank heaven!" Julia would never have forgiven herself if Jenny or Molly had come to harm because of her.

"You're shivering." Randall peeled off his coat and draped it around her shoulders. Body heat radiated from the garment.

"You'll freeze," she said, glad for the warmth but uneasy with the way the coat made her feel as if he was touching her.

He shrugged. "I've spent enough time living rough that I don't notice temperature much."

Taking him at his word, she put her arms into the sleeves. The coat was almost cloak-sized on her, and she welcomed every heavy woolen inch of it.

He led her into a copse on the left of the road. She thought the horse tethered there was Charles Townsend's mount, though she couldn't be sure. Randall slid his weapon into a saddle holster and mounted, then offered his hand. "Best ride astride."

She took his hand and he lifted her with unnerving ease. Swinging her right leg over the saddlebags was awkward, but she managed. Randall set the horse into a walk and they returned to the road, heading back toward Hartley.

She reluctantly set her hands on his lean waist for balance. "The man you struck, Haggerty. Is . . . is he dead?"

"No, but he'll have the devil's own headache. Why do you care?"

"He was the most decent of the lot." She closed her eyes, shaking, still not quite believing that she was free. Randall was dangerous and uncomfortable, but he'd saved her life. He was a hero, and rescuing females was what heroes did.

Shouts rose behind them, with Crockett bellowing, "The damned bitch has escaped!"

Her hands tightened on Randall. He said, "Don't worry. By the time they realize that you didn't head off into the pasture away from the coach, we'll be well away."

"Won't they come after us in the carriage?"

"They'll try." He chuckled. "They'll find that the harnesses have been cut, so they won't be going anywhere very soon."

"You did that first?" she exclaimed. "How very efficient!"

"Military experience has its uses."

"I thank God and you for that, Major." She drew a deep breath, still not quite believing she was safe. "I thought I was doomed."

He shrugged and didn't reply. All in a day's work for a hero.

The road curved around another hill, and he set the horse into a canter. Despite Turk's smooth strides, she had to tighten her hold on Randall. They'd never touched before this night, and now she knew why. Being so close to him was . . . disquieting. "Are we returning to Hartley?"

He shook his head. "Even if Turk wasn't carrying double, he's too tired to go that far. And if they followed us and tried to get you back in Hartley . . ."

He didn't need to complete the sentence. She would not call down violence on the town that had been her home for years. "I'm sure you have an alternative plan."

"I noticed a track leading up to a shepherd's hut not far from here. We can go to ground there and get some rest."

"Rest. What a lovely thought." She tilted her head against his back and relaxed. Disquieting the man might be, but she had complete faith in his competence.

Wearily she wondered what she would do next, now that they'd found her. She'd worry about that tomorrow.

Not long after, they swerved from the road onto a nearly invisible track that led up and around the tall hill. Patchy clouds were beginning to obscure the moonlight. For once, the chronically damp weather was welcome.

They reached the dark square of a hut and he pulled the horse to a stop. "We're in luck. Not only a roof, door, and four walls, but a lean-to for Turk."

"I'd be happy in a cow shed as long as Crockett and his men can't find us." She slid from the horse, swaying as she reached the ground. Randall steadied her with one hand. She pulled away from his touch as soon as she regained her footing.

"The chances of them finding us are vanishingly small." He dismounted himself. "If they do, I shall deal with them in a more emphatic fashion."

"Four to one odds don't bother you?" she asked, more curious than surprised.

"They're amateurs. I'm not." He unfastened the saddlebags and carried them into the hut. "Better and better. There's a small fireplace and some stacked wood. If I give you my tinderbox, can you start a fire while I tend to Turk?"

She followed him into the hut, glad to be inside. "Do you think a fire is safe?"

"We're well concealed here, and the wind will carry any smoke away from the road." He handed her the tinderbox and moved toward the door. "There will be rain by morning, and that will wipe out any hoof marks if they look along the road then."

As she knelt by the hearth, a glimmer of moonlight glowed through a parchment-covered window. The single-room hut had an air of disuse, but at least it was dry and they were protected from the wind. Though her hands were clumsy with cold and exhaustion, she had a small fire burning by the time Randall joined her.

He opened his saddlebags and pulled out a small blanket. "Take this."

She returned his coat, then wrapped herself in the coarse woolen fabric as she settled to one side of the fire. Randall dug into the saddlebags again. "Are you hungry?"

She thought about it. "Starving, actually."

"Here's some cider." After giving her the jug, he used his knife to divide bread and cheese.

She sipped the tangy cider gratefully. "You are well prepared. Military experience again, I presume."

"The first lesson of campaigning is to insure supply lines." He handed her chunks of bread and cheese, setting some aside for himself and repacking the rest.

She bit into the cheese with more enthusiasm than elegance. Her energy began to revive as she ate. There was silence as they demolished the bread and cheese. The cider was cool, tart, and welcome.

In the light from the fire, Randall's handsome face was remote and enigmatic. She had no reason to fear him when he'd just saved her, but he was too powerful, too male, to be comfortable company. Even with her eyes closed, his presence was as vivid as the heat of the fire.

She wrenched her thoughts away from the major. The urgent issue was deciding what to do now that she was not heading to likely death.

She was so absorbed that she jumped when Randall asked, "Do you know why those men kidnapped you?"

He had a right to know, but she hated revealing the sordid story of her life. "I do."

"Jenny said they called you a murderess," he said bluntly. "Is that true?"

Her mouth tightened as she met his intent gaze. "Yes."

# Chapter 5

Randall studied Julia's delicately lovely face. It was very hard to imagine her as a murderess. "Whom did you kill?"

Her gaze slid away to the fire. "My husband."

"Did he need killing?" he asked coolly.

Her head shot up again. "No one has ever asked that."

"Anyone can react with violence if sufficiently provoked. You don't strike me as a woman who would kill for anything less than the most drastic of reasons." He offered the cider jug again. "Tell me about it."

Relaxing a little, she took a long swallow of cider. Had she expected him to toss her back onto the road for the kidnappers to find? As a soldier, he'd had more experience with killing than most, and accepted that sometimes it was necessary.

He'd wondered what Julia Bancroft's story was. Now he'd find out. Perhaps that would explain why he found her so damned compelling.

She pulled the blanket tight around her as if it was a shield. "I was barely sixteen when I married. The match was arranged. Everyone agreed it was very suitable."

Randall put another branch on the fire. "How did you feel about the match?"

"I'd been raised to believe that arranged marriages were best. I assumed my father would pick me a good husband." Her smile was wintry. "My betrothed was young and good-looking and charming. I was quite pleased."

"But . . . ?"

"My handsome, wellborn, eminently suitable husband was a monster." Though her voice was flat, her body betrayed her by shuddering.

Making an informed guess, Randall said, "Violent and abusive?"

"Yes." She pulled even further into herself.

Randall clamped down on his rage at that unknown husband. "Did you have to kill him to save your own life?"

Wearily she brushed a wisp of soft chestnut hair from her face. "At first, the violence was rare and he would apologize very earnestly. But the marriage went from bad to worse. He was jealous and accused me of wanting to lie with every man I met, so he kept me in the country and made sure I had only female servants. Gradually I realized that hurting me aroused him." Her voice broke. "How was I to know how to deal with such a man? I was a *child,* raised to be dutiful!"

"It is not a woman's duty to allow a man to hurt her." Now Randall understood why she was so self-effacing, and why she flinched every time he came near her. She didn't trust men, and justly so. "How did it end?"

"After about a year, I found that I was with child. I prayed for a boy so my husband would have his heir, and told him I wanted to live apart until after the birth." Her gray eyes were stark. "He went berserk. He swore he'd never let me go, that I belonged to him, all while giving me the worst beating yet. I was sure he was going to kill me. I shoved him while frantically trying to get away from his riding whip. He had been drinking and his balance was off. He . . . he fell and smashed his head into the edge of the fireplace. He died instantly, I think."

Randall winced. A riding whip? "So it wasn't murder, but an accident that happened when you were defending yourself." He forced his voice to stay level. If he allowed his anger to show, she might bolt into the night. "And the child?"

"I miscarried that same night." Her breathing was swift and ragged. "My husband kicked me. Repeatedly."

He winced again. He would give a great deal to draw her into his arms to offer comfort, but he doubted she could bear a man's touch at the moment. "How in the name of heaven could anyone accuse you of murder under such circumstances?"

"Crockett, the man who kidnapped me, was my husband's companion and acolyte. They had a strange, intense relationship." She gazed at the fire, her expression remote. "Crockett was the one who found my husband's body, with me bleeding beside it. He acted swiftly to cover up what happened so there would be no scandal."

"So no one knew the real story?"

"There was an inquest. The official verdict was death by misadventure, but Crockett told my father-in-law I'd murdered his son. Naturally he was devastated by the death of his only son. He had to blame someone, so he blamed me. Ever since that day, he has wanted me dead."

"He was the one who arranged your kidnapping?"

"Yes." She closed her eyes briefly. "I don't know what he had planned for me, but I doubt I would have survived."

Randall thought about what she had said, and what had not been said. "Surely your own family is powerful. Couldn't they offer you protection?"

She laughed, unable to control her bitterness. "As soon as I could stumble from my sickbed, I fled to my father. My father-in-law had written to say I'd murdered my husband. They were old cronies, so my father chose to believe him rather than me. He disowned me. Said I was a disgrace to the family name. After that, I was fair game for my father-in-law."

Julia fell silent again, her mind caught in the past. Randall asked, "What then?"

"I faked my own death. I was near the sea, so I went to the shore and wrote a note saying how distraught I was at my husband's death. I took what money I had, left my shawl and bonnet on the shore, and let the world think I had drowned myself."

A mark of desperation, and of fierce strength. Intensely interested in the way the pieces of her story were shaping up, he asked, "How did you escape?"

She shrugged. "I bought a ticket on the first coach I could find, not caring where it took me. But I hadn't recovered from the beating and miscarriage. When I started bleeding all over the coach, the driver put me off at a village near Rochdale in Lancashire. The local midwife took me in. I was thought to be dying."

"Let me guess. Her name was Bancroft?"

Julia's face eased. "The real Mrs. Bancroft. Louise was rich in years and experience, and had snatched other females from the jaws of death. I asked if I could stay and help her until I was stronger. Soon I was her apprentice. I took the name Bancroft and we told people I was a cousin. I had an aptitude for the work, and it was very satisfying. She taught me all she knew, and I took care of her as her health declined."

"You moved to Hartley after she died?"

"I wanted a location as remote as possible. As Mrs. Bancroft was failing, she got a letter from a friend saying a midwife was needed in this part of Cumberland, so I moved here after her death."

Julia's mouth twisted. "I'm guessing that my visit to London with Mariah is what alerted my father-in-law to the fact that I might be alive. If I'd stayed in Hartley, I would still be safe."

"You can't live there again." His attraction to this small, self-effacing woman was no longer inexplicable. He'd noted her quiet beauty, but there were other beautiful women and most of them weren't doing their best to be invisible. What made Julia unique was the steel at the center of her soul.

He felt an intense urge to protect her. Protect, and a good deal more. "Have you thought what you'll do next?"

"I doubt I'll be safe anywhere in England." She brushed her hair again, her expression bleak. "Perhaps one of the colonies. Midwives are useful everywhere."

"I'm guessing that you were married to Lord Branford," he said in a conversational tone. "Your murderous father-in-law is the Earl of Daventry."

She gasped and shrank away. "Dear God, you're part of *that* Randall family. I had wondered, but Randall is a common name, and you don't resemble them." White-knuckled fingers clenched her blanket. "Are you going to turn me over to Crockett?"

He caught her gaze. "Never."

Watching as if he might transform into a wolf,

she asked, "What is your relationship to Branford and Daventry?"

"Since several cousins have died over the years and Daventry is childless, I'm currently the heir presumptive to the earldom." His face hardened. "My father was a younger half brother of the present earl. They never got on. My resemblance is to my mother's family. My parents died when I was small, so I was sent to Turville Park to share a nursery with Branford."

"What was he like then?"

Randall thought back to his arrival at the Daventry estate. He'd been grief-stricken and confused and desperate for a new home. "Branford made my life hell. He was older and larger than I, or I might have killed him myself."

She stared at him. "No wonder you joined the army."

"So I could learn to fight really well? I hadn't thought of it in those terms," he said. "Certainly I fought everyone at Turville. Daventry shipped me off to various schools as soon as he could. I was expelled from one after another until I ended up at the Westerfield Academy."

"Where Lady Agnes Westerfield worked her magic," Julia said softly.

"She did indeed." Randall had been a furious, snarling hedgehog of a child before Lady Agnes. She hadn't tried to restrain him. Instead, she asked why he was so angry. His rage and hurt tumbled out of him as he spoke of the pain and humiliation, the ugly dangerous pranks he'd suffered at Turville. She had listened quietly. Most important, she told him that he had good reason to be angry. After that, he had started to heal.

"I used to wonder if Branford's behavior was my fault. That something about me triggered that violence in him. But it wasn't me, was it? He was always brutal." Julia sighed. "I wonder how many other people he injured. Too many, I fear."

"I know you didn't intend to kill him, but you did many people a favor when that happened." Randall smiled wryly. "There is justice in the fact that he died by accident at the hands of one of his victims."

"I wish it had been other hands. Daventry is a formidable enemy."

"I was in the army and estranged from the family for years, and had only a vague knowledge that Branford married, then died a year or two later." Randall searched his memory. "His wife was Lady Julia Raines, daughter of the Duke of Castleton?"

"Your memory is good." She smiled mockingly. "I can't say that being a duke's daughter has done me much good."

A startling idea struck him. He had been attracted to her since the moment they met. He desired her, but he also respected her strength and he had a powerful desire to protect her from the threats she didn't deserve. God knew that she needed protection. "I have a solution to your situation," he said slowly. "You could marry me."

She stared. "Are you *mad?* Even if you aren't insane, your Uncle Daventry will go berserk if you marry me."

"When I was badly wounded in Spain, I was sent to London and placed in his care," he said with acid amusement. "I would have died of neglect in his attic if Ashton hadn't invaded Daventry House to rescue me. The idea of enraging the old devil does not distress me."

Expression horrified, she said, "I understand your anger, but I do not wish to be the instrument of your revenge on your uncle, Major."

"That is only a minor reason," he said seriously. "The Randall family has treated you abominably. Because of Branford, you lost your name, your rank, your home, and your child. As my wife, you could regain all those things, as is only just."

"So you would marry me for justice's sake?" Her smile was twisted. "That is honorable, but a marriage is made between a man and a woman, not two principles. We don't even like each other, Major Randall. Thank you for your most flattering offer, but I must decline."

Her refusal hurt far more than it should have. So much that he recognized that his offer had not been casual. "You have reason to dislike me,

Lady Julia. I was appallingly rude to you in the past. But not because I don't like you. Rather . . . the contrary."

They stared at each other and the unspoken emotions both had tried to ignore flared to insistent life. She swallowed hard. "I admit that since the first time we've met, there has been this—this connection between us. But it is awkward and difficult, and not the basis for marriage."

"No?" he said softly. "The connection is attraction. The difficulty has come from fighting it. Perhaps it will become easier if we stop fighting. Our mutual attraction might become the foundation of an admirable marriage."

She frowned. "Why did you fight that attraction, Major Randall? You've acted as if you hated me from the moment we met."

"As a serving officer, I was in no position to marry." But that answer wasn't good enough. He forced himself to go deeper. "And . . . the degree of desire was alarming. I've never been drawn so strongly to a woman. It was profoundly unsettling. But I find that the idea of marrying you feels very right."

Tears glinted in her eyes. "You leave me no choice but the ugly truth, Major. Perhaps if we had met when I was sixteen, simple attraction would have been enough. We might have married happily and had a nursery full of children by now.

"But I am not that girl any more." She closed her eyes in pain. "I can't bear the idea of marriage. The thought of lying with a man makes me want to run screaming. You have saved my life, Major, but I am no damsel rescued from the dragon. I am too old and scarred to be an innocent bride. If you wish to help me, escort me to Liverpool and lend me enough money to take a ship to America. As heir to Daventry, you will have no trouble finding a wife who is suitable. A sweet-tempered young woman like Sarah Townsend. Not a battered widow with nothing left to give."

"Damnation!" he snapped. "Why is everyone trying to pair me off with Sarah Townsend? She's a lovely girl, but a girl. You are a woman, and the one that I want."

"You are accustomed to having what you want," Julia said dryly. "But surely a little thought will persuade you that a woman who won't be a wife is not what you want."

He studied her slim figure and weary, indomitable eyes as he thought about her words. "What you say is entirely sensible, yet marriage is not a matter of sense. I want you to be part of my life, Julia. We have both survived great pain. I don't want a bright, uncomplicated girl who has no understanding of shadows. You and I can know each other in a much deeper way. Does that have no value? Might we not develop trust and friendship enough to eventually become husband and wife in truth?"

"Perhaps that is possible," she said, her voice aching. "But even if it is—I must reveal the final truth because it is an insurmountable obstacle. I don't believe that I will ever be able to bear a child, Major. Branford . . . damaged me. You are heir to an earldom. You owe it to your heritage to marry a woman who can give you a son."

So Julia, who would know, believed herself barren. Unable to sit still, he rose and moved restlessly across the hut. There wasn't even room for proper pacing.

The principal duty of a lord was to breed another lord for the future. Yet Randall wasn't a lord now, and his life had never been about the earldom of Daventry.

Julia had leaned back against the wall, eyes closed and her expression drained. In his previous experience of her, she had always been relentlessly self-effacing. Now she stood revealed with quiet strength and delicate beauty. Before her catastrophic marriage, she must have been a strikingly attractive girl. A major prize in the Marriage Mart. Daventry would want nothing less for his heir.

This discussion had to be even more difficult for her than for him. Yet she had revealed painful truths because of a bone-deep honesty that called to him. The more they talked, the more he wanted her as his wife.

He also wanted her as a lover. Attraction was mysterious. Her quiet grace and petite, perfectly proportioned body had entranced him the first time he saw her. Could he bear a wife he desired, yet could not touch?

If there was any chance she would overcome the horror of her first marriage, he'd be willing to take the risk. He'd taken far worse ones.

# Chapter 6

After such a long. traumatic day, Julia had barely enough energy left to be tense, despite Randall's bizarre suggestion. She watched as he moved restlessly around the small room. His limp was the worst she'd seen it, probably from his hard riding to rescue her after he'd already traveled all day. She hoped he was right that Crockett and his men wouldn't find them. Taking on four enemies at once was a lot even for Randall.

Her feelings were confused. On a purely emotional level, being in the presence of a powerful man who was skilled at violence made her want to cower in a corner. Yet he had none of the mad cruelty of her husband. Randall had behaved—was behaving—with impeccable honor and courage.

Strange to think that he and Branford were cousins. She saw no similarity between them. Randall was a warrior, intense and sometimes prickly. Yet that violence was controlled. She couldn't imagine him hurting a person for his pleasure.

Bringing their awkward, unwelcome connection into the open had been a relief. As Randall gazed down at the small fire, one hand braced against the wall above, she was reminded of Greek statues of athletes. No, he had a leaner, rangier build than the Greek ideal, and his blond hair and chiseled features were Nordic. A Viking deity, not one born of the Mediterranean.

She wondered what he was thinking. Likely he was readjusting his view of her now that he knew who she was, and that she was unsuited to be any man's wife. If he felt disappointment at her refusal, he'd recover quickly. He could have any woman he wanted. She'd realized that the first time she'd seen him smile.

He raised his gaze, expression pensive. "There are no certainties in life, Julia. Many healthy young couples are not blessed with children. Fertile couples may have only daughters. The fact that you are barren doesn't persuade me that I don't want you for a wife. Will you marry me, Lady Julia Raines?"

Her jaw dropped from shock. "You really are insane! Children might not interest you now, but that may change in the future." She shook her head, having trouble believing he was serious. "Even if you don't care about children, you can't possibly want to marry a woman who won't share your bed. Unless you want to marry a duke's daughter so flawed you have a license for adultery?"

His brows arched. "Hardly. I agree that if it's unthinkable that you might ever feel differently, there could be no true marriage. But as you say, things change. I swear that I would cut off my hand rather than hurt you. Try to believe that. With enough trust and enough friendship, perhaps you will overcome your distaste for men."

"I'm not sure there is enough trust in the world for that," she said helplessly.

Yet as she studied his cool, handsome face, she realized how powerfully she *wanted* to be different. She would give twenty years of her life to be normal, as happy and uncomplicated as she'd been before she married. At sixteen, she'd yearned for a man's touch. She'd enjoyed stolen kisses with the dizzy delight of the nubile girl she'd been. God help her, she'd gone to her marriage bed eagerly.

Wanting to be convinced that she wasn't insane, she asked, "Even if it's possible for me to change, how can I marry a near stranger? I don't even know your given name!"

"Alexander David Randall."

Alexander. She turned the name in her mind. It had edges, like he did. "Does anyone ever call you Alex?"

"Occasionally. Mostly I'm Randall. Does knowing that make a difference?"

"Alexander the Conqueror," she said wryly. "How much of your persistence is to prove that you can win even against impossible odds?"

"That's a fair question." He thought before shaking his head. "My offer isn't about winning. It's about being with you. You have some quality I find . . . soothing."

"I've been told that I'm soothing by women in labor, but never by a man in the prime of life. As a quality, it's the opposite of passion, I think." Yet she liked that he thought of her that way. "You strike me as a passionate man, Major Randall. I still can't believe that you would be happy in a marriage without physical intimacy."

"There would have to be an agreement between us that you are willing to try to change how you feel." He cocked his head thoughtfully. "If you will grant me permission to touch you, in return I will promise to stop whenever you tell me to."

They were venturing into very deep waters here. Remembering how crazed Branford would become when he was aroused, she asked, "Wouldn't that be difficult? Desire is not easily controlled."

"I'm extremely good at control." There was a glint in his cool blue eyes. "It's one of my most irritating qualities."

That surprised a laugh out of her. "I can see

why. I'd say stubbornness is another. Marriage is binding, Major. We can't just walk away if we find the result unsatisfying."

"Actually, we can walk away. Not easily, but it's possible." Folding his arms, he leaned against the rough wall. "Scottish marriage law is different from English. Females can request a divorce on equal terms with men. If we marry there, you can divorce me for adultery or abandonment, or demand a legal separation for cruelty."

She frowned. "It seems wrong to take marriage vows while keeping one foot outside the door."

"Perhaps. Certainly it is a gamble. But marriage is an honorable estate." His gaze was steady, his voice surprisingly gentle. "Do you want to spend the rest of your life running from Daventry and Crockett? You might succeed if you go to another country, but now that they know you're alive, they might pursue you anywhere.

"If you marry me, you can return to the world you were raised in. I'm not wealthy, but I have a comfortable income and a small estate. As my wife, you could visit London and wear pretty gowns and be Lady Julia Raines again. Isn't that worth a risk?"

To have her life back! The picture he painted was painfully tempting. "The risk is great, especially for you. I know you're a powerful protector, Major, but we could both wind up dead." She shivered. "I don't want your death on my immortal soul."

"As Daventry's heir, I have a certain amount of influence with him. Though he doesn't like me, he loves tradition and his earldom," Randall said with dark humor. "If you are my wife and the only hope for an heir after me, that's powerful protection."

"Except I can't give you an heir." She couldn't keep bitterness from her voice.

"He wouldn't know that." His mouth twisted wryly. "There would be ironic justice if the title goes extinct because of Branford's brutality. But I am not proposing marriage simply to punish Daventry. I think we would both benefit if we wed."

"You tempt me, Major," she said softly. "But this discussion is so cold and rational. Should marriage be a cool calculation of protection and possibilities?"

Without moving a muscle, he changed. She could *feel* emotion radiating from him. "My feelings for you aren't cold, Julia," he said, his voice as soft as hers. "I've never met another woman I've wanted to marry. The prospect of choosing a 'suitable' bride sent me running to hide in Scotland. I came to Hartley in theory to consider Sarah Townsend, but in truth, because I wanted to see you. Your situation is more complicated

60

than I realized. Yet the more I see of you, the more I want to be with you."

Moved and unnerved, she asked, "When did you start to call me Julia?"

"Somewhere earlier in this conversation." He folded himself down on the floor close enough to touch her, but not touching. "If you truly dislike me so much that you don't want to live under the same roof . . . well, I must accept that. I won't trouble you again. But if you think we might someday be more to each other . . ."

She saw vulnerability in his eyes. That was perhaps the greatest surprise of all. "I am not indifferent to you, Major," she admitted. "You were right about the connection between us. I also feel it, and I know you much better than I did an hour ago."

"An hour's acquaintance is about right," he said promptly. "More might increase your doubts."

"Finding you have a sense of humor is a definite plus." She gazed into the fire, amazed that she was actually considering marriage. And to Randall, of all men. "You say I must be willing to 'try' to make a true marriage. What do you mean by that?"

He set another piece of wood on the fire. "I think we should both commit a year to the attempt. I'm allowed to touch, while you have the absolute right to tell me to stop. Until . . . say, the next day?"

"That seems reasonable," she said cautiously.

"I will be faithful to my vows as long as we both feel our marriage is real. If we separate—that's a different matter. But I want very much to try, Julia."

She turned and met his gaze. "It's been so long since I've touched a man for any reason except patching up injuries," she said uncertainly. "Your terms are generous, yet even so, I don't know if I can meet them."

"No?" Slowly, as if she was a skittish foal, he reached out and took her right hand in his. "Is this unbearable?"

She closed her eyes, shaken by his touch. A virile male who wanted to marry her was holding her hand. Deep-seated fears were triggered, yet the warmth and strength of his grip were comforting. Most disturbing of all was the undeniable attraction. She opened her eyes. "Disconcerting, but not unbearable."

"And this?" He raised her hand and brushed the back with his lips.

She shivered as long-forgotten sensations jangled through her, as appealing as they were frightening. "Not . . . unbearable. Though the limit of what I can accept now."

He gave a slow, deep smile. "Again I ask. Will you marry me, Lady Julia?"

Even with his promise to always respect her wishes, she would lose the walls of privacy that had protected her for years. She hated knowing that would happen.

But she would never get such an amazing, unexpected offer again. She believed Randall was being honest. Despite all the reasons any sane man would walk away, he wanted her enough to risk the likelihood that marriage might be a disastrous failure.

And . . . he intrigued her. Though he was an alarming man in many ways, she paradoxically felt safe with him. She was tired of living in fear. The prospect of running away to a new continent made her want to weep.

As a girl, she'd had a reckless streak. For too long, she'd suppressed that, but now she felt a mad desire to risk her future. If he was willing to dare marriage, she could do no less. But she had to know that she could escape if necessary. "I have a condition also. That you give me a signed, undated letter saying that you agree that the marriage has failed and that you also want a divorce."

His brows drew together formidably. "I . . . see."

She looked away. "I'm sorry, I don't want to suggest that you're untrustworthy."

"But you don't trust me," he said wryly. "Very well, I shall give you such a letter before we head to the altar. Is that sufficient?"

For a proud man, he was accepting a great deal. She could do the same. Voice unsteady, she replied, "I believe that it is. If you truly wish it, Alexander David Randall, I will marry you."

"I'm glad," he said simply. He squeezed her hand, then released it. Wise man.

"Where do we go from here, Major?" She smiled crookedly. "First step, I imagine, is to get away without Crockett and his men seeing us."

"I'll listen for them the rest of the night. They'll spend time searching for you in the area where you escaped. Eventually, they'll have to head back to Hartley or go on toward Carlisle, based on their best guess of where you might run."

"They probably think that as a weak female, I'll head back to Hartley since it's where I have friends."

"Very likely," he agreed.

She bit her lip. "I hope they don't hurt anyone there."

"They've already attracted enough attention, so that's unlikely," Randall assured her. "I imagine they'll station themselves on the road and fields outside the village so they can catch you before you return home."

She was unable to repress a shudder. "I feel like a mouse being stalked by cats."

"They won't find you. Since they might be anywhere along the road, we'll go to Carlisle cross-country. I'll hire a carriage there. You can send a note to Hartley that you escaped your kidnappers but won't return."

She hesitated. "There are a few items at my house I wish to retrieve. Mementos from my mother and the like."

"We can stop for them later," he said, "but first Scotland and marriage."

She made a face. "A Gretna Green marriage? Vulgar but necessary, I presume."

"Gretna Green is neither necessary nor desirable," he said firmly. "The town is famous for runaway marriages because it's the most southern spot in Scotland, but we have time to go farther. I think we should marry from the house of my friend Kirkland. You've met him. His respectability will lend countenance to the marriage."

Kirkland had been one of the three friends who had come north to find Ashton. Dark and clever and contained, he had treated Julia and Mariah with courtesy and tolerance. Marrying from his house would be far better than a scandalous Gretna Green ceremony. "By marrying you, I come under the protection of all you Lost Lords of Westerfield, don't I?"

"Indeed you do." That glint showed in his eyes again. "We're a formidable lot in both practical and social terms."

"Believe me, I appreciate that." She had been alone for so long. The idea of protection was gratifying. "We shall need to agree on a story of how we came to marry."

"Something less than the truth since part of the exercise is to reestablish you socially." He thought. "Distraught from the tragic death of your husband, you left society and took up residence with a distant cousin in the country. Later, you became friends with the Duchess of Ashton—that part of the story is very important, you are a very dear friend of a duchess—and we met through her, since I'm close friends with the duke. Having sold out of the army, my thoughts turned to matrimony, so I sought you out and proposed to you."

"You mentioned earlier that you'd sold out. That must have just happened?"

He nodded. "Daventry informed me the last intervening cousin had died and I must return to England and prepare myself for my future responsibilities by finding a wife and establishing a household."

"I'm surprised you were willing to do anything he suggested," she said dryly.

"I forced myself since it was in accord with my own wishes," he explained.

"It's a good story," she agreed. "Simple enough that we can keep it straight."

"It's not that far from the truth," he observed. "I did sell out and determined I should be looking for a wife, and I thought of you."

She studied his face. "Yet you traveled to Hartley to visit Sarah Townsend. Does my exalted birth make me more marriageable? A village midwife would be far beneath your station."

"You were never less than a lady, even as a village midwife," he said slowly. "Granted, your rank will make it easier for others to accept you as my wife, but the main reason I looked elsewhere was because you appeared to want nothing to do with me. I didn't think I could change your mind, but I did want to see you again. Just in case."

She looked down at the embers of the fire. "You humble me, Major. I don't deserve your regard, but I'm grateful for it."

"To say you don't deserve my regard implies that I have poor taste," he said with lurking humor. "Quite the contrary."

She laughed. "My apologies." Her laugh turned into a yawn.

"Sleep now. You must be exhausted."

"I am." She raised her gaze to him. "I would never have imagined such a day as this one."

"Nor would I. Yet here we are." He gave one of his rare, surprisingly sweet smiles. "I think we shall deal well together, Julia."

"I hope so." She lay down and wrapped the blanket around her, so tired that she didn't mind the unyielding floor. Agreeing to marry a virtual stranger was madness. But it was good to have someone concerned on her behalf. She'd been alone so long.

# Chapter 7

Randall eased down next to the door and leaned against the wall. His damaged leg ached abominably as he stretched it out. He had demanded far too much of his body today, but it had been worth it. Julia was safe, and he'd see that she stayed that way.

He opened the door a few inches so he could listen to the night. Any travelers on the road far below would be audible, but at this hour, there were none. Only the sounds of small animals rustling about their business, and the implacable softness of falling rain.

Strange how important Julia had become to him, given that they might never be able to have a real marriage. Yet important she was.

He studied her sleeping form where she lay wrapped in the blanket by the fire. With the strain gone from her face, she looked very young. Fragile. Even knowing Branford's cruelty as well as he did, Randall still couldn't understand how his vile cousin could have brutalized a gentle young bride.

But he didn't doubt a word of her story. He guessed that she couldn't speak of the worst things she'd suffered. Like a soldier after battle, she might never be able to reveal the full horror of what she had endured.

But by God, he would never let anyone hurt her again. He was amazed that she had agreed to marry him. He doubted that was because of his dubious charms. More likely, she wanted to feel safe, and to regain the life she'd lost. No matter. Though she was quite right to say he was insane to take on such a damaged bride, he had no regrets.

A whimsical thought struck. Back in his school days, he'd loved the medieval tales of courtly love. Lady Agnes, headmistress of the Westerfield Academy, had specially ordered more books for the library because of his interest. The idea of a knight's selfless devotion to a matchless woman who was far above his station had struck him as profoundly noble and romantic. That ideal had become part of him. Julia was his lady, and he was the knight sworn to her service.

He smiled a little. They had updated the story to modern times, but finally he had the chance to swear service to a woman he cared for deeply.

Caring was the key. When he lay neglected in Daventry's London house, waiting for wounds and fever to kill him, he'd gone a long way on the journey toward death. Though Ashton had rescued him, he'd not fully returned to life in the months since.

He'd lived the year since then in a dank fog of pain and emptiness. He kept moving forward, one step at a time, because life was too precious a gift to waste. But he'd known damned little happiness or satisfaction.

That was one reason he'd been so easily persuaded to sell out. A soldier who didn't much care if he lived or died wouldn't last long on the battlefield. On some level, he retained the hope that in time he'd move beyond melancholia.

Now he had someone to care about. He wanted Julia to feel safe and happy. He wanted to be with her because in her presence, he felt a blessed sense of peace.

If she reclaimed her life and decided to live without him—well, there would be satisfaction in knowing what he had done for her. The purest service was selfless, though he doubted he would ever be that pure. He would gain from their marriage no matter what strange path it took.

He stretched out full length, using his saddlebag as a pillow. Despite his aching body, he felt better than since the French had come near killing him in Spain. Tomorrow, they would travel to Scotland and marriage.

Tonight, he dozed with listening ears.

Julia's exhaustion helped her sleep, but she woke stiff from her night on the hard floor. It took a moment for her to remember where she was, and why. Ah, yes, her carefully constructed life had been blown to pieces yesterday.

The hut was no longer dark, and she guessed that dawn was breaking. No sign of Major Randall.

She got to her feet creakily, trying not to wonder too much about what the future held. Wrapping the blanket around her shoulders, she headed outside. The rain had passed and the sky was cool and clear, with just enough light along the eastern hills to show approaching dawn. The road was somewhere below, out of sight but not out of mind.

Randall joined her, silent as a shadow. He stood close enough that she could feel the warmth radiating from his body, but he didn't touch her.

Her affianced husband. The thought was not quite as bizarre as it had been the night before. Voice low so as not to disturb the dawn peace, she asked, "Any sign of Crockett and his men?"

"I heard a pair of horses riding west along the road a little earlier. It might have been them. If the carriage harness was unrepairable, they might have split up and be heading in both directions."

She shivered at the thought. "A good thing we're traveling cross-country."

"With luck, they'll think you ran off into the hills and that you'll die of exposure, being a helpless female on her own."

"People do die like that in this wild country,"

she agreed. "But surely Crockett will know I must have had help to escape?"

"Not necessarily. The fellow I hit on the head probably won't remember exactly what happened. They might assume that you clipped him with a rock and cut the horses' harness before you ran."

"Would that I was so intrepid!" She bit her lip. "I hope Crockett didn't hurt Haggerty for letting me escape."

"There are better objects for compassion than Haggerty," Randall said dryly. "Time we had a bite to eat and got started."

Hoping Crockett would eventually decide she'd gone to her doom in the hills, Julia returned to the hut. They each had a couple of bites of bread and cheese and a swallow of cider. After Randall saddled and loaded the horse, he turned to help her into the saddle. "You'll have to ride astride."

She frowned, thinking of his bad leg. "Aren't you going to ride?"

"Turk had a hard day yesterday," he replied. "I don't want to ruin him by riding double today. It's only about ten miles to Carlisle. We should be there by early afternoon."

Knowing better than to argue, she let him help her into the saddle. When she was settled, she tugged at her skirts, but they barely covered her knees. Randall's gaze slid away from her indecent display of leg, for which she was grateful. Taking the horse's reins, he headed into the hills away from the road.

They soon picked up a sheep track that led in the right direction. Mists pooled eerily over lower ground, gradually dissipating as the rising sun brought warmth and light to the wild landscape. She thought wryly that the ride would be pleasant if she wasn't fleeing for her life, hungry, cold, and in dire need of a wash.

Major Randall was an easy companion, and he always knew exactly where he wanted to go. Sometimes they had to vary their course when a hillside became too steep, but he never hesitated in choosing a direction. After an hour or so of riding, she asked, "Do you have a compass?"

"The one in my head suffices. I never get lost."

"That must have made you popular for leading patrols in the Peninsula."

"It did. We always made it back to camp." He gestured at the green hills. "It's a pleasure to travel overland without having to worry about French cavalry."

"I think I'd prefer the French to Crockett." His limp was worsening. Guessing he would rather die than admit weakness, she said, "Hold up for a minute. I want to walk."

He halted, but said, "You can stay in the saddle. You weigh so little that Grand Turk hardly notices."

"I like walking. Especially since I spent yesterday cramped in a carriage with criminals." She swung her right leg over the saddle and slid off. Turk was a tall horse, and she stumbled when she reached the ground. Randall caught her arm to steady her, letting go before a suffocating moment of discomfort could flair into something worse.

Glad she had been wearing sturdy half boots when she was abducted, she fell into step beside him as they resumed their trek. It felt good to stretch her legs. And very odd to be traveling toward her wedding to a near stranger.

This close, she saw the lines of pain in his face, and the limp was noticeably worse. "Grand Turk doesn't seem particularly tired. Why don't you ride for a while?"

"I don't need coddling," he said shortly.

Julia always shrank back when a man was angry with her, but bad temper from someone in pain was a different matter. "It's not coddling to give an injured leg some rest when it's having a bad day."

"There are no good days," he snapped. "Only bad and worse."

"Then you definitely need to be riding," she said mildly.

He scowled at her. "Pray oblige me by minding your own business."

She had to laugh. "If we are to marry, you are

most certainly my business. As you have made me yours."

After a startled moment, he gave her a reluctant smile. "That's hard to argue with. Sorry to be such a bear. As you observed, my leg is acting up today, but for now, it's better to walk so it doesn't tighten up."

"What kind of wound was it?" When he glanced at her askance, she said, "For lack of anyone better qualified, I was Hartley's surgeon and physician as well as its midwife. I've dealt with all sorts of illnesses and injuries."

"I've been poked and prodded by experts," he said without enthusiasm. "The general opinion is that I should be dead, and not losing the leg borders on the miraculous. I doubt you could do anything to help."

She gave him a cheerful smile. "Probably not. I'd just like to satisfy my ghoulish curiosity since disease and injury have always interested me." That had been true even when she was a child. In a better world, she would have been able to study medicine rather than marrying too young.

"Since you put it that way . . ." Another brief smile. "I was chewed up by shrapnel at the Battle of Albuera. The surgeons did their best, but there are still bits of sharp metal moving around in appalling and uncomfortable ways."

She supposed that was all the explanation she was likely to get from a military stoic. "That's

75

the wound that sent you to Daventry's attic?"

He nodded. "Heavy bleeding, infection, fever. I was out of my head when someone decided I should be sent back to my uncle's tender mercies. My batman, Gordon, would have stopped that if he could, but he was wounded, too."

"That battle was in May last year, wasn't it?" At his nod, she said, "Wasn't that about the time Daventry's younger son died?"

Randall sighed. "Unfortunately, yes. The boy had always been sickly, and he died of a fever just before I landed on Daventry's doorstep. My uncle was wild with grief. I suspect that's why he sent me to the attic to die—because I was alive and his sons weren't. He's never liked me, but he wasn't murderous."

Julia winced inwardly at Randall's flat acceptance of an appalling situation. "Since you were the heir, one would think he would want you to survive."

"At the time, there was still a cousin or two in line, so I wasn't needed."

"I hope you're right that he'll find you more valuable now that you're the last heir," she said dryly.

"He does now that he's had time to recover from the loss of his son." Randall replied. "I never even met the boy. He was born after you ran away. His mother, the second countess, died a few days later."

"Your uncle has been unlucky in his children and wives," Julia observed. "I never met the current countess, but I was told the first two endured numerous miscarriages and stillbirths."

"His third wife is a widow who had three healthy sons with her first husband. My uncle must have hoped that would guarantee fertility, but it didn't. So if he wants the Daventry title to continue, he's stuck with me." He glanced at her. "And with you."

Who would be another Lady Daventry who would produce no heirs. Perhaps the title was fated to become extinct. "It will be interesting to see how this family drama works out." Julia studied her future husband's face. He looked gray, and was obviously in pain. "Perhaps now riding would be better than walking?"

He muttered an oath under his breath. "Perhaps, but I'm not capable of riding when a lady is walking."

She didn't mind walking while he rode, but since he did, she addressed the horse. "Turk, are you willing to carry two people? No more than three or four miles."

The horse turned its head and nosed her chest in a friendly way. She smiled and buried her fingers in his mane. "I think he just said yes."

"He does seem to be moving well despite the hard riding yesterday," Randall conceded. "Turk is a first-class horse. I wonder if Townsend would sell him?"

"He already refused an offer from a duke, so I think not."

"Ashton tried and failed? Then Townsend certainly won't sell to me. Very well, Turk, since you look willing and we don't have to move fast, we'll try." He mounted, wincing at the strain on his leg, then offered his hand to Julia. She put her foot on his and swung up to perch pillion style behind him. The horse made no objections.

She rested her hands on Randall's lean waist and they resumed their journey. Was touching him as unnerving as it had been the day before? She decided not. Modest progress had been made. Perhaps there was hope for her.

After a mile or so, she asked, "Do you have a plan for when we reach Carlisle?"

"Not really. We need to find transportation so we can continue as quickly as possible. Do you need to do anything besides writing your friends in Hartley?"

"There's a used clothing shop on the edge of the old town. I'd like to stop and acquire some more clothes." She made a face. "But I'll have to borrow money from you. I haven't a penny to bless myself with."

"It's not borrowing when you're about to become my wife." He frowned. "And as my wife, you should not have to wear secondhand clothing."

"I've been wearing used garments for years. A

little longer won't hurt me," she said mildly. "A bonnet and cloak will make me less conspicuous."

"Very well. But I will do better by you in future." He patted her hand where it rested on his waist. "I think you've earned some pampering."

"Pampering. What a remarkable concept." She thought of the long hours of work, the scrimping to make ends meet. Her life in Hartley had been rewarding, but not easy. "I think I would quite enjoy that."

They continued in peaceable silence until they intercepted a grassy lane that led in the right direction. They'd progressed from wild country and sheep tracks to cultivated fields and recognizable roads.

They crested a ridge and saw Carlisle ahead of them, the cathedral presiding majestically over the town. Randall said, "Time for a break. I need to stretch my legs."

He helped Julia down and dismounted himself, his face tight with pain. Julia wished she could help, but without her supplies, she couldn't even make willow bark tea.

A stream ran by the road, so horse and riders refreshed themselves. After drinking and splashing cold water on her face, Julia glanced longingly at the town in the distance. "Will there be time for a proper meal before we continue?"

"There will." His glance was admiring.

"You're a trooper, Lady Julia. Not a single complaint despite ample cause."

"You haven't complained, either, Major, despite your leg acting up," she retorted.

His mouth quirked. "Yes, but I *am* a trooper. Stoicism is expected."

She chuckled, thinking that either his sense of humor was improving or she was becoming more attuned to his dry wit.

Randall pulled out his wallet and handed her several banknotes. "Here's money for clothing. Do you ride? It's possible that I'll have to hire riding hacks if there's no carriage available."

She tucked away the notes, hoping he'd be able to find a carriage. The last thing the man needed was more hours on horseback. "I haven't done much riding in recent years, but I can manage. I'll see if there's a riding habit at the shop."

He glanced at the town with narrowed eyes. "With rivers on three sides of Carlisle, there are only a few roads in, which makes it easier if someone is looking for you. Which route do you think is least likely to be observed?"

Her brows furrowed as she thought about the town's layout. "If we circle around to the east, there's a small bridge that leads into the old section of town. The clothing shop is on an alley off that road."

"That's our route then. I'll leave you at the shop while I visit the liveries." He pulled a gold signet ring from his right hand. "We'll be less noticeable if we travel as husband and wife, so here's my ring. Turned around, it will look like a wedding band."

The body warmth in the gold was curiously intimate as she slid it on her ring finger. "We won't look as if we belong together. You are expensive and beautiful and aristocratic while I am drab and plain and easily overlooked. Women will feel sorry for you and think they would make you a better wife."

He stared at her, aghast. She wouldn't have believed he was capable of blushing. "What an absurd idea. My clothing might be expensive but I've traveled and slept in it, your aristocratic blood is superior to mine, and I am certainly not beautiful."

"I thought you were beautiful from the first time we met," she said thoughtfully. "In a bad-tempered sort of way."

He was even more beautiful when he laughed.

# Chapter 8

There wasn't a single damned carriage in Carlisle available for hire that afternoon. At least none that Randall could find. If he was willing to wait until the next morning, he would have his choice, but he had a prickly desire to get Julia out of town as soon as possible. Carlisle was an obvious place for the kidnappers to hunt her.

Luckily he located two sturdy riding hacks. Randall was not enthralled at the prospect of hours more riding, but he'd manage.

He returned to the shabby shop where he'd left Julia. Though he watched for men who might be the kidnappers, he saw no one likely. Probably Crockett was still searching the hills near where Julia escaped. But that could not be relied on.

The shop was small, neat, yet cluttered. Tables were dedicated to garments for men, women, or children. A particularly handsome lady's outfit hung on the back wall with gown, shawl, and bonnet. But he didn't see Julia. Surely she hadn't been fool enough to go out alone!

A movement caught his eye and he turned to see Julia sewing in a corner. With her head bent and dressed in drab clothing, he'd overlooked her entirely. "Are you finished here, my dear?" he asked, trying to sound like a fond husband.

"Your timing is good." She knotted her thread and bit it off. "I just finished basting this hem." She stood and shook out a dark gray cloak, then draped it around her shoulders. The garment was singularly devoid of style. She picked up a battered carpetbag and called through an open door at the back of the small room, "I'm leaving now, Mrs. Rown. Thank you so much for the tea."

"My pleasure, dearie," a woman called in a strong northern accent. "You have a safe journey now, and thankee for the advice."

Randall took the carpetbag and offered Julia his arm. When they were outside on the street, he said, "Did you know the proprietor already?"

Julia glanced up from under a depressing black bonnet. "No, but she's increasing and appreciated a few suggestions on how to feel better."

He studied her outfit. The colors were dull, the fabric worn, and the fit poor. "Your ensemble makes you as close to invisible as humanly possible. Well done."

"I've had years of practice in invisibility." Her fingers tightened on his arm. "I thought I'd hidden so well that the past would never find me. Yet when Crockett appeared—I wasn't really surprised."

"Soon you won't have to hide any more. Once we're married and Daventry has accepted your right to exist, he'll call off his dogs."

She bit her lip. "Do you really think he will?"

"Yes, though not happily." A lifetime of wariness had given Randall some understanding of his uncle. "For the sake of the earldom's survival, he will."

"I hope you're right," she said softly.

He hoped so, too. Though Randall spoke to Julia with confidence, he knew better than anyone that Daventry was an unpredictable old devil. "Were you able to purchase a riding habit? There were no carriages available, so I hired horses. They're waiting at an inn where we can dine and write our messages."

Her glance went to his damaged leg, but she knew better than to mention that. "I did find a habit, though it's large. I can change at the inn."

They stepped into the high street. Julia gasped and retreated to flatten herself against the bricks of the corner building. "He's out there! Crockett and one of his men!"

"Did he see you?" Randall scanned the people moving along the street.

"I . . . I don't think so." Julia's hands knotted into fists as she struggled for control. "He was looking toward the cathedral."

Randall's gaze settled on a tall man with a predator's face. "He's wearing a black hat and a bottle-green coat?"

"That's him."

Crockett's companion was a rough, menacing fellow who lacked Crockett's feral intelligence. Randall memorized their faces. "They're heading in the opposite direction from our destination. We can use a back street to get to our inn. Roads lead in all directions from Carlisle so we should be safe once we're away."

She forced her fists to relax and took his arm again. "I'll do my best to increase my invisibility."

A few minutes of walking brought them to the White Lion. The inn was bustling, but a private room was available and a substantial dinner was served quickly. Randall tried not to fall on the food like a starving wolf. He wasn't sure he succeeded. Julia, though more restrained, was equally enthusiastic.

"I feel more optimistic now that I've been fed." Meal finished, Julia rose and drifted to the window. "No sign of Crockett out there."

"Your bonnet is so deep he probably wouldn't recognize you even if we ride right by him." He finished his ale and stood. "I'll tell the ostler to saddle the horses. Grand Turk will spend the night here and be led back to Hartley in the morning, along with any messages you want to send with him."

"I'll write my notes and change into my riding habit." Julia dropped the curtain and turned from the window. "It's hard to believe that yesterday morning I woke up in my own bed in Hartley. It seems like a lifetime ago."

"It's been an eventful day."

She smiled. "You have a gift for understatement."

If that made her smile, he was grateful for it.

Even with her bonnet's veil drawn over her face, Julia felt horribly exposed as they rode from the inn's courtyard and turned north. She told herself that Crockett was looking for a lone woman on foot, not a couple on horseback, but her nerves were taut to the screaming point. Despite her attempts to look six ways at once without turning

85

her head, she still felt itchiness between her shoulder blades.

Luckily she didn't carry the burden of keeping watch alone. Randall looked casual, but she was sure he noticed everything and everyone around them. So far, all the benefits of their relationship were on her side.

She began to relax when they got outside Carlisle. This was the main road to Scotland, and there was steady traffic in both directions. Plodding farm carts were punctuated by riders, carriages, and once, a swift mail coach.

Randall also relaxed, though his eyes were watchful. A couple miles north of the town, he said, "You ride well despite your lack of practice."

"As a child, I was as horse-mad as my brother," she admitted. "Not being able to ride was one of the hardest parts about running away. I had the sweetest mare . . ." She bit off her words and patted the neck of her staid, unpretentious gelding. "In Hartley I had a pony cart, but I couldn't afford a riding hack."

"You still have light hands and an excellent seat."

"Perhaps, but I guarantee that when we stop for the night, I'll be aching in places I've forgotten I have!" she said ruefully.

He grinned. "We must hope for a shop that sells liniment."

She smiled back, but was reminded that he would be aching far more than she. They both fell silent as the afternoon wore on endlessly.

The sun was descending when they approached a low stone toll bridge that led into a town. "Welcome to Scotland and Gretna Green," Randall said. "I understand there's a marrying room in the tollhouse for those who don't want to wait to get all the way into town."

"You're joking!" Julia glanced at her companion. "No, I see you aren't. Some couples must be very impatient indeed."

"For a scoundrel who wants to secure an heiress before her guardians can rescue her, the sooner the better." Randall paid their toll and they rode forward. "We still have a couple of hours of daylight. There's a village about five miles north with two coaching inns. If you're game to ride farther, we can spend the night and hire a carriage for the rest of our trip."

Stifling the impulse to whimper that she wanted a bed and she wanted it *now,* Julia said, "If it puts more distance between me and Crockett, I can manage."

He smiled. "Good lass."

"Your speech is turning Scottish now that you're north of the border," she said, amused. "This is my first visit to Scotland, even though I've lived so close. So far, it looks much like Northern England."

"Except that here, you can become married by declaring your intention before two witnesses," he pointed out. "What a difference a border makes."

Glad they were waiting for Edinburgh to marry, she studied the famous blacksmith's shop in the town center as they rode by. "This is where so many marriages take place? I've never understood the custom of having a blacksmith perform the ceremony over his anvil."

"Kirkland says it's because a blacksmith joins two pieces of metal into one." Randall replied. "As marriage is supposed to join a man and a woman."

She studied Randall from the corner of her eye. Remote, handsome, controlled. A man to be reckoned with. Would he and she ever be joined as thoroughly as the molten metal that caused two separate pieces to become one? That closeness with a near stranger seemed impossible now.

Yet in the past day she had come to accept him as a protector. In time, perhaps he might seem like a husband.

# Chapter 9

The five miles to the next village felt longer. By the time they reached their destination, Julia ached all over. "We've earned a good night's rest in a proper bed."

"We have indeed."

Randall's face was as weary as hers must be. Thankfully an old stone inn called the King's Arms was on the left. They rode together into the courtyard. Creaking in every joint, Julia dismounted from her sidesaddle as soon as the gelding halted.

Randall swung from his horse. When he touched ground, his right leg crumpled under him. He swore and grabbed his mount to stay upright.

"Randall!" Julia threw her reins at the approaching ostler and darted to his side. To her horror, she saw that the right thigh of his buckskins was saturated with blood.

Head bent, he panted, "Just . . . a piece of shrapnel cutting its way loose."

And he had been riding with that? Idiot man! To the ostler, she said, "Take care of the horses and bring our luggage in when you can."

She drew Randall's arm over her shoulders. "Can you make it into the inn?"

"Give me . . . a moment." After a dozen harsh breaths, he raised his head. "You're too small to be a crutch."

"I've hauled around other men who were too pig-headed to know when they were injured," she retorted.

Randall gave a ghost of a laugh as he straightened and let go of his saddle. "Your rudeness is refreshing. You're usually so ladylike."

"You have an odd sense of humor." Moving slowly, Julia helped Randall up the steps into the building. He was limping heavily, and she guessed he was dizzy with pain.

Inside, a capable woman in an apron came out to meet them in the hall. "I'm Mrs. Ferguson, the landlady," she said with a broad Scots accent. Her gaze went to Randall's bloody leg. "Trouble?"

"My husband, Major Randall, needs a surgeon," Julia replied. "Is there one near?"

"In Gretna Green."

Julia uttered a mental oath. They should have stopped in Gretna. "We need a room, hot water, clean linen, honey, laudanum if you have it, a couple of sharp knives, and a bottle of the strongest spirits in the house."

"That would be the local whiskey." The landlady took some of Randall's weight as she guided them along a passage toward the back of the building. "There's one room empty here on the ground floor. How did your husband injure himself?"

"The French did it for him."

"Och, the poor man. My youngest is with a Highland regiment." Mrs. Ferguson released Randall and moved forward to open the door to a small bedroom with plain white-washed walls. "Give me a moment to cover the bed."

The landlady pulled two heavy old blankets

from a wooden chest and shook them over the coverlet while Julia peeled off Randall's coat. He more or less collapsed onto the bed. His blond hair was damp with sweat.

"I'll be off for your supplies, Mrs. Randall."

"Thank you." Julia pulled off her cloak and bonnet and tossed them over the back of the chair that stood near the bed. Technically she had also been Mrs. Randall when she was married, but she'd always been called Lady Branford. She liked being Mrs. Randall a good deal better.

"Your invisibility has vanished," Randall said, his eyes closed. "You sound like Lady Julia Raines."

"Actually, I sounded like Mrs. Bancroft, well-trained midwife and de facto physician and surgeon." She pulled off Randall's boots, grateful that they were well broken in instead of fashionably tight.

"You asked for a knife. Are you going to perform field surgery?"

"If necessary." She examined the right boot. "I see you have a rather wicked little dagger sheathed here. Why am I not surprised?"

"I assume that question is rhetorical."

"Quite. I'd be shocked if you weren't armed to the teeth." She stripped off his buckskins, then used the knife to slit the gore-saturated right leg of his drawers. Blood was oozing from a wound

91

on the outside of his thigh. She touched it very carefully, jerking her hand away while she muttered something unladylike. "You were right about the shrapnel cutting its way out. I can feel sharp edges."

"This isn't the first time shrapnel has emerged." His fingers clutched the blanket spasmodically when she folded a thin towel from the washstand and pressed it over the wound to stop the bleeding. He drew an unsteady breath. "You might want to use the razor in my saddlebags."

That sounded better than a knife. The ostler arrived with the baggage then, so she thanked him and knelt to dig through the saddlebags. She had just located Randall's shaving kit when Mrs. Ferguson entered with a tray of supplies, followed by a maid with a canister of steaming water. "There's a full bottle of whiskey, along with large and small knives and plenty of bandages. Do you need anything else, Mrs. Randall?"

Julia glanced up. "This should do. Thank you."

Mrs. Ferguson looked at Randall uneasily. "Do you need my help?"

"We'll manage," Randall said hoarsely. "My Lady Julia is most competent."

Looking relieved, Mrs. Ferguson and the maid escaped. Julia saturated a cloth with whiskey and wiped down the razor and knife blades.

His gaze locked on the bottle. "A waste of good whiskey."

"My apologies." She propped him up with a couple of pillows, added a dose of laudanum to a glass of whiskey, and handed it over.

He swallowed half the glass in one gulp. "You could probably use a good swig yourself," he said, "but maybe it's better if you don't."

"I'll indulge gratefully after you're sorted out." She examined his thigh inch by inch, pressing gently on the hard muscles to find the still harder pieces of buried metal. Much easier to think of him as a patient than as a man. "You certainly have a lively assortment of scars."

"The surgeon who cut out most of the pieces told me that my battered hide set his personal record." Randall drank again, this time more slowly. His fingers whitened on the glass when she touched the area around the wound.

When she finished her examination, she said, "Besides the big piece that's bleeding so nastily, there's another piece above your knee. It hasn't broken the skin, but it feels loose. Active."

"So that's what's been hurting like bloody hell," he muttered. "Excuse my language. Will you cut that out, too?"

She wiped damp hands on her skirt. "I'd like to. From what I know of shrapnel, there are probably other pieces that have become immobilized and won't cause problems, but this one is trouble waiting to happen."

"And likely sooner than later." He exhaled

roughly. "You've had cutting experience?"

"With no proper surgeon in Hartley, I was the one who removed buckshot, pieces of wood, and any other foreign objects that became imbedded in human flesh. Usually male flesh." She folded a clean linen rag and used the hot water to wash the blood from his thigh. "Men are much more injury prone. If it's any comfort, I've never accidentally removed anything a man wanted to keep."

He smiled crookedly. "A *great* comfort."

His color was better, whether it from banter, whiskey, or because he was finally lying down rather than on horseback. "This is going to hurt," she warned. "Do you think you can keep still? I can ask Mrs. Ferguson for a male servant to hold you down."

He grimaced. "I doubt you'll do anything that will hurt much worse than the way my leg feels already. Just give me the whiskey bottle."

"Be careful," she said as she complied. "The combination of ardent spirits and laudanum can be dangerous."

"I'm hard to kill." He swallowed a mouthful. "In middling amounts, the whiskey and opium put a pleasant distance between my mind and your knife."

Feeling qualms, she said, "It's not too late to send for a proper surgeon."

He shook his head. "Proceed, my dear wife. I

trust you at least as much as the sawbones who hacked me about on the Peninsula."

She smiled unevenly, pleased at the trust but unnerved by the responsibility. "Not your wife yet, and after I get through cutting, you might want to cry off."

He laughed, his eyes lightening. "In Scottish terms, we're already married, Julia. We have presented ourselves as husband and wife before two witnesses."

"Married?" Her voice squeaked. She hadn't been quite ready. Still . . . "Perhaps it's just as well. With no proper ceremony, I didn't have to promise to obey you."

"Now I'm the one who is not surprised," he murmured. "I shall make a note of that. No obedience expected."

Ignoring his comment, she prepared for the surgery, placing folded cloths near to hand so she could blot the blood, and packing rolled towels on both sides of his thigh to steady it. His razor and the smaller of Mrs. Ferguson's knives were the sharpest, so she cleaned them with whiskey again. As she prepared to start cutting, he said, "Talk to me."

She paused. "About what?"

"Anything. How did you learn surgery?"

"I found the subject interesting. As a child, I would sneak off to the village surgeon's house to watch what he was doing. He's the one who

taught me to use spirits to clean instruments."
She blotted the blood from the jutting shrapnel
and prepared to cut. "I would have studied surgery if females were allowed. But midwifery is
equally fascinating, and it's a woman's trade."

She continued talking as she worked. She'd
learned the first rule of surgery early: quickness.
The faster she worked, the sooner the procedure
would be over, the less blood would be lost, and
the better the patient would fare.

She found that shrapnel was more difficult than
buckshot because the piece was larger, irregular
in shape, and all jagged edges. Wishing she had
forceps, she cut around the ugly lump of metal.
"This must have been working its way out for a
while. If it were close to the surface originally,
your army sawbones would have had it then."

"I've felt it gnawing through my leg for
months. Damnation!" He flinched as she got her
blade under the shrapnel and popped the frag-
ment from the muscle, but he managed to hold
his thigh reasonably still.

She blotted the raw wound clean, poured on
whiskey and blotted again, then dressed it with
honey. He asked, "Honey?"

"I learned that from Mrs. Bancroft. Wounds
are much less apt to fester if it's used." She tied
the bandage around his thigh. "That's done. Are
you still willing to have me remove the other
piece?"

"Might as well." He took a deep swallow of whiskey. "Cut on, Lady Macbeth."

"She didn't wield the knife herself. I wonder if she resented having to give the job to her husband? My governess made me memorize speeches from all Shakespeare's plays. I still remember them, too. *Give me the daggers!* That was Lady Macbeth. She was definitely a frustrated surgeon." Julia recited other speeches she'd learned so many years ago, which left most of her attention free to concentrate on her surgery.

This incision was more difficult because it wasn't as obviously needed, and she had to use the razor to cut unbroken skin. Reminding herself that she would save Randall—her husband? really?—pain later, she cut around the shrapnel. It was smaller than the first piece, but situated near vital tendons and ligaments. Praying she would do no harm, she loosened and removed the wicked piece of metal.

Thanking God she didn't seem to have done irrevocable damage, she dressed the wound and set her knives precisely on the tray. Then she folded onto the wooden chair by the bed. She felt dizzy and exhausted and for some reason, on the verge of tears.

"Have a drink." Randall offered her the whiskey bottle.

She accepted the bottle and tilted her head back

for a serious swig. Her swallow was followed by a fit of coughing. "Dear Lord," she gasped when she could speak again. "This could fell an ox!"

He chuckled. "That's rather the point."

She swallowed a smaller amount and handed him the bottle, then got to her feet, swaying a little. "It's getting dark. I'll ask Mrs. Ferguson for a lamp."

"Find yourself some food as well. And please pull out the chamber pot."

She frowned. "Are you in good enough condition to use it?"

"Well enough. Then I intend to sleep the clock around." Randall smiled at her with surprising sweetness. "Thank you, my indomitable lady. You are . . . quite amazing."

A little flustered, she fled the room and headed to the kitchen. Given the way he'd rescued her, she was glad that finally she could do something for him.

Her *husband?*

She followed the scent of food to the kitchen at the back of the house, where Mrs. Ferguson presided over two scullery maids. "You look rolled up," the older woman said briskly. "How is your husband?"

"Resting now. He'll do." Julia managed a smile.

"Naturally he wouldn't admit anything was wrong until he collapsed. Men!" The landlady snorted. "Sit you down, lass, and have something to eat before you collapse, too. Cutting shrapnel out of a husband looks right tiring."

Julia considered. "Not so bad as attending a two-day labor, but bad enough."

"You're a midwife?" Mrs. Ferguson needed no encouragement to talk about her own confinements and the fine, healthy bairns she had produced.

Julia was happy to sit quietly and let the talk flow around her while the landlady provided her with thick cock-a-leekie soup, fresh bread, cheese, and a pot of tea. By the time she finished eating, it was full dark. Mrs. Ferguson sent her back to the room with a lamp and the promise to arrange carriage hire for the day after tomorrow. Randall would have to rest for a day whether he wanted to or not.

Her brand new husband was dead to the world when she entered their room. He'd obviously managed to get up safely, for he was now sprawled under the covers. He looked . . . peaceful. She realized she'd never seen him without an undercurrent of pain in his expression.

Wryly she thought that she'd agreed to marry, not share a bed. But since she didn't want to sleep on the hard, cold floor, she didn't have much choice tonight.

Glad her shabby brown riding habit scarcely

showed the blood stains, she stripped down to her shift. It was a relief to be out of her stays and stockings. Even her head was relieved when she let down her hair.

If presenting themselves as married before witnesses meant that today was their wedding day, she supposed this was their wedding night. She winced as she remembered her first night with Branford. This wedding night was as different as humanly possible, and thank God for that.

She checked Randall's temperature and the bandages. No sign of fever. No further bleeding, either. As she'd told Mrs. Ferguson, he'd do.

After turning the lamp down to a faint glow, she slid under the covers on Randall's left, keeping as far away as possible. She was too tired even to feel alarmed at sharing a bed with a large male. Luckily, he was practically in a coma.

Even without touching, she was aware of the warmth of his body. As she closed her eyes, she had to admit that warmth was pleasant. Very pleasant.

Randall drifted to awareness slowly. His head suggested a little too much drink and his right leg ached, but the pain was no longer acute. His internal clock said it was around four in the morning, so he'd had a good night's sleep already. Not that he felt inclined to move. Not with a warm, soft female cuddled against his left side.

The fact that Julia hadn't chosen to sleep on the floor gave him hope for their evolving relationship. She fit under his arm nicely. Her own arm was draped around his waist. He wondered which of them had moved during the night. Both of them, perhaps, since they seemed to have met in the middle.

Enough moonlight came in the window to illuminate her face. She looked like a sleeping angel with dark hair flowing softly over her shift-clad shoulders. He felt a stirring of emotions. Awe. Gratitude. Tenderness.

Neither of them would feel properly married until they had a real wedding in Edinburgh. Yet here they were, sharing a bed. Part of each other's lives.

He was startled by another stirring that was purely physical. Thinking back, he realized that desire had been muted to almost nothing since he was wounded at Albuera. That muting had been mental as well as physical. Now, finally, the black cloud that had engulfed his life was beginning to dissipate.

Gently he stroked Julia's back. He'd wanted her since first seeing her. That desire had been rooted in mind and emotions. Now it was strengthened by unabashed lust. Desire would complicate their situation greatly. Yet he couldn't be sorry.

He wasn't sorry at all.

• • •

Julia woke slowly, feeling peaceful and . . . safe. She floated in a contented haze until she realized that she was pressed against Randall's side, her head on his shoulder and his arm around her.

She stiffened, wanting to withdraw, until his deep voice said, "No need to run off. Even if I forgot my promise to leave you alone, I'm not in any condition to assault you." He rolled his head on the pillow so their gazes met. "Unless you hate being held?"

"Actually, no." She relaxed again. "I quite like being cuddled up on a cool morning."

"Of which Scotland has an abundance."

"Hartley had its share." And her bed had been much less cozy. Her cat did her best to bring warmth, but Whiskers was only little.

"I think this is one of the main reasons people get married," Randall said reflectively. "For touch. For warmth and closeness. Passion is all very well, but it's brief. Affectionate touching can be done much more often."

She tilted her head up to study his face, surprised. "I didn't know you were a romantic."

He laughed. "I'm not. This kind of closeness is more of an animal pleasure, like kittens or puppies piling together."

Branford had never touched her with that kind of pleasure in mind. He was more interested in pain. Tensing, she changed the subject. "Have you had mistresses who gave you the taste for puppyish pleasures?"

"I think it came from my mother," he said thoughtfully. "She loved hugging. I hadn't realized it before, but you remind me of her a little. Not so much looks or personality, but there's a warmth of the spirit that you have in common."

She knew from her patients that many long-term marriages had little physical intimacy. If Randall could be content with an affectionate mothering female rather than a passionate wife, they might suit very well.

"My mother also loved to hug. Not very duchesslike." Which might be why Julia also loved this warm, undemanding embrace. She had spent many years without enough touching. "I would like to lie this way for the next week."

"So would I," he said with regret. "But we need to be up and on our way."

"We won't have a carriage until tomorrow." She burrowed deeper under his arm. "So resign yourself to a day of eating and sleeping."

He laughed, the rumbling in his chest reminding her of a purring cat. "Outmaneuvered, I see. Very well then, today we rest. We should be safe enough here."

As Julia dozed off again, her body molded to his, she decided that if this was Randall's idea of marriage, she liked it very well.

# Chapter 10

Julia gazed out the window as their carriage rolled from the King's Arms' yard and swung north toward Edinburgh. "After so many quiet years in Hartley, now I feel like I'm in constant motion. Yet it's been only three days since I was abducted."

"Three very eventful days," Randall reminded her. "But yesterday was peaceful."

Blessedly so. Randall had proved himself an undemanding husband by sleeping most of the day, surfacing twice to eat voraciously before returning to his slumbers. But his body had its own wisdom. When she'd checked the dressing on his thigh late the previous afternoon, the surgical wounds were halfway to being healed.

"You're a very satisfactory patient," she observed. "This morning you're so hale and hardy you barely need that twisted old cane Mrs. Ferguson provided. I can tell myself that I'm a masterful healer."

He laughed. "You are. I've been chopped by experts, and not only do you measure up well against them, but you're much better looking."

She looked away, uncomfortable with the compliment. "A gallant lie, Major."

"Truth, Lady Julia. You've been practicing invisibility so long that you've forgotten what an attractive woman you are."

She kept her gaze on the dramatic Scottish hills, torn between pleasure that he thought her attractive, and extreme uneasiness.

His warm hand enfolded hers. "You really are lovely, Julia," he said quietly. "Once, before you married, you must have known that, and surely you enjoyed being admired. That's natural. Though you had reason to forget during the years since, reclaiming your life means accepting all that you are. And that includes lovely."

She smiled crookedly. "I can't manage that yet. Let me work on accepting the idea that I'm passable."

"Very well, my lady." His voice was warm with humor. "You look quite passable today. Such a very passable complexion. Pray remove your bonnet so I can admire your passable chestnut hair."

Laughing, she was able to look at him as she took off her bonnet. She had once found his austere, chiseled features intimidating, but no longer. "I can't believe how very agreeable you are, Major. You were so prickly when we first met."

"You're right, it's most unlike me to be agreeable," he said solemnly. "For your sake, I hope I don't revert to my usual surly self."

Though his expression was sober, humor lurked in his eyes. No longer was pain shadowed in his face. "Ever since we met, you've had metal bits slicing out of your body. That would explain a fair amount of surliness."

He sighed. "I'm hoping that you got the last of shifting shrapnel. Though my leg aches, for the first time in over a year, there's no acute pain."

"My blades stand ready if needed to cure your bad temper again."

His brows arched. "Is that a promise or a threat?"

"A threat," she said sweetly.

"I'll bear that in mind." He turned thoughtful. "I think it also helps that once I stopped resisting you, I became much more relaxed. For many years, my life had been about pain and war. With you, I can now imagine a life beyond that."

"The life of a country midwife is about as far from war as can be imagined," she agreed, understanding better why he was drawn to her. "Now that we've moved beyond our old lives, what lies ahead? Not being the intrepid sort, I'm glad not to follow the drum, but where will we live? You said you have a small estate?"

"I inherited Roscombe from my mother. It's near Cirencester, and I lived there as a boy. Though nothing like so grand as where you were raised, I think you'll like the place." He grinned. "I'm looking forward to pottering around my own estate and learning more about sheep and crops. Perhaps I shall become a hunting squire. A pack of hounds, side whiskers, and a red face."

She laughed. "Now that I cannot imagine. But I like the idea of a gentry life, comfortable and not too grand. I suppose there would be occasional visits to London?"

"Of course. As you know, Ash has given me the use of a suite of rooms at Ashton House, but we could lease a house if you prefer."

"I might not like London well enough to want a home there. If Ashton doesn't mind, it would be pleasant to stay with him and Mariah when we're in town." She looked pensively at the rugged Scottish hills. "The north is beautiful, but I've missed the friendly fields and villages of southern England. I'll be happy to return there."

"Will you continue as a midwife?" His voice was casual, as if the question was no great matter.

Her head whipped around. "You would allow it?"

"After marriage to my despicable cousin, I think you've earned the right to make decisions about your own life," he said peaceably. "Besides, if I try to lay down the law too often, you'll leave me. I'd rather that didn't happen."

She realized her hand was still in his, and she was squeezing hard enough to cut off the blood flow. Gently she released her grip. "I hadn't thought that far ahead, but you're right. I like delivering babies, and I will never live in a cage again."

"Nor do I want to put you in one." His gaze

was intent. "You have a gift for healing. I don't want to deprive the world of your skills. But Gloucestershire doesn't lack physicians and surgeons, so perhaps you could restrict yourself to midwifery. That way you could deliver babies and still have time to be the lady of the manor."

"That sounds like a very sensible plan," she agreed, marveling that he accepted the value of her work, and understood what it meant to her. "I've had no experience of men who don't simply lay down the law and expect women to obey."

"I have spent most of my adult life both giving and receiving orders that were often half-mad or tragic," he said wryly. "I find the gentle art of compromise appealing."

Under his dry humor, she heard the weariness produced by years of war and command. Her lips curved into a slow smile. "I begin to think, Major Randall, that perhaps a marriage between us would have a real future."

More surprisingly—she was starting to really want this match.


Their journey to Edinburgh was fast and efficient, made in one long day with post horses and brief stops for refreshment. Despite the bouncing of the coach, Randall managed to sleep for a good part of the journey. Julia envied him. It was a useful gift, and would aid his healing.

At dusk, they rolled to a stop in front of Kirkland's handsome town house. Randall had offered commentary as they drove through Edinburgh, which was attractive and more rugged than Julia had expected. She hoped they would have a chance to visit the castle that loomed portentously above the city.

As Randall helped her from the post chaise, he said, "This is where I stayed with Kirkland on my recent visit. Since he travels a great deal for his shipping business, his favorite aunt lives here and looks after the place. You'll like Mrs. Gowan, and she will love helping you prepare for a swift but respectable wedding."

She looked up at the stone façade uncertainly. "You're sure Lord Kirkland won't mind you bringing me here?"

"Quite sure." Randall took his cane in one hand, then offered her his other arm. "He likes you. He said that having you and Mariah with us vastly improved the journey from Hartley to London."

She took his arm and they climbed the steps. He was hardly limping at all. "Apart from you scowling at me, it was an enjoyable trip."

"As I've said, life is much easier now that I've stopped resisting your charms." Randall knocked on the door, then said to the butler who answered, "You thought you were free of me, Tanner, but your relief was premature."

The butler chuckled. "A pleasure to see you again so soon, sir. Lord Kirkland will also be pleased." His curious gaze went to Julia.

"My plans changed," Randall said with a smile.

The butler bowed them in. "If you would care to wait in the salon, I shall inform his lordship of your arrival." He opened the door on the right.

Julia entered the salon while Randall lingered to talk to the butler. She was stripping off her gloves when she saw a familiar figure at the writing desk in front of the window. "Lord Masterson?"

The large, calm major was another of the Westerfield friends who had searched for the lost duke, and he'd been the most accepting of her and Mariah. "I had thought you were campaigning in Spain."

The man glanced up, then stood and moved away from the window. "Sorry, I'm not Masterson. I'm his less respectable, not to mention less legitimate, half brother, Damian Mackenzie. And you are . . . ?"

Without the glare of the window behind him, she recognized her mistake. He and Masterson had similar features and broad, muscular bodies, but this stranger had more auburn in his hair and a roguish gleam in his eyes. Which were of two different colors, she saw as he approached. One brown, one blue. Startling and a little distracting.

She wondered briefly how to introduce herself.

Highborn Lady Julia Raines wouldn't deign to do so, but despite Randall's desire to reclaim her rank, she didn't feel like that ducal daughter any more. She had never really been Mrs. Bancroft, she refused to be Lady Branford, and she was not yet Mrs. Randall. She settled for, "I'm Julia. Quite boringly legitimate."

"Well played," he said lightly. "Yes, my esteemed brother is in Spain, having the sense to duck quickly when necessary, I hope."

"Did you also go to the Westerfield Academy, Mr. Mackenzie?" she asked. "I gather the friendships made there tend to be enduring."

"Please, call me Mac. I hate it when people take me seriously." His smile was distinctly wicked. "Yes, I'm another product of Westerfield, two years behind Will."

"Mac is living proof that even Lady Agnes can't work miracles on all her bad boys," Randall said as he entered the room behind Julia. He came forward to offer his hand. "Good to see you. It's been"—he thought—"a lot of years."

"I was sorry when Kirkland said I missed you by a day," Mackenzie said as they shook hands. "What brings you back to Edinburgh?"

Randall rested a warm hand on the small of Julia's back. "We're betrothed, and I thought Kirkland would help us arrange a Scottish wedding."

"You're marrying this girl?" Mackenzie exclaimed, jaw dropping.

"I hope you didn't mean that to be as insulting as it sounded," Randall said coolly.

"Sorry, no insult intended." Mackenzie bowed to Julia. "I just never thought of you as the marrying kind, Randall. My best wishes to you both."

Julia nodded thanks while wondering if Mackenzie was covering up surprise that a man as handsome as Randall would marry a drab sparrow like her. A fair question, but not something even a self-professed rogue would ask.

The awkward moment ended when Kirkland entered, as dark, handsome, and enigmatic as she remembered. "Randall, what brings you back . . . ? Julia!" He dropped his usual detachment to smile broadly and clasp her hand. "Randall is the bad penny that will always return, but it's a most unexpected pleasure to see you."

"Julia and I are betrothed, and I hoped we could be married from your house," Randall said. "It's . . . rather a complicated story."

Kirkland also looked surprised, though he hid it better than Mackenzie. "My Aunt Maggie loves a wedding, and she'll be delighted to help you plan yours. She's out for the day, but she'll be back this evening. Let me show you to your room, Julia. After you've refreshed yourself, come down and we can discuss complications over dinner. Randall, you're in the room where you stayed last time. Mac, will you tell Tanner to increase the place settings to four, please?"

An efficient man, Lord Kirkland. As he escorted her upstairs, Julia tried to recall the little she knew about him. His title was from his English father, but his mother had been the daughter of a wealthy Scottish merchant. As a boy, he had been regrettably intrigued by his Scottish relatives, and trade, so he'd been sent to the Westerfield Academy. Instead of turning respectable, he'd become a shipping magnate himself.

Kirkland took her to a spacious guest room with a splendid view of Edinburgh Castle in the distance. "I believe the room is in fit shape. A maid will come to check."

"I'm sure it's fine." More than fine. A quick survey showed that Kirkland kept his guests in comfort. "You're very generous to take us in so unexpectedly."

"I've had far more unexpected guests than you." His eyes twinkled. "And less respectable ones, too."

On impulse, she said, "Randall tells me that in Scotland, a woman can sue for divorce on equal terms with a man. Is that true?"

"It is." Without moving a muscle, Kirkland became very intent. "Did you doubt Randall's word? You shouldn't. He's alarmingly honest."

"I don't question his honesty." She turned away to remove her cloak. "But he might have been misinformed."

"He's seldom wrong." Kirkland regarded her thoughtfully. "It's odd to be inquiring about divorce on the eve of a wedding. Are you having second thoughts?"

Though his tone was neutral, his concern for his friend's future was clear. "I like Randall very well," Julia assured him. "I'm not sure I like marriage as much."

"Samuel Johnson said a second marriage is the triumph of hope over experience," Kirkland said. "Where would we be without hope? Randall can be prickly, but he's one of the most perceptive men I know, and his loyalty is absolute."

"So I have found. I'm fortunate." She smiled wryly. "He is less so."

"Doubt is natural when contemplating such a major step, but I think you might suit rather well." A knock on the door announced the entry of a maid, who entered with Julia's modest bag of belongings and a pitcher of steaming water. Kirkland headed for the door. "I shall see you downstairs when you are ready."

After Kirkland and the maid left, Julia poured water into the basin and began to wash up. So one of Randall's old friends thought he and Julia would suit? Perhaps hope really would triumph over experience.

# Chapter 11

By the time Randall finished writing the letter that would help release Julia from their marriage, he judged that she'd had sufficient time to freshen up. He crossed the hall and tapped on the door, identifying himself. His leg ached some from the long, hard day of travel, but he needed the cane much less today.

He entered when Julia called permission. Even in her worn, ill-fitting gown, his bride looked thoroughly delectable. The shining chestnut hair that fell past her shoulders was a good deal better than passable, and her delicate features and flawless complexion made him want to touch.

In fact, he wanted rather intensely to cross the room and take her in his arms, but her withdrawn expression made it clear that she was not in the mood. The fact that she had invited him into her bedroom without hesitation was progress enough for this day. "I'm just across the hall. Near, yet too far."

She gave a swift smile. "We really can't sleep together here since we're not precisely married. I hope the night isn't too cold."

"Two or three more days and we'll be legal in the eyes of the world." Even though they'd only shared a bed for two nights, tonight he would miss having her there. He handed her the letter he had just written. "As you requested."

She unfolded the paper and scanned the brief lines. "Very good. Thank you." Expression unreadable, she set the letter aside and began pinning back her hair. He hoped that after they were married, she might consider a less austere style.

"I didn't know Will Masterson had a brother," she remarked.

"Mac is the daughter of an actress, and the reason why Will ended up at Westerfield," Randall explained.

"I've wondered about that," she said, her hands moving swiftly as she tamed her hair into severity. "It's easy to see why the rest of your lot were sent to a school for difficult boys, but it's hard to imagine Will as a serious troublemaker."

"Mac's mother died when he was quite young, so he was sent to his father's house where Lord Masterson could decide what to do with him," Randall explained. "Will, who is a couple of years older, became very attached to his little brother. I think their father would have preferred to send Mac to a foster home where he could be forgotten, but Will wouldn't allow that. He refused to go away to school unless Mac could come, too. As you say, Will isn't a troublemaker by nature."

"Unlike you," Julia said with that quick smile again.

"Unlike me," Randall agreed, amused. "But he can be quite remarkably stubborn. Lord Masterson wasn't keen on sending his bastard to a fashionable school like Eton or Harrow, so the Westerfield Academy was a good alternative."

"Mr. Mackenzie was fortunate to have Will for a champion." Julia ruthlessly pinned down the last dark waves. "But he seemed rather disrespectful about his brother. Flippant."

"That's just Mac. He would give his life for Will without a second thought. Mocking all the way." Randall offered his arm. "Shall we go down?"

She tucked her hand around his arm. He loved these small signs that they were now a couple.

"Why did Kirkland and Mackenzie look so surprised at the idea of your marrying?" she asked as they left the room.

"I used to be quite vehement that I'd never take a wife, particularly if doing so would gratify my Uncle Daventry." He smiled wryly. "It was only recently that I recognized how foolish it would be to deny myself something I wanted merely because he wanted it, too."

"The unglamorous wisdom of maturity." They shared a warm glance. As they headed for the stairs, he said, "I think it best to explain to Kirkland and Mackenzie that Daventry is after you, and why. Shall I do the talking?"

She sighed. "Please. Just—don't tell them the more humiliating details."

"I won't," he promised. "And neither of them will speak of anything you prefer to keep private." They began to descend the stairs. "Now, Lady Julia Raines, it's time to leave the shadows and move into the light."

"We won't need you again, Tanner," Kirkland said. After the butler left the dining room, he continued, "I hope I get credit for controlling my curiosity through dinner. Julia, have you ever yearned to see what the gentlemen talk about over port? This is your opportunity."

"I think I'm better off not knowing." She was about to rise and take her leave when Randall's gaze caught hers. She could almost hear him thinking that if she was to face down London society, she should be able to face two men who were his friends. "But I suppose I should stay since the conversation concerns me."

Kirkland nodded as if that was natural. "If you're not familiar with port etiquette, I am allowed to serve a lady on my right"—he poured her a half glass of ruby wine—"but otherwise, the custom is to always slide the decanter to the left"— he demonstrated, pushing the crystal decanter down the polished mahogany to Randall—"and never to lift it unnecessarily, since a gentleman who has drunk too much might spill some."

"Which would be a grievous waste," Mackenzie said piously.

As Randall poured his port, Kirkland said, "You mentioned that the story behind your betrothal is complicated, Randall. Care to elaborate?"

"Though you know Julia as Mrs. Bancroft, her real name is Lady Julia Raines," Randall said succinctly as he slid the decanter to Mackenzie.

Mackenzie caught his breath, so startled he temporarily forgot to fill his glass. "You were married to Branford, Lady Julia?"

Julia winced inwardly. "Yes."

"You have my sympathies."

"On his death?" she asked dryly.

"On having been married to him." Mackenzie looked as if he'd tasted sour wine. He poured himself a drink, then passed the decanter back toward Kirkland. "He would have made the very devil of a husband, and that's putting it charitably."

"Exactly," Randall said, mercifully drawing attention from Julia. "One day when he was drunk and violent, Julia shoved him while she was trying to escape. He fell and hit his head and died. Unfortunately, his father, my Uncle Daventry, blamed Julia. The situation became so untenable that Julia faked her death and ran away."

Kirkland's brows arched. "I suspected that your background was unusual, Julia, but I didn't guess this. If you're a Raines, you must be Castleton's daughter?"

"I was once," she said tersely. "He disowned me."

"You're still his daughter, no matter what the old curmudgeon chose to do with his will." Kirkland studied her intently. "So you hid in the wilds of Cumberland and became a midwife. Randall coaxed you out of hiding?"

"I would have been content to stay in Hartley forever." She thought wistfully of her peaceful, useful life and the friends she'd made. "But I must have been recognized when I visited London with Mariah because four days ago I was abducted by Daventry's men. Randall happened to be visiting in Hartley and came after me when he heard the news. He rescued me from four villains, suggested we marry, and here we are."

Kirkland and Mackenzie were both staring. "Only four, Randall?" Mackenzie said ironically. "Hardly worth mentioning since there were fewer than six."

Randall shrugged. "No combat was involved. While the carriage horses were resting, I located Julia and we decamped under cover of night."

"Let me see if I understand this properly, Randall," Kirkland said slowly. "You are marrying the widow of your cousin. Your uncle, whose heir you are, considers her a murderer and wants to seek vengeance now that he knows she's alive. Do you look for trouble, or does it just find you?"

"I'm not sure that wanting to marry Julia falls into either category," Randall replied. "While it's a complication that she is my cousin's widow, I wanted to marry her before I learned that. Even if I hadn't, I could hardly stand by when I heard that men had broken into her home, tied up her apprentice, and carried her off in broad daylight."

"Certainly not." Kirkland frowned. "Is Julia still in danger? It seems likely."

"I think Daventry will call off his dogs after I visit him and tell him of our marriage. He wants to see a healthy heir to the earldom before he dies, and that means accepting Julia as my wife." Randall's brow furrowed. "I doubt that Daventry's men will find us now that we're away from Cumberland. But until we reach London and I've talked with my uncle—yes, there might be some danger."

"I'm about to return to London," Mackenzie said, serious for once. "If you like, I can travel with you."

"I can't say that I ever imagined having you along on my honeymoon, Mac," Randall said, his mouth quirking up. "But yes, that would be very helpful. Just in case."

Mackenzie smiled beatifically, seriousness abandoned again. "Splendid! A long journey is much more interesting if there is a possibility of mayhem."

"We will be taking a detour into Cumberland to collect some of Julia's belongings," Randall warned. "That will add a couple of days to the trip."

The other man shrugged. "I shall see a part of the country new to me."

The dining room door opened and a well-dressed woman of middle years swept in. "I can't leave the house for the day without matters getting out of hand!" She smiled affectionately at her nephew as she scanned the guests. "Tanner says Major Randall has returned with his betrothed, and I am to organize a wedding?"

Kirkland chuckled as the men arose to their feet. "He spoke true, Aunt Maggie. Unless Randall's betrothed prefers to make other arrangements. Lady Julia Raines, meet Mrs. Margaret Gowan, the most alarming of my aunts. I shall leave it to the two of you to work out wedding plans."

Julia rose. "Since my presence is no longer needed, I'll bid you good night so you gentlemen no longer have to be on your good behavior."

"Your suspicions wound me," Mackenzie said soulfully.

Randall grinned. "I would say she's taken your measure, Mac. Sleep well, Julia." His glance said clearly how much he wished he could join her later.

Surprised at how much she wanted the same

thing, Julia joined Mrs. Gowan. "Let's have a nice pot of tea while you tell me what you'd like for your wedding," the older woman said. She had a cheerful, no-nonsense quality that reminded Julia of Mrs. Ferguson at the King's Arms.

After ordering tea to be delivered to her private parlor, Mrs. Gowan led the way to a comfortably furnished sitting room. "Make yourself comfortable, Lady Julia." She waved toward the chairs. "I'm sure you have an interesting tale to tell if you wish to tell it, lass. Major Randall had no thoughts of marrying when he left here last week."

"The decision was sudden, but we've known each other for some time," Julia said, deliberately vague.

Disappointed not to learn more but still hospitable, Mrs. Gowan said, "Tanner gave the impression that you wanted the wedding performed as quickly as possible. What kind of ceremony would you like?"

Julia hadn't considered the question, so she had to think. "A small church ceremony. Nothing elaborate."

"I imagine you and Major Randall are Anglican." The older woman picked up a sheet of paper and a pencil so she could make notes. "Do you require an Anglican chapel, or will Church of Scotland do?"

Julia hadn't thought about that, either. Since

the whole point of marrying in Scotland was to give her the right to divorce, they might as well be Scottish all the way. "The Church of Scotland will do very well, and surely be easier."

"Indeed it will." Mrs. Gowan nodded approvingly. "Our parish church is only a street away, and it will be easy to arrange a ceremony there. What else?"

Julia grimaced at her worn, unattractive clothing. "If there's time, I'd like to get a nicer gown. I have nothing suitable with me."

"That's easily done. My youngest daughter is about your size, and she'd be happy to give away a gown or two since it would give her an excuse to buy more." Mrs. Gowan made a note. "No matter how small a wedding is, anything so important needs to be done right. Do you have any friends in Edinburgh you'd like to invite?"

"No one but Kirkland. I'm a widow and have always lived in England," Julia explained. "My first wedding was very grand. I'd like this to be as different as possible."

"It will be, lass." The tea arrived, and Mrs. Gowan poured them each a cup. "Now tell me what else you'd like for your wedding day."

When she'd married Branford, all the arrangements had been made by Julia's elders. She'd had almost no say. This wedding would be small, but to her own taste. And, please God, the marriage that resulted would be, too.

# Chapter 12

After Mrs. Gowan swept Julia away, Mac finished his port and got to his feet. "I'll take my leave now. There's a gaming house I need to inspect."

"Keep a tight hand on your purse," Kirkland advised.

When Mac was gone, Randall said, "Is he visiting on your official, or your unofficial, business?"

"A little of both. Plus some of *his* official business." Kirkland grinned. "We aren't all as straightforward as you."

"War reduces life to basics." Randall thought of what lay ahead. "Matters are more complex now that I'm out of the army."

Kirkland leaned back in his chair and laced his fingers together on his midriff. "Are you as confident that you can tame your uncle as you appeared?"

"No, but I thought I might as well appear confident until events prove otherwise." Randall's smile was ironic. "No battle plan survives first contact with the enemy. Daventry is capable of reason, but it's also possible that he'll pull a pistol from his desk and take aim. I can handle that. Hired assassins in dark alleys are harder to guard against. For Julia's sake, I hope the danger can be removed. She's suffered enough because of the Randall family."

Kirkland's eyes narrowed. "I never met Branford, and you never talked about him. He was that bad?"

"Worse." Randall knew he could never fully understand what it was like to be a young girl at Branford's mercy. Julia had been scarcely more than a child. But he knew enough of his cousin to be chilled at the thought of what she'd endured.

"Would you welcome an excuse to kill Daventry?" Kirkland asked quietly.

Frowning, Randall considered the question. His uncle had refused to acknowledge or check his son's cruelties. Because of that, Randall and Julia had both suffered at Branford's hands. And of course, there was Daventry's desire to let his nephew die of neglect. "Perhaps I would. But the provocation would have to be great."

"I shall hope that he can be tamed. If you have to kill him, it would be the damnedest scandal."

"You have a gift for understatement." Randall refilled their glasses. "Before I forget, thanks for your support. We could have married in Gretna Green, but I didn't want this to be a hole-in-corner wedding."

Kirkland swirled his port glass without drinking. "I think highly of Julia, but are you sure this marriage is wise? She seems a rather uncertain bride."

"Which is why we're in Scotland," Randall said wryly. "She's only willing to marry me if she's sure there's a way out."

Kirkland relaxed. "I should have realized you were aware of her misgivings."

"If there was time I'd court her in the usual way, but that isn't possible. I can best protect her if she's my wife." Which was true. But he wondered if his courtship would have been successful if she hadn't been in fear of her life. He suspected not.

"Still the knight in shining armor, I see." The other man hesitated. "Though she needs and deserves protection, sacrificing your future is not the only solution."

"Marriage is no sacrifice on my part," Randall said flatly. "She has not been out of my mind since the first moment we met."

Kirkland studied him. "Then it is better to marry than to burn." He raised his glass. "May you both find the happiness you deserve. Preferably with each other."

Randall could drink to that. Especially the latter part.

Julia was working at the writing desk in her room when she heard quiet footsteps accompanied by the tap of a cane. Randall was coming up to bed. He would be able to see the light under her door. Would he come in to say good night?

She was pleased when he knocked on the door. "Come in," she called as she rose from her chair to greet him. "I'm making lists. Mrs. Gowan suggests that we marry two days from now? With a wedding breakfast here after the ceremony."

"Very good." He glanced at his travel-stained garments. "I need to find myself some decent clothes. Maybe I can borrow something of Kirkland's. We're around the same size." He smiled a little. "You haven't decided to take flight? Every time I see you, I'm half-surprised that you haven't slipped away."

Though he spoke as if it was a joke, she recognized his underlying seriousness. "I am nervous," she admitted. "But I give my word that I won't run away. You're my best chance of a normal life."

That surprised a laugh from him. "I'm not sure if I'm pleased or alarmed to be seen as normal."

"You should be pleased."

"Then I will be. Sleep well, Julia." He started to turn away.

"Wait." She rose on her toes and gave him a goodnight hug, her arms sliding under his coat. His cane fell to the floor with a clatter as he hugged her back, strong arms enfolding her.

Though they'd slept together for two nights, this was the first time they'd embraced while standing. "Ahhhh . . ." she breathed as she leaned into him, resting her head on one broad shoulder.

She felt the beat of his heart, the rhythm of his breathing, the hard muscle and bone beneath her gently caressing hands. "This would be more convenient if I were taller."

"I think you fit very nicely." He stroked her head, his fingers kneading gently. She didn't realize that pins were falling out until her hair fell around her shoulders.

"You have extremely passable hair," he murmured as he ran his fingers through it.

She laughed a little, feeling feminine and attractive and—unafraid. Randall made her feel safe. As Hartley's unofficial physician, she'd cut and sewed and patched male bodies, but embracing a healthy man was very different.

His hands smoothed down her arms to her back, making gentle circles. "I'm glad you're getting used to my touch," he murmured.

"I like your touch." Which was quite amazing, really. But true. She wasn't sure how long they held each other. A long time, though not long enough. Randall seemed as content to be peaceful as she was. Thank God he wasn't a lustful, pawing boy. It was becoming ever easier to imagine a marriage of affection and companionship.

Finally he sighed and released her. "I'll be asleep on my feet in another few minutes." He bent and retrieved his cane, barely wincing as he bent his right leg. "Good night, milady."

There was a caressing tone in his voice that made her feel like a cat being petted. Regretting his departure, she said, "Only two more nights in separate beds."

He paused, and for a moment she thought he was going to kiss her. She withdrew a little, not ready for that much intimacy.

Perceptive, he brushed a kiss on her forehead. Light. Unthreatening. "I'll sleep better knowing you're not going to run away."

He was gone before she could say that she no longer wanted to run from him.

# Chapter 13

Randall experienced his wedding in flashes of clarity, surrounded by a haze of unreality. Julia looking lovely as the dawn in a rose-colored gown with soft waves of chestnut hair framing her delicate features. Mackenzie, one of the guests, coming alert as he noticed how attractive the bride was. Julia's ice cold hands as she tucked a sprig of her white heather nosegay into Randall's coat, whispering unevenly that it was for luck.

He felt nervous as a cat on a griddle. She must feel even more anxious since this was her second trip to the altar, and the first had been a disaster. *The triumph of hope over experience.*

His mind was very clear on how much of a

gamble this marriage was—but his heart, soul, and every particle of his body wanted her. He'd given up trying to understand why. What mattered was that she was willing to trust him enough to say yes.

The wedding breakfast at Kirkland's house was actually a wedding luncheon and lasted for several good-natured hours. As the guests and newlyweds laughed and joked and ate excellent food, Randall relaxed and the world began to seem normal again.

The feast ended when Kirkland stood to make a toast. Raising his glass toward the bridal couple, he said with a grin, "I've known you for over twenty years, Randall, and I never thought you would show such good sense as to marry a woman like Julia."

"I hadn't yet met Julia, so I was unaware that I would want to marry." His gaze found hers, and they shared rueful amusement over all the complicated reasons that had brought them together.

More seriously, Kirkland continued, "For this Scottish and English wedding, I offer a blessing in Gaelic and English." After uttering several sentences in rolling Gaelic, he said in English:

*"May you be healthy all your days.*
*May you be blessed with long life and peace,*
*May you grow old with goodness and with riches."*

"Thank you." Randall would settle for health, long life, and peace. Riches weren't necessary. As for the goodness—Julia had enough for both of them. His gaze moved to the other guests. There were only a handful. Apart from Mac, they were friends and family of Kirkland, all of whom had met Julia and fallen in love with her.

Raising his glass, Randall continued, "My thanks to all of you for coming and making today special." He finished his toast in one long swallow, then stood and bowed to his wife, unable to restrain his smile at the thought. *His wife!* "Since we will be leaving Edinburgh in the morning, milady, would you like to spend the rest of the afternoon exploring the city? You've not had much time to see it."

"I'd like that." Julia rose and gave her own thanks to the guests, with a hug for Mrs. Gowan. Then she collected a shawl and bonnet, and they left the town house.

They stepped into the quiet residential street. As usual in Scotland, the day was a mix of sunshine, swift clouds, and brisk temperatures. Randall exhaled with relief. "It was a good celebration, but I'm glad to be alone with you. What would you like to see? Edinburgh Castle? Holyrood Palace? The twisty old streets and closes of the old town? Edinburgh isn't like any English city."

She took his arm. "I want to see it all!"

He chuckled. "Will you settle for as much as we can manage before we run out of time or stamina?"

"That will do." She frowned. "Or until your leg starts bothering you. You aren't using the cane today."

"Hardly a twinge left. You do good work." He studied Julia's face. Lovely, serene, and a little haunted. *My wife.* As they turned into Princes Street, he said quietly, "I'm glad you didn't bolt, Julia."

"So am I." Her expression was pensive. "I have trouble remembering why I was so anxious. Now I feel wonderfully free."

"Because the decision is behind you." He smiled ruefully. "It's trying to decide that ties one in knots."

She laughed, looking young and carefree. "You're right. I feel as if I've made a new start in life. Looking forward, not back." She released his elbow and took hold of his hand, interlacing her fingers with his. "You risk a great deal by marrying a woman whose only dowry is likely to be trouble. Thank you for daring to do it."

"You risk a great deal by marrying at all." He hesitated. "I don't know why, but I can talk to you about things I'd discuss with no one else."

"And I've told you things I've revealed to no one else. Not at all a bad foundation for a marriage."

Julia's expression was warm and vivid—like a happy bride. With a rush of excitement, he realized that tonight might be a true wedding night. She had changed a great deal in the last days. If she wasn't ready for intimacy, he would never force her. But it was impossible not to hope. The happier he felt, the more he wanted her.

As they turned into broad Princes Street, Julia said, "I liked the wedding vows. No nonsense about me obeying you."

He laughed. "Scottish women are an independent lot, and the wedding vows reflect that. They might have been designed for you."

Her hand tightened on his. "I'm glad we came to Edinburgh. The city and your friends have given our marriage a good start."

Randall thought buoyantly that someday they would tell their grandchildren about this wedding day. He sobered when he remembered there would be no grandchildren. He hadn't much cared when Julia told him she couldn't bear a child because he had never expected marriage and family. Nor did the Daventry succession matter much to him.

Yet now he found that he did care. He would like to have a daughter with Julia's sweet smile and quick mind. He'd like to raise a son with kindness instead of brutality. That would never happen, and the loss was sharper than he could have imagined a fortnight before.

But that loss didn't matter as long as he had Julia.

● ● ●

Julia couldn't remember when she'd last felt so lighthearted as she had during their exploration of Edinburgh. Randall was the perfect escort. He made her feel safe and cherished, and he knew the city well. It was a grand, dramatic place with more than its share of history, and very different from London.

Ever since Randall had proposed marriage, she had wondered if it was wrong to marry a man only because he was the best of a poor set of choices. Yet Randall had become so much more than bald necessity. He was amazingly kind to her, and amazingly patient. Though she was still uneasy about marriage, she wouldn't do better than Randall for a husband.

By the time they returned to Kirkland's house, the light was fading and she was pleasantly tired. Since Kirkland didn't use the spacious master suite himself, the rooms had been designated the bridal suite for tonight.

"I see Mrs. Gowan's hand at work here," Julia said when they entered the large bedroom. She touched the rose blossoms in the lavish bouquet set on a small table.

"She has a sense of occasion," Randall said appreciatively as he investigated the sitting area at the far end of the room. A table and two chairs had been elegantly set with covered dishes and a bottle of wine chilling in ice. "Shall we change for bed and share champagne and this cold supper? I thought I'd eaten enough food for a week after the wedding breakfast, but all that walking has made me hungry."

"Food, champagne, and rest." She smiled at him as she removed her bonnet. "The end to a perfect day. Will you unfasten my gown so I needn't ring for a maid?"

"Of course." He fumbled a little as he undid the ties at the back of her neck and her waist, his fingers warm against her skin. She smiled. Better a little clumsiness than a man with too much skill at undressing women.

When he was done, he bent to press a light kiss on her nape. His warm lips sent a shiver through her, and she wasn't sure if it was from pleasure or alarm. Perhaps some of both, which was itself alarming.

"Thank you." Not looking at him, she retreated to the small lady's dressing room. Though it wasn't late, the day had been tiring. She was ready to go to bed. And more than ready to share it with Randall. He had been a warm and pleasant bedmate, and it would be good to fall asleep in his arms again.

Julia let down her hair and brushed it loose over her shoulders. In the soft light, she didn't look much older than the sixteen-year-old innocent she'd been on her first wedding night. Except for her eyes, which showed too much bleak experience.

She turned and removed her rose gown, then donned the elegant muslin nightgown and matching robe that were Mrs. Gowan's wedding gifts. The sleeves were long and the neckline was not low, yet the layers of filmy material and white-on-white embroidery made her feel uncomfortably bridal.

Reminding herself that this would not be their first night together, she returned to the bedroom. Hands clasped behind his back, Randall stood at a window watching the last of the day's light fade behind the craggy heights of Edinburgh Castle. His dark blue dressing gown emphasized his blond hair, powerful body, and broad shoulders.

He was pure Viking warrior, and the knowledge that she'd married him—was alone with him in a bedroom—produced a sharp unease.

Her disquiet vanished when he turned with a smile. The hard-edged warrior who had intimidated her when first they met was real and born of necessity. But the kindness was also real. She suspected that kindness was the deepest, truest part of his nature, or it wouldn't have survived his childhood.

"You look very . . . passable," he said, humor in his eyes. "It must have been difficult to disguise yourself as a wren when you were meant to dazzle like a kingfisher."

"A kingfisher is too flamboyant, but perhaps I

might qualify as one of the more passable finches." She gave him a slow, appreciative smile. "You look rather fine yourself. Relaxed and healthy."

"Not being in constant pain is bound to improve one's demeanor." Though Randall's voice was light, his gaze was uncomfortably intense. She didn't want a man to look at her like that, not even her husband.

"Did you know Mrs. Gowan has been married and widowed three times?" Julia asked as she inhaled the scent of the rose bouquet. "I don't know how she managed it."

"According to Kirkland, all the marriages were happy, and she wouldn't object to a fourth. She is either very lucky, or has excellent marital judgment."

"I never thought I'd marry a second time, and I certainly will not do so again," Julia said firmly. "If I can't manage a decent marriage with a man as understanding and intelligent as you, I need to retire from the lists."

He gave a surprised laugh. "I wasn't fishing for compliments, Julia. I was thinking how lucky I am that you're willing to take a chance on me." He crossed to the table that held the food and wine. "Would you like some champagne?"

"Please." She enjoyed watching him. His smooth movements gave no hint of the months of pain and surgeries he'd endured. And he was very fine to look at.

He poured sparkling wine into the tall, narrow goblets and handed her one, his fingertips brushing hers. "To us, for better and for worse."

"And there are bound to be both," she said wryly as she took a sip, then a larger one. The fizzing celebration of the champagne began to relax her. "Alexander," she said thoughtfully. "Does anyone ever use your full name?"

"My parents did. Not much of anyone since. Alex or Randall is shorter."

"Alexander," she murmured. "Someday to be Alexander, Lord Daventry. That will look good on the nameplate of the grand portrait of you in your regimentals that will hang in the portrait gallery at Turville Park and impress future generations. Or perhaps the painter can portray you as a knight in shining armor atop a white horse."

He grinned. "You have a good imagination, milady."

"Do you call me that because I'm Lady Julia?" she asked curiously. "That is an accident of birth, of no great importance."

He looked a little embarrassed. "As a boy, I loved the old tales of chivalry. Gracious ladies and knights pledged to their service. You are my lady. Milady."

Was chivalry at the root of his desire to protect her when she was in dire straits? If so, she could only be grateful. "You are a secret romantic, Sir Knight."

He laughed. "Don't tell Kirkland or Mackenzie. I'd never live that down."

"God forbid they should think you anything other than as tough as hardened leather." She sipped more champagne, and realized that she was happy. Not just content, but happy about the exciting, unknown possibilities that lay ahead.

For tonight, she chose to believe that her husband would be able to protect her against her murderous father-in-law. She even believed that someday it would be possible for her and Randall to have a real marriage, in every sense of the word. She raised her champagne glass. "To the future!"

"To the future." Randall clinked his glass against hers. "Sometimes in the regimental mess we'd toast with our arms interlocked like this." He linked his right arm around hers, which brought their bodies together from waist to knee. "This way two drinkers can support each other when both are foxed."

"I'm not foxed, but I see the advantages." Acutely aware of the warm length of his body, she raised her right arm and brought the champagne to her lips. Randall did the same, his expression teasing. Why had she thought his eyes were icy cold? The clear light color was bright and true as diamond.

As the champagne bubbled through her, she began to relax. She liked how their bodies touched. He was all strength, solidity, and masculine Viking power. Greatly daring, she pressed a little closer.

His expression changed. He finished his champagne in a single swallow and set his glass aside. "Julia . . ."

He bent his head for a kiss and her pulse accelerated like a mad thing. Their first kiss. Shocking passion blazed through her, drowning all her senses.

She forgot to breathe. Her champagne flute tilted, spilling the last drops of wine on the carpet. Carefully he removed the flute from her hand and placed it on the table. Then he enveloped her in an embrace that locked their lower bodies together. "Milady wife . . ." he breathed.

The pressure of his hard erection spiked her pleasure with fear. Furiously she buried it. Randall was nothing like Branford, *nothing*. He wanted her, as was his right.

And she wanted him. She *did*. The passion she'd cut from her life flooded back, hot and demanding as his large, strong hands kneaded her back and hips. Ah, God, how could she have forgotten . . . ?

Her lips parted and their kiss deepened. His breathing was ragged. "You are so beautiful, Julia," he said hoarsely. "So rare . . ."

His hand slid down, pulling her gown and robe

from her shoulder. Cool air caressed her heated skin, followed by his searing hand.

Then he stiffened as he touched the hideous scars she'd tried so hard to forget. "Julia?"

Horrified memories erupted in a blaze of hell-fire emotion as past and present collided in an avalanche of pleasure, passion, and pain.

She began to scream.

# Chapter 14

Randall's delight in his bride's eager response was interrupted when he felt the stunning, incomprehensible ridged scar tissue on her lovely breast.

His happiness splintered as she frantically wrenched herself from his embrace. She stumbled blindly away until she banged into the corner of the room. There she folded over onto the floor in a sobbing ball, her dark hair falling over her face.

The change in mood was as sudden and violent as cannon fire. He had been so sure that she desired him as he desired her. They would become lovers and mates with the intimacy he had craved since he first saw her.

Hope died in an instant as understanding sliced into his heart like shrapnel. But his pain was nothing compared to hers. Her anguished flight defined her first horrific marriage with visceral power.

He knelt beside her, sickened by the knowledge that Branford could still reduce Julia to anguished terror a dozen years after his death. "Julia, tell me what happened. I need to understand."

She shook her head, her face buried in her hands. "It's . . . it's not you."

No, but Randall must deal with the consequences. Her left shoulder was still bare, so he was able to confirm the atrocity he'd discovered by touch. The soft curve of her breast was marred by an ugly ridge of scar tissue that formed an irregular letter B.

Grimly he pulled the gown up over her shoulder. "B for Branford, of course." His voice was unnaturally steady. "I wouldn't have thought even he could be so vile."

She seemed to shrink even further. "He carved a D for Daventry into my other breast," she said dully. "The night I asked for a separation. The night he died."

Hoping talk would pull her away from her inner hell, he said, "When you told me about that night, you said Bran was drunk?"

"Drunk and mad." She drew a shuddering breath. "After beating me within an inch of my life, he pulled out his knife and pinned me down with his knee while he slashed off my clothing. He used an antique Saracen dagger he was particularly fond of. He loved all knives."

"I know. He would sit around and sharpen them for hours." Randall's throat constricted as a long-buried memory surfaced. More than once, Branford had come after his younger cousin with one of his knives, but Randall was fast and he learned to fight back when speed wasn't enough.

He glanced down at the thin white line that twisted around his left wrist and up his forearm. That was a remnant of the incident that made it clear he must fight to survive.

Forcing down his rage so as not to upset Julia even more, he said, "No one should have to endure what you've endured."

"I was his wife," she said bitterly. "He could do with me as he willed. He said that repeatedly. I was his possession, and he had the right to mark me as his. After he cut the letters into my breasts, he raped me."

"Dear God, Julia!" Randall said, too anguished to pretend calm.

She laughed, a hysterical edge to her voice. "The rape was what saved me, actually. When Branford was done, he slumped down on me and I was able to push him off. I managed to get to my feet. Before I could escape, he grabbed at me, but I was slippery with blood and he couldn't keep hold when I shoved him. He . . . he fell into the edge of the fireplace then. I don't remember screaming, but when I thought back later, I always heard screams. Odd, don't you think?"

"Branford was evil," Randall retorted, unable to keep his voice calm. He took her hand. She tried to tug it free but he held fast. She needed to be tethered to the present so she wouldn't drown in the past. "You are not to blame for his madness."

"No, but I am to blame for my shameful stupidity." Her unsteady voice was barely audible. "I never should have married him."

"There is no shame in being young. You were hardly more than a child when you married. But you were never stupid." He squeezed her hand gently. "That I know."

"You think not? I told you I agreed to marriage willingly, but that was . . . less than the whole truth." She laughed bitterly. "The beastly, shameful reality is that I was mad for Branford. He was handsome, charming, every girl's dream prince. And I . . . I thought he loved me, too. I was foolish beyond redemption."

Knowing Branford, Randall understood. "So in the beginning, he was tender and loving. He would apologize sincerely if he hurt you, claiming it was accidental. He took pains to win your trust so that you would suffer the anguish of betrayal as well as physical agony when he turned brutal."

She became very still. "How did you know?"

"He was much the same with me. But the relationship between two male cousins is less intimate than between a man and his wife." Though

145

the betrayal had been bad enough. When he had first been delivered into Daventry's care, he'd looked up to Branford. He'd wanted to have a big brother who would be his friend. For a fortnight, he thought that he did. That belief had briefly eased his mourning for his parents.

It would have been easier if Branford had tormented him from the beginning.

"He was the master of betrayal," she whispered. "You can understand that as no one else."

Sadly, he did. If that understanding helped Julia, there would be some value to the misery Randall had endured. "I wish I had been the one to kill the devil."

She gave a dry laugh. "But I was the murderer."

"An accident while you were trying to save yourself is not murder." Though he understood that a woman dedicated to preserving life would feel that way. "Branford has wrecked years of your life already. Don't let him destroy the rest."

"That would be his triumph from the grave, wouldn't it?" She pressed her tearstained cheek against Randall's hand. "He would love knowing he'd ruined me for any other man."

She was shivering from shock like a battle-weary soldier. Randall asked, "Would you like some brandy?"

When she nodded, he said, "It's time to come out of your corner." He rose and used their joined hands to coax her to her feet.

Her fingers were icy and her face splotched with tears, but she'd mastered the shattering pain that had sent her flying away from him. In bare feet and her pale night robe, she was slight and beautiful and indomitable.

Glad he'd replenished his travel flask, he poured a small glass for her, then a larger one for himself. He wished he could block out the images of a bleeding, frantic young girl trying to escape her brutal husband, but there wasn't enough brandy in the world for that.

After several sips of her drink, she said in a stronger voice, "I thought I'd buried the worst memories, but I was wrong. Now I've given you my nightmares."

He shrugged. "They may be lighter for being shared."

"Perhaps." She finished the brandy, refusing when he offered more. "Tomorrow, I shall be sane again. I promise you that, Alexander. For now . . . I wish to be alone."

Though he wanted to comfort her, he wasn't surprised that she couldn't bear his touch. "I'll sleep on the floor."

She drew a shuddering breath. "I'm sorry, but I meant—really alone. I'll go to one of the other bedrooms."

Once more he reminded himself that it was not really him she was rejecting. She must deal with her past in whatever way she thought best. But he wasn't sure he could bear it if she decided she must leave her brand new husband. "You won't run away?"

"No. My word on that." She sighed. "I'm tired of running, tired of being terrorized by the dead hand of the past. I want to live freely again. I just wish that my struggles weren't hurting you."

"Together we can manage. Remember that, milady." He wanted to take her in his arms and hold her safe against the terrors of the night, but that wasn't possible. "Till morning comes."

"Till morning comes," she echoed. "Thank you, Alex. For everything. For understanding, for being here, and for going away."

He released her hand, but couldn't bring himself to leave before he brushed her thick glossy hair. The silken strands tantalized his fingertips. He dropped his hand and knotted it into a fist. "Sleep well, milady."

He slid the brandy flask into the pocket of his banyan as he walked out the door and headed numbly downstairs. He was entering his old bedroom when Mackenzie emerged from his room just down the hall.

The other man was dressed for some nighttime prowl, but he stopped, surprise and then speculation showing in his eyes. "I thought I heard a woman scream earlier."

"Probably courting tomcats," Randall said

tersely, wishing to hell that Mac wasn't here to see that the bridegroom had left his bride.

"I would imagine that any woman who had been married to Lord Branford would require . . . patience," Mackenzie said quietly.

Randall scowled. "I prefer it when you're shallow and insensitive."

Mac's face smoothed into amiable blankness. "As you wish." He turned to leave, but briefly touched Randall's shoulder as he left. Sympathy from the devil.

Randall locked the door behind him. The draperies were open and admitted enough light to show that the bed had been stripped of linens, but blankets and counterpane were neatly folded across the foot. Wearily he stretched out on the bare mattress. His leg ached from all the walking, though not as much as his heart ached.

So Julia had loved Branford. That made everything worse. Randall had believed it was possible for her to overcome her nightmares and become a true wife. For a few fleeting moments, she had seemed willing, even eager. But the nightmares had won.

Could she ever recover from that betrayal of love so that she could love again? Her past might prove insurmountable.

He took a long swallow of brandy. The flask didn't hold enough for drunkenness, but there was probably enough to take the edge off his pain.

# Chapter 15

Brandy wasn't enough to warm the chill in Julia's soul. After Randall left, she lit the fire laid in the fireplace, then curled up in a corner of the small sofa. The idea of crawling under the writing desk was appealing, but that lacked dignity. It was time she began acting like a rational adult rather than a terrified girl.

A small, cowardly corner of her mind longed to run away to a place where no one knew her and she could start over again. But she hadn't the energy for that, or the strength to face such loneliness.

Since suppressing the past hadn't worked, the only way forward was through the hellish wreckage of her first marriage. Which meant she must look at Branford and how she had felt about him.

Julia forced herself to pull down the loose fabric of robe and nightgown so she could stare at her scarred breasts. As a girl, she had taken her healthy young body for granted. Despite her lack of inches, it was a good body. Not extraordinary, but graceful and well-proportioned, worthy of male admiration. Nature designed young men and women to appeal to each other.

That natural acceptance of herself had been destroyed by her first marriage. The occasional sensual pleasure she had experienced in the early days was soon overcome by loathing for his body, and for hers.

The letters he had carved bloodily into her breasts had set the final seal on her self-hatred. She was ugly, mutilated. No man could want her, just as she wanted no man. For years, she had done her best never to view her scarred body. Her bedroom held no mirror, and she became expert in dressing herself without seeing or thinking about her physical form any more than was absolutely necessary.

Looking back, she realized that time, life, and her nursing work had mitigated much of her hatred of the human body. She had delivered so many babies who were conceived in love. She'd seen deep, satisfying sexual bonds between husband and wife. And she'd heard her share of bawdy, happily lascivious jokes, because married women didn't hold their tongues around a widowed midwife.

Branford's sprawling, irregularly shaped initials were about two inches long and carved on the upper curves of her breasts. It hadn't been easy for her to overlook them. Over the years, the angry red letters had faded to dense white ridges of scar tissue.

She felt no particular sensation when she traced the forms. "B" for Branford, gone from her life and from the world. "D" for Daventry. It was ironic that in the fullness of time, she might still become the Countess of Daventry. But with a mercifully different husband.

Julia pulled up her nightgown and robe and settled back into the sofa, her absent gaze on the flickering fire. She had been barely sixteen when her father announced that she was to marry Daventry's heir.

She'd been raised to expect such an arrangement because of her high rank. Though she would have resisted if she'd met Branford and found him repugnant, she had been delighted by her father's choice.

All too clearly she remembered the way Branford smiled when they first met. He was dark, handsome, and fashionable, and he'd professed himself rapturous to have such a beautiful, elegant bride.

Julia had wanted to believe she was beautiful and elegant. What young girl wouldn't? By the time he kissed her to seal their betrothal, she was halfway in love with him. Their wedding had been the grandest of the Season, attended by no less than seven members of the royal family. It was no more than the Duke of Castleton's daughter deserved.

With the benefit of hindsight, she could see there were early signs that something was very wrong with Branford. His glittering, dagger-edged charm sometimes made her profoundly uneasy. He would be oddly amused for reasons she didn't understand. Yet she had blindly ignored her instincts.

Her deflowering had been shockingly painful, but afterward he had held her tenderly and said that was normal. She hadn't realized until much later that he'd made no attempt to be gentle, and that under his false sympathy was pleasure in her pain.

She was a normal young woman, and at first there were times when she found some pleasure in intercourse. But more and more often, she had ended up weeping. Branford would apologize with apparent sincerity, and she would be left feeling that the fault was in her. She was too young, too small, too stupid to be a proper wife.

She found the situation too shameful to discuss with anyone else. She was Lady Julia Raines, Viscountess Branford, and she would not reveal her weaknesses.

Only gradually had she come to notice the unholy gleam in his eyes when she was suffering. Later yet came the recognition that he'd sometimes exerted himself to pleasure her so that she would become optimistic about their marriage. She would start to believe that her weaknesses were almost cured and that everything would be all right.

When she believed herself in love with him, she was vulnerable. Easier to hurt.

Julia had been devastated the first time he told her he'd lain with another woman who was an infinitely more satisfying bedmate. Yet soon she felt relief in the knowledge that he had mistresses. Unfortunately, he couldn't ignore his legal wife since it was their duty to produce an heir.

She welcomed his trips to London, when she was left at peace in the country. Alone, she was able to think and to recognize the wrongness of her marriage. She began to avoid him when he returned to their country home. Her growing immunity to his emotional manipulation infuriated him.

That was when the beatings began.

Her pregnancy was the breaking point, and also her door to freedom. Praying that she would bear Branford a healthy son and heir—and that she would have most of the raising of the child until he was old enough to be sent to school—she asked for a separation. That request triggered the excruciating violence that left him dead and her close to it.

Could she have done anything differently? She was too well-bred to cause a scandal so it had never occurred to her that she might run away. It wasn't uncommon for aristocratic couples to live separate lives. Her duty as a wife was to give her husband an heir. Since Branford despised her, surely he would be happy to allow her to keep her distance once he had a son.

But he hadn't wanted that civilized solution, and he'd tried to kill her. She began to shake as scenes from that last horrible night burned across her brain.

The glowing coals in the fireplace collapsed, and triggered a harsh realization. She was glad he was dead.

The knowledge that she'd caused his death had been a heavy burden for all these years. She would never have chosen to hurt another living being.

But if he had survived, her life would never have been her own. Was her guilt because of her relief? Perhaps. But guilt wouldn't change the past, and if one of them had been fated to die that night, she was glad that it was Branford.

Vile, tragic, half-mad Branford. She tossed another scoop of coals on the fire and watched sparks flare up the chimney. Her anger and pain were like those burning coals, scorching her soul. She imagined the anger consumed by flame, the ashes flying into the night. One by one, she fed her memories of pain into the flames. Branford could hurt her no longer, unless Julia allowed it.

She would allow it no longer.

A fragile sense of peace unfurled deep within her. She settled back in the sofa, knowing she owed that peace to her new husband's kindness and his acceptance of her flawed self.

If she had met Randall when she was sixteen,

would she have been drawn to him? She imagined him as thin, blond, quiet, and intense, not yet tempered into the formidable man he would become. How deplorable to think that at sixteen, she might actually have preferred the more dashing Branford.

But now she a woman grown, seasoned by life. What did her instincts tell her about her new husband? That he was an honorable man who would never intentionally hurt her. Branford had smiled when first they met. Randall had scowled. An honest scowl had served her better than Bran's charming, lying smile.

Though she had accepted Randall's proposal with the intention of bolting out the back door if the marriage went badly, she had underestimated the power of wedding vows. She had pledged him her word, both at the altar and again tonight before he left the room. For better and worse, there would be no easy way out of this marriage.

Would Randall be better off without her? He said he didn't mind her barrenness, but that might change now that he had left the army and was settling into a normal life. Perhaps she should leave him so that he could find a whole, undamaged wife.

*No.* She didn't have the right to make that decision for him. For whatever reason, she was his choice, and her abandonment would hurt him. He didn't deserve that.

Since she was dealing with truth, she admitted to herself that she would rather have him for a husband than any other man. She liked his dry humor and intelligence, and the companionability growing between them. More surprisingly, she liked his taut, powerful body and that handsome, sculpted face that was so good at hiding his feelings.

He had scars of his own. Together, they might find healing.

Since Randall's belongings had been moved to the bridal suite the day before, he had no choice but to head upstairs the next morning. He wasn't sure what he'd find, but at least Julia had given her word not to vanish in the middle of the night.

"Come in." Julia's voice seemed normal enough. He entered the room to find her dressed for travel in a neat blue gown. Her expression was calm, with no signs of the previous night's breakdown.

"My clothes are here," he said apologetically.

"I know. I was expecting you." She gestured to a tray that held a steaming teapot, cups, and scones. "A maid just delivered this. Would you like a cup of tea?"

"Please." He closed the door, glad that normality had been reestablished. "How are you this morning?" The question was not routine courtesy.

She reached for the teapot, her mouth curving

wryly. "I spent the night wrestling ghosts, but I believe I won."

He girded himself for what must be said. "Do you want an annulment? Since the marriage hasn't been consummated, that wouldn't be difficult. Our initial agreement was that I could touch you daily, and you could say no when you'd had enough. Perhaps . . . that was too much to ask." As his words hung painfully in the air, he added, "Whatever you decide, I will do my best to shield you from Daventry."

Julia's hand froze, halting the teapot in midair. "Do *you* want an annulment? That would be . . . understandable under the circumstances."

It would be gentlemanly to defer to what the lady wanted, but if ever there was a time for honesty, this was it. Conscious that what he said could change the course of his life, he said, "I most certainly do not want to end our marriage. But if you can't bear for me to touch you, perhaps that is the only solution."

Julia set down the teapot and crossed the room to stand in front of him. Her gaze searching, she cupped his face with one hand. He hadn't shaved, so whiskers must be rasping her palm. She looked very grave, and unbearably lovely.

"I'm sorry for last night, Alex," she said quietly. "It won't happen again." Hesitantly she leaned forward and slid her arms around his waist. She shivered a little as she settled against him, one soft section at a time. Her breasts molded against his chest, then her torso gently pressed into him. Finally her head came to rest on his shoulder.

He was moved to wordless tenderness by her trust. A soldier assaulting a walled city was no more courageous. The top of her head just reached his chin, and when he stroked her hair, it released a tangy scent of lavender. "Last night was interesting in an educational sort of way," he murmured. "But I'd just as soon not repeat it."

She laughed a little, her breath warming the shoulder of his banyan. "There are still hurdles ahead. But I think that one was the worst."

After that, neither of them spoke. They just held each other. Randall's right hand stroked gently down her back, feeling the arcs of her ribs and the steely strength of her spine. He closed his eyes, content to absorb the essence of his wife. Sweetness and lavender.

This wasn't the wedding night he'd hoped they would share. But it was a start.

# Chapter 16

Julia found her return to Rose Cottage anticlimactic. She knocked at the door several times with no response, and the door was locked when she tried to open it. During her years in Hartley, the cottage had almost never been locked.

"Probably Jenny Watson is just out for a few hours," Randall said.

"I hope you're right." Julia moved to her left and felt under the sill of the parlor window. Good, the key was still there. She unlocked the door and stepped inside, then gave a sigh of relief. "All looks well."

The house was neat and felt lived in. Julia could see bread rising in a bowl back in the kitchen. She smiled when her tabby cat appeared and stropped her ankles. Scooping up the cat, she asked, "How are you, Whiskers?"

"It doesn't look as if she's missed many meals," Mackenzie observed. The cottage looked very small with two large men in it.

"Life goes on, and Jenny and Whiskers seem to have adjusted to my departure." The relief was huge.

"Is it strange being back here?" Randall asked.

"Yes." Julia frowned as she thought about her reaction. "Everything looks the same, but my life has been turned upside down. I was Mrs. Bancroft for so many years, useful and safe. Now Mrs. Bancroft is gone forever."

"She never really existed," he said quietly.

"I suppose not." But Mrs. Bancroft had felt very real for years.

"Will it take long for you to collect your belongings?" he asked.

Julia shook her head. Few things from her

career as a midwife would be needed in her new life. "By the time I've finished, Jenny and Molly should be back from wherever they've gone so I can reassure them, and say goodbye."

Randall hesitated. "I need to go up to Hartley Manor. Everyone there will want to know that you're safe, and I need to be sure that Grand Turk was returned properly. But I don't want to leave you alone."

They'd all been watchful on the drive between Carlisle and Hartley. Though there had been no sign of Crockett or his men, Julia could see that Randall was still wary.

"I'll stay with Lady Julia," Mackenzie said. "I won't let her out of my sight."

Randall relaxed. "Good. On the way back through the village, I'll book us rooms at the inn. I won't be gone long."

"I'll be fine," Julia reassured him. "No need to worry."

"Probably not," he admitted. "But Hartley is the one place Crockett can watch where there's a good chance you will return."

Mackenzie looked hopeful. "I wouldn't mind a bit of excitement."

Julia shuddered. "I much prefer boredom."

Randall grinned. "I shall attempt to make our marriage as boring as possible."

As Mackenzie laughed, Randall kissed Julia's cheek lightly and left. As the carriage rattled away, Julia asked, "Would you like a cup of tea or a draft of my ginger beer, Mr. Mackenzie?"

"The ginger beer would be pleasant." Mackenzie strolled into the kitchen after her. She poured a tall flagon of the fragrant, slightly bubbly brew. When he tasted it, he said, "Excellent. If you ever run away from Randall to start a new life, you could become a brewer."

Julia winced as she poured herself a small glass. "I can't really joke about that."

"Sorry. My sense of humor is deplorable." His voice turned serious. "But I assure you, Randall is nothing like Branford."

"You knew my first husband?"

"Our paths crossed in London occasionally." Mackenzie grimaced. "Most memorably when I had the bad judgment to beat him at cards in some gambling hall. He accused me of cheating, but I was known there and Branford had made himself unpopular, so he was thrown out. Naturally he blamed me for the humiliation, so he and a couple of his cronies laid in wait and attacked me when I left. Pure luck that they didn't beat me to death."

That sounded horribly like Branford. "How did you escape?"

"Ashton was driving by on his way home from some more respectable establishment. He saw the fight and recognized me, so he stopped his carriage. Branford and his bully boys ran off."

Trust Ashton to be in the right place when needed. "Did you consider reporting the attack to a magistrate?"

Mackenzie shook his head. "I didn't think I'd get very far with criminal charges since he was Lord Branford, heir to an earldom, and I was a bastard of dubious reputation. Since I was about to leave London anyhow, I chalked up the incident to education and made a note to steer clear of bad losers."

Julia wondered if Branford could have been curbed if he had ever suffered consequences for his bad behavior. But family wealth and influence had protected him from justice. The only man who had the least influence with Branford was his father, and the earl believed his precious son could do no wrong. She finished her ginger beer. "Time I started packing."

She set her glass aside and headed to her old bedroom. Nothing had been changed. It looked as if Jenny had hoped Julia would return. Or perhaps she had trouble believing the house was really hers. After today, it truly would be. Julia had bequeathed the cottage in her hasty last will and testament. Since she wasn't dead, she would legally transfer the title before leaving Hartley. Jenny and her daughter would have the security of a home for the future.

Most of Julia's mementoes were stored in the bottom drawer of a small dresser. A few pieces of jewelry from her mother, not valuable but cherished. A book of poetry from her grandmother, other bits and pieces from her earlier life. A pebble from the shore given to her by Molly when the child had crawled happily on the beach. Nothing from her first marriage. Julia carried the mementoes of that on her body.

As she packed her past into the carpetbag, she thought about the two days that had passed since her spectacularly melodramatic wedding night. Traveling in the close confines of a carriage was not a bad way to become more relaxed with one's husband. With Mackenzie present, Julia and Randall didn't talk about anything important, but by the time they stopped at an inn for their first night on the road, she was able to face sharing a room with her husband. She had been embarrassingly grateful when he wordlessly made up a bed for himself on the floor.

One step at a time.

After packing the items from her dresser, Julia went through her desk and the rest of the cottage, but added little to her carpetbag. Even the medical notes she'd maintained on her patients needed to stay for Jenny to use.

Since neither Jenny nor Randall had returned, Julia sought out Mackenzie, who was sprawled comfortably in the front room. "Packing took even less time than I thought," she said. "I'm going to walk down to the shore to say goodbye to the sea."

He drained his flagon and set it aside. "I'll go with you."

"To be honest, I'd rather go alone. Really, I don't think protection is necessary."

"Randall would have my hide for a rug if I don't accompany you." Mackenzie got to his feet. His head almost touched the low ceiling. "Best write Randall a note so that when he returns, he'll know where we are."

She could imagine how Randall would react if he found the cottage empty, so she scribbled a note and pinned it to the front door. Then she set off, Mackenzie at her side.

"How far is it to the shore?" he asked.

"Only a ten-minute walk. There isn't a place in Hartley that isn't close to the sea." She'd loved that about her adopted home.

Julia led the way along a lane that ran between hills dotted with grazing sheep. They emerged onto a narrow sand and shingle beach bordered by the stone wall that kept the sheep from wandering into the sea. Mackenzie asked, "Is this where Ashton's drowned body washed up?"

"Not quite drowned, and no, he was on the other side of this little peninsula, just below Hartley Manor." She pointed to the south. "Thank God Mariah found him. By morning, he probably would have died of exposure."

She strolled along the firm, dark sand, avoiding the water-smoothed stones and tangles of seaweed. This little beach had been her private retreat, a place to visit when she needed peace. She loved the timelessness of the sea. Perhaps sensing that, Mackenzie stayed several steps behind her.

*Ka-bang!!* A sharp crack of sound echoed over the water, followed a moment later by a second crack. Sand spurted into the air inches ahead of her. Surely not bullets . . . ?

Swearing, Mackenzie grabbed Julia and yanked her down behind the stone wall that bounded the pasture. She gasped for breath as he sprawled half on top of her, protecting her with his own body.

Her watchdog magically produced a pistol from somewhere. With crisp efficiency, he primed the pistol and raised his head above the wall to snap off a shot. The report was deafening, so close to Julia's ears.

Mackenzie ducked below the wall as his fire was returned. Reloading, he said mildly, "I'd say your pursuers have found us."

Julia's heart hammered with shock, but she managed to keep her voice steady. "Apparently Randall was right."

Two more bullets cracked through the air. Mackenzie glanced at the sand to see where the balls were striking. "There are two men and they have us pinned down. We're safe for now because they aren't great marksmen. Since the pasture provides no cover, they can't come after us without getting shot, but we can't retreat, either. Stalemate."

"For how long?" She reached under her hip to remove a sharp-edged stone. She'd have bruises in the morning.

Mackenzie shrugged as he peered above the wall again. He ducked as another bullet cracked by. "Not long. Randall will hear the shots and take care of the villains when he returns from the manor."

Thinking he sounded too casual, she said tartly, "You have great faith in Randall's abilities."

"It's not misplaced." He fired over the wall. The shot was returned twofold.

There was something familiar in the way he moved, and after a moment she placed it. "You were in the army also?"

"I served under Randall in Portugal." Mackenzie gave her a pirate's grin. "But I was cashiered and returned to England."

Cashiered. Dismissed from his rank. But not, she was sure, for cowardice. "A woman?" she guessed.

He laughed. "You're entirely too perceptive."

When she moved to find a more comfortable position, Mackenzie placed a large hand on her shoulder and pressed her to the ground again. "Don't wiggle. This wall isn't very high."

"You're in more danger than I because more of you shows," she pointed out.

He shrugged again. "As I said, they're damned poor shots."

The next minutes passed with agonizing slowness. Every now and then, their attackers would fire again, and Mackenzie would shoot back to keep them from approaching. Julia lay on the cold sand, rough stones behind her back, wishing she'd been more appreciative of the quiet life when she'd had one.

Another shot rang out. Mackenzie cocked his head. "Randall is moving in."

She stared at him. "How can you tell?"

"The sound of his carbine. Different from what the other two are shooting."

"You have some interesting skills, Mr. Mackenzie," she said dryly.

"None of them useful for earning a respectable living." He checked his pistol, then rose to a crouch. "I'll go lend a hand. Even the odds."

She grabbed his arm to pull him down. "You'll be shot!"

"Randall will keep their heads down," Mackenzie explained as he detached her hand. "Since I have a good idea where the devils are, he and I should be able to finish this up quickly. You stay low until it's safe. Randall or I will come for you then."

Then he was gone, moving rapidly for someone who was bent over and using whatever cover he could find. Julia lay still as the stone wall, counting her heartbeats. Hard to believe that only minutes were passing when the time seemed endless.

There was a flurry of shots. She shuddered, unable to tell one gun from another. Worse, she heard a man scream. Another cry—the same man or another? Was it Randall's voice? She couldn't be sure.

Her instinct was to get up and see if anyone was wounded, but she'd be a fool to make herself a target. Her fingers bit into the sand as she fought to control her tension.

Julia closed her eyes and prayed that her husband and Mackenzie would be safe. She knew her anxiety was out of place—Randall was doubtless as confident of success as Mackenzie. But she was a civilian and entitled to be terrified.

*"Julia!"* Carbine in hand, Randall raced down to the small beach. Surely she was safe, but he needed to see for himself.

Her small form erupted from behind the stone wall as she hurled herself into his arms. "I was so worried you'd be hurt! What happened? Is Mr. Mackenzie all right?"

He caught her close, feeling her pounding heart. He was sorry that she had been so upset, but it felt amazingly good to know she had been concerned for him. "Two attackers," he said succinctly. "One dead, the other fled. Neither was

Crockett. Mac was grazed by a bullet, but nothing serious."

She exhaled with relief and held onto him for a moment longer before stepping back. "I'd better take a look at his injury. You're sure the other man is dead?"

"Quite." Guessing that Julia would just as soon not know any details, he kept a protective arm around her as they headed up the lane.

The dead man lay in the lane at the top of the hill, his coat draped over his face. Mackenzie sat on the stone wall a few feet away, his face white. Julia examined the crude binding Randall had done on Mac's left forearm before coming for her. There were scarlet stains on the cravat he'd used for the bandage, but the bleeding had stopped.

"This should be cleaned and dressed again, but you'll do for now." She studied Mac's face with a frown. "Is that your only wound? You look on the verge of shock."

"He doesn't like the sight of blood," Randall explained.

Julia blinked. "Surely that made life in the army difficult, Mr. Mackenzie."

"I don't mind other people's blood," Mac said indignantly. "It's *my* blood that makes me go all queasy."

Randall gave Julia credit for not smiling. Gravely she said, "Can you manage the walk back to my cottage? I can fix you up properly there."

"The sooner the better." Mac stood, swaying.

Randall grabbed the other man's arm to steady him. Mackenzie's queasiness when wounded might seem out of place on a large man of military bearing, but it was real enough. "The Townsends have returned home," Randall said. "We've been invited to spend the night, so after Julia fixes you up, we can go up to the manor."

"Good," Julia said. "I hoped to see them before leaving Hartley." She looked at the corpse, biting her lip. "I should see if he was one of the men who abducted me."

"If you wish." Reluctantly Randall knelt and flipped the coat from the man's face. A bullet had gone through the villain's skull, but his features were recognizable.

"He drove the coach," Julia said without expression. "I never heard his name."

Thinking it was a pity that Crockett wasn't the one shot, Randall said, "Townsend is a magistrate, which will be useful in sorting this out."

They turned away from the dead man and started walking toward Julia's old cottage, but she gave one last glance at the sea. Randall guessed that in the future she wouldn't feel quite the same way about her private beach.

# Chapter 17

Julia lowered herself into the steaming hip bath with a grateful sigh. The day had been long and tiring, but the Townsends had installed an impressive array of creature comforts at Hartley Manor since Charles won the estate at cards. This large bath screened in a corner of their bedroom was one such comfort.

As Julia cleaned and bound Mackenzie's arm at the cottage, Jenny and Molly had returned. The three females had had a royal reunion with hugs and tears. Though Jenny was delighted that her mentor was safe, Julia could see that her apprentice was finding her feet as the area midwife. Jenny Watson would do very well for Hartley.

After tearful goodbyes, Julia and her escorts traveled up to the manor. The Townsends had returned home just that morning. Charles Townsend had been on the verge of sending word of Julia's kidnapping to the Duke and Duchess of Ashton when Randall appeared and was able to assure them of her safety.

Much of the rest of the day was spent explaining Julia's rank and recent marriage. Sarah Townsend, twin to Mariah, thought it was a vastly romantic tale. Julia hoped the girl never had such "romance" in her own life.

While Julia was bathing, Randall and

Mackenzie had withdrawn with Charles Townsend to address the untidy details of killing villains in Hartley. Julia wondered which of the men had done the actual shooting, then decided she would rather not know. Both had been soldiers. Both did what needed to be done.

What would normal life be in the future? She hoped that Randall was right in his belief that the Earl of Daventry would call off his hounds after he learned Julia was now Randall's wife. She could not bear to live the rest of her life under the shadow of violence. Even worse was knowing that others might suffer because of Daventry's fury.

She closed her eyes, reveling in the fragrant lavender oil that had been added to the hot water. She must have dozed off because she came awake with a start when the door to the bedroom opened. "Julia?" Randall called.

Though the hip bath was behind a screen, she felt awkward being naked in the same room with her husband. She scrambled out, trying not to splash the carpet. "I was enjoying the hot water too much," she said as she reached for a towel.

There was a clink of glass on wood. "No need to rush," he said. "Townsend offered me the hip bath in his dressing room, so I bathed as well."

Her nightgown and robe were draped over the top of the screen, so she dressed hastily and emerged as she unpinned her hair. Randall had settled into one of the wing chairs. After his bath, he had just pulled on his trousers and left his shirt loose. His blond hair was darkened from moisture and he looked relaxed, happy, and criminally handsome. "You deal with assassination attempts much better than I," she said wryly.

"Like most actions, it's a matter of practice." He gestured at the table between the paired wing chairs, which held a brandy glass and a steaming mug. "I brought up brandy for me plus some concoction that the cook said that you liked. I think it's hot milk and spices and some form of spirits."

"Mariah's hot posset," Julia said with pleasure. She collected her hairbrush from the dressing table and sat in the chair opposite Randall. "How thoughtful of Mrs. Beckett. Mariah learned all kinds of home remedies from her grandmother, including this one. It's delicious and very soothing after a hard day. You might want to taste it."

He eyed the mug dubiously as she took a sip. "Another time, perhaps."

She set the posset down and picked up the brush to straighten the tangles from her damp hair. "Will there be any trouble over Crockett's man being killed?"

"Townsend thinks that three respectable witnesses like you, me, and Mackenzie are suffi-

174

cient to declare the death justifiable homicide." Randall grinned. "Though it may be stretching a point to call Mac respectable."

"Though you tease him, you trust him," she said thoughtfully. "He certainly looked out for me well today."

"I knew he would. He's sound on important matters." Randall frowned as he watched her brush out her hair. "You avoid looking in mirrors more than any other beautiful woman I've ever met."

She froze, her stomach clenching. It took several moments to reply. "That's because I'm not beautiful. I find it . . . more comfortable to avoid mirrors."

"But you are beautiful, Julia," he said quietly. "I know you've had to hide for too many years, but that's not necessary now."

Her hands clenched on the brush in her lap. "Since that night in Edinburgh, I've been trying to come to terms with my disfigurement. It . . . will take time."

"You're not disfigured," he said firmly. "Yes, you bear scars on your lovely body, but beauty doesn't require perfection, and your scars aren't even visible."

"I can't forget the scars are there, and they make me feel ugly," she said tightly, wishing he would drop the subject and never mention it again.

She heard him sip at his brandy. "I'm sorry you consider me ugly," he said. "I had hoped to be at least presentable in your eyes."

Her gaze snapped up to him. "Why did you say such a foolish thing? You are classically handsome. Unnervingly so. You can't possibly not know that."

"If scars cause ugliness, I must be repulsive," he said coolly. "You've seen the mangled mess of my right side and leg, but they are hardly the only scars I bear." He stood and pulled his shirt over his head, revealing his bare torso. "I doubt that you've ever come near a man who bears as many scars as I do."

She stared at him, riveted, as he turned around to reveal his back before he faced her again. His broad shoulders, hard muscled body, and lean waist were beautiful—and marked by scars of all sorts. Some were faint, others blatant. There were thin lines and ragged knots of scar tissue. His right side was marked with more of the shrapnel that had done such damage to his leg. His body was a road map of pain and injury.

Lips dry, she touched a long, thin white scar that curved around his right shoulder. "How did that happen?"

"A French sword on the retreat to Corunna. I bled, he died." He frowned down at his body. "Every scar must have a story, but to be truthful, I can't remember where I got them all. Minor wounds in most cases. I heal quickly, but scar easily."

"You have an amazing array of scars," she admitted. "Most of them are never visible in public."

His brows arched ironically. "But if even hidden scars make one ugly . . ."

"It's different for you! Your scars are honorable marks of bravery."

"They're proof that I wasn't always good at dodging." He knelt in front of her. Before she realized his intention, he drew her loose robe and gown down her shoulders and cupped her breasts with his large, warm hands.

She gasped, feeling as if she'd been struck by lightning. "Don't!"

"When we first agreed to marry, you gave me leave to touch you," he said quietly. "Is this so upsetting? I swear I'm not going to ravish you." He took a deep breath. "Though it's a test of my willpower. Is it the touching that bothers you? Or the fact that your scars are exposed?"

Julia wanted to bolt. Or kick the damned man. Instead, she stared down at the scar-tissue initials that marred the upper curves of her breasts, and forced herself to examine her reaction. "Your touch is . . . not unpleasant." Actually, she rather liked the warmth and the feel of his hard palms against soft hidden flesh. "But the scars make me feel flawed. Disfigured."

"What was done to you was ugly beyond belief. That doesn't make *you* ugly." He began a slow, gentle stroking of her nipples with his thumbs.

She felt another jolt, this time undeniable pleasure. The breasts she hated were still capable of sensual response. Her nipples tightened under the rhythmic stimulation.

"I'm sure that if you had married a reasonable man and were living your life in normal society, you would still be a lovely, kind woman," he said. "But you would not have the strength and individuality that make you so special."

Her mouth twisted. "I should be grateful for being tortured? For being forced to falsify my death and flee into poverty?"

"Grateful? No. But all those events are part of you, as much as your beautiful chestnut hair and your lovely, creamy"—he swallowed hard—"touchable skin. We are shaped by our lives. Yours has been hard, but the person created by those events is . . . fascinating."

Her, fascinating? She'd like to believe that, but the thought was too new and strange. "I . . . I thank you for what you are trying to do," she said unevenly as she pushed at his hands. "But I can bear no more tonight."

Accepting that, Randall gently drew up her gown and robe over her shoulders before getting to his feet and moving away. She exhaled with relief.

Since his bare torso was distracting, Julia took a mouthful of her cooling posset before she resumed brushing her hair. "I'm not sure if you're going to save my soul or drive me mad, Alexander," she said wryly.

"The former, I hope." He opened the clothespress and removed his blue banyan. Covering his handsome body reduced the distraction, but the color made his blond hair and blue eyes even more striking. She dropped her eyes again.

"I want our marriage to be a real one, milady, and I think that will happen only if we both accept our scars. The mental ones and the physical ones." He smiled faintly. "This means you have the right to confront me when I'm trying to deny the undeniable."

Her eyes narrowed. "Since you have the right to touch me each day, perhaps every day I shall ask the origin of one of your scars."

"Go ahead, though I don't think that will torment me as effectively as what I'm doing to you." He considered. "Though some of these scars represent emotional pain as well as physical. If you ask about one of those, you might produce a satisfactory amount of torment."

"Which scars are they?" she asked with interest.

"It's up to you to find them among all the rest." Randall removed two folded blankets from the clothespress and set them on the floor.

She realized that he was planning to make up another pallet. "Don't," she said. "I'd like you to share the bed again, though . . . no more than that."

"Then progress has been made," he said with a smile that made her want to melt. He thought she was fascinating. She liked the idea even if she didn't believe it.

Randall moved behind the screen to change into his nightclothes. Since he was much taller than Julia, the screen revealed his splendid shoulders.

Needing calm, not confusion, she looked away as she braided her hair and finished the posset. "I'm going to fall asleep as soon as I climb into bed." She stood and removed her robe, then slid between the covers, keeping to her side.

Randall emerged from behind the screen and began putting out lights. "Would you like to spend another day here? Charles Townsend suggested we stay longer, and that will give you more time to say your goodbyes."

"I'd like that, if you're not in a tearing hurry to get to London." Julia smothered a yawn. She hadn't been joking about her fatigue.

After extinguishing the lights, Randall joined her in the bed. The mattress sagged under his weight and Julia slipped down the smooth sheets into Randall's side. "Sorry!" She started to push herself back to her side of the bed.

"No need to run away." He slid his arm under her neck and tucked her against him. "Why share a bed if we're on opposite sides and not touching?"

His embrace was friendly rather than carnal, so she settled against him. Though Branford often wanted sex, he had no use for affectionate cuddling. She felt warm, relaxed, safe.

Until she moved her hand and her palm brushed against his hard erection. As he caught his breath and stiffened all over, she pulled away with a sound perilously close to a squeak. "I didn't mean to do that!"

"I know." He didn't pull her back, but he caught her hand and laced his fingers between hers. "Though progress has been made, we still have a long way to go." His fingers tightened on hers. "Have I mentioned how much I admire your courage in facing your own private hells?"

She smiled wryly into the darkness. "I don't think I've displayed much courage. Each time you've pushed me, I've wanted to run away." She considered. "Though tonight I briefly considered kicking you."

His laughter was deep and rich. "I'm glad you didn't, but fighting instead of running is a good sign, I think. You really are an amazing woman. We grow through adversity. That's why Mariah is more intriguing than Sarah, even though they're twins and equally pretty and good-natured. Innocence simply isn't very interesting."

"Surely there are few men who would agree with that!"

He shrugged. "Tastes vary. I like women who have journeyed through darkness."

"Because they understand you better?" Julia asked softly.

There was a long silence before he said, "I suppose that marriage is meant to be about two people sliding under each other's skins. You're rather good at that."

"As are you." Emboldened by the darkness, she asked, "Isn't it terribly painful to . . . to be aroused as you are and not satisfy yourself ?"

"I sense Branford's voice behind that comment," he said dryly. "Yes, continuing arousal is somewhat uncomfortable, but hardly unbearable. A grown man should not be ruled by his lusts."

Branford had been. And she was the one legally obliged to satisfy them. "As a midwife, I've spent much of the last years with women and small children," she said reflectively. "I'm beginning to realize how little I know of grown men."

"You're learning quickly." He squeezed her hand again. "At least, you're learning *me* quickly. As to being aroused—the good outweighs the bad. It reminds me I'm alive. For a long time, I'd forgotten that."

She didn't like to think of his private darkness. But if he hadn't endured that, he wouldn't understand or want her. She rolled onto her side and pressed a light kiss to his cheek. "Sleep well, Alexander."

His whispered, "Sleep well, milady," followed her into her dreams.

# Chapter 18

Julia shifted wearily on the carriage seat. She'd spent a dozen years living quietly in country villages, never traveling more than a few miles from home. She had lost the habit of long journeys. Randall and Mackenzie had much better endurance.

Randall glanced out the window. "We've made good time today. We're coming into Grantham now."

She glanced out her own window and saw nothing unusual. "I suppose you've been up and down the Great North Road often enough to recognize all the landmarks. Will we be stopping here, or going on for another stage?"

"You've been very patient with all these long days of travel." His smile was understanding. "Grantham has one of the Midlands' best coaching inns, so it's a good place to spend the night."

Mackenzie sat opposite them, idly tossing dice,

right hand against left. Not looking up, he said, "My mother died in Grantham."

"I didn't know that," Randall said, looking surprised.

"No reason why you should." Mac scooped up the dice and shook them between his caged hands. "As you know, she was an actress. We were heading north so she could join the theater circuit based in York. Her death was very sudden."

Julia caught her breath, remembering that Mac had been very young when his mother died. "You were there? How dreadful for you!"

He tossed the dice onto the seat beside him and studied the results. His expression was improbably neutral. "Luckily my mother's maid was a capable woman. She arranged for my mother to be buried in the parish churchyard, then packed me up and took me off to my father's country house."

"Had you met Lord Masterson before then?" Julia asked.

"Once or twice. I remember him saying I looked much like his son Will, but without the manners." Mackenzie grinned. "That has never changed."

They all laughed, but Julia said, "You were fortunate that the maid knew where to take you, and that she did it."

"She kept my mother's jewels and clothes as

payment for her efforts," Mac said dryly. "But yes, I was lucky she didn't abandon me to the parish here in Grantham."

"Lucky also that Lord Masterson recognized you as his son," Randall added. "Will Masterson's father might not have been a model of moral behavior, but he liked boys. I spent a number of school holidays with Will and Mac and the rest of the family."

Julia guessed that had been his way of avoiding Branford. A memory struck her. "I haven't thought of this for years, but Branford had an illegitimate son born shortly before I learned I was pregnant. He taunted me several times for being slow to produce a child, since he was clearly capable of doing so. I wonder what happened to that boy? He must be twelve or thirteen now."

Mac frowned. "Did the child live with his mother?"

Julia thought, then shook her head. "I had the impression that was the case, but I don't remember any more than that."

Mac frowned even more. "I hope the boy wasn't neglected after his father's death. He would have been just a baby."

"Presumably the mother could appeal to Daventry if she was in dire straits after Branford's death," Randall said. He was undoubtedly right, but still Julia wondered about the boy. Every child deserved a decent home.

They were on the Grantham High Street when Mackenzie signaled the driver to stop. "I think I'll get out now and walk the rest of the way to stretch my legs. I'll catch up with you at the inn. Will you book a room for me? I presume you mean to stay at the Angel and Royal."

Randall nodded. "If they're full, we'll go to the next inn down the high street. I forget what it's called, but it's just beyond the Angel and Royal."

"I'll find it." The carriage rattled to a halt and Mackenzie swung out.

After he closed the door and strode off, Julia said, "I'm tempted to join Mr. Mackenzie. I'd like to stretch my legs, too."

"I doubt he'd want the company." Randall gestured out the window at an unusually tall, slender church spire. "He said his mother was buried at the parish church. My guess is that he's going to visit her grave."

"Then I shall leave him in peace." She settled back in her seat. "I've stayed at the Angel and Royal, though it was long ago, of course. Grantham was a regular stop for my family on our way north, until my father became angry with the innkeeper for some reason. After that, we stayed elsewhere." She shook her head in bemusement. "The innkeeper's name was Beaton. Strange that I remember that."

"The present Mr. Beaton is probably the son of

the one you remember." Randall took her hand since they were private. "Was your father often angry?"

"I'm not sure he was ever *not* angry. Which made it very easy for him to be angry with me when I proved such a disgrace to the Raines family."

The carriage pulled to a stop in front of the wide stone façade of the Angel and Royal. Randall climbed from the carriage and helped Julia down. "Anger is such a tiring emotion. Refusing to patronize an excellent inn is downright foolish."

"With friends in the north, you must make this journey often," Julia remarked as they entered the inn and waited for the landlord to appear.

"Too often. Usually the Great North Road is a tedious blur of fields and villages and posting houses." He grinned teasingly. "The very worst journey through England I ever made was accompanying Mariah and Ash from Hartley to London when you were acting as Mariah's chaperone. I wanted to be anywhere else."

She laughed. "You scowled as if you wanted *me* to be somewhere else."

"This journey is far better since I've accepted my fate and married you." His voice was still light, but his eyes were serious. "The miles are still long and roads rough, but the beds are more comfortable."

She blushed, but smiled back. Since rejoining her in their bed, Randall had proved himself a gentleman of his word and never forced unwanted attentions on her. He'd been downright embarrassed the morning they woke and his hand was on her breast. Knowing it was an accident of the night, she'd calmly moved the hand and they'd cuddled a few more minutes before rising. The more she trusted him, the easier it was to believe that someday they might be lovers. Though not yet.

The landlord appeared, a younger man than the one Julia remembered, but with a similar affable expression. "Major Randall, how good to have you with us again. Will you be staying long?"

"Just a single night," Randall replied. "I need a room for myself and my wife, and another room for Mr. Mackenzie, who will be here shortly."

Mr. Beaton's face lit with real pleasure as he bowed to Julia. "Allow me to congratulate you, Major. My felicitations, Mrs. Randall." The landlord consulted his guest book. "You're in luck. A large party is expected, but the corner room you like is available, and there's a smaller room two doors down for Mr. Mackenzie."

A heavy rumble of carriages pulling to a stop sounded outside. Julia guessed that it was the large party Mr. Beaton was expecting. As Randall signed the register, Julia removed her bonnet, thinking that with luck and good weather, they'd be in London in a day and a half. She fervently hoped so.

A grand footman entered the inn and turned to hold the door open for his master. A compact, dominating man of inbred arrogance swept into the Angel and Royal, his entourage dimly visible behind him.

Julia's gaze met his, and she made a strangled sound, scarcely able to believe her eyes. Dear God, no! Of all the inns in England, why this one?

The newcomer stopped in his tracks as shock, disbelief, and finally fury rippled across his face. The moment stretched until he spat, "You're supposed to be dead!"

Julia wished she could faint to escape the horror of this meeting, but there was no way out. A tremor in her voice, she said, "I'm sorry to disappoint you, Father."

The Duke of Castleton's contemptuous gaze swept over Randall, who had turned when she spoke. "Is this your current lover, Julia?" her father sneered. "I presume you've been supporting yourself on your back since you're good for nothing else."

The virulence in his voice was like a physical blow. She swayed, on the verge of collapse. Then Randall's large, warm hand locked onto her elbow. Eyes narrowed, he said, "You may be a duke and Julia's father, but I will allow no man to insult my wife."

"Did she tell you she murdered her first husband, a most distinguished young gentleman?" the duke snapped. "For all I know, she's murdered a dozen husbands since!"

"That's absurd and you know it," Randall said calmly. "Any normal father would rejoice to see his long lost daughter alive, but if you were a normal father, you wouldn't have abandoned her to cruelty. You are a disgrace to your name and lineage."

The duke gaped at him. "How dare you, sir! Who are you?"

Randall gave a slight, mocking bow. "I'm Major Randall. If you wish satisfaction, I shall be happy to oblige you. But you should be aware that I am generally considered to be a crack shot and expert swordsman."

The duke's eyes narrowed. "Are you related to Daventry?"

"His nephew and heir." Randall gave a glinting smile. "So your daughter will someday be the Countess of Daventry, but with a husband of her choice, not yours."

His glare poisonous, the duke snarled, "Remove these creatures, Beaton. I will not stay under the same roof with them."

The innkeeper, who had been watching with shocked fascination, said politely, "I'm sorry, your grace, but they are already registered guests. I assure you that there is no need to see them again since your rooms are at the opposite end of the house."

The duke stared at Beaton incredulously. "You prefer their custom to *mine?*"

"I have no grounds to expel Major Randall and Lady Julia," the innkeeper said. "And they're courteous." The implication that other guests weren't was unmistakable.

"You're as bad as your father!" the duke spat.

"I am honored by the comparison," Beaton said, still unruffled. "I admired him in all ways."

"I shall never set foot in this pestilential place again!" Her father's icy gaze shifted to Julia. "I had a certain amount of respect for you when I believed you took your own life as expiation of your sins. Now I find that you're deceitful and cowardly. You are no daughter of mine."

The duke was pivoting to stalk from the inn when Randall said in a hard voice, "Julia is better off without such an unnatural father, Castleton. But she has property rights that cannot be denied by you. Prepare to honor those obligations. My solicitor will communicate with yours."

Her father cast a fulminating glance over his shoulder before he slammed out of the inn, accompanied by his entourage. After a moment of vibrating silence, Beaton said mildly, "His grace stopped coming here in my father's time but decided to give me another chance when I inherited. Once more the Angel and Royal has failed to meet ducal standards."

"I'm sorry for the loss to your business," Randall said.

The innkeeper shrugged. "Castleton doesn't stop often and he has always been a difficult guest. You and your friends are frequent visitors, and always most welcome." He returned to business. "Would you care for a private dining room tonight?"

Randall studied Julia's face. "We shall dine in our room. I'll order later."

Julia nodded gratefully. She wanted nothing more than to go to ground like a hunted fox.

Randall added, "Please tell Mr. Mackenzie what happened when he arrives, but I would prefer that you not discuss the matter with anyone else."

"Naturally one does not wish family difficulties to be made public," Beaton murmured. "If you'll follow me, Major, Lady Julia."

Julia was barely aware of climbing the steps, other than that Randall's steadying hand was on her lower back. She was not alone.

When was the last time a man had defended her?

Never.

# Chapter 19

As soon as Beaton left them alone in the spacious bedchamber, Julia turned into Randall's arms, burying her face against his shoulder. Her slim body felt fragile. He enfolded her, wishing he could have spared her that horrific scene.

"I'm sorry you were subjected to that," she said dully.

"You are not the one who should be offering apologies," Randall said acerbically. He took the bonnet from her numbed fingers and tossed it on the bed. "Was your father always this bad?"

She considered. "I'm not sure. As a girl, I was too well behaved to be the target of his wrath. I seldom saw him, and when I did, he was always very stern and formal. I usually thought of him as 'the duke,' not as my father. I don't think he likes females much." A shiver went through her. "Then I went to him after Branford's death, and he . . . he was vile. I hadn't known he was capable of such viciousness."

"I understand better now why you ran away from your life." Randall curbed a powerful desire to go after Castleton and beat him senseless. A man really shouldn't do that to his father-in-law, no matter how much it was deserved. Instead, he pulled the pins from Julia's hair and combed it loose over her shoulders with his fingers. "It's a tribute to your strength that you didn't walk into the sea in truth."

"I was tempted. Very tempted." She gave a little choke of laughter. "But I was too stubborn to surrender. I'm not sure that's the same as strength."

"Close enough." He began massaging her scalp with his fingertips, and was rewarded by the easing of her tight features.

"I knew my father would be outraged when I returned from the dead, but I assumed he'd learn some other way," she said ruefully. "Unexpectedly seeing me alive brought out the worst of his nature. I suspect that much of his fury was because I'd deceived him by not really killing myself."

"At least the worst is over now." Randall ran a warm palm soothingly down her spine. "I doubt that even Daventry could upset you as much."

"True."

Since she was calmer, he asked, "Do you want me to leave?"

"Not this time." She tightened her arms around his waist, as if she feared someone would try to pry her away from him. Randall found it most gratifying.

"Since you don't want to send me away, I'd say you and I are making progress." He scooped Julia up and settled onto the small sofa with her on his lap. She made a small, endearing squeak before relaxing against him, her head against his shoulder. "Castleton, Daventry, Branford. Have all the men in your life been so difficult? What about your brother?"

"Anthony? I don't know how he'll react to knowing I'm alive. We were close as children, but I haven't seen him in so long. He was sent off to Eton as soon as he was old enough, and he was only fourteen when I married and left home." She bit her lip. "I haven't wanted to think about Anthony. He was a darling little brother, but after so many years of being Marquess of Stoneleigh, he might be as insufferable as my father."

"What a depressing thought. I imagine you'll find out soon." Randall frowned. "Until now, I haven't thought much about how you'll deal with your family when we arrive in London. Since Stoneleigh is your closest relative, you might want to write him directly rather than let him find out from your father."

She winced. "You're right. I'll send a letter to Anthony in the morning mail, though it might not reach him before he receives word from the duke. I should write my grandmother as well. I need to let her know that I'll be calling very soon, and that she can now reveal to people that I'm alive."

"You will be the most sensational topic in the beau monde for at least a week," Randall predicted. "Perhaps even a whole fortnight."

"Surely not that long." Julia tilted her head up to look at his face. With her dark hair loose around her shoulders, she looked young and delectable. "How did you know I was entitled to family money? When I walked away, I put my inheritance out of my mind and haven't thought of it since."

He shrugged as his hand wandered over the soft curve of her hip. "Your mother was surely wellborn, so there must have been a marriage settlement that provided portions for all children of the union. Perhaps you've inherited other property as well."

"My mother was a Howard." Julia smiled without humor. "I have some of the bluest blood in Britain. Far superior to the Hanoverian upstarts who sit on the throne."

So she was related to the Duke of Norfolk, the premier duke in England. Randall wasn't surprised. "Your parents' marriage contract probably rivaled treaties between small countries for complexity."

"I'm sure you're right." A touch of dryness entered her voice. "Marrying me could prove to be very profitable, since a wife's property belongs to her husband."

"I don't blame you for being wary of male motives, Julia." Randall's eyes narrowed as he caught her gaze. "I am quite capable of supporting a wife without your inheritance, or Daventry's

196

fortune. But now that I've met your father, I think you need to have your own money so that you will never have to feel dependent on a man again. I shall place any property pried loose from your father into a trust for your exclusive use."

She ducked her head, her cheeks coloring. "I know you're not a fortune hunter, Alex. Being around my father brings out my worst nature, just as I bring out his."

"Your snappishness is nothing compared to what Daventry does to my temper," Randall assured her. His caressing hand moved over her hip. Julia was petite, but every part was exactly right. "Didn't you visit your grandmother when you came to London with Mariah? I assume she was on the maternal side."

She nodded. "Grandmère is the only one in my family who knew I was alive. She was very ill earlier this year, and I feared I'd never see her again. That was much of the reason I risked going to London."

"That visit must be how Daventry discovered you were alive, and sent Crockett after you."

"Yes," she said slowly. "But I'm not sorry. For all the tumult of the last weeks, I'm glad I'll be able to live as myself again."

Randall never would have met Julia if she'd refused to be Mariah's chaperone. "But if you were safe in Hartley, you wouldn't have needed to marry for protection."

She tilted her head back and studied his face, her gray eyes serious. "You are the only man who has ever protected me," she said softly. "The only one. I hadn't known how much I wanted that." She leaned up and kissed him.

It was a serious kiss with parted lips, not a formality. He responded in kind. Julia was a warm, sensual armful, and the restraint he'd been exercising since he freed her from the kidnappers began to crack as his hands moved over alluring curves.

She caught her breath. "I feel like a cat being petted."

"And like a cat, I imagine you'll leave when you've had enough." He bent to kiss the tender skin beneath her ear. "But for now—Julia, can you trust me enough to relax and see if I can give you pleasure? Though it's too soon to become lovers, I'd like to see if I can persuade you a few more steps in that direction."

"My mind and body still have fears, but my heart trusts you," she said as she raised her hand to his cheek. The light brush of her fingertips was startlingly erotic.

Clamping down on his reaction, he recaptured her lips, deepening the kiss until their tongues touched. Her hesitation began to fade and he felt the quickening of her breath. The quilted padding of her stays was firm beneath his palm. Because she was traveling, the corset was a lightweight version that ended at her waist. Which meant that when he moved his hand down her body, he felt the ripe curve of her hip and the taut length of her thigh under a mere two layers of fabric.

She tensed when his hand came to rest on her knee, so he concentrated on learning how sensitive her elegant ear was. Very, as it turned out. As he traced the edge with his tongue, she released her breath in a pleased sigh.

When his hand glided up her thigh under her skirts, he felt the faintest of tremors go through her, but she didn't try to stop him. The smoothness of her stocking gave way to the silky warmth of female flesh.

When they were skin to skin, he again stilled his hand so she had time to get used to where it was placed. Her head fell back, her breasts rising and falling, as he trailed his lips down her throat. He felt the purr of her pleasure under his tongue.

He slid his hand between her thighs, kneading his way slowly higher. She jerked and gave a sharp gasp when he first touched the hidden heat and moisture at the juncture of her thighs. "Is this unpleasant?" he whispered as he lightly pressed the edge of his hand into the delicate folds. "Do you want me to stop?"

"Not . . . unpleasant," she said unevenly. "Don't. Stop."

"As milady wishes." He caressed her with

increasing depth and intimacy, altering pressure and speed as her breathing grew harsher and her legs separated to allow him greater access. His own breathing was equally harsh as her excitement kindled his.

She arched her back, eyes closed, and her hips began to rock in a timeless, involuntary rhythm. "Alex . . ." she said, taut and needy.

Then she cried out, her nails digging into his arm and back as she convulsed around his right hand. The heat and scents of sexuality nearly overpowered him. More than anything on earth, he wanted to be joined with her, to share that wild pleasure.

Not yet, not *yet*. But there was delight and satisfaction in having brought her to this point. Surely the day was coming when he would be able to go the final step, and bury himself inside her.

She opened dazed eyes. "I didn't know," she breathed. "All those lusty women I've cared for over the years, and I never really understood what they meant when they talked about how much they desired their men."

"This is just one step, Julia." He kissed her damp forehead. "There are many more." Her lovely round backside was pressed into his erection, tempting him to the outer limits of his control. He shifted, uncomfortable, but not wanting to distress Julia.

Even sated with pleasure, she was observant. She slid from his lap onto the sofa beside him, staying under his encircling arm. "I'm sorry. You made me forget about meeting my father, and in return I'm distressing you."

He tightened his arm around her shoulders. "The distress is minor compared to the satisfaction of pleasing you."

"Nonetheless . . ." Her eyes narrowed as she studied his taut breeches. Then she drew a deep breath and began to unbutton the fall.

"Dear God, Julia!" He froze, lightning searing through his veins as her fingers clasped hard, pulsing male flesh. "You . . . you don't have to do this."

"I know." Biting her lip, she stood and moved to straddle his lap, her skirts cascading over them both. "That's why I can."

She eased slowly onto him, stopping with a gasp. Before he could react, she said, "I'm all right. It's just—I'm tight and you're large."

She rolled her hips a little, almost sending him over the edge. His hands clamped on her hips and waves of sensation surged through his body.

When she began lowering herself again, they slid smoothly together. He was too paralyzed by shock and raging lust to move.

She leaned forward to press her cheek against his. "That wasn't so bad." Her voice was shaky, but determined.

"Not . . . not bad at all." He wrapped his arms around her waist, sure that this intimacy was costing her a great deal. Yet he couldn't bear for this mind-numbing, guilty ecstasy to end if she chose to pull away.

For the space of perhaps two dozen heartbeats they held each other, adjusting both physically and mentally to the irrevocable change in their marriage. Then Julia raised her face into a kiss. She filled his senses with touch and taste and scent. His wife, the fulfillment he had longed for and feared he would never find.

He wanted the moment to last forever, but she rocked against him, murmuring, "I wonder . . ."

He was fire and she was tinder as madness seared through him. He shattered, his mind vanquished by sensation.

The firestorm passed, and every fiber of his body vibrated with scalding awareness. "Dearest God in heaven," he managed as he crushed her to his chest.

Julia laughed a little. "I think you're taking the Lord's name in vain."

"No." He buried his face in her dark hair. "Prayers come in many forms. You're the answer to prayers I didn't know I'd made."

"That's either powerfully romantic or borderline sacrilege." Julia gently untangled herself so she could stand and pull two towels from the washstand.

Accepting one, he said, "I didn't expect this to

happen tonight." He studied her face. "Are you all right? I didn't hurt you?" What he really wanted to know was if she was sorry, but he wasn't sure he wanted to hear the answer.

His heart sank when she frowned, but when she spoke, her voice was thoughtful, not distressed. "There was some discomfort, but no more than might be expected." She cleaned herself, then brushed her skirts down. "I'm glad that's over. Next time will be easier."

It was a crashingly unromantic statement, but at least she was thinking in terms of doing it again. "Next time will also be better," he promised as he buttoned his breeches.

"Tonight was already very fine." She raised her gaze to his and her voice warmed. "You did indeed pleasure me. Even more important, fears that possessed me for too long are gone."

That was a good start. Feeling optimistic, he stood and wrapped an arm around her shoulders, drawing her against his side in a hug. "Shall I order supper and a bath?"

"That would be lovely." She turned her back to him. "Could you unfasten my gown and stays? I'm looking forward to a quiet, relaxed evening with you." Glancing over her shoulder, she said softly, "Thank you for your kindness, Alex. For your patience."

He went to work on the laces. "You're worth patience, milady."

She blushed and ducked her head. Her hair fell away from her nape so he bent and kissed it, overwhelmed by tenderness. She trusted him.

He felt truly married.

# Chapter 20

It was nearly dark when the carriage arrived at Ashton House. Julia had forgotten just how large the ducal mansion was. Reading her mind, Randall said, "This sprawling great pile is said to be the largest private home in London, which is why Ash can give me a set of rooms and never even notice."

"I shall be glad to stay in one place for several days at a stretch," Julia said fervently as her husband helped her from the carriage. Well-trained footmen arrived to carry their bags inside.

Mackenzie climbed from the vehicle to say his goodbyes. "Lady Julia, it's been a pleasure to make your acquaintance." He kissed her hand with a flourish. "Though I'm sadly disappointed that the trip was so uneventful."

Her brows arched. "You think a mere single assassination attempt is uneventful, Mr. Mackenzie?"

"Downright boring," he agreed. "Trouble is my middle name, you know."

Randall laughed and shook Mackenzie's hand. "Thank you for the escort service, Mac. And for everything else."

"It was my pleasure," the other man said, his voice serious for once. "I owed you a favor or two."

Randall said, "In that case, since someone is bound to want to throw a ball in our honor to reintroduce Lady Julia to society, will you attend if you receive an invitation?"

"I don't owe you that large a favor!" Grinning wickedly, Mackenzie swung back into the carriage and signaled for it to set off again.

Julia took Randall's arm as they climbed the steps to the front door. "Does Mr. Mackenzie's birth prevent him from moving in society?"

"Not really. His father was a lord, he's acknowledged by Will Masterson and the rest of the family, and he was popular with the other troublesome lordlings at the Westerfield Academy. But he has always preferred to distance himself from the ton." Randall made a face. "I did the same, but that is no longer possible."

"You were a serving officer, which is the best of excuses for avoiding Almack's." She glanced up at his profile. Her handsome husband, whose intimidating exterior concealed remarkable kindness and patience. "A good part of the reason for coming to London is to return me to society, but that will mean you have to attend balls and routs as well. Will you hate it too much?"

"I'm not sure," he admitted as the doors swung

open before them. "I've never spent much time moving in such circles. In moderate amounts, the social routine might be amusing. Have you been yearning for the delights of the beau monde?"

"Since I went into an arranged marriage when I was young and then I was isolated in the country, I have no idea if I'll enjoy the ton. If I do, I'll probably prefer moderation, as you do." Her hand tightened on his arm. "It's fortunate that we're here at the start of the autumn social season. The spring season might be too much for me."

The butler approached with the faint smile that meant gushing good humor by his standards. "Major Randall, Mrs. Bancroft, how good to see you again. The duke and duchess are dining in tonight. I shall inform them of your arrival."

"Don't interrupt them if they're eating, Holmes," Randall said. "After dinner is soon enough."

"It would be worth my job if I didn't inform them of your arrival immediately," Holmes said, his expression stern.

Randall glanced down at Julia, humor lurking in his eyes. "In that case, tell them Major Randall and his wife have just arrived."

Holmes was so startled he actually raised his brows before saying, "Indeed I shall." He bowed and withdrew.

"That will bring them both quickly," Julia predicted as she removed her bonnet. "Especially Mariah."

Her prediction was accurate. By the time she'd removed her cloak, swift light footsteps were approaching. The duchess called merrily, "Randall, you rogue. Did you change your mind about my sister Sarah and whisk her off to Gretna Green?"

Mariah swept into the entry hall, her sunny nature filling the high-ceilinged hall with golden warmth. Dark and reserved, Ashton was several steps behind, but his smile was equally welcoming.

On seeing the new arrivals, the duchess stopped so quickly that her husband almost ran into her. "Julia! You and Randall have married?"

"Indeed we have," Julia said mildly.

"Adam, you owe me five guineas!" Mariah launched herself into Julia's arms with an exuberant hug. "I told you Randall fancied her."

"Whereas I, being a mere male, thought they disliked each other." Ashton clapped Randall's shoulder as they shook hands. "Kind of you to bring Mariah's best friend into the family, Randall."

"Julia didn't seem interested, but after she repaired my bad leg, I decided I must marry her so she'd be available the next time I damaged myself," Randall explained.

"You are walking rather well." Ashton's green

eyes showed amusement. "I quite see why you'd want Julia. It's more surprising that she said yes."

Julia was reminded that the duke was a remarkably perceptive man. "I was content with widowhood, but Randall changed my mind." She made a face. "There were . . . extenuating circumstances."

"That sounds interesting," Mariah said. "Take a few minutes to freshen up, then join us for dinner. No need to change. We're very informal tonight."

"Ten minutes then." Randall offered Julia his arm. To the footman, he said, "Place Lady Julia's bags in my rooms."

"Lady Julia?" Mariah exclaimed.

"I told you it was complicated!" Julia tossed over her shoulder as they headed up the staircase.

She hadn't seen Randall's rooms when she'd visited Ashton House earlier in the year, so she looked around with interest when he ushered her into the sitting room. It was spacious and well furnished in restful shades of blue and cream, with windows overlooking the garden behind the house. "This is lovely! No wonder you're so comfortable here."

"It's incredibly generous of Ash to allow me to treat the house as my own," Randall agreed. "The bedroom is through there and that door leads to a dressing room."

The dressing room door opened and a wiry, dark-haired young man emerged, one of Randall's coats folded over his arm. "Welcome home, Major." Then he saw Julia. He knew her from the earlier trip to London, and his expression was vivid with curiosity as he bowed a welcome. "Mrs. Bancroft. It's a pleasure, ma'am."

"No longer Mrs. Bancroft." Randall placed his hand in the small of her back. "She's now Lady Julia Randall. My wife."

Julia knew that valets often felt jealous when their masters married, but luckily she and Gordon had been on friendly terms. Though his expression was startled, he didn't appear upset. "Congratulations, sir!" He bowed again. "Will I be meeting your lady's maid soon, Lady Julia?"

"It's good to see you again, Gordon." After a dozen years of looking after herself, Julia had half-forgotten that a maid would be expected. "I haven't a maid at the moment, but I imagine I will be looking for one soon." She glanced at her husband.

Randall nodded. "Since you'll be acquiring a new wardrobe, a maid is essential."

The thought of interviewing applicants made Julia feel tired. "Perhaps the duchess has a junior maid ready for a promotion."

Gordon looked hopeful. "I know a young female who might be suitable, Lady Julia. She isn't as experienced as some, but she's good with clothes, expert with a needle, and she's bright and good-natured and willing."

Randall grinned. "Is this the girl whose praises you sang throughout Portugal?"

Gordon blushed. "Yes, sir. But truly, I think Elsa would suit you, Lady Julia."

"Then I shall certainly interview her," Julia agreed.

"Thank you, my lady! She can call tomorrow afternoon for an interview." He ducked his head. "Your bags have been delivered. You'll be sharing these rooms?"

"We will indeed," Randall replied. "After you've unpacked us both, you may have the evening off. It's been a long journey and we'll retire early."

"Yes, sir!" Gordon left the fresh coat over the back of a chair and withdrew.

As soon as they were alone, Randall drew her into a hug. "I expect he'll be off to tell the fair Elsa that they might be able to work in the same household. I could tell you more than you would ever want to know about the girl, her appearance, her relations, and how she and Gordon met."

Julia laughed. "Then I hope she will do." She relaxed into Randall, loving the growing familiarity of his embrace, his scent, and strength. "With any encouragement, I'll go to sleep here," she murmured.

"You need food and good company, both of

which are waiting downstairs." His hands stroked over her hips, pressing her closer. "The trip was tiring, but easy compared to all we have to do here in London. I shall be glad of an early night."

Recognizing that it wasn't sleep he had in mind, she said hesitantly, "I shall also be glad to sleep."

Hearing her unspoken reservations, he said, "As you wish."

She felt his embrace change subtly. It was still affectionate, but no longer anticipating more. "You're so patient with my foot dragging," she said ruefully. "I keep thinking a soldier would want to conquer."

He laughed. "A soldier needs patience more than the ability to attack. I was prepared to spend a year hoping you would be willing to lie with me, so I think we're progressing very well."

"That's true," she said thoughtfully. "In another fortnight, my skittishness might be gone forever and you can seduce me whenever you choose."

"I'm hoping that a fortnight after that, you'll be seducing me." He kissed the sensitive spot under her left ear.

She caught her breath as desire curled through her. Though she'd never imagined initiating intimacy herself, the idea was as intriguing as it was bold. "An interesting thought, Alexander. For now, though, we should freshen up and join our hosts."

"How much do you want them to know?" Randall asked as he released her and peeled off the coat he'd worn all day.

She considered. "Everything but the most sordid bits, I suppose. Not about the scarring and my . . . barrenness, but they should know about the kidnapping and the circumstances of Branford's death."

"They can be trusted with as much truth as you want to reveal." He poured water into the basin so he could wash his face. After drying himself, he added, "I assume that the public story will be more discreet? We need to agree on the details."

Julia brushed out her hair and tied it back, intensely grateful to have friends she could trust to be on her side. Randall was the first among those friends, but Mariah and Ashton were close behind. "The world can be told that Branford died of injuries from a fall, which is true. I was so devastated that I ran away and let everyone believe I was dead, which is a kind of truth."

"True enough to be easy to remember," Randall agreed. "What shall we use for the official story of our marriage?"

"We can say we met in Hartley and I revealed who I was after learning you were my late husband's cousin." She splashed water on her face. "After a dozen years of mourning, I was ready to consider marriage again, and how could I resist you?"

Randall rolled his eyes. "Remember that we should keep close to the truth. The fewer details, the better. Since you didn't go out socially when you were in London earlier, you will be an intriguing surprise to society."

Julia had been teasing a bit when she said he was irresistible, but it was true. As she enjoyed the way the light linen shirt revealed his lean, powerful body, she recognized that any normal woman would have been riveted at first sight. Julia hadn't been normal when they met—but her female nature was recovering steadily.

Randall pulled on the fresh coat, then offered his arm and they headed downstairs to join the Ashtons in the small salon. Mariah looked radiant when they arrived.

Julia studied her friend as she and Randall entered, recognizing that radiance. "You're increasing!"

"How do you know?" Mariah exclaimed. "But of course you would. I'm so glad you're here. I'm delighted but a little panicked."

"The same is true of me!" Ashton added fervently.

Suppressing painful envy, Julia said reassuringly, "Having babies is the most natural thing in the world. You'll manage splendidly."

"Congratulations!" Randall shook Ashton's

hand, then kissed Mariah's cheek. "Your families must be quite pleased."

"They will be when they learn," Mariah agreed. "We hadn't told anyone yet. But I'm glad Julia guessed so I can talk about it!"

"Now that our news has been shared, shall we drink a round of sherry in a fashionable sort of way," the duke asked, "or fall ravenously on our dinners?"

"The latter! I'm ravenous all the time now." Mariah made a face. "Except in the mornings, when I'm green."

Laughing, both couples moved into the family dining room, which was much cozier than the majestic state dining room. Conversation was general and lighthearted until the meal was finished. After Mariah ordered tea for the ladies and port for the gentlemen, Ashton waved away the servants so they could talk privately. "About those complications? Unpleasant ones, I gather."

Randall glanced at Julia. She nodded at him to start the story.

"The first complication was arriving in Hartley to learn that Julia had just been abducted." Having captured the attention of the Ashtons, he kept them riveted as he tersely described rescuing Julia, and their marriage in Edinburgh. The duke's eyes narrowed, a reminder that his mildness concealed a core of steel.

When Randall finished, Mariah said in a hushed

voice, "Thank heaven you visited Hartley at the right time. Would Daventry have murdered Julia?"

"I don't think he would plan to kill her in cold blood. But if he lost his temper . . ." Randall shook his head, expression grave. "Julia, you knew him. What do you think he intended to do if Crockett brought you to him?"

"I presume Daventry ordered the abduction so he could scream and swear and tell me what a wicked woman I am." Julia tried to sound calm, as if the subject was no more important than the weather. "He probably didn't plan murder, but he might easily have lost control."

Ashton asked, "Will Daventry drop his persecution when he learns Julia is his heir's wife?"

"I think so," Randall replied in a steely voice, "but I'm not sure. If he won't—well, I will do what is necessary to protect my wife. He should be in London now, so I'll send a message and ask him to receive me at his earliest convenience."

Julia took a deep breath. "When you call on him, I'm going with you."

Randall frowned. "Daventry is going to explode in all directions when he learns I've married you. Your presence will make it even worse."

"I might as well get the meeting over with." Her smile was rueful. "If we're both going to be mauled by the encounter, it might be easier if we're together."

His expression eased. "You're probably right."

"Enough of problems. It's time to discuss amusements," Mariah announced. "We must introduce you both to society with a ball. In about a fortnight, which will allow time to have a truly splendid gown made, Julia. I'll arrange for the modiste to call here. Randall, you must wear your uniform. The sight of you in your regimentals is enough to make strong women swoon."

Randall groaned at her words, though Julia privately agreed. Ignoring him, Mariah continued, "Adam, is our social credit strong enough to overcome Castleton's disowning Julia?"

"I believe so." Ashton smiled fondly at his wife. "Castleton isn't very popular, whereas you, my golden duchess, are all the rage in the polite world."

"Golden duchess?" Randall asked.

"The beau monde loves to give nicknames." Mariah grinned. "Considering my rather dubious upbringing, I find it vastly amusing to be considered fashionable."

A thought occurred to Julia. "Would it help if my grandmother is co-hostess? That would demonstrate that not all my family has cast me off."

Mariah nodded. "An excellent idea. Who is your grandmother?"

"The Dowager Duchess of Charente."

Ashton, who knew London society best, burst into laughter. "The most exclusive, reclusive, and sought after noblewoman in London! Her presence will surely smooth your way if she's willing to cooperate."

Randall's brows arched. "I see that you weren't joking about having the bluest blood in England, milady."

Julia shrugged. "To me, she is simply Grandmère. She said during my earlier visit that it was time I returned to the world, so she will approve of your efforts, Mariah."

Her friend's eyes gleamed. "Society is a game, and we've just been dealt the cards to make this the most talked about ball of the autumn season!"

# Chapter 21

Randall sent a note to Daventry first thing the next morning, explaining that he had married and would like to bring his wife to call. His uncle replied immediately, setting a time that very afternoon.

When Randall handed Julia into an Ashton carriage, his wife said admiringly, "You look so calm. I'd be biting my nails if I wasn't wearing gloves."

He grimaced. "If I look calm, it's a lie. When I was a boy and sent to live in Daventry's household, he was God and the devil rolled into one. I preferred playing least in sight to engaging pitched battles, so I am not looking forward to this."

His uncle had definitely played the devil when Randall lay dying in the attic of Daventry House. Was it possible to have a civil, adult relationship with the man? Probably not. Marrying Julia might end his relationship with his uncle forever.

If so, good riddance. "You were right to come," he told her. "We can face him better together than separately."

She gave a tight smile when he took her hand. Even in gloves, her fingers were icy. They didn't speak for the rest of the journey.

When they reached Daventry House, Julia gripped Randall's arm after emerging from the carriage. "I hate this house," she said under her breath as they started up the steps. "Branford and I stayed here for several days after the wedding before moving to his estate near Bristol."

Randall didn't like to think what her wedding night and honeymoon had been like. "I'm not fond of the place, either. I believe it's part of the entailed estate and can't be sold, but no reason why the house can't be leased out after I inherit. We can choose a home that *we* like."

Her expression lightened. "What a splendid idea!"

They reached the door, which swung open to admit them. The butler bowed respectfully.

"Lord and Lady Daventry will receive you and your wife in the morning room, Major Randall."

If the countess was present at the meeting, his uncle must have decided to treat his heir with courtesy. Randall wondered how long that would last after Daventry recognized Julia.

They were ushered into the morning room. The Countess of Daventry sat behind a tea tray. The earl's third wife was an attractive blonde of middle years with natural elegance and calm reserve. She nodded a welcome to the newcomers but didn't rise.

Daventry dominated the room. Tall, white-haired, and forceful, he always reminded Randall of a sputtering rocket on the verge of ignition. He rose when Randall and Julia entered. Julia lagged a little behind Randall, and he guessed that she was delaying the moment when recognition became inevitable.

"Good day, Randall," Daventry said stiffly. "I had expected you to consult with me over your choice of a bride. I trust you chose a suitable female."

Clamping down familiar resentment at his uncle's domineering ways, Randall replied, "I'm the one who must live with my wife, so I thought the choice should be mine. But there is no question she has the breeding you require of the next countess. Uncle, Lady Daventry, allow me to introduce my wife, Lady Julia Randall."

Julia stepped forward so that she was in clear view of her father-in-law. "Good day, Lord Daventry, Lady Daventry."

The countess smiled pleasantly and returned the greeting, but the earl froze at the sight of Julia. "Damn you, boy!" Daventry gasped. "How *dare* you bring that murderess into my house! Is this some vile joke?"

Randall's temper kicked up several notches, but he maintained his control. "Not at all, sir. Julia and I were married in Edinburgh."

Daventry swore with vicious fluency. "I thought you'd finally grown up enough to recognize your responsibilities. Instead you married the bitch who murdered my son!"

It was time to set the record straight. Randall took Julia's hand, not sure which of them needed the comfort more. Her face was white, but she didn't drop her gaze despite the fury raging around her.

"Branford's death was an accident caused when Julia was fighting for her life," Randall said flatly. "He was a monster, Daventry, though you have always refused to see the truth. He hurt people for pleasure. I felt lucky to escape your household with my life. Julia very nearly died at your son's hands."

"You *lie!*" Daventry roared. "Branford was the best of sons, respectful and obedient. You were always jealous of his strength and superiority.

How dare you slander him when he isn't here to defend himself !"

"He was respectful to you because you controlled the money," Randal retorted. "To everyone else, he was a brute and bully. After his death, you made accusations against Julia that caused her to be cast off by her father." His grip on her hand tightened. "She managed to survive despite the worst you and Castleton could do to her. Now she is my wife, and I will not allow you to hurt her again in any way."

"So the sly slut cozened you with her lies." Daventry stared at Julia, his mouth twisted bitterly. "She looks as young and innocent as the day she married my son. Don't blame me when she decides she's tired of you and kills again."

Randall's temper snapped, but it was Julia who exploded. *"Enough!"*

Releasing Randall's hand, she stalked toward Daventry, a slim furious figure. "A dozen years ago, I made allowances for the way grief warped your judgment, but no longer!" she spat out. "Branford almost succeeded in murdering me. Last summer, you nearly killed Randall because of your angry neglect. Branford was mad and I pitied him almost as much as I feared him. But you are not mad, sir. You are a selfish, arrogant, bullying *brute,* and that is far more wicked than madness!"

Daventry flinched backward from her words.

"Did you know your pious midwife was such a dangerous shrew, Randall? If you believe her lies, you're an even bigger fool than I thought!"

"Do you wish proof of what your innocent, honorable son did? See the evidence for yourself!" Julia ripped the fichu from her gown, exposing the ghastly scars on the upper curves of her breasts. "Branford carved his initials on my body the night he almost killed me." Her voice dropped to a haunting whisper. "The night he kicked me until I lost the child I carried. The night he died."

The countess gasped and put her hand over her mouth. "Merciful heaven!"

"You did that yourself to garner sympathy," Daventry said after a shocked pause, but his voice was uncertain. His gaze was riveted to the scars.

"Don't be a damned fool, Daventry." Fighting the urge to knock his uncle to the ground, Randall wrapped his arm around Julia's shaking shoulders as she tucked the loose fichu back into place. "Julia is not the only one to bear the marks of Branford's madness. Shall I show you the scars he carved into me when I was a boy half his size?"

Daventry's face twisted with rage and anguish, but the countess said, "I know you loved him, my dear, but Branford was . . . not normal." Distaste flickered across her face for a brief moment. "I found it best not to be alone with him."

As her husband swung around to stare, she continued, "Though Branford could be charming, too many people had beastly stories for all of them to be false. Servants who fled his household came to me, as did shopkeepers and tenants whom he had injured. None of them dared go to you because you refused to listen." Her compassionate gaze moved to Julia. "Stop blaming this poor girl for what happened."

His face vulnerable, Daventry said, "*Et tu, Louisa?*"

"It is time to stop looking back," she said in a gentle voice. Her hand crept to her stomach. "The future is more important than the past."

"You're right, my dear." Competing emotions showed in Daventry's face. Triumph won. He turned to his visitors. "Randall, I was prepared to accept you as my heir of last resort, but I've recently learned that I can disown you. Louisa, stand up."

The countess rose, revealing that she was well along in pregnancy. The news struck Randall like a body blow. But he'd be damned if he would let that show. After a pause of several heartbeats to collect himself, he said, "My congratulations, sir, your ladyship," he said coolly. "This is very good news for you."

"But not for you." Daventry's voice rang with conviction. "It will be a son, I know it. I have only ever sired sons, and this one will be healthy.

Once again I shall have an heir of my blood for Daventry!"

Taking advantage of his uncle's changed mood, Randall said, "You are free to disown me, but you must stop persecuting my wife. Call off Crockett and his men."

He glanced at the countess, guessing she didn't know what her husband had done. "In the last month, Julia has been abducted from her home, terrorized, and shot at by your men. All because you refused to accept the truth about Branford. As Julia said, *Enough!*"

His eyes narrowed into his fiercest officer gaze, the one that made armed men pale. "Or there will be blood, and it won't be Julia's or mine."

"The major is right, Daventry," the countess said, looking appalled at Randall's recitation. "You really mustn't be terrorizing your nephew's wife. It's most improper."

The earl looked as if he'd bitten into a lemon, but after a glance at his wife, he said grudgingly, "I shall tell Crockett to leave her alone in the future."

"Do I have your word as a gentleman on that?" Randall asked.

"Yes, damn it, you do!" Daventry snarled. "Now get out of my house, and I hope to God I never see either of you two again. Don't expect to inherit a penny from me!"

"You never gave me anything in the past," Randall said, letting his anger show. "I never expected anything in the future. Being disowned merely makes it official."

"Damn you both!" Daventry gave his visitors a last fulminating glance as he stalked furiously from the room.

The countess broke the shaken silence first. "That certainly wasn't pleasant. Will you two join me for tea? Very soothing, tea, and my cook makes excellent cakes."

Randall exchanged a glance with Julia. Her expression echoed his anger and exhaustion, but she nodded acceptance. "Thank you, Lady Daventry," he said. "That would be most welcome. You've never met Lady Julia, I believe?"

"No, and I am most anxious to do so. Please, take seats." The countess gestured to chairs on the other side of the tea table. This close, Randall saw the fine lines around her eyes and haunted tension in her face, but her graciousness was impeccable.

"Would you like oolong tea?" The countess's hand hovered between two handsome teapots. "I also have a quite nice lapsang souchong. It's my favorite variety."

Her calm social manner seemed rather mad under the circumstances, but Randall supposed that an ability to ignore wild moods was essential to living with Daventry. "I'd like the lapsang souchong, please." Though he doubted she was a poisoner, it wouldn't hurt to drink what she was having.

Perhaps sharing the thought, Julia said, "I'll have the same."

Lady Daventry poured, the fragrant liquid arcing gracefully into the cups. "Lady Julia, please accept the silk shawl draped over your chair as a gift. The color suits you."

"Thank you, Lady Daventry." Julia draped the shawl around her shoulders, completely covering the crumpled fichu. "You're very generous."

"It's the least I can do." The countess passed out the teacups. "I knew your mother when I was a girl, Major, and admired her greatly. You resemble her."

Randall felt an unexpected tightness in his throat as he accepted a delicate porcelain cup. "Thank you. I'm glad to take after her family."

"And so you should be. The Blairs are a more reliable lot than the Randalls." The countess stirred sugar into her own tea, looking down at the silver spoon. "But Daventry's not mad, you know, nor evil. His blindness is because he cares so deeply."

"Blindness that profound might not be evil, but it produces evil results," Randall said dryly. "Branford was surely mad, but the fact that his father left him unchecked greatly increased his destructiveness." He stirred his tea, the spoon clinking against the delicate china. "Marrying him to an innocent child like Julia was a crime."

"Indeed it was." The countess's grave gaze moved to Julia. "I was so glad when Daventry said you were alive. From the stories I'd heard about Branford, I can imagine the horror of sharing a bed with him."

"No," Julia said softly, her eyes bleak. "You really can't."

Lady Daventry became very still. "I suppose not. It was very wrong for my husband to arrange a marriage for Branford, but he desperately fears that his bloodline will die out. His fear is not unjustified. All three of his wives, including me, suffered multiple miscarriages and stillbirths. I didn't tell him I was increasing this time until I was far enough along to be confident the child would go to term."

"Did Branford's madness come from the Randall side of the family?" Julia asked.

The countess shook her head. "It's from his mother's people. The first countess was more than a little mad, but she apparently had a wild charm that made her irresistible. Daventry thinks of her as the love of his life. She died in child-birth."

Amazed at Lady Daventry's detachment, Randall said, "Yet my uncle married twice more."

She offered a plate of iced cakes. "He was

determined to see his bloodline carry on. He had great hopes for his younger son, Rupert, who survived infancy, but the poor boy was always sickly. Daventry was mad with grief when Rupert died at age ten." The countess's face was shadowed. "I was sorry, too. He was a good lad. No madness in him. He was a child of Daventry's second marriage."

Julia asked in an edged voice, "You seem a sensible woman. Where were you when your husband was killing Randall with neglect in his very house?"

Lady Daventry looked directly at Randall. "I was at Turville Park recovering from a miscarriage when you were brought back from Spain with your wounds, Major. Please believe that I would not have allowed such ill-treatment and neglect. I was horrified to learn of it later from the servants. You have my deepest apologies."

So not only had Daventry lost his one living son, but his wife had miscarried, magnifying the earl's desperate sense of loss. No wonder he'd hated his nephew's tenacious ability to survive. But his raging grief had damned near cost Randall his life. "The fault was not yours, Lady Daventry," Randall said. "But I would have died if Ashton hadn't invaded the house and taken me away."

"That was a dreadful summer for everyone. I am truly sorry for how you were treated, and very glad that you have a friend like Ashton."

The countess turned to Julia, her face intent. "Lady Julia—Daventry said you were a midwife. Can that be true?"

So that was what this conversation was about. Lady Daventry's hospitality was real, but her interest in Julia's midwifery skills was burning.

"Indeed it is." Julia took a ginger cake, but her gaze was on her hostess. "I shall be happy to discuss your condition, but surely you have a physician here?"

"Sir Richard Croft, considered the best physician in London for such matters." The countess crumbled a seed cake between anxious fingers. "I had my other sons when I was young, without any problems for them or me. I wanted another child. That was one reason I married Daventry. But now . . . I am over forty."

"I've had a number of patients who delivered safely at your age," Julia said reassuringly. "It's not that uncommon."

"I had hoped we would have a chance to speak privately." The countess gave Randall a sidelong glance.

Julia nodded, a hint of smile in her eyes. "This will be the sort of conversation that sends strong men fleeing for the hills, Randall."

He didn't even want to imagine what they would discuss. He scooped up his teacup and a small plate of cakes. "There's a salon through that door, I recall?"

"It's now my private parlor. Daventry never goes there," the countess replied. "He probably went out to his club where he is safe from females. Or perhaps he's riding too fast in the park."

Randall hoped the damned man would break his neck, but the devil protected his own. As he retreated to her ladyship's private parlor, he prayed that he'd never have to enter this house again.

# Chapter 22

Julia emerged from Daventry House jangling with nerves. "That was the strangest tea party of my life," she said after their carriage door closed and the vehicle rumbled into the late afternoon traffic. She pulled off her bonnet and ran stiff fingers through her hair, displacing several of the pins.

"Strange indeed." Randall's expression was as impenetrable as when they first met in Hartley. "How is Lady Daventry's health?"

"Reasonable. The baby is very active and close enough to term that it will likely survive even if born early." Julia thought of the lively kicks she'd felt at the countess's invitation. "Beyond that, I can't say. There seems to be a weakness in Daventry's seed that has prevented him from fathering a truly healthy child."

"Is the countess in danger? She seemed very worried."

"She's terrified that the delivery will kill her." Julia pulled the shawl Lady Daventry had given her more closely around her shoulders. "And it could, of course. Much can go wrong."

"You said you'd delivered many women safely at her age."

"Yes, but I've also lost some." Sometimes Julia dreamed—or had nightmares—of patients who had died. One's best wasn't always good enough. "Lady Daventry was gravely ill after her last miscarriage. This delivery will probably be harder on her."

"What about the expensive physician Daventry has engaged?" Randall said rather dryly. "His precious heir will surely get the best care possible."

"Sir Richard Croft has an excellent reputation. He's been bleeding her and he has her on a reducing diet. It's not what I would recommend." Julia frowned. "I know that having male physicians in attendance is the fashion, but a competent midwife is as good or better than a physician. Of course, I'm biased."

"A woman would have more respect for the territory," Randall said with a faint smile. "I hope the countess comes through. I'm amazed that any woman would want Daventry for a husband, but she seems to see him clearly and still likes him." He shook his head. "Women truly are extraordinary."

Julia laughed. "Men and women are so often mysteries to each other. I succumbed to vulgar curiosity and asked why she married him. She was quite candid. She found him attractive in a Byronic sort of way."

"Byronic?" Randall asked incredulously.

"As you say, women can be odd creatures, and they're often attracted to powerful men. After her ladyship was widowed, she didn't feel ready to languish into embroidery and good works. Marrying Daventry made her a countess, with wealth and influence. That also appealed to her, of course."

"Of course." His dryness had increased.

Julia's thoughts moved from the countess's health to the implications for Randall. "Are you upset to be displaced and disowned?"

"I think we've done rather well." His profile was like marble as he glanced out at the crowded street. "Between us, we've been disowned by two of the most powerful men in England within the space of three days."

"My father had virtually disowned me a dozen years ago, so hearing the words doesn't change my situation," she pointed out. "But you've not only been disowned, but likely lost an earldom. That does make a difference."

Outside, an upraised Cockney voice shouted at

another driver. Several rounds of insults were exchanged before Randall said, "I was getting used to the idea of becoming the next earl. There was a kind of justice to it." He turned from the window and took her hand. "I would have liked to make you a countess."

"That would be a lower rank than the one I was born to, so it's no great loss to me," she said lightly. "But you would have made a very good earl. Fair and wise and used to commanding men."

He shrugged off the compliment. "For most of my life, I never considered the possibility of inheriting—there were too many others in line before me. So it shouldn't take me long to readjust to being a mere major."

"You earned your army rank, which is more than a peer can say."

"The peerage is all about inheritance," he agreed. "Even when I was heir presumptive, I always knew the estate would come to me only because it was entailed. Daventry would never voluntarily leave me any of his personal fortune. So as in your case, being disowned just makes official what was already the reality."

Thinking his voice didn't sound quite right, she studied his face. The carriage lurched forward and sunlight poured in the window, revealing his expression clearly. She was shocked by what she saw in his eyes.

Losing the earldom might not concern Randall overmuch, but Daventry was the powerful man who had ruled his childhood. Though Randall had stood up unflinchingly to his uncle's fury and abuse, he was not unaffected by it. Just as she had not been able to shrug off her father's rage and revulsion.

A wounded spirit could ache far longer than physical injuries. Daventry's grudging acceptance when he'd thought Randall was the heir wasn't much, but she suspected it was the closest thing to approval her husband had ever known from his guardian. Today, Daventry had smashed that fragile bond into bleeding pieces.

Randall could not be as sensitive to her if his awareness hadn't been honed by his difficult childhood. She imagined him as a wary boy, always watching his surroundings for safety's sake, just like she had always been vigilant when Branford was near. Now Randall was hurting. It was time she took care of him as he'd cared for her.

"The ride home will be a slow one at this hour." Julia pulled the shade down on her window, then reached across Randall to lower the shade on his side. "Let's use the time to forget about our rather difficult visit to Daventry House."

In the dim remaining light, she could see his brows rise. "What do you propose?"

"I was thinking about kissing." A little hesitantly, she lifted her head and pressed her lips against his. "I've always been the kissed, not the kisser, so I hope you don't leap away from me."

"Why would I want to do a foolish thing like leap away when I've been campaigning to lure you closer?" His mouth opened and the kiss deepened.

She reveled in the touch and slide of tongues, which made it easy to forget the voices of angry old men. Reality was *this* man, who made her pulse quicken as they pressed together. His hands kneaded her back, causing her fingers to bite into his arms as pleasure simmered through her. No wonder chaperones tried to protect girls from kisses. Such drugging delight drove out good sense. But this dangerously attractive man was her husband, so there was no need to be sensible.

Under the colorful shawl the countess had given her, his hand curved over her breast, his stroking thumb bringing sensitive flesh to startled life through the layers of fabric. Wanting to explore his body as well, she slid her hand down his torso, enjoying the feel of taut flesh and bone under the tailored garments of a London gentleman.

Her wrist brushed the hard bulge in his breeches. To her surprise, she was pleased, not alarmed, at such undeniable proof that he found her attractive. Loving the effect she had on him, she began to unbutton his breeches.

He caught her hand. "You needn't do this, milady," he said roughly. "It's enough that you are kissing me."

She tilted back her head and caught his gaze. "Alex, so far this marriage has mostly been about me and my fears. Now I want to do something for you."

He drew an unsteady breath. "If you're sure . . ."

"Entirely sure." She returned to the buttons, releasing the taut, hard shaft into her hand. She knew from experience that male flesh could be used as weapon, but that knowledge was distant memory, no longer relevant.

What mattered was how his hands gripped her shoulders, the immense enjoyment she found in pleasing him as she stroked and squeezed and teased. In the early days of her first marriage, she'd learned how to satisfy a man.

The teaching had been harsh, but she'd learned well. Later she'd used those skills in self-defense, hoping that if Branford was sated, he wouldn't hurt her.

Now she remembered those sensual skills, and she was with a man who wouldn't hurt her. When it occurred to her that she could give him even greater pleasure, she hesitated, not sure she was ready for such intimacy. It took long moments to recognize that her desire to please was more powerful than her misgivings. She drew a deep breath, then bent and took him into her mouth.

"My God, Julia!" His hands spasmed on her shoulders.

Startled, she raised her head. "Do you want me to stop?"

*"No!"* His breathing was ragged. "Dear God, no!"

Gratified, she bent again, her mouth and tongue remembering the subtle techniques she hadn't used in so long. To her surprise, she enjoyed this intimacy, not only for the pleasure it gave him, but for the power she felt in creating that pleasure. The very air of the carriage was saturated with passion as her own excitement echoed his. His harsh pants and rigid body made her feel like his sexual equal, a true partner rather than a victim or a passive recipient.

In her enthusiasm, she triggered his climax sooner than she'd intended. He cried out and knotted his hands in her hair, his pelvis rocking. When his body stilled, she rested her head against his belly, feeling vastly pleased with herself.

His fingers loosened in her hair, becoming a caress. "You are the most extraordinary woman, Julia." His voice was less than even. "If you will permit me . . ." He scooped her across his lap. "You are just the right size for holding. "

"I enjoyed that," she said as she settled comfortably in his arms. "I trust you've forgotten your visit to Daventry House?"

"Never heard of the place," he said promptly. His left hand stroked down her leg, shaping calf and ankle before sliding up to her knee under her skirts.

She caught her breath as his warm palm on her inner thigh stirred her from contentment to yearning. He parted her knees so that his hand could move higher, higher. She gasped at the sensual shock when he touched her most intimate flesh. Sensation hazed her mind as he caressed more deeply. Yet this time pleasure was not a surprise. It was . . . anticipated.

He knew what she wanted better than she did, and the searing climax blazed through her entire body. Her fingers bit and her lower body rocked hard against him as unbearable need culminated, then unwound swiftly, leaving her collapsed against him.

"Oh, my," she breathed. "I've been royally rewarded for wanting to please you."

"Mutual pleasure is better." He kissed her damp temple. "Next time we should try this in a bed. More comfortable, and we can go to sleep after."

"That would be nice." She covered a yawn as her eyes closed and she felt the steady throb of his heart against her cheek. "I hope this is the worst tangle of traffic in London history and that we don't get back to Ashton House until midnight."

He laughed and raised his shade a couple of inches. "No such luck. We're out of the worst of the traffic and will be home in a few more minutes."

But neither of them was in a hurry to move. Julia realized with amazement that she wasn't just content. She was happy.

She was also curious. He knew all he needed to know about the one man she'd shared a bed with, but she knew almost nothing about his romantic experience. "I probably shouldn't ask, but where did you learn so much about pleasing women?"

"There hasn't been an endless stream of lovers, if that's what you're wondering." His hand lazily stroked her nape. "An officer on campaign has limited opportunities."

"Limited, but not nonexistent?"

"I avoided the camp followers because I didn't want the diseases," he explained. "A decision practical rather than moral. But I had one significant affair during those years. I rescued a French officer's widow and her maid from Spanish partisans who wanted to take vengeance on anyone French, even two helpless women."

Major Randall, the protector. Of course. "The lady must have been very grateful."

"She was, but the affair was with her maid." He smiled reminiscently. "Celeste was pretty and saucy and very French. She said I wasn't her type, but she missed having a man and I'd do for the time being. She and her mistress spent a long winter quartered in Portugal near my regiment until they could return to France and their families."

Julia regretfully acknowledged that no one had ever thought of her as saucy. "Celeste must have been quite an education for an Englishman."

"She was." He grinned. "Her best piece of advice was to pay attention to what a woman says—and to what she doesn't say."

"A wise woman," Julia said. "I hope they both made it back to France safely."

"They did. Madame sent me a note that eventually made its way through enemy lines. They were both home and safe in Lyon. Celeste married a young man she'd known for years who had been invalided out of Napoleon's army."

"She sounds very amusing and uncomplicated." Also words not usually applied to Julia.

"But you're much more interesting." His voice changed. "We're entering the gates now. Idyll over." He transferred her to the seat beside him. "Time we made ourselves at least marginally presentable."

"I can smooth down my hair, but I don't think I can get rid of my cat-in-a-cream-pot smile," she said as she straightened her clothing.

He returned her smile. "I have one, too, I think."

"I can almost see you licking the cream from your whiskers," she agreed.

"Licking?"

She blushed, embarrassed but more pleased.

"I'll never get into a carriage again without remembering this ride," he murmured provocatively as the vehicle stopped and a footman opened the door.

Julia's contentment lasted until they entered Ashton House and the butler approached. "Lady Julia, you have a guest waiting in the small salon." He handed her a calling card. "He has refused to leave until he sees you."

A guest? Surprised that anyone in London knew she was alive, she read the calling card. The blood drained from her face. *Lord Stoneleigh.* "Merciful heaven," she whispered. "It's my brother Anthony."

"You don't have to receive him if you don't want to." Randall's gaze was steady. "And if you do want to see him, you don't have to face him alone."

Julia thought despairingly of her appearance. She must look like a well-tumbled dairy maid, with flushed cheeks and rumpled clothing. But this was another meeting she couldn't avoid.

Jaw set, she drew Lady Daventry's shawl around her shoulders as if it was protective armor. "I might as well get this over with. Please . . . come with me?"

"Of course. You're a trooper, milady." Randall placed a comforting hand on her back. "To the small salon we go. I hope your brother doesn't much resemble Castleton."

So did she.

# Chapter 23

When Julia and Randall entered the small salon, she stopped dead in her tracks, shocked by how much her brother had grown to look like their father. "Anthony," she whispered despairingly.

Her brother had been a schoolboy when she last saw him, all big hands and feet that he hadn't yet grown into. Now he was a man, expensive and aristocratic to the bone. He was taller than her father but with the Raines features and the Raines coloring—and an anger that scorched the room. She wanted to weep. Or run away.

Randall placed a warm hand on the small of her back, reminding her that she wasn't alone. No matter how much her family despised her, Randall was on her side. That conviction made it possible to stand her ground in the face of her brother's anger.

Randall spoke to fill the silence when she couldn't. "Lord Stoneleigh?" he said easily as he closed the door behind them. "I'm Major Randall." He offered his hand. "I presume you've heard that we are now brothers-in-law."

Ignoring Randall as if he was invisible, Anthony stalked forward, his gaze never leaving Julia's face. She glimpsed Randall beside her from the corner of her eye. He was cool and composed—and quietly prepared to stop her brother dead in his tracks if the younger man threatened harm.

"It really is you, Julie," Anthony said tautly. "I couldn't believe it when the duke wrote that you were alive."

She tried to smile. "Indeed I am, Anthony. A dozen years older. I hope a little wiser. I . . . I thought of you often."

"Then why did you let me believe you were dead?" His cry from the heart splintered his polished façade to reveal the boy who had been her dearest friend. A boy who had suffered greatly from the loss of his only sister, and now felt betrayed.

Julia blinked back tears, but her gaze didn't drop. "I didn't dare, Anthony. It was too large a secret for a young brother to bear."

"Perhaps you were right then." His mouth twisted. "But in all the years since?"

"The only way I could survive was to turn away from my past, because remembering was too painful," she said haltingly. "And . . . I feared that if you learned I was alive, you would despise me for my deception. Apparently I was right."

"Damn you, Julie!" Voice breaking, Anthony

stepped forward and wrapped her in a crushing embrace. The top of her head barely reached his chin. "How could you think I would despise my own sister?"

"You . . . you've grown," Julia choked out before she began to weep from relief. Because she had expected nothing good from her father, his contempt was painful but predictable. But she and Anthony had been close. His rejection would have been devastating.

After her tears slowed, Randall said, "I gather this means that even though your father has disowned Julia, you won't be giving her the cut direct if you meet socially."

"Of course not." Anthony's voice was husky as he stepped back a little to study Julia's face. His eyes were his father's, but his caring expression came from their mother. "You are my sister, Julie, and I'm proud to tell the world that. Castleton can cut you, but he can't actually disown you since your inheritance is from Mother."

"I don't care what Castleton thinks about my wicked ways." Almost giddy with relief, Julia sat on the sofa, tugging Anthony down next to her. "What matters is that you are welcoming me."

"I'll talk to the family lawyer about transferring your inheritance." Anthony gave Randall a wary glance. "Of course a settlement should be drawn up."

The wariness was understandable. Because Julia and Randall were already married, he was legally entitled to complete control of all her property. In a properly arranged marriage, there would have been negotiations and a prenuptial contract. Julia trusted Randall to be honorable, but Anthony didn't know him.

"I didn't marry your sister because of any possible inheritance," Randall said coolly. "I'll waive my claim so she can control her inheritance herself."

Anthony relaxed. "That's decent of you, Randall. Too many men would be itching to get their hands on her fortune."

"How much is my portion?" Julia asked. "I was never told."

"I don't know the exact figure." Her brother thought for a moment. "But it's close to a hundred thousand pounds."

"Good God!" Randall exclaimed, staring at Julia. "You're probably the greatest heiress in England."

"I had no idea it was that much." She shrugged uncomfortably. "It's hard to imagine such money when I've been bartering my services for chickens and eggs."

Anthony blinked. "How did you survive all these years, Julie?"

"I was a midwife in Cumberland." Julia smiled wryly. "It's a long story."

"One I want to hear," her brother said firmly. "I want to know *everything*."

"You two have much to discuss." Randall clasped Julia's shoulder with a warm hand before moving away. "I'll leave you now."

Julia glanced up at him, hoping her smile would convey her gratitude. "Thank you, Alex. For everything." Then she turned back to her brother to exchange the tales of their last dozen years.

Numbly Randall closed the salon door. In a day with far too much drama, the size of Julia's inheritance was the greatest shock of all. He'd been glad he could offer her a comfortable life and a modest but pleasant estate. It was unnerving to realize that she could buy and sell him several times over.

He turned to see the Duchess of Ashton, who waited in the hall with a concerned expression. "How is Julia's meeting with her brother going?" Mariah asked. "I assume you wouldn't have left her if he was behaving badly."

"Stoneleigh is upset that Julia let him believe she was dead for so many years, but once that was addressed, they fell into each other's arms," he said succinctly. "Though her father will cut her, Stoneleigh won't. She's happy and relieved, and they'll probably talk for hours."

"Oh, good." She took Randall's arm and

steered him back toward the front hall. Glancing up, she said, "You look particularly granite-faced. Daventry?"

Randall shrugged. "He showed off his pregnant countess and announced that I was not only superceded but disowned. A typical interaction with my uncle. I fondly hope it's the last time I shall ever have to deal with him."

Mariah winced. "You've had far too eventful a day."

"Indeed." The high point had been in the carriage, but he could hardly tell Mariah about that. "The biggest shock was learning how much Julia's portion is. The world will say that she married beneath herself."

"What nonsense!" she scoffed. "Who cares what the world says? When she was the midwife of Hartley, society would have said that you were the one who had married beneath your station. But you are both the same people now that you were then."

Mariah was right, but Randall still wished that his wife's dowry was less extravagant. Obviously he preferred to feel magnanimous and broadminded rather than like a fortune hunter. "Actually, I'm not the same person. Being around Julia is improving my disposition."

"I've noticed," Mariah said with a smile. They entered the front hall at the same time that Holmes was admitting a visitor, a white-haired lady garbed in black silk and shimmering pearls. She swept into the hall—petite, beautiful, and with a command presence that rivaled Wellington's.

"Her grace, the Duchess of Charente," Holmes announced.

Mariah made a strangled sound before sinking into a deep curtsy. "Your grace. Welcome to my home. I didn't expect you to respond to my note so quickly."

"Naturally I wish to see my granddaughter now that she is officially alive again," the older woman said with a tart French accent. "Stand up, girl. Respect for your elders is all very well, but one duchess should never grovel to another."

"I stand corrected." Mariah rose, eyes dancing but voice demure. "But I am the newest and most inexperienced of duchesses. I can't begin to match your . . . your duchessness."

"You will in time," her grace said grandly, but her lips quirked with amusement.

Randall had expected Julia's grandmother to be frail, perhaps an invalid. Clearly the lady's health had improved since Julia had visited her in the spring. Julia resembled her grandmother—and she would be just as beautiful when she was the duchess's age.

Mariah continued, "Julia and her brother are in the small salon, renewing their acquaintance after so many years of separation."

The duchess sniffed. "Stoneleigh is here? I trust he is behaving appropriately."

"He welcomes his sister's return," Randall said. "They were very close, and will be again, I think."

The duchess turned her gimlet gaze on Randall. "I suppose this is Major Randall, Julia's husband?"

He bowed. "Indeed I am, ma'am."

"Daventry's heir, I believe?"

"Heir presumptive," he said, "but unlikely to inherit. Daventry and his wife are expecting a blessed event."

The hazel eyes sharpened. "I hadn't heard that. A pity that you're being superceded. Julia should be at least a countess. What makes you think you're good enough for my granddaughter?"

"I'm not," Randall said. "But sometimes the gods smile."

"They did in your case," the old lady said dryly. "My granddaughter is the richest prize in England."

"I didn't marry the richest prize in England," he said with equal dryness. "I married a winsome midwife who owned no more than the roof over her head."

The duchess gave a crack of laughter. "You'll do, Major Randall. Now take me to my grandchildren."

Randall accompanied Mariah and the Duchess

of Charente to the salon. He was curious how Julia and Stoneleigh would react to her entrance.

When the door opened, two voices chorused, "Grandmère!"

Looking over the heads of the two duchesses, Randall saw Stoneleigh leap to his feet and bow. Julia rose and swept gracefully into a formal court curtsy before moving forward to embrace her grandmother. She was taller, but only slightly.

For a moment, tears glinted in the eyes of the fierce Duchess of Charente. "I'm so glad you're out of the shadows, my dear," she whispered. Then she blinked and stepped back to study her granddaughter. "You're looking well, Julia. Less mousy. I suppose I should thank this great hulking male creature you married?"

"Indeed you should, Grandmère." Julia glanced over the duchess's shoulder to give Randall a smile that did strange things to his insides. "He is an amazingly tolerant man who was willing to marry me even after I explained all the reasons he shouldn't."

"Not tolerant. Wise," the duchess said approvingly. Her attention shifted to her grandson. "You are not going to treat Julia like your fool of a father, Stoneleigh?"

"It would be disrespectful of me to agree with your assessment of my sire, Grandmère," he replied, his eyes glinting. "But I assure you that

I will support my sister in all ways I can." Like Julia, he obviously respected his grandmother without being intimidated by her.

The duchess nodded. "Very good." She turned to Mariah. "You and I have a ball to plan. I will permit the children to catch up a bit. Then you will join us for the planning, Julia." Her gaze shifted to Randall. "You will best serve by staying out of our way. This is women's business."

"I wouldn't dream of interfering," Randall said fervently. "The Duchess of Ashton has already informed me that I must attend wearing my regimentals. I am at your service for any other orders you wish to issue."

The Duchess of Charente chuckled. "You're a scamp, Major. Orders will be forthcoming after I have conferred with my adjutants. Now be off."

Randall obeyed. He'd never been called a scamp before. Coming from the duchess, he suspected that was a compliment of sorts.

He collected several letters that Holmes had set out for him and retreated to his rooms. Some of the letters had followed him to Spain and back. Knowing that many were from his business manager, he added the new letters to the pile of correspondence that had landed on his desk during his adventures in the north country. It was time to settle down and behave like a responsible property owner.

He took a Spanish dagger from his desk drawer and began slicing open the seals, but he had trouble concentrating on routine matters of business. He'd started the day as heir to an earldom with a bride who was rare, intriguing, and penniless. Now he was an untitled gentleman with a modest income who had married a woman who was heiress to almost unimaginable wealth.

It was said that Sarah, Lady Jersey, had gone to her marriage with a hundred thousand pounds because her mother was the only daughter of Robert Child, founder of Child's bank. Lady Jersey was her grandfather's principal heir and she'd been an enormous prize in the marriage mart. His quiet Julia, who had dug bits of shrapnel from his damaged thigh, was equally wealthy.

He'd told both Julia and Mariah that it was no great matter that he was being superceded, but apparently he did care. Though he'd lived most of his life not considering the possibility that he'd inherit the earldom, in the last few weeks, he had become used to the idea. He'd even grown to like the prospect. He had too much pride to admit that to anyone else, but in the quiet of his own mind, he must be honest.

What happened when the knight errant rescued his lady, and it turned out that after the rescue she didn't need him any more?

# Chapter 24

At the end of the afternoon, Julia returned to their rooms. She paused in the doorway to admire the picture that Randall made as he worked at his desk by the window. Late afternoon sunshine touched his hair to gold and silver, and lovingly illuminated the strong, austere planes of his face. She felt a pleasant internal shiver at the knowledge that she was becoming very familiar with that lean, well-muscled body.

He glanced up at her entrance. "You look like a girl just emerged from the schoolroom," he observed. "Young and happy and excited about new possibilities."

"I feel that way." She crossed to Randall and bent to hug him. "I knew that Grandmère would be glad to see me, but I feared that Anthony would disown me forever, like Castleton."

"He's a better man than your father." Randall wrapped an arm around her waist and pulled her to his side. Since he was seated, the side of his head rested very pleasantly against her breasts.

The energy that had buoyed her up evaporated, leaving her tired but happier than she'd been in . . . forever. "I'm sorry that my family was so much more rewarding today than yours."

"My expectations of Daventry have always been

253

low," Randall said. "What matters is that he ordered Crockett to stay away from you so you can live without always looking over your shoulder."

"I feel as if a great weight has been lifted from my shoulders." She brushed her fingertips through his thick blond hair, thinking how much she owed her husband. "Considering that I had to be coaxed into marriage like a skittish filly, I've benefited remarkably from marrying you." She hoped he'd say that he had also benefited, but when he didn't, she continued, "What did you think of Grandmère?"

"She enjoys terrifying people," he said promptly. "But her sense of humor occasionally undermines that."

Julia laughed. "You understand her well. She said you weren't at all like a Randall, which means she liked you."

One corner of his mouth turned up. "That's quite a compliment. I think."

Since Randall didn't seem inclined to pull her onto his lap, Julia moved to the adjacent wing chair to continue their talk. He looked calm and handsome—and too blasted detached, given what they'd done in the carriage earlier.

Reminding herself that detachment was his natural expression, she said, "Gordon's sweetheart, Elsa Smith, came by to be interviewed. She's a bit inexperienced, but bright and keen to learn. I think she'll do very well."

Randall gave an approving nod. "Gordon will be ecstatic. Can she start soon?"

"Tomorrow." Julia frowned as she thought about the interview. "Her current master has been making Elsa's life difficult, so she's desperate to leave. I told her she could move here tonight and I'd make up whatever wages she lost by not giving notice. She and Gordon were going to her former household right away to collect her things."

Randall regarded her curiously. "Given her bad situation, would you have hired her even if she didn't seem like a promising lady's maid?"

"Probably," Julia admitted. "I hated knowing she had to dodge her master to avoid being assaulted. At least she's free to leave, unlike a wife."

"Unlike most wives, you are free to leave," he pointed out. "You made sure of that before accepting my offer."

"I had to know the door was open if I needed to run." Was it only weeks since she'd insisted he give her a letter agreeing to a divorce if she should want one? How quickly she'd grown to trust him. Julia continued, "Elsa's situation got me thinking. If I really have this huge amount of money, I'd like to use some of it to create shelters for women who need to flee male violence but have no place safe to go. Not every woman can fake her own death in order to escape."

"And most wouldn't be lucky enough to be taken in by someone like your Mrs. Bancroft." Randall's expression was thoughtful. "That's an ambitious plan, but such shelters would literally save lives. Would you establish them in all the major cities?"

"I haven't thought that far," she admitted. "They would need to be widespread since abused women are everywhere."

"What if the shelters were affiliated with parish churches?" he suggested. "They really are every-where."

She frowned. "Yes, but I'm not sure that would be the best plan. The church is run by men, and male views of a woman's place often differ from female views. I suppose I could talk to the Archbishop of Canterbury. He's some sort of cousin."

"Naturally the Archbishop of Canterbury is a relative," Randall said with wry amusement. "I should have guessed."

"None of my exalted relatives helped me when I needed it," she said tartly. "Grandmère was the only one who might have taken me in, but her husband was dying then and I couldn't burden her further." Nor had Julia been able to face the difficulties of staying in her old world.

His amusement faded. "So you stayed with Branford until he almost killed you. You're right, there should be refuges for women so they can escape before it's too late. Perhaps you might want to affiliate with the Methodist chapels. They aren't as widespread as Anglican parishes, but they already have shelters to take women from the streets and give them training and education to build better lives."

She felt a tingle of excitement. "You're right, the Methodists might be better partners. May I have a piece of paper and a pencil so I can make notes to myself?"

He pulled paper and pencil from a drawer and handed them over. "You might want to start by talking to Mariah and your grandmother. They will approve and have good ideas, I'm sure. They would also be very influential supporters."

"Another good idea." She scribbled that down, other ideas beginning to bubble into her mind. "I'll start with Mariah."

"This will be a way where you can help many more women than you did as a midwife," Randall said, his eyes warm. "You've traveled a hard road to get here, but it's made you a better, more compassionate woman."

"I'd like to think so." She hesitated, not wanting to chase away that warmth. "Something has been bothering me all day. Lady Daventry mentioned the earl's obsession with carrying on his bloodline. When she and I talked privately, I asked her if Branford had left any by-blows. She didn't know of any, so perhaps Branford never told his father."

Randall's expression hardened. "And you're worried about that boy."

Julia bit her lip. "With any luck, he's living happily with his mother with financial support from Daventry, but I'd feel better if I knew he was well."

"Assuming he's even alive," Randall pointed out. "Many small children don't make it to adulthood."

"Yes, and if that's the case, the boy is in God's hands now. But what if he's alive and mistreated?" Julia knew that some of the nobility's illegitimate children were reasonably well treated, like Mackenzie. But others were not so lucky.

"Why do you care about the fate of a child who was sired by an abusive bully who almost killed you?" Randall said with exasperation. "If he's alive, he might be a monster like his father."

"Perhaps, but as you've said, Branford surely would not have been so bad if he'd been raised better. The same could be said of Daventry himself."

"This boy would be what—twelve or thirteen? His character must already be set."

Julia searched for words that might persuade Randall. "Perhaps. But no matter what his nature, every child deserves to be cared for properly. Though Daventry was a poor guardian for you, at least you had food and a roof over your head, and an education. Who is caring for Branford's son? You have no reason to love Branford, but the boy is also your cousin. A Randall by blood. Someone should care about his welfare."

Randall sighed. "Perhaps Daventry does, but we can't be sure, since his wife was unaware of the boy, and I can hardly ask the man directly. Very well, I am reluctantly convinced that I owe some responsibility to Branford's bastard. What do you wish to see done? Do you have any idea of where the boy is?"

Julia thought back to Branford's taunts. "I think the child was born early in the year twelve years ago, probably near Branford's estate, Upton Hill, near Bristol. I had the impression that the mother was a servant who lived in the area, but didn't work at the manor." She thought some more. "Maybe a barmaid? He told me more than once that I was a scrawny little wench who would never be noticed if a barmaid was in the room."

"Proving once again what a fool he was," Randall said acerbically as he made notes on a fresh piece of paper. "Branford would have wanted a convenient woman for when he was at Upton Hill, so that's a good area to start looking."

"Is this enough information to find the boy? I'd be willing to go to Upton to search, but I don't know if I'd be any good at it."

"My friend Rob Carmichael is a Bow Street Runner. He's good at this sort of thing." Randall made another note. "I'll set up a meeting with him."

"Tomorrow morning Mariah's modiste will come to make me fit for society." Julia made a face. "Grandmère will also be here, and Elsa Smith, and Mariah, of course. I suspect they'll all have strong opinions about my new wardrobe."

"It sounds like I should leave town." Randall tapped the papers in front of him. "I need to visit Roscombe. My steward is good, but some things I must deal with myself. I'd planned on going there after visiting Kirkland in Scotland, but as you know, I was sidetracked." His eyes glinted. "In the most interesting possible way."

Julia felt a pang that he was going away, but said cheerfully, "As long as you return before the ball. Mariah will never forgive an absence. I don't think I would, either. I won't be a demanding wife, but . . . I'll need you then."

"Of course I'll be back for the ball, Julia. It's the goal we've both worked for—making you safe and returning you to your rightful station." His tone matched hers in lightness. "After the ball, you won't need me any more."

"I think that a fortnight of frivolity will be enough. After that, I'll be yearning to settle in Roscombe." She wondered what kind of life they would build together, but found she was afraid to ask. Did he honestly think she wouldn't need him?

Or did he really mean that *he* wouldn't need *her?*

After dining with Mariah and Ashton, Julia retired early and fell asleep right away. She had a vague impression of the bed sagging and a warm embrace when Randall joined her, but she woke to find him gone, leaving only an indentation in the mattress.

When she got up, she discovered on the washstand a brief note saying that he was leaving early to meet Rob Carmichael. After that meeting he would head on to Roscombe. There was no trace of feeling in the brief words. Would he miss her? She would surely miss him.

She had no time to brood because Elsa, her new maid, shyly entered the room to begin her duties. The girl was quick and pleasant, and she had a good way with hair. Julia went down to breakfast feeling a little more like a London lady.

Mariah was alone in the breakfast parlor. She glanced up from her plate with a smile. "Oh, good, company. Adam is off doing something useful, while I'm eating everything in sight. Of course, I was sick when I woke up, so I now need to fill the empty spaces. How long will this phase last?"

"About three months. Then about three more months of bouncing energy, followed by the slowest three months in the history of the world." Julia studied the dishes being kept warm on the sideboard. "Any recommendations?"

"The sausage is very good," Mariah replied. "So is that kedgeree."

Julia lifted the silver cover and saw a mixture of rice and fish, topped with chopped hard-cooked eggs and pleasantly perfumed with exotic spices. Beside the warmer was a small dish of orange-colored chutney. "This looks good. Kedgeree is Indian, isn't it? My father would never allow anything so foreign into our house."

"Then he missed some good food," Mariah said. "We hired an assistant cook with experience in India so we can have curries along with the English fare. The Indian side of Adam's family loves to dine here. His mother threatens to hire away the cook."

Julia smiled as she helped herself to a spoonful of kedgeree, adding toast and a soft-cooked egg just in case. But the kedgeree was tasty, as was the mango chutney.

Mariah finished eating first. Glancing at the clock, she poured herself more tea and spread marmalade over a piece of toast. "We have about an hour before the modiste arrives. Are you ready for the ordeal?"

"I suppose so." Julia chuckled. "The mere

mention of the modiste sent Randall flying off to his estate early this morning."

Hearing something in Julia's voice, Mariah asked, "Did you two quarrel? You look a little tense."

"Not a quarrel." Julia toyed with her teaspoon, wondering how much to say. "But yesterday was difficult. I'm not sure if Randall was more upset about being superceded for the earldom, or finding out that I'm a considerable heiress."

"If he's upset, it's about your inheritance," Mariah said shrewdly. "He'd never planned on the earldom so he can shrug that off fairly quickly. Your becoming so wealthy is much more disturbing. Heaven knows that I found Adam's wealth alarming. I would be happy if he had less. Yet the ton is full of envious women who see me as a triumphant fortune hunter."

"But you didn't know that Adam was a duke when you met him," Julia pointed out. "Neither did he, for that matter."

"No one wants to let facts get in the way of a good story. The more ambitious young misses have been copying my dress and trying to bribe my maid to learn what kind of scent I wear." Mariah laughed. "One terrible old dowager studied me through her lorgnette before announcing, 'Beauty for wealth. Mankind's oldest bargain.' Then she swept grandly away. I'm not sure if it was a compliment or an insult, but she did Adam a disservice. He's rather beautiful himself, though it would pain him if I said so in public."

"The dowager's logic could be applied to me," Julia said ruefully, "with Randall having the beauty and me the wealth. But neither of us expected my inheritance." She crossed her knife and fork meticulously on her plate. "Randall promised to return in time for the ball."

"Are you worried that he won't?" Mariah said in surprise. "He just needs time to adjust to the new situation. The reasons he married you are as true as they ever were."

Julia shook her head. "He married me mostly to protect me from Crockett and Daventry. That protection isn't needed any more."

"He could have protected you without marriage. He's the noble sort, but he wouldn't take a wife he didn't want," Mariah said crisply. "Though your fortunes are unequal, he was raised as a gentleman and you as a gentlewoman. That's more important than who has the greater inheritance. You are closer in background than Adam and I were."

Since the Ashtons' marriage seemed to be flourishing, Julia hoped Mariah was right. "I came up with a plan to get rid of some of that disturbing money. I'd like to create shelters for women so they have somewhere to go when they are threatened or abused."

Mariah blinked. "What a splendid notion. May I be a sponsor?"

"Of course," Julia said, startled. "The Duchess of Ashton will lend luster to the enterprise. But where do we start?"

"Right here. Right now," Mariah said, eyes gleaming. "Tell me more!"

As they threw ideas back and forth, Julia's nerves began to calm. She wasn't sure how good she would be as a wife or a society lady, but helping women was something she knew how to do.

# Chapter 25

Julia was on her third cup of tea and regretfully thinking the modiste would arrive soon when the door to the breakfast room opened. A beautiful young woman swept into the room, the skirts of her scarlet riding habit foaming around her.

"Good morning, Mariah!" the newcomer said gaily. "It started to rain, so I thought I'd take refuge here and see if you have any of that lovely kedgeree available." She stopped in her tracks. "I'm so sorry! I didn't realize you had company, Mariah."

"You're always welcome, Kiri." Mariah rose and hugged the young woman. "Julia, you've met Adam's sister, Lady Kiri, haven't you?"

"Indeed I did. Last spring." Julia rose with a

smile. Like Ashton, Lady Kiri was half Hindu, and she had his dark hair and startling green eyes. Unlike her brother, she was outgoing rather than reserved, and her voice had a hint of musical accent. "London seems to agree with you, Lady Kiri."

"Mrs. Bancroft," the younger woman said with pleasure, "will you be staying in London longer this time? I should like to become better acquainted."

"She's Lady Julia Randall now," Mariah said. "She and Adam's friend Major Randall married in Scotland and are now in London for the autumn season."

Kiri's eyes rounded. "I do hope all of Adam's handsome friends don't marry before I've had a chance to look around! Well done, Lady Julia. Randall is a truly splendid specimen. But—*Lady Julia?*"

"My father is the Duke of Castleton, but he disowned me." Julia gestured toward the sideboard. "Don't let me keep you from the kedgeree. Mariah said earlier that the Indian branch of the family loved to eat here."

Lady Kiri laughed as she picked up a plate and helped herself. "Neither I nor the kedgeree are entirely Indian, but this is much better than porridge."

Mariah poured tea for her sister-in-law. "We shall have to leave shortly when the modiste arrives. I'm holding a ball for Julia and Randall in a fortnight, so there's no time to waste in ordering a suitable gown. You're invited, of course."

"Splendid!" Kiri seated herself and attacked the kedgeree with enthusiasm. "I have been longing for excitement. May I stay for the fitting with the modiste? I love looking at the fabrics and style books."

Mariah looked thoughtful. "Would you mind, Julia? Kiri has a marvelous eye for color. She also does custom perfumes, including the scent all the young fortune hunters wanted to copy."

"Would you like it if I blended a custom scent for you, Lady Julia?" Kiri asked. "As a wedding gift."

Kiri looked so eager that Julia said, "I should love that." Which meant she must allow the girl to come to the fitting. Not that Lady Kiri was precisely a girl; she must be in her early twenties. But her happy directness was youthful. When Julia was in her early twenties, she'd felt eons older.

The modiste, Madame Hélier, arrived just as Kiri was finishing her second breakfast, and the fitting began in Mariah's private parlor. Madame was accompanied by three assistants loaded with fabrics, trims, and fashion books. Two Ashton House footmen were pressed into carrying still more bolts of fabric upstairs.

Elsa appeared, looking intimidated by all the grand ladies. While she found a spot in a corner of the room, Grandmère swept into the parlor, commandeered the most comfortable chair, and began speaking to the modiste in rapid French.

Luckily, it was a large parlor.

Mariah produced a sturdy wooden stool for Julia to stand on so the seamstresses could work more easily. "Care to step onto the sacrificial altar, your ladyship?"

Julia laughed as she stepped onto the stool. "I feel rather like a lamb for the slaughter. I'm really only here to provide a cause for this gathering."

"Nonsense," Grandmère said firmly. "You are here to be made utterly dazzling. Girl"—she collected Elsa with a glance—"help your mistress remove her gown so we can start draping fabric. So fortunate that you aren't a young chit who must wear insipid white muslin, Julia."

"A deep, rich blue," Lady Kiri suggested. "With a touch of green in it." She crossed the room to the bolts of fabric and tapped one with a long forefinger. "This one."

"A fine color," Madame Hélier said approvingly. She gestured to one of the assistants, who obediently collected Kiri's choice and several other blue fabrics.

Julia held out her arms so Elsa could unfasten the gown and pull it over her head. Julia was not uninterested in clothing, but at the moment, most of her attention was engaged by the shelter project. Perhaps a woman and her children could be moved to another city if there was a danger that a brutal husband might pursue her? What kind of arrangements would be needed for that?

Grandmère said, "You have a fine little figure, *ma petite*, and you should show it off. Girl, tuck your mistress's shift down so it's like a ball gown."

Julia hardly noticed Elsa's gentle fingers turning down the edge of her shift. Then the maid gasped, shocking Julia back to the present. She glanced down, horrified to find that her maid had uncovered the scars.

Julia wanted to cover herself and flee. Instead she clenched her fists and stood stock still, grateful that her back was turned to most of the women. Only Elsa and Mariah could see the ugly ridged tissue.

Mariah's brown eyes showed an instant of shock, swiftly followed by understanding. She gave Elsa a sharp hold-your-tongue glance before saying easily, "I don't think Julia should wear low décolletage." She stepped forward to raise Julia's shift over the scars. "She has a perfectly good husband, so she needn't advertise her wares. I think a style of rich but modest elegance will suit her best." She grinned. "Not like me. I prefer to look like a refined trollop."

"Your grace!" Madame Hélier exclaimed, horrified. "Never, never would anyone call you a trollop!"

Kiri laughed. "A trollop, yes, but certainly the most refined sort! It is a style I aspire to!" Grandmère permitted herself an amused shake of the head.

Mariah's comments had drawn attention away from Julia, for which she was profoundly grateful. Elsa couldn't be her maid without knowing about the scars, but Julia couldn't bear for her humiliation to become public knowledge.

After Julia's breathing steadied, she asked, "If I am permitted an opinion, I like Mariah's suggestion. I'm much more comfortable with quiet elegance than with being a glittering belle of the ball." She inclined her head to Mariah. "Or a golden duchess."

All seven women studied her, weighing her words. Julia felt like a side of beef being priced for the market. Madame Hélier, unintimidated by so many duchesses and duke's daughters, gave a decisive nod. "*Très bien*. A modest décolletage, but perhaps cut lower than usual in back because you have such beautiful skin, Lady Julia. Like porcelain. To reveal a little of your back will be more subtle, but most effective. Betsy, drape the Chinese silk around Lady Julia's shoulders."

As an assistant moved forward to comply, Julia joined the discussion to ensure that she didn't end up tricked out like a circus pony. The ball gown was settled first with an exquisitely simple style suited to her lack of stature. Julia was swaddled in at least a dozen fabrics, but in the end they all agreed on the silk Lady Kiri had singled out.

The fashion team swept onward to walking dresses and cloaks and riding habits, and all the other accoutrements of a grand lady. At midday, Mariah rang for refreshments for all, from dowager duchess to assistants to lady's maids. The atmosphere of feminine frivolity was enough to drive any male mad, as was proved when Ashton stopped in, took one appalled look, and headed for safer precincts.

When all the decisions of fabric, style, and trim had been made, Julia descended from her perch. Lifting a bolt of fabric, she tossed a length over Mariah's shoulder. "I've noticed you eyeing this changeable mantua silk. The way the green shimmers gold is perfect for you." She glanced at the other women. "See how the gold brings out the gold flecks in her grace's eyes?"

Mariah stroked the silk. "Adam says I should spend more on myself."

"By all means, spend more of my brother's money." Lady Kiri smiled mischievously. "He will be very happy to see you in that silk. With emeralds."

"Onto the stool, Mariah," Julia ordered. "Now it's your turn."

Mariah complied, choosing a style that would

allow room for an expanding figure. By the time Madame Hélier and her minions had left, Grandmère and Lady Kiri had also chosen fabric and ordered gowns.

Julia poured herself a cup of tea. "Since I never had a proper season before I married, I didn't realize how much work it is to dress like a grand lady!"

"The polite world must recognize your rank," Grandmère proclaimed. "After that, you may dress as badly as you please and merely be considered eccentric."

"I wish to be unobtrusive, not eccentric, Grandmère." Julia exhaled. "I hope I needn't do this again!"

"That shouldn't be necessary now that you have laid the foundations for a proper wardrobe," Mariah said reassuringly. "You have chosen classic styles that will always look splendid."

Grandmère rose and gave Julia a hug. "Madame Hélier has been instructed to send the bill for today's session to me," she said quietly. "My gift to my favorite granddaughter."

"Grandmère, it is too much!" Julia gasped.

"I have many years to make up for." A quaver sounded in the older woman's voice. "I haven't enjoyed a day so much since . . . since your mother died, *ma petite*. Though I am proud of how you kept yourself all these years, I am so very glad that you've come home."

Julia blinked back tears. "So am I, Grandmère. So am I."

Randall had half-forgotten how beautiful Roscombe was. He halted his horse on a hill that offered sweeping views of the Cotswold hills, and of the mellow stone manor where he had been born. Roscombe was a gentleman's residence, not a grand castle. It had been home to generations of his mother's family.

After his parents were gone and Daventry became his guardian, Randall had spent little time at Roscombe. How long since the last visit? Good God, more than two years, since before being wounded.

He set his horse down the hill. Most of his recuperation had taken place in London. From there he traveled to Scotland in search of Ashton, and afterward he'd shipped out to the Peninsula again.

Yet even though he'd spent little time at Roscombe in recent years, it was still home as nowhere else could ever be. He rode through the old iron gates which were never closed, then up the long drive that led to the house and its outbuildings.

Small ornamental deer scampered away, not looking unduly worried by his presence. All was orderly and well kept. To Daventry's credit, he'd hired a good man to look after the estate.

Caldwell was so competent that Randall had never considered replacing him.

In the morning he would call on Caldwell to discuss tenants' cottages and drainage and the cost of new farm equipment. He'd probably accept all of Caldwell's recommendations, since the man had kept Roscombe profitable and the land in good heart for over twenty years.

There had been no real need to make this trip, but Randall wanted to get away from London for a few days. Gordon had looked plaintive at being abandoned again, but he'd recover soon enough with his Elsa under the same roof.

Randall circled the house to the stables and dismounted, leading his weary mount inside. The groom, Willett, was in the tack room, repairing a piece of harness. After glancing up, he rose and ambled out to greet his master as if Randall had been here just last week. "Good day to you, Major. Will you be stayin' long this time?"

"Not long, but soon I'll be living here." Randall unsaddled his horse and began grooming it, enjoying the horseman's ritual. His leg ached from the long ride, but was in no danger of collapse. Soon he would be taking his recovery for granted. "I've married, so I wanted to make sure Roscombe is in fit condition for my new bride."

Willett's expression sharpened. "Will you be needing more inside servants? My youngest daughter is almost ready to go into service."

"My wife will do the hiring, but I'll tell her your girl"—Randall searched his memory—"would that be Nancy?—might be interested."

"Aye, 'tis my Nancy. You've a good memory, Major." The groom turned back to the tack room, adding, "Welcome home, sir. 'Tis time the house was lived in."

Time and past time. After Randall settled his horse, he headed into the house, surprising his cook-housekeeper in the kitchen. She was baking a shepherd's pie for herself and her husband, and he assured her that a slice of that would do nicely for him.

Then he wandered through the familiar rooms, trying to see the house as Julia would. The place had been well maintained. There were no leaky ceilings, no dry rot nor woodworm.

But neither had any decorating been done since his parents died. On Randall's rare visits, he'd liked the familiarity of knowing that his childhood home was unchanged. As a result, paint was faded, furniture needed reupholstering, and some of the carpets were worn. There was much to keep a new mistress busy.

Randall entered the drawing room and gazed out at the rolling vale, his hands clasped behind his back. What would his life have been like if his parents hadn't died? He would have grown up here, perhaps had younger brothers or sisters. He wouldn't have become such a difficult boy that he'd ended up at the Westerfield Academy.

Yet the friendships he'd made there had enriched his life beyond measure. Would he have become as close to his classmates if he'd been sent to one of the usual schools of his class? Probably not. Lady Agnes Westerfield's damaged students had needed each other more than most schoolboys.

Would he have gone into the army? Not likely. If he had grown up here, he wouldn't have had that angry edge of violence that made battle so appealing. Neither would he have felt such an intense desire to get away from England.

He would have gone to university and lived like most young men of his class. He would have learned the land from his father here at Roscombe, and spent some time sowing a few wild oats in London. He would be married by now, probably a father. But the mother of his children wouldn't have been Julia.

There was no point in thinking about the life he might have had. The life he did have included scars, friends as close as brothers, and Julia.

He tried to visualize her living here. Would she read in the small library? Make preserves in the still room? There would be no children giggling in the nursery, a thought that hurt more than he would have believed possible a month before.

Julia had made her small cottage a warm and welcoming place. She could do the same here.

Yet he had trouble imagining her in these rooms. Was that failure of imagination, or was he being foolish to think they would ever live here together?

In some ways, his marriage was going well. Better than expected. But he couldn't ignore the fact that Lady Julia Raines was a great heiress. Wealth gave her freedom and choices that few women could dream of. She could buy an estate of her own if she wished. Or her own house in London. Or she could travel.

Starkly he recognized that he had wanted her to need him for financial support and protection, because God knew he needed her. He didn't really want her to have choices if that meant she didn't choose him.

He felt pressure against his leg and looked down to see a large, confident cat leaning against his ankle. The beast was mostly dark tabby with white chest and feet, and it was busily shedding white hair on the master of Roscombe.

He smiled wryly and scooped up the cat. It purred fiercely under his stroking fingers. His mother had always had cats, and this one must be a descendant. Even if Julia never came, he wouldn't be alone.

# Chapter 26

Preparing for her introduction to London society kept Julia busy during the next several days, though nights were rather lonely. She liked sharing a bed with her husband, even during warm weather. When winter arrived, he'd be indispensable.

Four days after Randall left, she received a letter from him, delivered by Elsa on the morning tea tray. He said briefly that affairs at Roscombe were being sorted out and he looked forward to bringing her there soon.

She smiled ruefully after reading it. The man was a soldier and protector of a high order. She shouldn't expect romantic words from him as well. At least this note was a little more personal than the one he wrote the morning he left.

Julia and Mariah had a shopping trip planned for the day. Officially the goal was for Julia to buy some small items she needed, but mostly the trip was for fun. Anthony had set up an account at his bank so Julia now had pin money. She would have access to her full inheritance in a month or two.

Her brother reported that their father was enraged, but Castleton had no legal right to block his daughter's inheritance. Plus, the family lawyers prudently recognized that the future lay with Lord Stoneleigh, so they didn't throw spurious roadblocks in the way.

After dressing, she moved into her private parlor. Formerly a bedroom with a connecting door to Randall's sitting room, the space was now dedicated to Julia's use. After the bed was removed, Mariah and Julia had raided the attic for furnishings. Her new parlor was a charming room done in shades of cream and rose, and it was slightly larger than Julia's main living space at the cottage in Hartley.

She sat down at her delicate French writing desk and glanced over her shopping list. Someday she would take money in her purse for granted, but now it was a delicious luxury. If she'd lived her whole life within the aristocratic circles in which she'd been born, she would never have fully realized how lucky she was.

Julia was about to head downstairs for breakfast when sunlight touched her wedding ring, illuminating the swirling Celtic patterns molded into the gold. A thought struck her, so she rang for Gordon.

The valet appeared almost immediately. "Do you have a task for me, my lady?" he asked hopefully. "I've had little to do."

She laughed. "Surely educating Elsa about the household is keeping you busy."

He smiled. "Yes, but I feel I'm not fulfilling my duty to the major."

"When he returns, he'll need you to make him handsome for London society."

Gordon shook his head. "He needs no help to be handsome. I merely make sure his clothes look good."

Very true. Randall was amazingly handsome no matter what he wore. Or didn't wear. Reminding herself to stick to business, Julia said, "I want to buy a ring for my husband. Can you supply me with a ring that the jeweler can use for sizing?"

"I shall get one straight away." Gordon bowed and withdrew, returning a few minutes later with a gold signet ring.

Julia tucked the ring in her reticule. Randall had done so much for her. She wanted to give him a token of her appreciation in return.

As an Ashton footman took possession of a wrapped bundle of silk stockings, Julia observed, "I'd forgotten how convenient it is to have someone carry everything."

"And deliver it to our carriage, which is well on its way to being full, I suspect. Not that I haven't contributed my share to filling it!" Mariah covered a yawn with one hand. "I'm tiring easily these days. Have we reached the end of your shopping list?"

"One last stop. I want to visit a jeweler or goldsmith to order a ring for Randall. One with the same pattern as my wedding ring." Julia smiled shyly. "I hope he won't think it's too dreadfully sentimental of me."

"What a fine idea. I think Adam would like it if I gave him a matching ring," Mariah said thoughtfully. "I rather fancy marking him as *mine*."

"It seems only just, since women wear rings to mark that they've been claimed," Julia agreed. "Where would be a good place to have the rings done?"

"There's a goldsmith just around the corner." Mariah led the way out into Bond Street. "Mr. Rose made my wedding ring, and he knows what size Adam wears." She pulled off her glove and showed the ring to Julia. "Though this looks like a plain gold band, an Indian pattern that incorporates our initials is engraved inside. I'll show you when we get to the shop."

"Perhaps we can start a fashion for matching wedding rings." Julia gave her friend a teasing smile. "After all, you are the very, very fashionable Golden Duchess."

Mariah laughed. "That won't last more than a season or two, but this"—she held up her bare left hand, the golden band as bright as her shining hair—"is forever."

Naturally Mr. Rose was delighted to welcome two highborn ladies to his shop. Ordering the ring for Adam was simple since Mr. Rose had made Mariah's, but a ring for Randall was more complicated. The goldsmith examined the gold band carefully. "In order to copy the pattern accurately, I'll need to keep the ring for a day or two."

"No!" Julia's fingers curled around the ring. She smiled apologetically. "I'm sorry, but I haven't had this very long."

Mr. Rose's dark eyes twinkled. "I understand, my lady. My wife would feel exactly the same. If you can part with it for a half an hour, I'll make a wax impression."

Julia glanced at Mariah, who was looking tired. Interpreting that, Mr. Rose said, "I have a private parlor where you can wait and refresh yourselves."

"Thank you, that would be lovely." Julia and Mariah were escorted to a pleasant salon on the floor above. They could watch the ebb and flow of fashionable traffic in the street below in comfort.

After a maid brought in a tray of tea and cakes, Julia asked her friend, "Have you become accustomed to having such service everywhere? After years of being a widow of modest means, I'm finding it strange to be treated with such deference."

"I'm not used to it yet," Mariah admitted. She patted her still slim waist. "It's strange to think how this child and any others Adam and I may have will be raised in such luxury. We'll have to work hard to ensure that the next generation has a proper sense of perspective. Maybe it will be a little easier for you and Randall since your children won't be born with titles."

"There won't be any children for us," Julia said quietly. She crumbled an oatcake into small pieces. She had wanted to tell Mariah, but speaking the words was still painful. "I . . . can't have them."

Mariah caught her breath. "I'm so sorry." After the space of half a dozen heartbeats, she said, "I assume Randall knows."

Julia nodded. "It's one of several reasons I gave him to explain why he shouldn't marry me. He said that didn't matter."

"And you worry that he's not a romantic." Mariah turned thoughtful. "Though not quite the same as having your own flesh and blood, if you want to raise a child, there are always babies in need of homes. You were wonderful with all the children you met through your work, and you positively doted on Jenny Watson's daughter Molly."

Julia frowned. "I hadn't really thought of that. I'm not sure how Randall would feel about raising a child not his own. But it's worth considering."

"Personally, I think it would be splendid to acquire a baby without morning sickness," Mariah said firmly. "The usual method leaves a lot to be desired!"

Julia laughed. "I promise that you will be amazingly pleased with yourself when you finally hold your baby in your arms."

"I expect you're right." Mariah looked down at her teacup. "When my time comes, will you be with me, Julia? Please?"

"If you want me, of course I'll be there," Julia said. "I'm honored."

"Thank you." Mariah smiled ruefully. "I think I'm only averagely nervous, but that's nervous enough."

Before Julia could offer more reassurance, Mr. Rose entered the room. "Lady Julia, here is your wedding band. The gentlemen's rings will be ready in a week's time."

They thanked him and stepped into the street, where the Ashton footman, Timms, waited. He bowed. "I shall go around the corner and summon the carriage, your grace."

"We'll head in that direction and meet you there." Mariah looked tired, and Julia guessed that the sooner her friend was home and resting, the better. Side by side, they walked along the street after the footman.

"Oh, look at that lovely bonnet!" Reviving, Mariah turned to her left to look into the bay window of a very fashionable milliner. "Do you think it would suit Kiri? She's been so helpful with the ball that I'd like to give her a token of my appreciation."

Julia joined her, visualizing the bright confection of ribbons and flowers on Lady Kiri's dark hair. "The style would suit her, but those aren't quite the right colors, I think. There should be green ribbons to bring out the color of her amazing eyes."

Mariah considered, then nodded. "You're right. I'll bring Kiri here after the ball, and if she likes the style, we can choose the best colors for her."

As they moved back out onto the sidewalk, Timms's voice rose in a terrified shout from ahead of them. "My ladies, look out! Behind you!"

Other voices were shouting. Julia spun and looked back the way they'd come. Her heart jumped into her throat when she saw that a runaway carriage had exploded out of control and swerved onto the sidewalk. Only yards away, the wild-eyed horses were crashing toward them at lethal speed.

Mariah was only half-turned and hadn't yet seen the danger. For Julia, time seemed to slow as it always did when disaster was imminent with her patients.

The milliner's shop. Two bay windows projecting out over the sidewalk with the door indented between.

Knowing it was their only hope, Julia hurled herself to her right, wrapping an arm around Mariah to pull her along to safety. Julia's bonnet went flying and they tumbled hard against the shop door an instant before the carriage and pair hammered by.

The carriage sideswiped the bay windows and glass shattered on both sides as Julia and Mariah fell to the ground. The horses were so close Julia could feel the heat of their bodies. The ironclad carriage wheels were closer yet.

Then the carriage was past. Julia lay stunned for a moment as glass shards tinkled to the sidewalk within inches. Realizing she was sprawled on top of her friend, she cautiously pushed herself to a sitting position. "Mariah, are you all right?"

"Bruised but otherwise well, I think," her friend said shakily as she levered herself up against the shop door. "Thank heaven you were so quick! I once saw a peddler's cart crushed by a runaway carriage. One forgets how dangerous streets can be."

"I've lived in the quiet countryside too long, I think," Julia said ruefully. "Look at my poor bonnet. Today is the first time I wore it, and now it's crushed and ruined."

Mariah caught her breath, her face ashen. "There are wheel marks on your skirt! If you'd been any closer to the street . . ." She shuddered.

Julia stared at the long dark streaks on the dove gray fabric. She'd felt a powerful yank on her skirts as the carriage roared by. The wheels had passed within inches of her legs. She would have been crushed as thoroughly as her pretty bonnet.

The footman, Timms, reached them, his face like chalk. "Your grace, my lady, have you been injured?" He offered his hand. "Look out for the broken glass, my lady."

Julia winced as the young man helped her up, knowing she'd have major bruises. "I'm fine, thanks to your warning."

She glanced along the street as Timms helped Mariah to her feet. The carriage had vanished around the corner. "The carriage didn't crash so the driver must have got his horses under control. Then he kept going so he wouldn't have to face the consequences of his bad driving."

"It will cost the milliner a pretty penny to repair those windows," Mariah agreed. "But thank heaven no one was injured."

The footman collected Julia's ruined bonnet and guided both women through the crowd that had gathered. Julia was grateful for his strong hand on her arm since her knees were weak.

Even more upsetting than the accident was the fear that it hadn't been an accident.

With the efficiency characteristic of Ashton House, by the time Julia and Mariah entered the building, the duke had been informed of the accident. He rushed from his study and met them just inside the door. He caught Mariah up so energetically that her feet were lifted from the floor. "Mariah, you're all right?"

"Indeed I am, my love," she said with a laugh, though she didn't move from his embrace even after her feet were on the ground again. "Thanks to Julia. She got us both out of the way in the nick of time."

"Thank God!" Ashton wrapped an arm around Julia and hugged her close. Julia clung to him, glad he was strong enough to support two distressed women.

"I hate to think what Randall would do to me if you were damaged while under my roof, Julia," he said with a crooked smile. "Come into my study and have a brandy." An arm around each of them, Ashton led the way to his study.

Julia sank into a deep leather-covered sofa while the duke poured three brandies. After handing them out, he sat on the sofa opposite with his arm around his wife.

Julia swallowed a mouthful of brandy. "Your footman, Timms, called a warning. If he hadn't, we mightn't have been able to get out of the way of the carriage."

"I'll see that he's rewarded," Ashton said, his perceptive gaze on Julia's face. "Something more is troubling you?"

Julia sighed. "I wonder if it was an accident, or a deliberate attempt to run us down. To run *me* down."

"I wondered, too," Mariah said quietly. She stared at her brandy, not drinking. "Runaway horses would be more likely to bolt down the center of the street rather than come so close to buildings."

The duke's expression turned grim. "Do you think Daventry tried to kill you?"

Julia thought before shaking her head. "He said he would call off his dogs, and I think he meant it. But maybe his dogs don't take orders well."

Ashton frowned, and she remembered how very dangerous he could be. "I shall have the incident investigated," he said. "There must have been a number of witnesses. Until we know exactly what happened, I suggest you ask merchants to call on you here."

"An excellent idea." Mariah's hand moved unconsciously to her abdomen. "There is too much at risk to be careless."

Julia agreed. She would be very, very glad when Randall finished his business and returned.

Randall picked up his morning mail with anticipation. Julia had written him a brief note every day, always an amusing description of the trials and tribulations of becoming a grand lady in a handful of days.

Today's letter described how the modiste had descended with her minions for final ball gown fittings. Julia finished with:

*Tomorrow, as a reward to ourselves, Mariah and I are going on a deeply frivolous shopping excursion. Life in London definitely undermines one's moral character.*

He grinned, hearing her voice sparkling through the words, then set the letter aside and turned to the rest of his correspondence. There were a couple of pieces of routine business, but more interesting, a letter from Rob Carmichael.

He broke the seal and read the Bow Street Runner's terse words.

*Haven't time to write in detail, but I think I found your lost boy near Upton. I wouldn't leave a dog in his situation. I'll get him out of there if you're too busy. Think about how much you're willing to do for a young cousin you've never met. Rob.*

Randall frowned at the note. The flat truth was that he wanted nothing to do with any child of Branford's, but the boy was blood kin. If Rob thought the situation was so bad he was willing to rescue the boy himself, it must be very bad indeed.

Since Rob was difficult to locate at long distance, it was time to return to London.

# Chapter 27

Guessing that Randall would return to London the day before the ball, Julia assumed that she must wait three more days until he returned. With a sigh, she settled into the deep hip bath, which was large enough for her to immerse herself entirely. The gently steaming water was redolent with floral scents, courtesy of the shockingly expensive bath oil she'd bought the day before on Bond Street.

Though Ashton was planning to have several luxurious bathing rooms installed in the mansion, for now Julia was content with the hip bath. The hot water eased the bruising on her right hip and elbow. So did the goblet of port reposing on a low table within easy reach. She lifted the glass and took a sip, feeling deliciously decadent.

The evening was well advanced and she'd dismissed Elsa for the night. The girl was working out well. Her good nature made her pleasant to have around, and it was useful to have a maid to care for Julia's rapidly growing wardrobe.

Still, years of being on her own had given Julia a taste for privacy. Since her husband was away, she would indulge herself with peace, water, and wine. She sighed contentedly and savored another swallow of the port's heady sweetness.

The port was gone and she was half-dozing in

the cooling water when the door to the suite opened. She came instantly awake. Neither Gordon nor Elsa would come at this hour unless summoned, and Mariah or Ashton would knock if they came calling.

A few seconds passed, and the door to the bedroom opened. A soft, deep voice said, "Julia?"

*Randall!* She scrambled from the hip bath, wrapped herself in a large, luxurious bath towel, and darted around the screen. There was only a single lamp lit, but it was enough to show that her husband had shed his boots, probably so he wouldn't wake her if she was sleeping. In the dim light, his golden hair and lean, broad-shouldered figure reminded her again of a glorious Nordic god.

"I'm so glad you're back!" Julia went straight into his arms, half-knocking him over in her enthusiasm.

His weary expression vanished. Laughing, he fell back a step to catch his balance, but his arms went around her with satisfying swiftness. "I've been gone less than a week, milady. Not that I mind such a welcome." He buried his face in her damp hair, which she'd pinned to the top of her head. "Mmm . . . you smell like a bouquet in springtime."

He smelled like . . . himself. Safe and familiar and masculine. All her senses were wide open, absorbing his presence thirstily. She tilted her head back and kissed him with unreserved pleasure. His instant of surprise was immediately followed by fierce response. He kissed her back with matching intensity, tugging the pins from her hair so that it tumbled sensuously over her bare shoulders.

Heat blazed through her, pooling in her loins and breasts. She had felt stirrings of desire for him before, but this was a full-fledged inferno. The calm, reserved woman she'd become over her years in exile was gone, replaced by an eager, shameless wench.

His hand slid seductively down her bare back under the towel. "You aren't wearing very much," he said a little breathlessly as he squeezed her bottom.

"And you're wearing too much." She put her hands on his lapels and pushed his coat off his shoulders. Her loosely tucked towel sagged open halfway to her waist.

He turned rigid as he stared. "If you have any doubts about where this is heading, milady, the time to retreat is now."

But she didn't want to retreat. "I have no doubts, Alex," she said softly. "Tonight I want us to come together like lovers who have never known shadows."

He took a deep breath. "I would like that more than anything on earth."

She smiled and dropped the towel so that it

crumpled to the floor around her bare feet. She didn't feel like a flawless, unscarred young girl. She felt feminine and experienced and powerful.

Her scars were unimportant, a remnant of the past. *Now* was the hot beat of desire that drew them together like opposite poles of a magnet. "About those clothes . . ."

She tugged his coat off the rest of the way and let it drop while he untied his cravat and tossed it away. Swiftly she undid the buttons at his throat and stretched up to kiss the smooth, faintly salty skin. His pulse hammered under her lips and he made a choked sound of pleasure.

Richly pleased with herself, she attacked his other garments. Since he was doing the same, their hands tangled and fingers wandered in a glorious welter of touch and laughter. As a way of undressing, their mutual efforts lacked efficiency, but it was delicious fun, and the absence of fear was the greatest aphrodisiac she'd ever known.

Unclothed, he had a hard male beauty that put Greek sculptors to shame. She ran her hands over his shoulders and torso, feeling the changing textures of skin and scars and pale hair. "I've never seen all of you at once before," she breathed. "What was I waiting for?"

"For the right time." He scooped her up and deposited her in the middle of the bed. "Having had a long ride today, I'm hungry. And you, milady, are a banquet as well as a bouquet."

Before she'd finished bouncing on the mattress, he was stretched out beside her, the length of his body pressed against her from ribs to calf. He bent into a deep, openmouthed kiss. Her toes and fingers curled at the wanton carnality of their mating tongues and lips.

The kiss went on and on until they were both breathless. He lifted his head. "You taste most deliciously of Ballard tawny port."

Julia laughed giddily. "You can identify the maker?"

"Ashton only stocks Ballard port since it's made by a friend," Randall said with a grin. "And very good port it is, too. But you taste sweeter and more intoxicating than the finest spirits." He pressed his lips to her throat as his hand came to rest on her breast.

As his thumb stroked her nipple, she arched against his palm. He began nibbling his way down her body in a slow blaze of kisses.

She gasped when his mouth fastened on her left breast and he sucked hard on her nipple. Her hips rocked against him. After kissing her other breast with matching thoroughness, his mouth moved lower, lower, over her belly.

Surely he wasn't going to . . . she gave a strangled shriek and almost leaped out of her skin when his skilled lips and tongue reached her most private parts. *"Alex!"*

She'd learned how to pleasure a man with her

mouth, but never once considered how it would feel to receive rather than give. Her fingers knotted in his hair as her body coiled tighter, tighter, tighter, her need so frantic it was almost pain.

Release ripped through her with shattering power. She cried out, every muscle in her body rigid. As the tide of sensation ebbed, Randall rested his head on her thigh, his breathing soft against her groin.

"Alexander the Great indeed," she said weakly as she released her grip on his hair and stroked the thick gold waves back from his forehead. "No wonder you liked it so much when I did that to you."

" 'Like' is far too pale a word for such an experience." He tilted his head so their gazes met. "I've wanted to devour you since the first time I saw you."

She could feel a hot, delighted blush coloring her face. "I'm glad I didn't know. You were quite fearsome enough as a disapproving soldier." She traced his ear with her fingertip. "But surely we're only half done?"

"If you've had time to recover your breath . . ." He raised himself over her, using one finger to delicately stroke the moist, exquisitely sensitized folds of flesh between her legs. Small shocks of pleasure tingled through her as he found the center of sensation. "Are you ready to provide me with a second course, milady?"

"And to think I read your letters and thought you had no poetry in your soul!" she said with a laugh.

"Not poetry, perhaps. But a deep and abiding appetite that only you can appease." He settled between her legs carefully, stroking with unerring skill until she was writhing against his fingers. "Now?" he asked.

"Now!" She pulled him down hard against her, raising her hips to receive him. Amazing how she yearned for him to fill her after so many years of fearing male invasion. But when he buried himself inside her, it wasn't invasion. It was completion.

She rocked against him, startled that desire was rising to match what she'd felt before. But this time the tide carried them both, the mad rhythms of their bodies matching until he shuddered and poured himself into her with a deep groan. She echoed his release, uncertain which of them had culminated first.

His harsh breathing slowed and he rolled onto his side, drawing her tight against him. She relaxed with her face against his shoulder and her arm across his waist. Once she had been grateful for her celibate life. Never would she have believed she might experience such a stunning explosion of desire and release. But the evidence of their bare, intertwined bodies proved that this was no dream.

He curled his hand around her head, his fingers sliding into her tangled hair. "I wonder if I sensed that you were capable of such generous passion?" he murmured. "Or am I merely the luckiest man on earth?"

"I'm the lucky one." Julia gave a choke of laughter. "Lucky, and selfish. You probably really are hungry if you rode all day. And I had to go and distract you."

"Actually, I stopped in the kitchen for a bite before coming up." Gently he massaged her head. "But even if I hadn't, you are a more satisfactory meal than any other I could have found."

"That's good, because I haven't the strength to go down two flights of stairs to raid the pantry. I barely have the energy to choose a scar for you to identify even though there are so many to choose from." She traced a line over his ribs with her forefinger. "This, if I recall correctly, was a bayonet slash you received on the retreat to Corunna."

He nodded. "Half the military campaigns of the last fifteen years are engraved on my hide. I've been lucky that in all that time, there has only been the one serious injury."

She shivered. "I'm trying not to think of all the times you might have been killed, Alex. I would never have met you."

"That means you wouldn't miss me, either," he pointed out, a smile in his voice.

"I refuse to think philosophically tonight." She frowned as her fingers moved down to his groin. She'd never seen him entirely naked before, so she was discovering new scars. "These faint lines are odd. There look to be a dozen or more and they're roughly parallel." Her fingertips skimmed lightly over the ridged flesh on his groin. "What on earth could create such a wound? A few inches more to the left and we would not have had such a delightful evening."

"Not a weapon." He sighed. "Branford."

She snapped to full attention, pushing herself up with one hand so she could study the scars more closely. "Good God, he cut you deliberately?"

"It was when I first arrived at Turville." Randall's voice was flat. "He would declare a hunt and start to chase me. When he caught me, which he always did because he was older and taller and faster, he would pin me to the ground. Then he dragged down my breeches and sliced me with his stiletto. Each time this happened, he cut a little closer. He said that when he reached my cock, he'd cut it off."

Julia gasped in horror, her hand over her mouth. "Why did no one stop him?"

"He was the young master. No one dared cross him."

"So you learned to fight, and how to behave so badly that you'd be sent away." She pressed her lips to the scars, aching at the picture of a small boy being tormented and having no one to turn to. No wonder Randall had become a protector.

As she kissed the scars, she felt him stir a little in response. He said wryly, "Leave it to Branford to ruin a perfect moment even now. We need to talk, milady, and that means you'd better put some clothing on, or I will be useless for rational speech."

"Then you must cover yourself as well, Major," she said tartly. "Do you think women immune to such distractions?"

"I'm glad you're not," he said warmly, his hand stroking down her side. She flinched at the pressure on her bruises.

Frowning, he leaned over her for a closer look. "Good God, what happened to your hip? I can't believe I didn't see these bruises earlier!"

"The light was low and we were both otherwise occupied." Julia sat up, more aware of the injury now. "A runaway carriage almost struck Mariah and me when we were shopping yesterday. I fell getting out of the way." She took a deep breath, wishing she didn't have to break the mood. "It was probably an accident, but . . . we're not sure. Ashton is having the incident investigated."

Randall exhaled roughly. "One can't shut out the world for even one night, apparently. Is there any port left? We have even more to discuss than I realized."

# Chapter 28

Since a hip bath full of water was available, Randall had a quick wash before he poured two glasses of port, donned nightclothes, and rejoined Julia in the bed. Her dark hair was in a neat braid falling over one shoulder and a modest muslin nightgown covered her thoroughly, but she was still distractingly attractive.

In fact, knowing what lay beneath the muslin made her even more irresistible. Perhaps the reverse was also true, since she watched him with unabashed enjoyment even though he was now as thoroughly covered as she was.

He handed her the wine, then slid under the covers next to her. Leaning back against the piled pillows, he draped an arm around her. "Drinking wine in bed with a beautiful woman is a soldier's dream, especially when slogging through the mud of a military campaign."

She smiled. "Is wine the first thought on a soldier's mind?"

"The second." He kissed her lingeringly, ending it with great reluctance. Now that the barriers to intimacy had been annihilated, he wanted to make love to Julia until he was too weak to even crawl out of the bed.

Reminding himself that there would be other

nights, he asked, "Has Ash found any witnesses to the carriage incident?"

"Yes, but so far, nothing that proves whether or not it was deliberate." She sipped at her port, her brows furrowed. "If it was an attempt to kill me, I don't see how it could have been planned. Even Mariah and I didn't know we'd be at that place at that time."

"A man who was following you might have seen an unexpected opportunity to attack, and acted on impulse," Randall said slowly.

"Perhaps that's it," she agreed. "Usually those streets are too crowded for a carriage to build up much speed, but the incident took place during one of the lulls in traffic that sometimes happen. A stalker might have decided to seize the chance to run me down." Her fingers tightened on her goblet. "He might have killed Mariah, too."

Mariah, and the child she was carrying. If the two women had been hurt, Randall and Ashton would have been fighting each other for the chance to administer justice to the culprit. "You knew Crockett. Might he ignore Daventry's order to leave you alone if he still wanted vengeance?"

"It's possible. Crockett's loyalty was to Branford. They had a strange attachment that I never understood." Her expression was troubled.

Randall tightened his arm around her shoulders. "While Ash is investigating the accident, perhaps I'll start at the other end by tracing Crockett's movements. He seems the most likely to want to do you harm."

Julia sighed. "I'd like to think that the carriage really was an accidental runaway and Crockett was nowhere near London. I don't want to have to be afraid for my life."

"I shouldn't have left you here alone."

"Since I'm firmly planted in the middle of Ashton House, I was hardly alone," she pointed out. "No harm was done except to a very nice bonnet, and I ordered another like it as a replacement. But what about you? You also had something to discuss, I think?"

Randall swirled his goblet, watching the lamplight reflect through the red-gold liquid. "At Roscombe, I received a letter from Rob Carmichael. He believes he's found Branford's son near Upton. He also recommended that the boy be removed from his present situation immediately."

Julia straightened so abruptly that she almost spilled her port. She didn't even notice when Randall rescued the goblet. "What else did he say? What kind of bad situation is the child in?"

"You know as much as I do," Randall replied. "Rob isn't much of a correspondent at the best of times, and I gather that he was in a hurry when he dashed off this note. I'll have to track him down, which could take several days. I was lucky to find him so quickly before going to Roscombe."

"We must go to Upton and get the child," Julia said vehemently.

"Not before Mariah's ball—she'd never forgive us." Randall frowned. "Julia, why do you care so much about the bastard child of a husband you hated? There are many children in dire straits and if you establish your shelters, you will help a good many of them. Why this child?"

"I . . . I'm not sure. But surely the boy needs care." She bit her lip. "He's close to the age my child would have been."

And Julia would never have another child. Randall could dimly understand her sense of connection to this particular lost boy. But he was Branford's child. "Julia," Randall said. "What if the boy is mad like his father?"

"I hope he isn't." Julia looked at him with pleading eyes. "But even if he's troubled . . . Alex, you've said yourself that if Branford had been raised better, he might not have been so destructive."

"Perhaps not. But perhaps he would have been vicious no matter how he was raised." Randall remembered the horror of lying pinned down while his large cousin gleefully wielded the glittering stiletto. His mouth tightened. "If this boy is like Branford, I don't think I could bear living under the same roof. Could you?"

Her eyes squeezed shut. "I don't know," she whispered. "But even if he's difficult, surely we could find a better place for him than where he is. What about the Westerfield Academy? All of you speak of how Lady Agnes performs miracles."

"Only if the basic human material is sound under the bad behavior," Randall said. "A fair number of boys arrive at the academy on the verge of explosion, but they get over that when they're treated well. Lady Agnes won't keep a student who takes pleasure in hurting others."

"I suppose not. But he's your uncle's only grandson. Surely Daventry would want to take charge of the boy?"

"Perhaps, perhaps not. Why should he care about an unknown bastard when his wife is about to give him the son he's wanted for so long? Even if he is willing to do his duty by the boy, Daventry might turn the child into as great a monster as Branford," Randall said bluntly. "If the boy is violent, the best solution might be to hand him over to a press gang. On a Navy ship, he'd have to learn discipline or die."

Julia shuddered.

More gently, Randall said, "Not everyone can be saved, Julia. I'm willing to look for him. As you say, he's my cousin. But if he's a monster like his father, I won't let him endanger others."

"I know you're right," she said, her voice

almost inaudible. "But there's a good chance that the boy is normal. We must find out. Can we go the day after the ball?"

"That depends on when I locate Rob Carmichael." Randall drew her against him. She relaxed on his chest with a sigh. "For the next two days, don't think about this boy. Concentrate on the ball, your friends, and your new life."

"That's good advice." She covered a yawn. "For now, I'm ready to sleep."

So was he. He'd sleep, and dream of Julia.


Randall awoke with Julia burrowed against him, her hand resting in a very personal place. His body was responding, too. He shifted a little, rubbing against her hand, and she came awake.

Her eyes fluttered open. After the briefest moment of surprise, her hand slowly squeezed around him. He caught his breath as he became rock hard. "I hope you weren't planning to get out of bed immediately," he said in a choked voice.

"Definitely not." Her smile was teasing, her hand more so. "I have a dozen years to make up for, Alexander."

"I shall do what I can to help you get caught up. But this morning you must do the work." He caught her around the waist and pulled her over on top of him.

His brave, dignified lady wife giggled. Then

she bent into a kiss, her soft body molding to him. They made slow, satisfying love until the end, which wasn't slow at all.

Passion temporarily exhausted, they stayed joined together, her hair spilling down his throat. "I didn't know what I was missing," she breathed. "I didn't know."

Randall had known passion, but never had it been so infused with tenderness. He gently kneaded her back from smooth shoulders to slim waist to ripe derriere. Fairly early on, their night-clothes had been tossed aside so that they lay skin to skin. "I knew I wanted you from the first moment I met you, milady." He laughed. "I didn't understand why then. Now I do."

They lay contentedly for a few more minutes before Julia said regretfully, "We really must get up. You have to look for Mr. Carmichael and I have to help Mariah with a few thousand details for the ball." She slid off Randall and sat up, a delicious naked nymph. "Also, Lady Kiri is coming by this morning, partly for the kedgeree and partly to give me a perfume she has blended especially for me. Mariah says she's very good, too."

"I doubt she can make you smell any better than you do now." He rolled onto all fours and began stalking Julia across the mattress.

She laughed and descended from the bed. "You are seeking to undermine my plans for the day, Major."

"Indeed I am." But he had much to do himself. "I shall be out until dinner."

"Anthony wants you to sign a quitclaim waiving your husbandly rights to my fortune." Julia looked a little uncomfortable. "You did say you would."

"Of course." He didn't mind signing away his legal right to her money. He just wished that she didn't have it.

Lady Kiri arrived as Julia and Mariah were having a last cup of tea over breakfast. But not before the kedgeree was removed from the dining room. Julia smiled at the younger woman. "You have a fine instinct for arriving while food is still available."

"The mysterious wisdom of the Orient," Kiri said loftily as she served herself a portion of the Indian dish and added a slice of toast. After setting down her plate, she pulled a lovely cut crystal perfume bottle from her reticule. "Here's the perfume I blended for you, Lady Julia. I do hope you like it."

Julia would never be rude about a gift, especially when accompanied by the giver's anxious expression. Mariah had told her that Kiri was very serious about her perfumes. "I've never had a custom-blended perfume before, so I will certainly love it."

Kiri still looked concerned. "Usually when I

blend perfume for someone, I let her try different scents and talk about what she likes. But Mariah speaks of you often, that I know you a little. When I saw you the other morning, inspiration struck, and I went home and started blending like a painter running mad with watercolors in the Lake District." She handed the bottle to Julia. "This is just the first version. Scents react differently on different people, so they must often be adjusted. With Mariah, it took several attempts to get it just right."

"Five, but it was a wonderful experience. You mustn't worry so, Kiri," Mariah said soothingly. "I'm sure you've never had anyone dislike your blends."

"No one would say so to my face," Kiri said tartly. "But people lie all the time. Especially those in 'good society.'"

Deciding it was time to end Kiri's worry, Julia unstoppered the bottle and put a dab of perfume on her wrist. Then she sniffed the heady fragrance.

She froze as she was transported back to her childhood. Her throat closed, and tears formed in her eyes. "Oh, my . . ." she whispered.

"I've never had anyone cry from my perfume before!" Kiri exclaimed, aghast. "I'm so sorry, Lady Julia!"

She reached for the bottle, but Julia shook her head. "The scent makes me think of my mother," she said, her voice choked. "She was beautiful and bright and . . . and safe." After her mother died, Julia hadn't felt safe again for many years. Not until now, with Randall.

"That's all right then." Kiri relaxed and took a bite of kedgeree. "Does it remind you of other things?"

Julia sniffed the fragrance again, trying to be more analytical. "There seem to be layers of fragrance here. Like flowers, only more complex. I'm reminded of lilacs, which I love, but there is also a richer scent of rose and a hint of . . . of a dark forest at night." She raised her wrist again. "And through it all, there is something wild and fragile that reminds me of an oboe threading its way through violins and cellos."

Kiri nodded her head with satisfaction. "You describe well, Lady Julia. I wanted that kind of complexity for you. Now to see how it wears on your skin."

Mariah took the bottle and inhaled. "Mmm, wonderful, Kiri." She smiled mischievously. "Randall will like this, Julia."

"I think he will." Julia smiled to herself. Her husband would particularly like the perfume if she was wearing nothing else.

# Chapter 29

Rob Carmichael responded to Randall's note by setting up a meeting at Rob's home on the morning of the ball. Randall was glad it would be daylight. The area near Covent Garden wasn't the worst in London, but it certainly wasn't the best.

Randall's hired cab dropped him off on a nearby street and he walked the last blocks. The neighborhood was quiet at midmorning, but he stayed alert.

Not alert enough. He'd almost reached Rob's home when a hard object was jammed into his back. A deep voice growled, "Yer money or yer life!"

Randall slammed an elbow into his assailant's ribs. The man made a strangled sound.

Whirling, Randall knocked his attacker's legs from under him with a scythe kick, then whipped out his concealed knife. The man, a roughly dressed laborer, went sprawling. Ashton had taught his classmates *Kalarippayattu*, an Indian fighting, when they were boys. Randall had later acquired practical battlefield fighting experience. The results were usually quite adequate.

Randall sheathed the knife when he got a good look at the ragged laborer. "Lucky I recognized you before serious damage was done, Rob," he said with dry amusement.

"I always underestimate how fast you are," the Runner said in his normal voice as he rose lithely to his feet. "I thought I'd be home and cleaned up before you arrived for our meeting, but my previous business took longer than expected."

"And naturally you couldn't resist testing me." Randall scanned his friend as they resumed walking. "I'd shake hands, but I might catch some revolting disease. What did you stick in my ribs?"

"A *kottukampu*. It's a short stick used in *Kalarippayattu*." Rob showed him a shaped piece of wood as thick as a thumb and about a handspan long.

Randall studied it with interest. "I never saw Ashton use anything like this."

"It's an advanced technique that he didn't know." Rob tucked the small weapon inside his coat. "I learned how to use it while I was in India. I prefer to keep this handy rather than a knife because I'm less likely to kill someone accidentally."

"And they say that soldiers live dangerous lives," Randall remarked. "I suspect that life in Wellington's army is peaceful compared to what you do."

"Most of my days are peaceful enough. But a Bow Street Runner who expects safety will have a short career." The old building where Rob lived had a pawnshop on the ground floor and a flat above. Rob unlocked the door to the stairwell beside the pawnshop and ushered Randall inside.

When they'd climbed a flight of shabby stairs and gone through another locked door, they reached Rob's quarters. The main sitting room was surprisingly comfortable and furnished with military neatness. Rob's man, Harvey, came out to check who'd arrived. Battered and broad with muscle, he was formidable despite his wooden leg.

Recognizing Randall, he gave a nod of recognition. "G'day, Major." Then he disappeared into the rear of the flat.

"Give me a few minutes to restore myself," Rob said as he followed Harvey out.

Randall settled into a chair by the window and took one of the day's newspapers from the stack on the side table, but he had trouble concentrating on the news. Tonight was Julia's grand ball, and she would enjoy the evening more when the uncertainty about Branford's bastard was resolved. Randall was reluctantly curious about the boy himself.

Ten minutes later, Rob returned carrying a tray with a steaming pot of coffee and two cups. Gone were the wild hair and the ragged, filthy garments. His friend wore the neat, unobtrusive clothing of a gentleman of modest means. This was as much a disguise as the beggar's outfit, but the mode of dress allowed him to travel in places high and low without attracting much attention. His lean build and brown hair were unremarkable. Only Rob's cool blue eyes suggested that he was more than he seemed.

Randall accepted a cup of coffee and stirred in cream. One sip confirmed that it was burning hot and strong enough to stun an ox. He added sugar as well. "Tell me about my misbegotten young cousin. Was it hard to locate him?"

"Not really." Rob poured himself coffee, adding nothing to soften the taste. "Lady Julia's recollections were accurate. The boy's mother, Sally Thomas, was indeed a barmaid. She worked in a tavern several miles north of Upton. It was no secret who the boy's father was. Branford visited Sally Thomas regularly for years, and the child resembles him enough that no one doubted the relationship."

So the boy looked like Branford. Not an appealing fact. But Randall doubted that would deter Julia. He could hardly criticize her for her warm, nurturing heart, since he was a beneficiary. Thinking it was time to stop saying "the boy," Randall asked, "What is his name?"

"Benjamin Thomas. Known as Ben, or that bastard Benny." Rob downed half a cup of the scalding coffee with one swallow, then topped it up again. "He lived with his mother in the tavern until he was about nine. She died in childbirth and Benjamin is her only surviving child. Sally

Thomas was a fine, strong wench, I'm told, and apparently tolerant of Branford's uglier traits. She came from somewhere in the West Country, but no one knew where. No known family, so Benjamin was left alone in the world."

"Where is he now?"

"The parish didn't want to support him, so he was basically sold as slave labor to the most brutal farmer in the area," Rob scowled. "No one wants the boy. No one cares if he lives or dies."

Randall felt an unwelcome twinge of sympathy. "Was any attempt made to inform Daventry that he had a grandson?"

"That I couldn't learn. If the attempt was made, it failed for some reason." Rob swallowed more coffee. "The farmer, Jeb Gault, is a nasty piece of work. He had a wife but she left him. He has trouble keeping laborers, which is why he generously offered to take in a hungry boy so the parish would be spared the expense of supporting him."

"It sounds like a bad situation for any child." Randall thought again of the boy's resemblance to his father. "Does Benjamin have his father's crazy violence?"

"I don't know. I didn't speak to him myself." Rob frowned. "But one of the locals I talked to said that everyone assumed that sooner or later Gault would kill the boy, or the boy would kill Gault."

A bastard who looked like Branford and who might be a killer. Wonderful. Randall sighed. "I'll go down to Gloucestershire and get him away from the farm. After that, it will depend on what young Benjamin is like. I promise that he'll end up in a better situation than he's in now."

Rob poured himself more coffee. "Family can be hell."

Too true. But they were still family.

Julia took the news about Benjamin Thomas calmly. "Let's leave first thing in the morning, Alex."

He laughed. "I guarantee you'll be exhausted from tonight's ball. So will Mariah. She'll want to spend a quiet day dissecting the events of the evening and as a good friend, you should indulge her. There will also be guests calling to offer appreciation of the ball. I don't think that leaving tomorrow will work."

Julia frowned. "I suppose you're right. The next day then."

Part of Randall wanted to avoid this journey as long as possible. A different, better part of him wanted to get his unknown, baseborn young cousin away from the brutal farmer. No child should be a victim of violence.

The irony that Randall's brutalization had come at the hands of young Benjamin's father did not escape him.

• • •

As Julia prepared for the ball, her dressing room was crowded with people ensuring that she would look as good as she possibly could for her debut in London society. Julia stood patiently while Madame Hélier and a seamstress dressed her in the ball gown and made small adjustments. The modiste had forbidden Julia to go near a mirror until her appearance was perfection.

Naturally Mariah's personal maid was present to aid Elsa in the grand production. Mariah, exquisite in gold brocade, had come to offer encouragement. Lady Kiri appeared, splendid in scarlet. In theory, she'd come to offer help should any be required, but really, she admitted cheerfully, because she wanted to be part of the fun. Lastly, Grandmère swept in, looking more regal than the queen, in black satin lavishly trimmed with silver lace that matched her hair.

As Elsa pinned up Julia's hair, Julia murmured to Mariah, "I've become superfluous, I think. If I slipped away, no one would notice."

"They would eventually," Mariah said with a laugh. She glanced at the clock on the dressing table. "I need to go down and greet the first guests. Don't appear for another quarter hour, and be sure to enter with Randall. The two of you together will look even better than you do separately."

Julia closed her eyes. "Is too late to cry off from the evening?"

"It most certainly is!" Mariah patted her friend's arm. "I know that you're not fond of being the center of attention, but I promise this will go well. You have friends here, and by the end of the evening, you'll have more."

Mariah collected Grandmère and Lady Kiri and politely herded them from the room. Elsa finished styling Julia's hair while Mariah's maid used a hare's foot to dust the faintest blush of color on Julia's cheeks. A rosy salve gave similar color to her lips.

"Very well, Lady Julia," Madame Hélier said with approval. "You may now look at yourself. You look very splendid indeed."

Julia crossed the room to the tall mirror. The image reflected back at her was a stranger—a startlingly fashionable stranger. The sea-tinted blue silk Lady Kiri had picked was perfect for Julia, bringing out the delicate color in her face and auburn undertones in her dark hair. The neckline was high for a ball gown, but as the modiste had promised, the back was cut so daringly low that custom-made stays and shift were required.

The lines of the gown were simple, and her only jewelry was a pearl necklace and matching earrings. They had been a gift from Grandmère, who had inherited them from her own grandmother.

A string of smaller pearls had been woven

through Julia's upswept hair, along with tiny rosebuds fashioned of the same silk as the gown. A single teasing lock curled down to her shoulder. The effect was exactly what Julia had wanted: modest but stylish, attractive but not blatant. Turning, she said warmly, "Thank you all. I look better than I ever dreamed I could."

Madame Hélier gave a satisfied smile. "If you continue to let me dress you, Lady Julia, you will be considered one of the great beauties of the beau monde."

The dress might be modest, but not the modiste. Suppressing a smile, Julia dismissed Madame Hélier and the maids. She applied Lady Kiri's perfume at the base of her throat and the nape of her neck. Then she went in search of her husband.

She stepped into the sitting room from her dressing room just as Randall was entering. Her breath caught at the sight of him. She'd always found him strikingly handsome, even when they first met and he was scowling half the time. He looked even better now that he'd remembered how to smile.

Mariah had been right. In his dress uniform, Randall was a sight to make strong women swoon. The tailored scarlet jacket emphasized the width of his shoulders and the buff pantaloons set off his powerfully muscled legs, while candlelight burnished his golden hair and sculpted the fine planes of his face. A Nordic god, and he was *hers*.

Randall stopped in his tracks when he saw her, his gaze riveted. "You look . . . magnificent." He cleared his throat. "Even though I wanted you from the beginning, I hadn't actually realized what a beauty you are, milady."

Julia laughed with delight. "I have never been a beauty, but I'm glad if you think so." She moved forward to take his arm. "You, sir, will have impressionable females following you around the ballroom like dazed ducklings. Shall we go down to the ball?"

Ignoring the remark, he bent and pressed his lips to her nape, then trailed a kiss down her shoulder. "You smell wickedly delicious. Shall we be late to the ball?"

Sharp, sweet desire spiked through her. "I know you're teasing," she said breathlessly, "but beware. I may take you up on it."

He looked hopeful. "I am always at your service, milady."

Julia thought of the nights they'd shared since his return to London, and desire became even sharper. Now that the barriers were down, they were discovering intoxicating new ways to pleasure each other. "Don't tempt me, Alexander! Too many people have worked on this ball. We must play our roles."

He smiled and led her to the door. "Duty calls.

It always does for both of us. But I warn you, after the ball is over, I shall do my utmost to seduce you into my bed."

Laughing, they walked down the sweeping stairs together.

# Chapter 30

Julia knew they made a striking picture as they walked down the sweeping stairs to the entrance hall—any woman would look striking on Randall's arm. But her stomach was knotted and she felt on the verge of becoming ill. All the pain, rejection, and misery around her first marriage and her exile from her childhood home had become intertwined with this grand return to society.

Mariah glanced up the staircase and gestured Julia to come to her side in a receiving line by the entrance to the ballroom. Ashton was there chatting with Grandmère, whose presence signaled her approval of her long lost granddaughter. Randall escorted her down the final steps and stationed himself beside her. She was surrounded by friends, and her anxiety dissolved between one heartbeat and the next.

"This isn't so bad, is it?" Mariah whispered when there was a lull after the first rush of guests.

"Not bad at all," Julia admitted. "I'm glad you forced me into this, your grace."

Mariah laughed, then greeted another guest. There was intense curiosity about the duke's daughter who had returned from the dead, but Julia sensed no hostility. As Ashton had said, her father was not popular with society and the Dowager Duchess of Charente inspired awe. The beau monde was prepared to like Lady Julia Randall.

"Anthony!" she exclaimed as her brother appeared. She hugged him exuberantly. "Will you dance with me later?"

He laughed and hugged her back. "Yes, even if you do step all over my toes. I don't suppose you did much dancing in the wild north country."

"No, but Mariah engaged a dancing instructor who drilled me ruthlessly." She surveyed Anthony, who looked as handsome and elegant as a future duke should. "If you weren't my brother, I'd say you looked madly attractive."

Anthony's eyes twinkled. "I would say the same of you if you weren't my sister." He moved on to Randall. The two men shook hands and slipped into easy conversation.

The next guest, to Julia's shock, was Lady Daventry. An invitation had been sent to her and her husband, but Julia and Randall had assumed the earl would rip the card into pieces and toss it into the nearest fire.

Yet here was the Countess of Daventry, looking as elegant as a very pregnant woman could in a sky blue gown and splendid sapphires. She was on the arm of a handsome young man. After a quick glance over the countess's shoulder, Julia said warmly, "How lovely to see you again, Lady Daventry."

"Don't worry," the countess said with a mischievous smile. "My husband isn't here. He had to go off to Turville for a few days." She patted her belly. "I'm not allowed to travel, of course. But when I received the invitation, I couldn't resist coming."

"I'm glad you did." Julia studied the countess's escort. "This handsome young man is one of your sons, I think? He looks very much like you."

As the young man blushed, Lady Daventry said, "Yes, my oldest, Lord Morton. He'll be back to Oxford soon, but he consented to escort his aging parent tonight."

Lord Morton smiled. "My mother is the most dreadful tease. I'm very pleased to make your acquaintance, Lady Julia."

When his admiring gaze went to Randall, Julia guessed that the young man might be army mad. She introduced him to her husband, then turned back to Lady Daventry. "Will Daventry be angry that you came here even though he's disowned my husband?"

"Yes, but it's not the first time I've enraged him," the countess said tartly. "He rages and stomps about furiously, but he's never laid a finger on me in anger. I would not tolerate that."

At least the earl wasn't as mad as his son had been. Julia said, "You're a brave woman, Lady Daventry."

The countess's animation vanished, and she spread her hand on her belly. "Not brave at all."

"How have you been feeling?" Julia asked with quick concern.

"Huge. Slow." Lady Daventry swallowed hard. "I was very young when my first son was born, and the others came within the next five years. My body isn't as strong and resilient as it was then."

Julia took the countess's hand. "That doesn't mean you won't be safely delivered of a fine, healthy baby. Have faith, Lady Daventry. A hopeful spirit will encourage a good outcome."

"I'm having trouble being hopeful," the older woman said in a low voice. Her hand tightened on Julia's for a moment before she released her. "But enough about me. When we first met, you mentioned that you were curious if Branford had spawned any by-blows. I wondered myself."

Attention caught, Julia said, "Did you ask your husband?"

"I sounded Daventry out on the subject, but he said no. Regretfully." The countess sighed. "It would be comforting to know he could have healthy descendants. You're lucky your husband has the good blood of his mother's people."

In other words, Randall could probably sire

strong children . . . if he had a different wife. Julia suppressed the thought. It sounded as if Daventry didn't know of Benjamin Thomas's existence. Perhaps he'd be willing to accept the boy. Julia hoped so.

But first, they must find him.

Randall swept his wife into the first waltz. "Obviously your practice with the dance instructor paid off. You dance well and you haven't missed a set yet."

His wife laughed, her expression vivid with delight. "I love dancing! I do believe that I am learning to enjoy London social life. Especially when I can have the first waltz and the supper dance with you."

Gossamer strands of dark hair had loosened to fall around her face and shoulders. The effect was startlingly erotic. He wanted to lick her slender throat, but settled for saying, "Since we're married, we could dance more than twice without scandal."

"As a good guest of honor, I shouldn't spend too much time with you." She smiled mischievously. "They might think that I'm trying to seduce you. Would it be horribly indelicate of me to admit they would be right?"

He grinned. "We'll probably both be too tired to care by the time the night is over, but we can lie in late in the morning."

She moved a little closer in his arms, her gaze sultry. "You were right. I don't want to take off for Gloucestershire first thing tomorrow. The day after will do."

They spoke no more, but he savored the heat between them. Disapproving dowagers were right to condemn the waltz—it was indeed inflammatory to spin around the ballroom with a beautiful woman in his arms. Knowing that they would be sharing a bed later was all that kept him from luring her out onto the terrace to steal kisses.

The dance had just ended and Randall was leading Julia from the floor when a familiar dark man came up to them. "Ballard!" Randall exclaimed, shaking his friend's hand. "I thought you'd be in Portugal by now."

"Business delayed me. I'm leaving tomorrow, but tonight, I can be here." Ballard turned to Julia. "And this lovely creature must be your wife?"

After Randall performed the introductions, Julia gave Ballard her hand. "It's such a pleasure to meet you," she said warmly. "I'm developing a definite taste for port that has been produced by Ballard House."

Ballard laughed. "A woman with a fine palate! You're a lucky man, Randall." The musicians were starting to play again, so Ballard offered Julia his arm. "May I have this dance, Lady Julia?"

"With pleasure." She gave Randall a roguish glance as Ballard led her away. "I want you to tell me disgraceful stories about my husband."

Randall watched her go, his heart tight in his chest. She was laughing and radiant, perfectly suited to this milieu. The gown's neckline was modest, but the low back was tantalizing and the fitted bodice proved that her figure did not lack femininity.

Now that she'd mastered her fears and discovered her passionate nature, she attracted the attention of every man who saw her. Lady Julia Raines was the belle of the ball. She had high birth, beauty, dazzling charm, and an extravagant fortune. She could have any man she wanted. The knowledge was like a weight in his belly.

The fact that she currently had a husband was a minor impediment, given that he'd carefully arranged for her to be able to end the marriage in a year if she chose. He'd signed the quitclaim that waived his husbandly rights to her fortune. Why should Julia stay married to a man of no great fortune or distinction?

Granted, they had turned out to be very compatible lovers. But as he watched her laughing with Ballard, he bleakly acknowledged that she could easily find satisfaction elsewhere. He wasn't jealous of Ballard, who would never betray a friend, but the world was full of men who would happily bed a woman as lovely and sensual as Julia. Could his marriage survive when there was such a disparity of fortune and there would be no children to bind them together?

Knowing he was being morbid and foolish, he forced himself to stop watching his wife. As he turned from the dancers, he saw Lady Agnes Westerfield, founder of the Westerfield Academy. Tall and masterful, she stood on the edge of the dance floor watching the other guests with benign amusement.

"Lady Agnes!" He crossed to her and bowed. "Ashton said he'd invited you, but he didn't think you would be able to come."

When he straightened, Lady Agnes gave him a hug. "You're looking very well, Randall." She picked a thread off his scarlet sleeve. "Splendid as you are in this uniform, I'm glad you've left the army. I worry."

Lady Agnes was a visionary headmistress and a gifted teacher, but even more important was the caring she gave her students, who often came to her angry and neglected. She wasn't precisely a mother to her boys, but she made a splendid aunt.

"What brings you to London?" he asked. "Just the ball, or other business?"

She laughed. "Much as I love my boys, I was in need of a few days of adult conversation. It's summer and only a handful of students are at the school, so I decided to come up to town. I'm staying at my brother's house and indulging myself." Her gaze went to his wife. "I talked a bit with Lady Julia last spring when I was here.

A very sound young woman. She has turned from a quiet caterpillar into a shimmering butterfly in the months since. Is that your doing?"

"Perhaps a little. But mostly it is Julia herself. She was born to this life, and now she is finally claiming it." He offered his arm. "May I take you off for an ice?"

She took his arm. "Wicked boy! You know how fond I am of ices."

As they headed to the refreshment table, he said, "I may have a student for you. Apparently my cousin Branford had an illegitimate son that the family hasn't known about. Rob Carmichael thinks he's located the boy, Benjamin Thomas. Julia and I are going to Gloucestershire to see."

"The illegitimate son of your wife's first husband?" Lady Agnes's brows arched. She knew of Branford's violence because of what Randall had told her when he attended the academy. She was quite capable of deducing what that had meant for Julia. "Lady Julia has a generous spirit if she wants to help the child."

"Julia is generosity personified, especially since it seems likely the boy is being ill-used." Randall collected two ices and a pair of spoons at the refreshment table, then led his companion to a small table under a towering palm. When they were seated, he continued, "The local parish handed young Benjamin over to a brute farmer as labor. Probably the child hasn't a trace of education or manners. I know you have a reputation for working miracles, but there are limits. Would you be willing to take the boy on?"

"Branford's mother came from unsound stock," Lady Agnes looked intrigued. "But that doesn't mean Branford's son is mad. He must be twelve or thirteen?"

"From what we know, yes."

"Young Benjamin would present a challenge, but not an impossible one if he's willing to work to better himself. We could give him private tutoring if needed," Lady Agnes said thoughtfully. "Once you have the lad in hand, bring him to me for an interview. If he hasn't the background and temperament for academic pursuits, I presume you could find him an apprenticeship or some other suitable situation."

Relieved by her calm acceptance, Randall said, "I had hoped you would be willing to look him over. Will you be in town very long?"

"About a fortnight, I think." She tasted a mouthful of her lemon ice and smiled blissfully. "I'll return to Westerfield Manor just before Michaelmas term begins."

"Then I will bring the boy to you here rather than in Kent." With that settled, Randall concentrated on his ice. But his gaze kept searching out Julia on the dance floor.

What did the gallant knight do when the princess didn't need him any more?

# Chapter 31

Julia danced every dance, but it would take more than one night to make up for all her years of deprivation. She was on the sidelines ruefully examining her hem when Randall approached bearing two glasses of champagne. From the way female gazes followed him, Mariah had been right about how magnificent he was in his uniform. Just looking at him caused heat in unmentionable places.

He offered her a glass of champagne. "A problem with your gown?"

"My last partner stepped on the flounce at the bottom of my skirt and it tore loose." She accepted the champagne and swallowed a mouthful with pleasure. "I'll go to the ladies' retiring room. Elsa is working there and she can pin it up."

"Let's go up to our apartment," he suggested. "I can manage if you provide the pins. I could use a break from all this concentrated humanity."

The look in his eyes made her feel even warmer. She finished the champagne in a single swallow and set the glass on a nearby table. "I'd like that." She took his arm and they headed across the ballroom. "I noticed that you danced most of the dances. Were you enjoying yourself, or being a good guest?"

"Mariah gave me my marching orders before the ball," he explained. "I've danced with every wallflower and frisky dowager in Ashton House."

"I hope they didn't all fall in love with you." Her tone was light, but she had been very aware of his other partners. Though he claimed to be merely doing his duty, some of those "wallflowers" had been young and more beautiful than she would ever be.

"If they were attracted by the uniform, I'm sure my stern expression discouraged any romantic fantasies. Mostly I was glad that you did such a good job repairing my leg that it is hardly aching at all." He smiled down at her. "You do very good work."

"The governess I had as a girl would probably say that my needlework lessons were good training for surgery," Julia replied. "She was always trying to persuade me to embrace ladylike accomplishments."

The cooler air outside the ballroom was a relief. As they started up the stairs, Julia caught up her skirt where the flounce was dragging. "It's convenient to be living in the house where the ball is being held. Sanctuary from all the noise and talk."

"I've been on battlefields that were quieter than a London ball in full spate," Randall agreed.

At the top of the staircase, they turned right

toward their apartment. When Randall opened the door to the sitting room, Julia realized that they were directly above the ballroom. She could hear the music and feel its vibration through her feet.

Closing the door, Randall said, "I've wanted to do this all night." He turned and drew her into his arms.

"Oh, *yes!*" She reached up to put her arms around his neck as passion crackled between them like heat lightning. All night she had been aware of Randall, not just where he was in the ballroom and how splendid he looked, but memories of his taste, his touch, his ability to make her melt with desire.

He drank her in as if she were a fountain and he was dying of thirst. Dimly she was aware that her back was pressed against the door as their mouths and tongues melted together with no beginning and no end.

Her hips rocked against him. She felt quick disappointment when he pulled back a little, until she realized that he had lifted her skirt. Cool air touched heated flesh as he sought and found the most sensitive parts of her body.

Exquisite though the sensations were, she wanted more. Blindly she fumbled with his breeches, managing the buttons with clumsy fingers until she freed the hard, pulsing shaft into her hand.

He groaned. She had thought they might kiss their way to the bedroom, but instead he caught her around the waist and lifted her high. Crushed between the door and his taut body, she was shocked into mindless pleasure as he slid into her slick, heated depths. For an instant they were both still, adjusting.

Then she wrapped her legs around his hips and ground frantically against him. Her nails bit his arms and her teeth sank into the scarlet wool of his shoulder as his harsh breathing sounded in her ear. More, more, *more* . . .

Such fierceness couldn't last. Her body convulsed and she smothered her cry against his shoulder. A heartbeat later he spilled into her with a wrenching groan.

The shattering release faded and sanity returned. Randall had intended a playful seduction, not mating with such raw need. Gasping for breath, he lowered Julia's feet to the ground. "I'm sorry," he gasped. "I hope I didn't hurt you."

"You didn't, Alex." Julia's pulse pounded in her throat as her palms skimmed down his arms, fingers opening and closing. "Not in any way I didn't want."

He was grateful for that. Though he hadn't expected to burn so hot or run so wild, at least they had been consumed together. But as passion ebbed, he realized bleakly that physical possession was fleeting. Julia was his for the moment. But for the future?

Only God knew.

Julia woke slowly the morning after the ball. If it was indeed morning. Her eyes were still closed, and for all she knew, it was high noon. Her muscles ached from so much dancing, and her stomach was a little queasy, probably from too much champagne. It was all quite wonderful.

Randall's body was warm and close, so she opened her eyes lazily. He was lying on his side, his tousled blond head propped on one hand as he studied her thoughtfully. His chest was bare, and so was she, now that she thought about it. Heavens, they were both thoroughly naked! She felt deliciously indecent.

Memory flooded back. After they recovered from their fierce coupling, they'd returned demurely to the ballroom to eat supper. She had felt sure that her wanton behavior was written all over her, but no one seemed to notice.

When she and Randall finally retired at some ridiculous early morning hour, she'd been ready to collapse into bed and sleep for days. Yet when he helped her disrobe, she'd returned the favor and all of their garments had ended in a pile on the carpet.

His skin against hers felt so lovely that when they climbed into their bed they had been unable to keep their hands off each other. Fatigue dissipated as they had made love with slow thoroughness. Julia had fallen asleep smiling.

When her eyes opened, Randall asked, "Did you sleep well?"

"I must have, since I remember nothing." She covered a yawn. "Do you have any idea what time it is?"

"I heard the church bells ringing noon not long ago." His hand stroked down her arm, then cupped her breast. "You were a great success last night."

"People were very kind. I'd feared rude stares and at least some caustic comments, but if that happened, it was out of my hearing." She exhaled with pleasure, feeling like a well petted cat. "No one seemed to care that my father disowned me."

"Your brother and grandmother's support mean more than Castleton's disapproval." Randall's thumb gently teased her nipple, creating a stir of pleasure. "After last night, you can have your choice of lovers. Half the men in aristocratic London desire you."

She jerked as if he'd splashed ice water over her. "Good God, Alex! Why would I want lovers? You above all should know that I'm a married woman!"

His eyes were profoundly sad. "Everything has changed since I proposed in that Cumberland hut. You were wise to want a door out of the marriage if it proved to be a mistake. Once we're sure there are no more threats to your safety, there's no need to stay married to me. There would be some scandal if we get a Scottish divorce, but nothing that a charming heiress couldn't weather socially."

She wanted to stammer that she *liked* being married to him, but her queasy stomach turned over. Feeling dizzy and confused, she scrambled from the bed and retched into the chamber pot.

Randall pulled a blanket from the bed and wrapped it around her. "I'm sorry," he said quietly. "I didn't mean to upset you."

When her stomach was empty, she sat back on her heels and pulled the blanket tight. "Why do you assume I'm going to want to end this marriage? I thought we were getting on rather well."

"So far." He scooped her up and tucked her back into the bed, blanket and all. Then he crossed to his wardrobe and pulled out his banyan. As he slipped it on, he continued, "But how will you feel after a year has passed? So much has changed in a few weeks. There will be more changes ahead."

"Does anyone know how they'll feel a year in the future?" she asked.

The mattress sagged as he perched on the edge next to her. "One can't know such things," he agreed. "But given the pleasure you took in dancing and flirting and socializing last night, you might prefer a fashionable life."

Julia closed her eyes, wishing she was still happily asleep. Had she been flirting? She supposed so, but it was just light, pleasant fun! "Flirting doesn't mean I wanted to bed any of my dance partners."

"Not now, perhaps, but you're only just discovering your own nature. You might want to lie with other men, and I could really not accept that while you are married to me," he said calmly. "Your wealth puts you in a rare position. You can do good works, take lovers, find a husband who will suit you better than I, or all those things at once."

Julia realized that she had created this situation by her insistence on keeping one foot outside the door of their marriage. It had made sense then, and she supposed it still did. Or did Randall's gallant willingness to let her leave conceal his own desire to be free?

Her voice edged, she asked, "Do you want me to dissolve this marriage so that you can find a woman who will give you children?"

After a brief pause, he said evenly, "You told me from the beginning that it wasn't possible. I accepted that."

Which was true, but his answer was a few seconds too slow in coming. "You're right, we've both changed a great deal in the last weeks," she said wearily. "So perhaps it was wise to leave that door ajar. But why did you raise the subject this morning?"

"Because your situation changed so dramatically last night." He sighed. "You married me because I was the best of a bad lot of choices. Now you have a life full of possibilities. From the beginning, we've both done our best to be honest with each other, so I thought it best to make sure that the situation is clear."

The damned, honorable man. Julia rolled away from him and buried herself in the covers. Her head knew that he was right. A year from now, she might be frantic to escape the marriage she'd made in desperation.

But since that was the case, why did she feel like throwing up again?

# Chapter 32

Randall halted the curricle and read the weathered sign. "Here's the drive to Jeb Gault's farm."

"We'll know soon," Julia said, her voice tight.

Very true. But just what would they know? Randall watched Julia from the corner of his eye as he turned the light carriage into the lane. It hadn't taken him long to realize that too much honesty could be a mistake in a marriage. The two days since his talk with Julia about her future had been full of strain. It wasn't in her nature to sulk, but she had been very quiet ever since.

When they'd gone to bed that night, she'd turned onto her side, presenting her back to him. The message had seemed clear, yet when he touched her shoulder in a silent good night, she'd rolled over into his arms and they'd made desperate, wordless love. The next night had been the same. He could find no fault with the passion, but he missed the talking, which created intimacy beyond the physical.

He wished he knew what she was thinking. Was she considering her choices for lovers after the marriage ended? Was she practicing her sensual skills for the benefit of future bedmates? Not that she needed to—her talent for passion was unsurpassed. Or was she merely irritated with his directness?

The thought of her leaving him was like a bayonet in the gut, but after seeing her pleasure at the ball, he'd realized she'd probably be happier with a man who was more lighthearted. More her equal in station and fortune. So he was forcing himself to be rational and detached, since the alternative might be turning crazily possessive. She'd suffered enough of that with Branford.

The last thing he'd wanted to do was upset her, but he had. And he couldn't unsay his words.

As planned, they left London in search of Benjamin Thomas on the second morning after the ball. This time they'd traveled in style, using two carriages to transport Gordon and Elsa and their luggage. Since Upton was a couple of hours beyond Roscombe, they'd traveled down to his estate and spent the night.

This morning, Julia had been so tense she'd had only a slice of toast and a cup of tea for breakfast. After, they'd set off in Randall's curricle.

The lane to Gault's Hill Farm was long and rutted. Randall drove with care, and found that the lane ran right into the farmyard. Feeding chickens beside the barn was a small, ragged boy who looked up suspiciously as the carriage pulled in.

With that face, the boy had to be Benjamin Thomas. Branford's bastard looked much like his father at that age.

Randall exchanged a glance with Julia, whose gray eyes were dark. She had also seen the resemblance.

Reminding himself that he was an adult, not a child trying to escape a vicious older cousin, Randall swung from the carriage. "Good day."

The boy edged back. "Mr. Gault be in the house." He pointed.

"I'm not looking for Mr. Gault." Randall handed the reins to Julia. "I believe I'm looking for you. You're Benjamin Thomas?"

"I didn't do nothin'!" The boy backed up farther, into the stable wall. He was small for thirteen, and didn't look as if he'd had a decent meal in years. His feet were bare and a rip in his shirt showed boney ribs.

"No one said you did." Julia's voice was gentle but her gaze was intense.

"I believe your father was my cousin, which means you and I are cousins also." Randall didn't move any closer since the boy was poised to run. "Just to be sure, might I ask your father's name?"

"Some bloke called Branford. I never met 'im." His gaze went to the curricle. "My mam said 'e was rich. Like you."

The door to the farmhouse opened and a burly man with a horsewhip in one hand strode out belligerently. He reeked of whiskey even though it was only midday. "Who the hell are you and why are you talking to my boy?"

"My name is Randall. I assume you're Mr. Gault." Randall's brows arched. "You're saying this is your son?"

"No, but I'm responsible for him. Benjamin was on the parish so I said I'd take him in and care for him." Gault scowled at the boy. "Useless little bastard."

"You haven't cared for him very well," Julia said tartly. "He's wearing rags and I could count every rib on his body."

Gault glared up at her. "Not my fault he ruins

342

his clothes! He gets plenty to eat but he's a growing boy so he looks skinny. Eats like a pig and too lazy to work."

Benjamin made a small sound that reminded Randall of a spitting cat. He glanced at the boy, who was staring at Gault with an expression that was . . . murderous. There were welt marks visible through holes in his ragged garments. The marks of a whip.

"Then you are in luck today, Mr. Gault," Randall said coolly. "The family was unaware of Benjamin's existence until quite recently. Now that we know, naturally we will take responsibility for him."

Benjamin's head whipped around and he stared at Randall. Despite his resemblance to Branford, he reminded Randall of someone else.

Of himself, when Randall had been a frightened, abused boy.

Gault's brows furrowed. "You want to pay for his upkeep? That would be right honorable of you. I'm willing to keep looking after him for say"—his gaze went to the expensive curricle—"fifty quid a year. He's a right handful, not fit for a gentleman's household, but I can handle 'im. 'Twould be a crime to take him away from Hill Farm when he's been with me for four years. He's like me own flesh and blood."

The sum was outrageous. If Randall was fool enough to agree to those terms, Benjamin would never see a pennyworth of benefit. "Generous of you, Mr. Gault," he said with only a trace of sarcasm, "but there is no need for your continued care. A child belongs with his family, so my wife and I will take Benjamin now. I assure you that he will be properly cared for."

Gault's anger thickened the air. "The parish gave him to me! You can't just take 'im away!"

"I'm sure the parish will be glad to be freed of responsibility for an orphan." Randall turned to the boy. "As I said, Benjamin, you and I are cousins. You also have a grandfather. You are not alone in the world."

The boy's face worked. "I don't have to stay here?"

"No. Do you have any possessions you wish to take with you?"

"Damnation!" Gault bellowed, his hand tightening on the whip. "You can't kidnap my farmhand! Who will take care of my stock? He's good for that, at least."

"Hire another hand." Randall had guessed that Gault wouldn't voluntarily give up free labor, and he'd come prepared. He pulled twenty pounds out of his pocket and held the notes so the farmer could see them. "I should think this would be good for a couple of years worth of labor."

Gault gazed at the money. "Very well. Take the little bastard and get out!"

Randall turned to the boy. "Benjamin, do you

wish to know more about me before climbing into my carriage? I give you my word that you won't be cold or hungry or whipped again."

"I'd go with anyone to get away from 'im!" The boy looked from Randall to Lady Julia and back. "You're really family?"

"We are." As Randall looked more closely at the dirty face, he saw a different inheritance beyond what came from Branford. Benjamin's jaw was more square, his eyes hazel, not blue. And if he wanted to do violence to Gault, he had good reason. "Do you need help bringing your things to the carriage?"

Blinking, Benjamin shook his head and darted into the barn. There was a sound of scrabbling feet, climbing a ladder, Randall thought. Gault said brusquely, "Give me the money!"

"When we're ready to leave." Randall gave the farmer his most intimidating stare and Gault subsided.

In less than five minutes, Benjamin emerged with a small bundle in one hand and a fluffy black-and-white cat draped over his shoulder. "The cat is yours?" Randall asked.

The boy gave a jerky nod. "He'd kill 'er if I left her behind."

"Damned right I would," Gault growled. "Worthless beast."

"Then the cat comes," Randall agreed. "Does she have a name, Benjamin?"

"Miss Kitty." Benjamin walked to the carriage, his wary gaze on Gault.

"That's a pretty name. She seems very much a lady." Julia transferred the carriage reins to her left hand. "Do you want to hand her to me while you climb in?"

Since Benjamin couldn't manage the cat, his bundle, and the step all at once, he reluctantly passed the cat up to Julia. "She won't run off as long as I'm with 'er."

"She's very calm." Julia stroked the cat, who turned around, then settled in Julia's lap. She was a large cat, with enormous tufted feet. "Such lovely silky fur!"

"I groom her every night with a comb I made," Benjamin said proudly as he dropped his bundle behind the seat.

A pity that Benjamin hadn't used the comb on himself, but no matter. Randall suspected that a boy who loved a cat and was good with livestock probably hadn't inherited his father's viciousness. Even if he had, Randall wouldn't leave a rabid hedgehog here with Jeb Gault.

Instead of climbing into the carriage, Benjamin turned and scooped up a stone the size of his fist. Then he darted across the yard and swung the stone at Gault's jaw.

The farmer howled when the stone slammed into his jaw. Grabbing Benjamin, he threw the punching, kicking boy to the ground. As

Benjamin skidded through the dirt, Gault unleashed his whip and slashed it viciously across the boy's arm.

The farmer was about to strike again when Randall wrenched the whip away. Gault turned on Randall, his huge fists slamming forward. Randall deftly stepped out of the way, then used a throw he'd learned from Ashton to put Gault flat on his back.

"God damn it!" the farmer snarled. "You saw how the little beast attacked me! He deserves one last beating before he leaves!"

Before Gault could scramble to his feet, Randall bent down and jammed two fingers into the man's neck, blocking the flow of blood to the brain. This close, the stench of whiskey was overwhelming. Gault gasped and the fight went out of him.

"Enough!" Randall snapped. "The boy is now my problem, not yours!"

As he straightened, Benjamin arrived and tried to hit Gault with the stone again. Randall caught him around the waist and lifted him into the air. "That's enough from you, too! Let go of the stone!"

Benjamin struggled to free himself. "I'm going to pay 'im back for beating me!"

"No!" Randall pried the stone from the boy's hand and tossed it away. He caught Benjamin's gaze, willing him to settle down.

As the wildness faded in the hazel eyes, Randall said quietly, "Learn to pick your fights carefully. This one is over. Forever. Do you understand?"

When Benjamin nodded, Randall set him on the ground but kept his hand on the boy's shoulder. To Gault, he said dryly, "You should pay me for taking him away, but since we had an agreement . . ."

He dropped the money by the farmer, then marched Benjamin to the curricle, where a worried Julia had one hand on the reins and her other on the cat. He gave her a reassuring smile. "All boys lose their temper."

She nodded, but still looked worried. Privately, Randall was also. Benjamin's violence might be understandable under the circumstances, but the wild attack on Gault was troubling in Branford's son. For Julia, the idea must be horrific.

Randall looked down at the boy, who stared back defiantly. "Sometimes fighting is necessary, sometimes it isn't, Benjamin. We will talk more about that later. But I am telling you right now that if you *ever* raise a hand to my wife or try to hurt her in any way, I will take a knife and peel all the skin from your bones. Is that clear?"

Benjamin's brows drew together. He looked surprised by an adult who talked rather than hit. "Won't 'urt 'er if she don't 'urt me."

Randall thought that was sufficient for now.

"Good enough. Now we'll be on our way." He lifted the boy into the curricle, then swung up into the seat. Benjamin, who was between the adults, reclaimed his cat, petting her with dirty fingers.

The farmer stumbled to his feet. "Get off my land and don't let that little bastard near me ever again!"

Randall inclined his head. "Good day, Mr. Gault." Then he expertly turned the curricle in the narrow quarters of the farmyard and drove back down the rough driveway. Benjamin, who sat between Randall and Julia, said pugnaciously, "You shouldn't a given 'im the money. He fed 'is pigs better 'n me."

"He doesn't deserve it," Randall agreed. "But the money made it easier and quicker. Particularly since you attacked him and could have been charged with assault."

"But he beat me all the time!"

"Yes, and he was very wrong to do it," Julia said. "But sometimes there is a difference between what is right and the law. Legally, men are usually allowed to discipline wives and children." A note of bitterness sounded in her voice. "Sometimes it is best to walk away."

The boy frowned as he pondered that. There seemed to be a sharp mind inside that ragged head. He had potential—if he hadn't inherited his father's madness.

As they rode toward the village of Upton,

Randall said, "I thought we should stop at the tavern to eat before driving home."

"Eat at a real tavern?" Benjamin said incredulously. "As much as I want?"

"Not that much," Julia said firmly. "Since you haven't been fed decently, you'd probably make yourself ill if you ate as much as you want. But you will have enough, and a good dinner when we get home."

"Home." The boy's expression flattened. "Where you taking me?"

"To Roscombe, my estate about two hours east of here," Randall replied. "Some of my old clothes will hold you over until we can get to a tailor to make new."

"New clothes?" The boy held the placid cat closer. Her plumy black tail thumped Randall's thigh. "Then what? You want me to work on your estate?"

"A lot depends on you, Benjamin," Julia said seriously. "Our first choice would be to send you to school. Do you know how to read?"

" 'Course I can read! My mam taught me reading and figgering."

"Excellent!" Julia said. "Would you like to learn more?" Her warmth was enough to draw out even the most suspicious boy.

Benjamin hesitated. "Mebbe. Depends."

This was promising. Randall had had doubts about finding Branford's bastard, but now that the boy had a face and a personality, it was impossible to dismiss him. If he wanted to learn, Lady Agnes would work with him until he did.

Benjamin looked up at Randall. "I'd like to learn how to fight like you do. Would you teach me?"

Reminding himself that it was normal for boys to have violent impulses, Randall said, "Perhaps someday. Not until you master your temper and prove that you won't bully people just because you can."

Benjamin scowled, but in a thoughtful way. Randall continued, "I'll also stop by the parish church and tell the vicar that you have been claimed by your family."

"My family," Benjamin said experimentally. "Tell me about my father."

Randall's gaze met Julia's over the boy's head. They had discussed this, and agreed that honesty without too many appalling details was best. "That can wait till later. We're coming into Upton now."

Randall's stop at the parish church was brief. The vicar was only mildly interested in the fact that Benjamin Thomas's family wanted to take him away. No proof was required. The fact that Randall looked prosperous was enough.

As he headed toward the village tavern, he reminded himself that finding the boy was the easy part. Knowing what to do with him would be harder.

# Chapter 33

After their luncheon, Randall considered finding a cage or box for Miss Kitty, but she seemed content to travel on Benjamin's lap. The cat had a pretty white face, her huge green eyes set off by a black cap and a comical black circle on her chin. She caused no trouble, though he guessed that the tomcat who ruled Roscombe manor would not be pleased to see her.

On the drive to Roscombe, Julia drew Benjamin into conversation. As he relaxed under her gentle questions, his answers got longer.

Sally Thomas seemed to have been an affectionate mother, and she'd given her son a solid basic education. She'd been barmaid in a posting house, and Benjamin started helping around the kitchen and as a pot boy as soon as he was old enough. Serving travelers of many kinds had broadened his experience, and made him more worldly than if he'd spent his life at Hill Farm.

His ambition had been to become a coachman. Then his mother had died and he'd been handed over to Gault. He'd considered running away, but was intelligent enough to realize that he had no place to go. Especially not with a cat.

Benjamin's eyes widened when they drove into Roscombe and pulled up by the manor house. He clutched Miss Kitty, not speaking. The groom,

Willett, took over the carriage and Randall, Julia, Benjamin, and Miss Kitty went into the house.

"Benjamin, you can put Miss Kitty down now." Randall said. "She'll be safe here and she'll want to explore."

Benjamin obeyed and his cat set off to look around. With unerring instinct, she headed toward the kitchen even though she'd been fed at the tavern two hours earlier.

Randall continued, "Lady Julia will arrange a room for you. But the first order of business is to get you bathed."

Benjamin looked appalled. "Don't need a bath! A basin and a bit of soap will do for me."

"A bath," Julia said firmly. "Perhaps in the laundry room? There's a large tub and it's close to the kitchen where water can be heated."

Benjamin started edging away, looking as if he was regretting leaving Hill Farm. "Don't need a bath!"

"You most certainly do." Seeing that the boy was on the verge of bolting, Randall caught his arm. The boy flinched and tried to yank himself free.

Guessing what Benjamin was thinking, Randall said pleasantly, "No, I won't beat you to make you obey, but I have no qualms about using my superior strength to dump you into a laundry tub." Benjamin stopped struggling to escape, but his breathing was shallow and he looked as if he still expected a blow.

Randall said to Julia, "Have Gordon find some clothes that will fit and bring them to me in the laundry." Turning to Benjamin, he said, "Cooperate with the bath, and you shall have tea and cakes after. In moderation."

The bribe worked. Benjamin went down to the laundry tub like Joan of Arc being tied to the stake, but he didn't fight.

Randall's mouth tightened when Benjamin stripped, revealing a thin body amply marked with bruises and scars. Randall should have used Gault's horsewhip on the man.

The bath was a lengthy process, with Randall threatening to scrub the boy with a kitchen brush if he didn't wash properly. Three tubs of warm water were required to remove all the buried grime. Randall stood guard to prevent him from bolting and suggested places that needed extra washing attention.

After Benjamin dried himself, he donned the outfit Gordon had brought. The garments were loose on his thin frame, but not too bad a fit. When the valet cut Benjamin's tangled hair, the boy quivered like a nervous pony, but again, he tolerated it.

Randall was increasingly optimistic that the boy had the intelligence to benefit by attending the Westerfield Academy. Washed and decently dressed, he looked downright presentable.

"Now it's time for the tea and cakes," Randall

said as he escorted Benjamin up the steps to the main floor. "We will join Lady Julia in the morning room."

"Lady Julia?" Benjamin frowned as he walked alongside Randall.

"My wife is the daughter of the Duke of Castleton," Randall explained. "It's a very high rank."

As they entered the drawing room, Benjamin said, "My mam told me that my father was married to a snobbish girl called Lady Julia."

"That was me." Julia glanced up from the tea tray. "Please take seats. I don't think I was snobbish, Benjamin. Mostly I was young, and had been raised very strictly. How old are you now—about thirteen?"

"Almost." He stared at her as he sat on the sofa. "In a few weeks."

"I was sixteen when I married your father." She poured three cups of tea. "Not much older than you are now."

Though Julia's words were true, she'd been a nubile young woman. Benjamin was still a child. Perhaps his growth had been slowed by hunger and ill-use. But some time soon, he'd start shooting up. He would become strong and dangerous. Randall hoped he could be tamed before that happened.

Benjamin accepted his tea rather awkwardly, as if fearing he'd drop the delicate china cup. "My mam said you killed my father." From his expression, he was having trouble reconciling Julia's demeanor with the idea that she'd murdered Branford.

Randall said to Julia, "He needs to know. Would you prefer I tell him?"

She shook her head and offered Benjamin the plate of cakes. "Your father was a very difficult man. Somewhat like Mr. Gault."

The boy frowned. "A drunk?"

"Sometimes, but even when he wasn't drinking, he could be frightening." Julia offered the cakes to Randall, and he saw that her hand was trembling.

Randall took over. "Your father could be very clever and charming, Benjamin, but he was a bully. After my parents died, I was sent to live at Turville Park, the family estate, and I shared a nursery with Branford. He was older and larger than I, and he made my life hell," he said bluntly. "Life was difficult until I went away to school."

Benjamin stuffed the iced cake in his mouth as if fearing it would be taken away. After he'd swallowed it, he said, "That's why you killed him, Lady Julia?"

Julia paled, but she didn't dodge the question. "It was an accident. He was hurting me, and I wanted to get away. I shoved him. He had been drinking, and he lost his balance. He fell and hit his head on the corner of the fireplace."

356

"He was like Gault?" After a wary glance, Benjamin took another cake.

"Scary and unpredictable?" she said. "Yes."

The boy devoured the second cake as quickly as the first. "Sounds like he deserved killing. Sometimes my mam whacked me when I was bad. I didn't mind that. Knew I deserved it. But someone who hits with no reason—that's different." He looked at Randall. "You could have killed Gault easy, but you didn't."

"Killing isn't hard," Randall said. "But it's not something to be done lightly."

Benjamin's gaze moved back to Julia. "Why did you come looking for me?"

She took a deep breath. "I can't undo Branford's death, so I suppose that taking care of his son is a way to make up for that. I needed to know that you were all right."

Benjamin's gaze narrowed. "If my mam was alive, would you have taken me away from her?"

"No. Children belong with their mothers. But we would have made sure that you and she were comfortable and lacked for nothing," Randall said. "I would have paid your school fees."

The boy made a face. "School again. Why?"

"Because education is the key to a better life. It opens doors." Randall smiled. "And builds friendships. Most of my best friends are the boys I went to school with."

"I had friends in the village when I lived with

my mam," Benjamin said belligerently. "Weren't nobody my age at Hill Farm."

"Then you might like school." Julia moved the cake plate out of Benjamin's reach before he could take a fifth cake.

Benjamin regarded the cakes longingly but didn't reach for another. "What school would I go to?"

"I'd like to send you to the Westerfield Academy," Randall said. "It's my old school, and a good place for boys who are a little different."

"You want me to go to *your* school?" Benjamin said, surprised. "How were you different?"

"I was stubborn and bad-tempered." Randall guessed Benjamin had trouble imagining that an adult who looked expensive and confident had been a problem child. "Remember how you asked if I would teach you how to fight like I do?"

After Benjamin nodded, Randall said, "You can learn that at the Westerfield Academy. The very first student at the school was the Duke of Ashton, who is half Hindu, and he was skilled in the Indian fighting skill of *Kalarippayattu*. He taught his classmates so he would have other boys to practice with. *Kalarippayattu* has become a school tradition, with older boys teaching younger ones once they are thought ready."

"I'd like that," Benjamin said cautiously. "But . . . will I be living at the school all the time?"

"No, you'll spend the holidays here at

Roscombe." Randall was amazed at how naturally he made such a sweeping promise to Branford's son.

Ben looked as if he wanted to believe, but wasn't yet sure. That would take time. Randall continued, "We need to go to London next week so Lady Agnes Westerfield can interview you for her school."

"London!" Benjamin breathed. "I'm really going to London?"

Randall nodded. "Assuming that Lady Agnes accepts you, we'll have about a week to holiday in London. See the lions, visit Astley's circus, get new clothes made up. But there is one other task to accomplish." He glanced at Julia, who gave a small nod. "We have to introduce you to your grandfather, the Earl of Daventry."

Benjamin frowned. "An earl? Isn't that very grand?"

"Yes, almost as grand as a duke," Julia said with a hint of dryness.

"Will he want to know me since I'm a bastard?" Benjamin said, worried.

"I don't know," Randall admitted. "Daventry cares a great deal about family, and it has been a sorrow to him that he has no surviving children. I don't believe that Branford ever told him of your birth. Daventry is . . . not an easy man, but I'm sure that he would have provided for you if he'd known of your existence."

"Might it be better to write Daventry instead of taking Benjamin to meet him?" Julia bit her lip. "With Lady Daventry close to her lying in, Daventry will be distracted."

"I wondered about that, but I think it's best if they meet," Randall said. "When they do, Daventry will immediately know that Benjamin is his grandson."

Julia nodded, but still looked worried. So was Randall. But withholding knowledge of Branford's son would make Daventry even more furious when he finally found out. Better to make the introduction as soon as possible. And if Daventry rejected the boy, no matter. Benjamin had a home now.

Returning from her explorations, Miss Kitty entered the morning room, plumy tail waving. She made her way to Benjamin and draped herself over his feet.

"She's very well behaved," Julia observed.

Belligerent again, Benjamin said, "She always sleeps with me."

"I'm sure you both enjoy it," Randall said. "When I was serving in Portugal, I was adopted by a dog who slept with me every night. Santa Cruz was good company. He was also warm on cold nights."

Julia laughed. "I didn't know that. Why was the dog called Holy Cross, and what happened to him?"

"I considered him my cross to bear," Randall explained. "When I was wounded and sent home to England, Santa Cruz transferred his affections to an ensign in my regiment. I'm told that ensign and dog are flourishing."

Benjamin giggled, sounding like a child for the first time since they'd found him.

The Roscombe tomcat strolled into the room. He was smaller than Miss Kitty, but he made up for that in arrogance. Randall said, "This is Reggie T. Cat, who mostly lives in the kitchen. I hope that he and Miss Kitty can negotiate a truce."

Reggie spotted Miss Kitty. Looking joyful, he swaggered toward her. His dreams of dominance vanished when she couched down and glared at him, fur fluffing up so much that she looked like a small black-and-white sheep.

When she growled with chilling intensity, Reggie stopped dead in his tracks. Then he hunkered down in a pose that mirrored hers as they stared at each other.

Randall had no idea what silent messages were being passed, but the duel ended when Reggie warily touched his nose to Miss Kitty's. Then he ambled out of the room, tail high, looking as if he'd lost a fight and didn't want to admit it.

"Cat politics in action," Julia said with a laugh. "I hope that means they won't fight in the middle of the night."

Benjamin swallowed the last of his tea and

stood. "Can I go now? I want to take Miss Kitty to my room so she'll know where it is."

"Of course," Julia said.

He scooped up the cat and exited. When he was gone, Julia asked, "What do you think of our wild child?"

"He'll do," Randall said thoughtfully. "He's a tough little devil, but he doesn't seem to have Branford's craziness. I met Branford when he was even younger than Benjamin, and it was already obvious that something was wrong with him. Benjamin has rough edges. He's wary, and with reason, but he's not crazy. He's clever enough to appreciate how much his situation has improved, and he wants to preserve that. Given education and opportunities, I think he'll turn out well."

"More like you than your cousin, in other words," Julia said.

Is that how she saw him? The strain that had been between them had eased, Randall realized. "I suppose. I'm sure Lady Agnes will be willing to take him on. A few days here, and then we can take him to London to meet her."

Julia smiled. "She will turn him into a proper young gentleman in no time."

"Perhaps not quite a gentleman." He smiled back. "But close enough."

One of the housemaids who had young brothers volunteered to look after Benjamin, who was too

362

old for a nursery maid but needed instruction on how to live in a proper household. Julia wasn't surprised to learn that at Hill Farm, the boy had slept in the barn on a pile of hay with a blanket and Miss Kitty.

Benjamin had had a tiring day, so Julia sent him to bed immediately after dinner. He didn't even argue, which was most unlike a young boy and proved he was tired.

After dining, Julia and Randall spent a peaceful evening in the library. She read while he wrote several letters. He didn't make any foolish suggestions about her finding new lovers, which was a relief.

When the clock struck ten, she rose and covered a yawn. "I'm going to bed, but I'll check on Benjamin first. I hope he doesn't find a real bed too strange."

Randall grinned. "As long as he has his cat, I imagine he'll sleep well."

Benjamin had been given a room in the opposite wing from the master's rooms. Not wanting to wake him, Julia opened the door without knocking. The maid had left a night lamp burning so he wouldn't wake and be upset by strange surroundings.

Benjamin was a small lump in the bed. Miss Kitty lay on his other side, and she raised her head to stare at the intruder. Julia was about to withdraw when she heard a muffled sob.

Frowning, she crossed the room. Benjamin instantly pulled the covers over his head, but he couldn't stifle his sobs. She perched on the side of the bed and laid a hand on his shoulder. "What's wrong, Benjamin? Too many changes?" Change was upsetting, even good changes, as she could attest.

He pulled the covers down enough to reveal his tear-smudged face. "I . . . I was thinking of my mam," he said haltingly. "What she'd think to see me here."

"Your mother would be happy," Julia said softly. "She wanted the best for you."

"It was best when I was with *her*."

"I know." Julia sighed. "I lost my mother when I was about your age." She stroked his blanket-covered shoulder. "I missed her dreadfully. But I had other family to care for me, and now you do, too."

Benjamin began shaking with more sobs. He'd learned to be tough to survive at Hill Farm, but he was still a little boy. Julia bent over to kiss the top of his head, and he swarmed into her arms.

"My mam would always come to kiss me good night," he said thickly. "Then she died and left me alone."

"You aren't alone now, Benjamin." Julia hugged him close. Though he was no blood kin of hers, she was beginning to feel that he was. Not as a surrogate for the baby she'd lost, but for himself: a lost child struggling for survival. "I swear it."

His sobs faded as she stroked his head, and he drifted into sleep. Julia tucked him back under the covers under the cool green gaze of Miss Kitty, who hadn't moved during the drama. The cat was adapting to life in a manor house with more ease than her master.

Julia left the room quietly. She and Randall had done a good day's work when they brought Benjamin home. Even Randall thought so, despite his initial doubts.

Feeling optimistic, she headed to her bed.

# Chapter 34

A week at Roscombe transformed Benjamin Thomas into a fair approximation of a young gentleman. Julia was amused and touched at how carefully Ben observed her and Randall, copying their speech and manners, and he had plenty of opportunities since the three of them took all their meals together. He was amazingly quick. His country accent was disappearing fast, though it reappeared when he was excited.

The boy's mind was as hungry as his body. Julia tutored him in the afternoons, working on his reading and arithmetic and giving him a grounding in history and geography. Roscombe had a good library, and Benjamin was usually to be found there when he wasn't otherwise engaged.

In the mornings, Randall took the boy riding. He reported that Benjamin was a natural with horses and would make a first-class rider.

In return, Benjamin hero-worshipped Randall. Julia tucked the boy in every night. They talked about his day, she answered some of his endless questions, then kissed him good night. It had taken only three days for Benjamin to outgrow his earlier ambition to become a coachman. Now, he confided to Julia, he wanted to become an army officer. She thought that might be a good career for him. But he would have plenty of time to decide.

He hadn't even gone to school yet, and already she was missing him.

The day before they were to leave for London, Randall announced at breakfast, "Benjamin, you've worked hard and deserve a holiday. The village fair starts today and it's so close we can walk. Would you like to go this afternoon? We can make a family outing of it."

"Oh, yes, sir!" Benjamin beamed.

Julia was equally pleased at the idea of the three of them being a family. Would Benjamin help bind her and Randall together? If so, all the more reason to love the boy.

"I swear that lad has grown an inch in the last week," Julia said fondly as she watched

Benjamin laughing at a Punch and Judy show with a group of other children.

"At the least, he's put on some much needed weight," Randall agreed. "He's making up for the hungry times."

Thinking of Benjamin's appetite, she asked, "Is the food good at the Westerfield Academy?"

"Very. Lady Agnes knows that well-fed males of any age are less likely to cause trouble." Randall's voice lowered. "Here come more neighborhood gentry to be introduced. You're a source of great interest, milady."

"It's only natural. You're a large local landowner and a local hero as well. Of course people are happy that you're finally settling down at Roscombe." Julia smiled at the older couple that approached.

Wisely, the gentleman introduced himself and his wife as Sir Geoffrey and Lady Bridges, probably guessing that after so many years away, Randall might be unsure of names. But his mother's family had lived in Gloucestershire for generations, and he was seen as part of the community. Sir Geoffrey and his wife were very welcoming.

After a few minutes of chat, the Bridges moved on and Julia took Randall's arm again. It was a beautiful day for a fair, sunny and with the first snap of autumn in the air. A good day to celebrate the last week of progress.

Julia had begun to relax since Randall had

made no more cool comments about ending their marriage. Perhaps their silent, searing nights were changing his mind. She wanted to believe their relationship was special. If it wasn't—she'd rather not know.

During the next hours, Julia met a dizzying number of people. She and Randall performed the traditional fair activities of admiring livestock and jugglers while sampling food from vendors. Julia skipped the sausage on a stick since her stomach wasn't in the mood, but she enjoyed the fresh lemonade, apple tarts, and the toasted cheese on bread.

Benjamin came to find them every half hour or so, as if fearing they might have vanished. Once he'd reassured himself, he would bounce off to join the local boys again.

After one such flying visit, Randall observed, "He seems not to have been damaged by his years with Jeb Gault. Getting along well with other boys is a good omen for his going to school and for life in general."

Julia nodded. "His mother gets the credit, I think. She had him for the first nine years of his life, and that set him on the right path." She covered a yawn. "I'm tired. Meeting so many people, I suppose."

"Are you ready to go home?" Randall asked. "We've seen just about everything there is to see, and it will be dusk soon."

"I'd like that." She shaded her eyes. "Where did Benjamin go?"

"Over there by the game booths. It looks like he's trying his arm on throwing the balls." Randall took Julia's arm and they headed in the boy's direction. "He's old enough to stay on his own longer if he wishes. I'll give him another half crown if he wants to treat some of his new friends to cakes."

Benjamin was intent on his target and didn't see them approach the ball-throwing booth. Stuffed heads of Napoleon in three sizes sat on a ledge. With his first throw, he knocked the largest off the ledge. There was a smattering of applause.

He tossed the second ball a couple of times, getting the feel of it, then threw again. The middle-sized Napoleon went flying. "Well done, lad!" the proprietor of the booth called. "Do you think you can get the smallest Boney? He's a tricky one, he is."

Eyes narrowed, Benjamin tested the weight of the third ball, then wound up and hurled it across the booth. The ball smacked Napoleon right between the eyes. This time the applause was louder. If the proprietor was disappointed to have a winner, he concealed it well. "Your choice of a fairing from that shelf. Maybe a toy soldier?"

Benjamin looked longingly at the small soldiers, but shook his head. "One of those ribbons. The blue-green one."

"Aha, you have a lady to please!" The proprietor extracted the long blue-green ribbon from a bouquet of differently colored ribbons and presented it with a flourish.

Grinning, Benjamin turned away, then blinked in surprise when he saw Julia and Randall behind him. Randall said, "We're going to leave now, but you can stay until dark if you like."

"No, I'll go with you." Benjamin said quick goodbyes to the boys he'd met, then set off beside Randall.

"You've got a good arm," Randall said as they left the fairground and took the path that led through the woods to Roscombe. "Have you done any cricket bowling?"

"Sometimes we'd play in the village when I was little. Do they play cricket at the Westerfield Academy?" Benjamin asked hopefully.

"Indeed they do. There are other sports, too."

"I'll like that." Benjamin glanced up at Julia, his expression shy. "I got the ribbon for you. I thought the color would look nice in your hair."

Julia's heart melted when he offered her the cheap ribbon. "How lovely!" she exclaimed. She immediately tied it around a lock of her hair. "You have good taste. A duke's daughter who understands fashion picked the same color for the gown I wore to my first London ball."

Benjamin looked as if he would burst with pride. As he skipped ahead of them on the path,

Julia said softly, "He really is a fine lad. He fits in so well here."

"I wouldn't have believed Branford could have such a good son," Randall agreed. "I hope that Daventry appreciates Benjamin. And doesn't try to take him away."

"Could he do that legally?" Julia asked with quick concern.

"I'm not sure. He was never named legal guardian. Since I'm also a blood relation, I would have some legal standing if there's a dispute." Randall's voice turned dry. "Daventry will probably be so excited about his new heir that he won't have a lot of interest in a bastard grandson."

"We can only hope." Julia wondered again if it would be best not to tell Daventry of Benjamin's existence. But he was bound to find out eventually. Like Randall, she hoped that the earl would be so absorbed by the birth of a new son that he would acknowledge his grandson, but not want to take possession of him.

Glancing up at Randall, she saw that his expression was very alert and he was scanning the woods on both sides. "Is something wrong?" she asked.

He gave her a quick smile. "As long as I live, I'll probably think of places like this as ambush territory. The perils of a military career."

She looked up at the trees, with beams of late

afternoon sunshine shafting through the branches. Birds trilled their songs and a squirrel scolded from a branch.

It was an immensely peaceful scene, but Randall's words reminded her of the carriage incident in London. Might danger be lurking among the bushes? The afternoon looked a little less peaceful.

She told herself not to be foolish, but couldn't help studying the windowless old hut by the path ahead. Some kind of farm storage structure, but as Benjamin scampered past it, Julia realized that the small building could provide cover for villains.

"Having an imagination is a nuisance," she said wryly as they came alongside the hut. "Now that you've made me aware of the possibilities, I can see danger everywhere . . ."

The hut exploded.

# Chapter 35

Ears ringing from the blast, Julia went flying through the air as Randall caught her in a rolling dive that carried them to the far side of the path, away from the explosion. Debris rained down around them, but she was safe under her husband's shielding body. Except for his blood, which was pouring onto her face. She gasped, "Alex?"

In the sudden silence that followed the explosion, Benjamin gave a wordless scream. She heard his feet pounding back along the path toward them as she dragged herself out from under her husband's still body.

Randall rolled limply onto his back, eyes closed and blood pouring from a long, jagged laceration on the left side of his head. Blood was so much more shocking against blond hair than dark, she thought dizzily. But he wouldn't bleed like that if he were dead.

Reminding herself that head wounds bled like the very devil, Julia dug a folded handkerchief from her reticule. Then, hands shaking, she yanked the scarf off her bonnet and used it as a bandage to secure the handkerchief pad over the bleeding wound. As Benjamin dropped to his knees beside her, she applied pressure on the pad over the wound, hoping to stop the bleeding.

"Lady Julia, what happened?" Benjamin gasped, his voice frantic. "Is Major Randall dead?"

Randall's eyes flickered open. "I'm well . . . enough. Not dying."

"But you will be." Grinning with satisfaction, Joseph Crockett emerged from the woods, a double-barreled shotgun in his hands. "You're quick, Randall. If you hadn't grabbed your bitch wife and jumped away from the explosion, you'd already be food for buzzards. Now you get to see death coming."

As he spoke, a similarly armed subordinate stepped from the woods at the left, his face like granite. Julia recognized the burly man as Crockett's most frightening associate when they'd kidnapped her.

Looking at Crockett's mad, hating eyes, she wondered how she could ever have believed he would be satisfied with anything less than her death. Shaking and dizzy, she stumbled to her feet, knowing there was only a faint chance she could save Randall and Benjamin, but she must try. "Shoot me and be done with it, Crockett. But leave my husband and the boy alone. They've done you no harm."

"Wrong." Crockett's eyes were hard as agate. "Your precious major killed one of my men and has caused endless irritation. You'd be long since dead if not for him." He gestured at Randall with his shotgun. "And if I leave him alive, he'll come after me."

"You're absolutely right," Randall said in a harsh whisper. Sprawled on his back and stained with blood, he already looked more dead than alive, but his gaze was icy as he watched Crockett. "But you don't want to kill the boy."

"Is he your bastard, Randall?" Crockett's eyes flicked to Benjamin, who glared back with feral intensity. "I'll enjoy wiping out your bloodline. O' course, maybe you've scattered other bastards around."

He transferred his gaze to Julia. "You'll die last, your precious ladyship, since you're helpless. I look forward to your screaming as you watch your men die."

"Benjamin isn't my bastard, Crockett," Randall said with a twisted smile. "He's Branford's. Would you kill Branford's only child?"

Crockett jerked in shock. "Branford left a son? He never told me!" His voracious gaze latched onto Benjamin's face. "My God," he breathed. "You're telling me the truth. Was your mother that blowsy barmaid? Come here, boy. You I'll keep. I'll raise you like my own."

"No!" Benjamin spat at Crockett, his eyes bright with tears.

"Do what he says, Benjamin." Randall heaved himself up into a sitting position. Taking Benjamin's hand, he said quietly, "If you want to be a soldier, you must learn to cut your losses. Crockett and his man are armed and we aren't, so Julia and I don't have a chance. But we'll die happier if we know you're safe. Do you understand what I'm saying? So go to Crockett. He'll be better to you than Jeb Gault was."

Benjamin blinked back his tears and nodded. Head down and hands shoved in his pockets, he moved reluctantly to Crockett's side.

Randall looked up at Crockett. "You were a soldier, weren't you?"

"Damned right. I was a sergeant, and I always hated bloody officers like you!" Crockett raised the shotgun to firing position.

Randall's voice wavered. "As one soldier to another, will you let me die on my feet rather than being shot like a dog?"

Crockett hesitated, then jerked a nod. "If you can stand, I'll shoot you then. But be quick about it. The explosion will draw people here any minute now."

Randall raised his hand to Julia and she helped haul him to his feet. His grip was surprisingly strong, and there had been something wrong with his speech to Benjamin. Would Randall ever admit defeat like that?

She was trying to puzzle out that sense of wrongness when violence erupted again. As Crockett aimed at Randall, Benjamin grabbed the barrel of the shotgun and dragged it down with one hand. His other hand slashed across Crockett's throat.

Blood spurted violently in all directions, including over Benjamin. Crockett made a horrible strangled sound, his expression stunned. Then he collapsed backward.

At the same instant that Benjamin attacked Crockett, Randall shoved Julia so that she once again tumbled to the ground. In one continuous flow of movement, he then hurled himself at Crockett's subordinate. The man's shotgun blasted as he fell backward, Randall on top as they crashed to the ground.

Shredded leaves exploded over the path as the pellets ripped into the tree, and the acrid stink of black powder filled the air. A moment later, Julia heard a horrible snapping sound and saw that the man's neck was turned at a lethal angle.

Julia threw up, sickened by so much violence. But there was no time to indulge her queasy stomach. She scrambled to her feet. "Benjamin, are you all right?"

He was shaking and white-faced as he stared at the man he'd killed, then at the blood dripping from his small knife. He made a strangled sound and threw the knife away before hurling himself against Julia. As she wrapped her arms around him, she cried urgently, "Alex, did the shotgun miss you?"

"Yes. Barely." Randall staggered to his feet, bracing one hand against a tree trunk when he wavered. "Crockett was right that people will be drawn by the noise any moment. Benjamin, you were superb, but let everyone think that I did all the killing."

Benjamin raised the face that had been buried against Julia's shoulder. "Why?"

"The authorities expect soldiers to kill. They get very worried when children do, even if it's justified." Weaving, Randall stumbled forward and half-fell into an embrace with Julia and

Benjamin. "Better that . . . they not wonder about you."

Especially since the boy was an orphan and illegitimate. Julia's blood chilled as she thought what might happen to Benjamin if the authorities decided he needed to be punished. Thinking that when this was over she would be sick again, she asked, "You passed Benjamin your boot knife when you took his hand?"

Randall nodded. "He was clever enough to understand that we needed to work together. You'll make a brilliant officer someday, Benjamin."

The boy closed his eyes and hugged them both more tightly. Randall whispered into Julia's ear, "He's like me, Julia, not Branford. He killed because he had to."

She knew her husband was right. In a distant corner of her mind, she was impressed at how perfectly Randall and Benjamin had worked together to stave off disaster. Almost like father and son.

But at the moment, Julia would like nothing better than to retreat to a convent full of gentle, loving women who wouldn't raise a hand to a mosquito.

Julia managed to keep from falling apart until everything essential had been taken care of. Men came pounding in from the fair before the black powder smoke had cleared. With the three of them battered and covered with blood, Sir Geoffrey, who was the local magistrate, accepted Randall's version of events without question.

Julia was quietly impressed at how Randall managed to explain what had happened, and imply that he'd killed both men without actually lying. He would have made a fine lawyer. Both Julia and Benjamin were largely silent. She was more than willing to take the role of frail, terrified female, and Benjamin was skilled in not talking.

It was almost dark by the time official statements had been made. After they returned to Roscombe Manor, Julia enlisted Gordon to bathe Benjamin. By the time the boy emerged from his bath, the local surgeon had arrived to bandage Randall's head.

Benjamin hardly protested when she ordered him to bed. When she came to tuck him in, he had one arm around Miss Kitty and looked tired enough to sleep through until the next morning. Julia smoothed back his brown hair. "It was quite a day, wasn't it? We'll postpone our trip to London by a day. We all need to recover."

"You don't want to get rid of me?" Benjamin asked in a thin voice. "I saw your face when I killed that man."

The boy noticed too much. She supposed it had been necessary for his survival. "I was upset," she admitted. "My job has always been to fight death. But I'd rather see Crockett and his man die than to have him kill you and me and Major Randall. You were very clever and very brave. Despite my husband's skill at fighting, I don't think he could have saved us without you doing what you did."

Benjamin reached up and patted the ribbon he'd given her, which was still tied in her hair. "That man Crockett deserved to die. I'm glad I killed him before he could hurt you or the major."

It was a chilling statement from a boy so young, but entirely, dreadfully understandable. Julia just hoped Randall was right that Benjamin wasn't like his father.

After kissing Benjamin good night, she went in search of the surgeon, who had finished examining Randall and bandaging his head properly. The injury was declared not life-threatening, and the surgeon gave Julia careful instructions on wound treatment. She didn't bother to tell him that she probably had experience equal to his.

Julia ushered the surgeon out and returned to their shared bedroom. She didn't want to disturb Randall if he was sleeping, but his eyes opened when she entered the room and turned down the lamp. She asked, "You really do need your own private surgeon. How are you feeling?"

"A headache and many fine bruises where bits

of timber landed on me, but generally I feel well," he said sleepily. "How about you? Being knocked to the ground twice surely left you with bruises, too."

"A few. Very minor considering what might have happened." She perched on the edge of the bed. "I should have known Crockett wouldn't quit until I was dead. Not realizing that might have cost you and Benjamin your lives."

"But didn't. Don't blame yourself. Even if we were sure that Crockett was behind that carriage accident in London, what could we have done about him until he showed himself?" Randall said reasonably. "Finding out where I live would have been easy. Then it was just a matter of waiting until we were vulnerable. I imagine he saw us walk to the fair and made his preparations to kill us when we returned home. Foolish of him to explode the hut, but perhaps he wanted our deaths to look accidental."

Her brows arched. "Do huts explode on their own?"

"Sometimes, especially if grain has been stored in a closed building." He covered a yawn. "It's rare, though. Conditions have to be just right. Luckily, my instincts said something was wrong and I reacted in time to get us out of the way of the explosion. How is Benjamin?"

"Shaken but handling his first killing better than I would."

"Benjamin really does have the makings of a first-class officer. The army is a good place for a young male with sharp edges. It worked for me." Randall took her hand and pulled her down beside him. His voice softened. "Relax, milady. You're safe now."

Weary to the bone, she rested her head on his shoulder and closed her eyes. Now that she was safe, would he think that she no longer needed his protection so he could leave at the end of the year?

Tonight, she was too tired to think about it.

# Chapter 36

As always, Lady Agnes Westerfield was an island of unflappable calm. Randall and Julia took Benjamin to meet her at Rockton House, the London home of her brother, the Duke of Rockton. Benjamin was dressed with painful neatness, anxious despite Randall's assurances that Lady Agnes would surely accept him to her school. He wanted so much to be like other boys.

Lady Agnes was expecting them, so the butler escorted them to the lavishly furnished morning room. Setting her newspaper aside, she rose. In her fashionable blue morning gown, she was more regal than any member of the royal family, but her expression was welcoming. "Good day, Lady Julia, Randall." Her gaze went to

Benjamin. "You, I presume, are Master Benjamin Thomas, Major Randall's cousin?"

He nodded. "Yes, Lady Agnes." His country accent was strong today.

Randall asked, "Should we leave so you can interview Benjamin privately?"

"That shouldn't be necessary. Please, take a seat." She settled back in her chair. "I'm returning to Kent in the morning, so it's good you could come today. Benjamin, why do you wish to attend the Westerfield Academy?"

He looked startled at her directness. "Uh . . . because Major Randall went there? And because he thought it would be a good school for me."

Lady Agnes nodded. "Randall will have told you the Westerfield Academy is unusual because all of the students have an odd kick in their gallop. What is yours?"

Benjamin looked uncertain again. "M-my mam was a barmaid, and I'm a bastard," he stammered. "I was born and raised in a posting house until she died and I was given to a farmer as slave labor. That's odd."

"You would not be the first illegitimate child to attend the Westerfield Academy, and other students have had backgrounds as unusual as yours," the headmistress remarked with a faint smile. "Major Randall's note yesterday said that you'd had basic schooling in reading, writing, and numbers, and that you love to read."

"Yes, but I don't know any Latin or Greek," he confessed. "Gentlemen are supposed to know Latin and Greek."

"One can be a gentleman without, but they are good subjects to know. With tutoring, you can catch up with those boys who've had more traditional educations." Lady Agnes regarded him thoughtfully. "I always ask two questions of prospective students. What at school would make you happy? And what would you hate most?"

"I have a cat," Benjamin said hesitantly. "Could I bring Miss Kitty to school with me? She's no trouble!"

"Other students have pets. Five dogs, three cats, a parrot, and two ferrets at the moment, I believe," Lady Agnes replied. "There's room for another cat if she's not a troublemaker and you take care of her, so that's doable. But what would you hate?"

Benjamin's lips thinned. "Being beaten for no good reason!"

"I assure you that will not happen." Lady Agnes gave a short, sharp nod. "I think you'll do very well at the Westerfield Academy, Benjamin. Classes will start a week Monday. Most boys will be arriving the Friday before to settle in before they start to work. Randall will know what you need"—she lifted a folder from the side table and offered it to Benjamin—"but here is general information on the school."

Benjamin stared at the folder, not taking it. "There's something else, Lady Agnes," he blurted out. "I killed a man three days ago."

For a moment there was absolute stillness in the morning room. Randall and Julia stopped breathing, but Lady Agnes asked calmly, "Why did you do that?"

"He was trying to kill Major Randall and Lady Julia."

"In that case, you did the right thing." Lady Agnes looked over at Randall, silently asking for information.

"A friend of Julia's first husband has made several attempts to kill her," Randall said tersely. "Three days ago, he and an associate ambushed us while we were walking home from the Roscombe fair, but Benjamin and I stopped them. The official story is that I killed both attackers, since I was unlikely to suffer any consequences for doing that. But Benjamin was very brave and very clever. I'm proud of him."

"It seemed better for Benjamin not to be seen as a murderer," Julia agreed. "Why did you tell Lady Agnes now, Benjamin?"

He bit his lip. "I thought she should know before accepting me as a student."

"That's very honorable of you, Benjamin," Lady Agnes said gravely. "I would suggest that you not tell anyone else for the reasons the Randalls have mentioned, but I do appreciate your honesty with me." Once more she offered the folder of school information. "Just remember that killing is not allowed at the Westerfield Academy. Do you have any other questions?"

"No, ma'am!" Benjamin took the folder, looking much more relaxed.

"Then I shall see you in Kent." She rose gracefully. "Much needs to be done before I leave London."

"Thank you for finding time to interview Benjamin," Julia said. As they left, she said to Randall, "Is there another headmistress in England who would accept such news so calmly?"

He grinned. "I doubt it. That's why Lady Agnes's school is unique, and a perfect place for Benjamin.

As they settled into their Ashton carriage, Julia said, "Well done, Benjamin. I almost fainted when you told Lady Agnes about Crockett, but your instincts were right. Honesty is preferable. Especially when one gets away with it."

"One of Lady Agnes's rules, which you'll probably find in that folder, Benjamin, is to always tell her the truth, no matter how appalling." Randall studied his young cousin, amazed at the boy's inherent integrity. Did it come from his mother? Or was it some special gift that was Benjamin's alone? "Are you pleased to be accepted?"

"I would rather be at Roscombe, but I need to go to school if I want to become a gentleman," Benjamin said pragmatically as he claimed the seat opposite Randall and Julia. "I though Lady Agnes was scary at first, but she has sparkly eyes and she says I can keep Miss Kitty. And she's had other bastards as students!"

"Indeed she has," Randall said, thinking of Mackenzie. "Those who have studied at the academy and gone on have done well."

Julia's brows furrowed. "I want to give some advice, Benjamin, but I'm not quite sure how to say it. Basically, it's that you should be true to what you are, but it's not necessary to make a point of tossing everything into the middle of the drawing room."

"I'm not sure I can say it better, but you're right," Randall said slowly. "At the Westerfield Academy, you will be judged primarily on what you do, not on your background. Are you a good friend, a good student, a good athlete? Those things are what are important to your class-mates."

Benjamin looked thoughtful. "I think I under-stand. But what shall I say when asked about my family?"

"You can say that your guardian is Major Randall of Roscombe Manor. That's not grand, but it's respectable," Randall said. "Or you can say that you're a connection of Lord Daventry. But that might invite more questions than you want."

"What if people think I'm your bastard?" Benjamin asked.

"I would be honored if they think that," Randall said quietly. "Would you mind? We are family, after all. The exact relationship is merely a detail."

"Oh, no, sir!" Benjamin looked ready to melt with happiness. "I won't mind."

Julia squeezed Randall's hand and smiled at him with such warmth that he started calculating how long it would take them to get back to Ashton House. Because of their assorted bruises, they had merely slept together the three previous nights. Now he needed to be skin to skin, as close as two people could be.

He was wondering if Julia might be persuaded up to their rooms for a romantic interval before luncheon when she said suddenly, "Daventry House is on this street, isn't it? Let's stop and see if Daventry is available to meet Benjamin."

"Now?" Benjamin said uncertainly.

Randall frowned, thinking he didn't want to ruin what so far had been a good day. Correctly interpreting his expression, Julia said, "Perhaps the earl won't be in. But if he is, we can get this meeting over with before we have time to worry more."

"I suppose you're right," Randall said without enthusiasm.

"I hope so." Julia gazed out the window again, her brows drawn together. "I have a strong feeling that we should call now."

Randall signaled the coach to stop. He had his battlefield intuition, and Julia had human intuition. She also had a point about getting this over with.

Anticipating the worst, he said to Benjamin, "It will be good if Daventry acknowledges you as his grandson, but remember that you will be no worse off if he doesn't."

Benjamin's nose wrinkled. "Your old earl can't be worse than Jeb Gault."

Which put the situation in perspective.

Julia's nerves were strung to jangling point as Randall knocked on the door of Daventry House. She'd felt this way before, usually when one of her patients was about to give birth. Her teacher, Mrs. Bancroft, had experienced the same with her patients. Though Lady Daventry wasn't Julia's patient, they had discussed the older woman's pregnancy. If the baby was coming early . . .

Her thoughts were interrupted when an agitated footman flung open the door. "Thank God . . . !" His expression changed when he saw who was on the doorstep. "I thought you would be Sir Richard Croft. Go away, the household is not receiving."

Lady Daventry's accoucheur! Julia was wondering if she should force her way in when a scream echoed eerily through the house. The young footman gasped and looked like he wanted to bolt.

"Lady Daventry is giving birth?" Julia asked, her voice sharp.

"Yes, and it's bloody awful! I think she's dying." The footman cringed at another cry. "Lord Daventry has gone to find Sir Richard Croft."

"I'm a midwife and have discussed Lady Daventry's pregnancy with her." Julia marched into the house as if she had every right to be there.

"But . . . but . . ." the footman sputtered, uncertain what to do.

Randall put a hand on Benjamin's back and they came in behind her. "Give thanks that an experienced midwife has arrived," Randall said tartly. "I assume Lady Daventry is in the countess's rooms?"

"Yes, but . . ."

Ignoring the servant's protests, Randall said, "I know the way, Julia."

She glanced back at Benjamin. "You might want to stay down here."

"I'm coming, too." Jaw set, Benjamin followed her and Randall up the stairs.

Randall's escort wasn't needed. It was all too easy to follow Lady Daventry's cries of pain. Julia turned left at the top of the stairs and moved down the corridor at a near run. Randall opened the door at the end and Julia swept inside.

In the middle of her massive canopy bed, Lady Daventry thrashed in agony across blood-stained sheets. A white-faced maid clutched helplessly at the countess's hand.

"Stay out of my way," Julia ordered. "Alex, I'll tell you if I need any help. Benjamin, go to the footman and get a bottle of brandy and a pile of clean towels."

As they obeyed, Julia approached the bed. The ghastly stains were more pink than red, indicating that the countess's water had broken and there was some bleeding. It was enough to make an unholy mess, but Julia guessed that the situation looked worse than it was. "Lady Daventry, it's Julia," she said in her most soothing voice. "Everything will be all right."

"Thank God you've come!" Contraction over, Louisa grabbed Julia's hand. Her sweaty face was twisted with pain. "Please, help me! Something is different this time." She was not a countess now, but a desperate, terrified woman. "Am I going to die?"

"You are not going to die," Julia said firmly. There was a bowl of water and a cloth beside the table, so Julia moistened the cloth and wiped perspiration from Louisa's face. "I'm a mid-wife," she told the maid. "And you are . . . ?"

The maid was about the same age as the countess. Now that someone knowledgeable had arrived, she tried to pull herself together. "I'm Hazel, her ladyship's maid, but I don't know what to do. The doctor was always here in plenty of time for her other babies."

Julia asked, "How long has her ladyship been in labor?"

"I . . . I'm not sure, ma'am. Maybe an hour?" the maid said uncertainly. "Her water broke and the contractions and bleeding came very fast. Today is the servants' half day off, so there's hardly anyone in the house. His Lordship went for help himself." As Lady Daventry moaned with another contraction, Hazel said worriedly, "She's been thrashing something terrible. It's all I've been able to do to keep her still."

"A woman giving birth isn't supposed to be still," Julia said. "Louisa, were your other labors quick?"

"Yes." The countess's gaze was locked on Julia, but she looked a little less terrified. "My youngest son was born after only a couple of hours."

"How fortunate you are," Julia said admiringly. "Let me wash my hands here in this basin, and then I'll examine you. I always wash thoroughly when I'm delivering a baby. The midwife who trained me said it can't hurt and it might well help since cleanliness is next to godliness. She was right, too. Mrs. Bancroft almost never lost a baby or a mother."

Julia continued talking as she washed up, surrounding the countess with warm, calming words to drive away the fear. Another thing Mrs. Bancroft had taught was that a woman who didn't think she was going to die was more likely to survive.

When her hands were clean, she said, "I'll examine you now, Louisa. It's undignified, but you've had three strong, healthy babies before, so you know what birthing is like."

"Yes . . . aahhhh!" Louisa convulsed in another contraction, her hand locking onto Hazel's until the knuckles whitened.

"Soon this will be over," Julia said soothingly. "Very soon. Remember that your body knows how to have babies and you have three fine strapping boys to prove it. Since this baby is coming a few weeks early, he'll be smaller and that's easier for you."

The world narrowed down to Louisa and the blood-stained bed as Julia felt her patient's distended belly with experienced hands. Her brows drew together when she felt the hard ball of the head at the top rather than down near the birth channel.

Seeing her expression, the countess asked fearfully, "Is . . . is the baby dead?"

Julia felt an impact against her left palm. "No, he

just kicked me, and he seems very vigorous. But the baby is turned around so his feet will come out first. That's why you felt something different."

Louisa fought for a breath. "A breech baby? That's bad, isn't it?"

"Not necessarily. As I said, the body knows what to do. An uncomplicated breech birth is no more dangerous that a regular one."

"I can't stand lying down like this," Louisa said fretfully. "I have to sit up."

"Then do so," Julia said encouragingly. She took Louisa's other hand. "As I said, a woman's body knows what it's doing. Hazel, help her ladyship sit up. We're going to let gravity help this baby be born."

# Chapter 37

Randall stayed by the door, glad that the bedchamber was large enough that he didn't have a clear view of the bed. He'd experienced more than his share of battlefields and the crude surgery that followed, but he'd never seen a more harrowing sight than Julia's fearless, utterly calm battle to save Lady Daventry and her baby.

Saving Daventry's heir. The situation was fraught with irony, but he would contemplate that later. For now he concentrated on maintaining a stoic face and being ready if Julia needed him.

Benjamin returned with the towels and a full bottle of brandy. Randall opened the bottle and set it and the towels on a table beside Julia. He was tempted to take a swig, but he guessed she meant to use the brandy to reduce the chance of infection, as when she'd operated on him. She barely noticed him as she spoke soothing words to the countess. Randall kept his eyes averted, feeling it was wrong to violate Lady Daventry's privacy.

He retreated to his position by the door. Benjamin was white-faced but calm. He must have seen a lot of life in a posting inn, and his mother had died in childbirth. He was a tough little fellow. But both of them flinched whenever Lady Daventry cried out.

"Are you sure you wouldn't rather be somewhere else? A birthing room is no place for men," Randall said quietly. "The carriage can take you back to Ashton House."

Benjamin shook his head stubbornly. "I want to stay with you."

Randall nodded and draped an arm around the boy's shoulders. Though this might be no place for males, he was selfishly glad for Benjamin's company. The large posts of the bed blocked much of the scene, but Lady Daventry seemed to be kneeling, supported by Julia and the maid.

The door downstairs opened again and footsteps pounded up the stairs. Had the society accoucheur finally arrived?

Lord Daventry burst into the bedroom, his face haggard. "Hold on, Louisa, the physician will be here soon!"

Then he saw Julia by the bed and stopped dead in his tracks. *"You!"* he said venomously. "Get away from my wife, you murderous bitch!"

The countess screamed with blood-chilling force. Raging, Daventry started across the bedroom.

Realizing why Julia had asked him to stay and be ready to help, Randall caught his uncle's arm in a steely grip. "Stop right here!"

Daventry's head swiveled around and he gasped in shock to see his nephew. "I should have known you'd be here, too," he snarled. "You've come to see that my heir dies, you and your devil-spawn wife! Well, you won't succeed, damn you!" He tried to jerk his arm free.

Randall's grip held firm. "Show some sense!" he snapped. "Julia isn't the midwife you would have chosen, but by a miracle, she's here. You should go down on your knees and give thanks that we decided to call. If your wife and son survive, it will be because of her."

Raging, Daventry swung his free had in a savage strike at Randall's face. Randall caught the other man's wrist and twisted it to the point of excruciating pain. "If you want to help your wife, behave like a man, not a savage. And if you go *near* Julia, I will break your arm."

Shaking with fury, the earl spat, "You have no right to keep me from my wife!"

Before Randall could respond, a cry sounded from the bed. This time it wasn't a scream of agony from the countess, but the thin wail of a newborn infant. Daventry turned his attention to the bed. "Louisa?"

Randall released his uncle and followed the man across the room, ready to stop him if he threatened Julia. They reached the bedside together as Julia crooned, "Splendidly done, Louisa! The worst is over and your pains have been rewarded."

As the maid helped the countess lie down, Julia patted the baby dry with a clean towel. The infant was bloody and rather small, but full of vigor and with an impressive set of lungs.

"My son? My son is healthy?" Daventry croaked.

"Congratulations, Lord Daventry." Julia gave him a cool glance as she laid the infant in the crook of his wife's left arm. "You have a beautiful, healthy daughter." To Louisa, she said, "She needs your warmth and to hear your heartbeat, so hold her close." The countess's face was pale as snow, but she was radiant as she looked at her child.

Daventry gasped, his gaze riveted on the infant, who was unquestionably female. "A daughter?"

Randall caught his breath, stunned. He'd been convinced by Daventry's certainty that this would be a boy. The earl's breeding record had supported that, but as always, God got the last word. Once more, Randall was Daventry's heir.

The countess glared at her husband defiantly, her arm tightening around her baby. "I know you wanted a son, but I have always yearned for a daughter. I will name her Sophia. If you don't want us, I'll take Sophia away to some place where you won't have to see either of us ever again." It was a clear threat.

Face working, Daventry reached out a shaking hand and touched the tiny toes on one perfect little foot. Sophia squeaked and pulled her foot away. There was awe on the earl's face as he looked at his new child. "A daughter for Daventry," he murmured. "It never occurred to me that I would have a daughter."

"In the nature of things, girls happen," Julia said dryly. "You said once that you'd only bred sons, Lord Daventry, and perhaps that was the problem. I've known women who have seen all their male babies miscarry or die young, while the females thrived. Some weakness in the male seed, I think. Sophia might not be able to inherit your title, but your bloodline will survive."

Daventry brushed his wife's hair with gossamer lightness, as if afraid she'd break. "Will Louisa be all right? She's lost so much blood."

"The countess will be very weak a while, but she should be fine." Julia turned to the basin to wash the blood from her hands. After her hands were clean and dry, she began rubbing the countess's belly with gentle firmness. "Hazel, watch what I'm doing so you can do this. Rubbing helps the womb contract. That will reduce the chance of any bleeding. You'll be able to feel the difference."

"Yes, ma'am," the maid said respectfully. "Anything you want me to do."

"You will visit us, won't you?" Lady Daventry asked hopefully. "My husband won't try to stop you. Will you, darling?" There was a definite edge to her final words.

Sounding as if he'd rather have all his teeth yanked from his jaw than have to thank Julia for anything, Daventry said reluctantly. "No, I won't. I suppose I must be grateful to you, Lady Julia."

Benjamin pressed close to Randall's side, his eyes huge and interested. Randall was bemused to think that tiny Sophia was his aunt.

Reminded of why he and Julia were here in the first place, Randall said, "Your bloodline will have more than one stream to carry on, Daventry. Julia and I called today to introduce you to your grandson, Benjamin Thomas. Branford's son, born a few months before Branford's death."

Daventry hadn't noticed Benjamin, but now his gaze dropped to the boy. "You want to foist this boy on me by claiming he's my grandson?" he growled.

His uncle's continual suspicion and anger were damned tiresome. Randall said coolly, "There is no foisting involved. Benjamin is my foster son and his home is Roscombe Manor. He'll start school at the Westerfield Academy in a week. He doesn't need you, but Julia and I felt that you have a right to know your grandson."

"He looks like Branford," the countess said drowsily. "But nicer. Hello, Benjamin. I'm your stepgrandmother. I have a son not much older than you."

For a long moment, Daventry studied Benjamin. His initial doubtful expression changed to intense scrutiny, then acceptance. "You *do* look like Branford. Just like when he was a boy." The earl looked like a boxer who had received one punch too many to his head. He shook his head and managed a crooked smile. "I have unexpectedly acquired a daughter and a grandson on the same day."

"My mother was a barmaid, but she was more of a lady than you are a gentleman." Benjamin scowled at the earl. "I don't know if I want you for a grandfather. You're mean and you yell at everyone."

Daventry's surprise was so great that it took all of Randall's control not to laugh out loud. The earl had met his match.

"Yes, I do yell a lot, and sometimes I've been mean," Daventry said seriously. "But since I seem to be your grandfather, we should get to know each other."

"It's time everyone left," Julia said firmly. "Lady Daventry needs her rest."

The door opened and a fashionably dressed man with a black bag swept in. "I came as quickly as I could, Lord Daventry," he said, concerned. "How is the countess?"

"The countess and her daughter are doing very well, Sir Richard." Louisa covered her yawn. "Courtesy of my friend Julia, who is a midwife."

Sir Richard Croft's nostrils flared as if he'd smelled something nasty. "A midwife delivered your child? You are fortunate to have had a good outcome." He stared suspiciously at Julia. "Who *is* this woman?"

" 'This woman' is Lady Julia Randall, trained midwife and daughter of the Duke of Castleton," Randall said, guessing that the society accoucheur was a snob.

Julia recognized that, too. A wicked glint in her eyes, she said to Lady Daventry, "Rather than hire a wet nurse, Louisa, I suggest you nurse Sophia yourself. It's better for the baby and better for you."

"Very well, if you say so," Lady Daventry said obediently.

Sir Richard looked horrified. "Ladies do not nurse their own children."

"Perhaps not," Julia said. "But mothers do." She bent and kissed the countess's cheek. "Sleep well, Louisa. You've done a fine day's work."

She straightened and swayed a little. Guessing that she was exhausted, Randall put his arm around her. "I'll take my wife home now."

She leaned against him, looking gray. Under her breath, she said, "A good thing I haven't eaten in hours."

If she felt unwell, the sooner he got her home, the better. She would hate vomiting in this company. He nodded to the group. "Congratulations on your new daughter, Lady Daventry. Rest well. Come along, Benjamin."

He and Julia and Benjamin were halfway to the door when Daventry said, "Wait. I'd like my . . . my grandson to stay this afternoon so we can get better acquainted." When Randall hesitated, the earl said, "I'll send him home before dinner."

"Benjamin, are you willing?" Randall asked.

The boy shrugged. "I suppose." But the spark in his eyes suggested he was pleased by his grandfather's interest.

"Very well. We'll see you at dinner." Randall escorted Julia downstairs and out of the house. The street was quiet enough that the Ashton carriage had been able to wait at the curb. How long had they been in the house? Less than two hours, he calculated. Once they were inside and heading back to Ashton House, he asked, "Feeling better?"

She gave him a crooked smile. "I just needed fresh air."

"How serious was Lady Daventry's condition?" he asked. "To an inexpert eye, the situation looked dire."

"Since I was there, all went smoothly," Julia replied. "She was afraid because of her age, and fear is dangerous. Also . . ." she hesitated.

"Also what?" he prompted.

"It may be unfair to Sir Richard to say this, but if he'd been in attendance, matters might not have turned out as well," she said reluctantly. "Males often prefer action to allowing nature a chance to do her job. Tugging at a breech baby can cause serious problems."

Under her measured words, he sensed that the delivery could have turned fatal very easily. "Lady Daventry is very lucky to have you as a friend."

"I was just doing what I was trained for. I hope Louisa does nurse the baby. It really is better for both of them." Wearily she rested her head on his shoulder. "I'm glad Benjamin was accepted by Daventry. He needs all the family and acceptance he can get."

"Doesn't everyone?" Randall said wryly. "Since Ash and Mariah aren't in London, let's enjoy a nice quiet afternoon together in our rooms. You'd like a bath, I'm sure, and I'll order up a luncheon."

Julia smiled. "Sounds lovely."

But the day was far from over. As he put his arm around her, he knew that the marital equation between him and Julia had changed.

But he wasn't sure just how.

# Chapter 38

Julia's bloodstained gown drew exclamation of shock when she and Randall entered Ashton House. While he ordered bath water and food to be delivered to their rooms, she glanced tiredly at the silver salver that held their mail.

Beside the letters was a small package from Mr. Rose, the goldsmith. Guessing that it had been hand-delivered, she opened the package. Inside was a velvet box containing the ring she'd commissioned for Randall.

She admired the twisting Celtic patterns, thinking that the ring was a good symbol for the complicated threads of their marriage. She closed the box and tucked it into her reticule, then took Randall's arm and headed up the stairs.

The hot water arrived in their rooms just after they did. Julia loved the efficiency of Ashton House.

When the servants who'd brought the hot water were gone, Randall moved behind her to unfasten the ties of her gown. "Try not to fall asleep in the hip bath."

"No promises." Even though Elsa was turning into a good maid, Julia liked the intimacy of Randall's fingers brushing her nape and lower back. "Birthing babies is tiring work." And never had it been so tiring as today. Julia must be out of practice.

She moved behind the screen that concealed the gently steaming hip bath. Lady Kiri had created a special bath oil scented with the perfume she'd created for Julia, so Julia poured a few drops into the water. Every time she used the fragrance, she discovered new layers of complexity.

With a happy sigh, she pinned up her hair, then stepped into the bath, enjoying the exquisite welcome of the hot water as she sank down. The tub was large enough for her to immerse herself up to her chin.

Randall stepped around the screen. "Ash's admirable cook heard that you just delivered Lady Daventry's daughter, so she sent up a lovely concoction of chilled champagne and orange juice. I thought you'd like some." He offered her a tall goblet of frothy orange drink. "To Lady Sophia. May she grow up with health and happiness."

"To Sophia." Julia accepted the goblet and sipped the tart sweetness. "Mmm . . . sensual pleasure doesn't get better than this."

He grinned wickedly. "Never?"

"Well, hardly ever." Julia studied her husband

with sultry pleasure. He'd taken off his coat and cravat and she loved the informal, bedroom intimacy of seeing him in his shirt sleeves.

He said in a conversational tone, "If you don't stop looking at me that way, you will find your bath cut short."

"I'll be out soon." She teasingly raised one leg out of the water, curving her foot like a dancer.

"Not soon enough!" He bent and kissed her forehead, then trailed fingers down the inside of her leg.

She gasped. "The water feels much warmer!"

"Don't stay in so long that anything cools," he said meaningfully.

She almost got out of the tub and followed him away, but there was no rush, and anticipation would make consummation all the more satisfying.

Julia returned to luxuriating in the warm, perfumed water and the champagne and cool, tangy drink. She must get the recipe for it.

Idly she glanced down at her breasts. The scars were mostly concealed by bath bubbles. Thanks to Randall, she was no longer repulsed by her body. She'd learn to accept that while the marks were ugly, they were part of her, and he didn't find her repulsive at all.

Julia sipped again, thinking that she was having a very good day. Benjamin had been accepted by both Lady Agnes and the Earl of

Daventry, a beautiful baby had been safely delivered, and she could look forward to an afternoon of mutual seduction.

Julia ran her free hand down her body. The bruises she'd received in the encounter with Crockett were turning interesting shades of yellow and green, but they didn't hurt much. She noticed that her nipples were unusually sensitive. It must be time for her courses.

*No.* She thought about the calendar and almost gasped aloud at the discrepancies she saw. There was only one likely reason.

But that one was impossible.

Yet when she looked at all the symptoms, the answer was the same. What should have been obvious had been covered up by her lack of belief, not to mention the considerable distractions of the last weeks.

Exhilaration bubbled through her veins like champagne. Though her heart was hammering, she stayed in the bath long enough to decide what she wanted to say. This would make all the difference in her somewhat uncertain marriage. Especially after today. She wondered how Randall felt about being heir to the earldom again, especially since he was unlikely to be superceded this time.

Her nerves knotted with hope, she climbed from the tub, dried herself, and donned her soft robe. Then she unpinned her hair and brushed it around her shoulders the way Randall liked. After slipping off her wedding ring in preparation for the scene she had in mind, she stepped out from behind the screen.

Randall was reading his correspondence in a leather upholstered chair by the bedroom window, but he set aside the letters and stood when she appeared. "You look as delicious as Aphrodite rising from the sea," he said admiringly.

She laughed. "The advantages of a classical education, and why Benjamin should learn Latin."

"Since he enjoys learning, he'll be a better classical scholar than I was. I wonder how he's getting on with Daventry." Randall's aquamarine eyes glinted. "Daventry and I will have to be civil to each other again. I'm not sure that's good. It was easier when he disowned me and I didn't have to deal with his moods."

"Now that Daventry has two descendents to carry on his bloodline, I think he'll be easier to get along with." She studied the way light from the window gilded his hair and silhouetted his broad-shouldered form as he leaned back against the sill. "At his age, being angry all the time must be tiring."

"I'm the heir presumptive again." With the light behind him, Randall's expression was impossible to read. "Is that a high enough rank to make this marriage worth maintaining? An earl is a better match than a mere country gentleman."

Julia's hand clenched around her wedding ring as his words splintered her jubilant mood like ice on a winter morning. Ice transformed to pure fire. Forgetting her carefully planned words, she snapped, "Alexander Randall, you are an *idiot*. Do you think I really care about whether or not you have a title?"

He was rocked back by her vehemence. "You should care, Julia. A great heiress can have any man she wants. Marriage to me offered you protection, but with Crockett gone, you don't need that any more."

She moved close enough to see his face clearly. Her anger dissolved. His bleak expression said more clearly than words that he believed no woman would want him for more than practical reasons. To be loved for himself was outside his experience.

She damned herself as she recognized that the conditions she'd demanded on entering the marriage had reinforced his belief. And she was no better than he was in this area. "We're both idiots, Alexander. If you'll excuse me a moment . . ."

With quick steps, she opened the connecting door that led to her private sitting room. It took only a moment to find the letter Randall had written that she could use in a Scottish court if she wanted a divorce.

Returning to the bedroom, she unfolded the letter and showed it to him. "Do you recognize this?"

"Of course." He watched her warily, as if she were a rocket on the verge of explosion. "The letter you required me to write."

She tore the sheet of paper into long strips with furious fingers. "I wish there was a fire in the fireplace so I could throw this damnable letter into the flames. Burning would be more satisfying than ripping." She crumpled the ragged pieces into a ball and hurled them into the empty fireplace.

"Excuse me if I'm not quite sure what your grand gesture means," he said carefully. "I don't want to misunderstand."

Julia sighed. "We are two very confused people, Alex. Worse than confused. Wounded. You worried that I want wealth and status. I worried that you would lose interest when I no longer needed protection. And once I saw how quickly you came to love Benjamin, I added the worry that you secretly hope I'll seek a divorce so you can find a woman able to give you children."

"I never secretly wanted you to divorce me, Julia!" he said sharply. "If our marriage ends, it will be by your wish, not mine."

"You are the one who keeps talking about ending this marriage, not me." She caught his gaze with hers. "But the fault is mine. Marriage isn't about money or passion or even children. It's a promise two people make to each other. A commitment, and it isn't quite real if one person is keeping her foot outside the door."

"Perhaps not," he said quietly. "But if the door hadn't been left ajar, you wouldn't have married me. More than anything on earth, I wanted you to say yes."

Julia felt tears stinging in her eyes. "Even after I told you I was barren. That was the greatest miracle of my life."

"Benjamin found a place in my heart on his own merits, not because I expected him to hold our marriage together." Randall's mouth twisted humorlessly. "But I did hope that would be one of the results. Though we can't have children of our bodies, there are other children who need a good home and people to care for them."

"I hoped you would feel that way." She smiled wryly. "And while I just said that passion alone doesn't make a marriage, it certainly helps. Or is the lovers' bond between us something that only I feel?"

"No." His knuckles whitened where his fingers curled around the windowsill. "No, that bond is not one-sided."

"Very well then." Julia retrieved her reticule from the table where she'd dropped it and dug out the ring she'd had made for him. Cupping it in her palm with her own ring, she extended her hand, sunlight flashing off the Celtic gold patterns. "Marry me again, Alexander David Randall. This time for always, with no open doors. I am not leaving you. Not now, not *ever*.

"And if you ever decide you want to leave me"—her eyes narrowed—"I have neither the intention nor the desire to commit adultery, so you'll have no legal recourse. You will be stuck with me forever."

He looked tense to the point of shattering. "Are you sure, Julia? I've tried very hard to fulfill my promise to let you go after a year if that's what you want. It hasn't been easy because from the first moment I met you, I've wanted to say, 'Mine, mine, *mine!*' If you commit yourself to being my wife, you won't be able to change your mind because I will never let you go."

"I'm sure, Alex," she said softly. "Now and forever, amen."

With delicate precision, he lifted the smaller ring from her palm and slipped it onto her third finger. "I love you, Julia, for better and worse, in sickness and in health, until death do us part." Taking her hand, he bent and kissed the golden band.

"And I love you, Alexander." Silent tears were streaming down Julia's face as she took the larger ring and slid it onto her husband's hand. "That's what we were missing. The ability to admit love, and to accept love in return." She raised his hand and pressed her cheek into it, shatteringly happy that he would willingly wear her ring.

His arms came around her with fierce intensity. He was warm and strong and finally, she knew, *hers*.

"I didn't believe in love at first sight," he said quietly. "So I couldn't admit it to myself, much less to you. Pure cowardice on my part. Far easier to charge a French artillery battery than to put my heart in your hands."

"You have a warrior's strength, Alex, but I don't think warriors are known for admitting to emotions," she said with a little laugh. "As a female, I should have done better, but I didn't."

"You have a woman's strength, which equals that of any warrior. Perhaps revealing one's deepest emotion must be learned." He rested his cheek on her damp hair, releasing a wisp of fragrance. "You radiate womanly warmth, which I've been seeking my whole life."

"While I sought a man I could trust." She exhaled softly against his throat, feeling utterly safe. "But brace yourself, Major Randall. I do believe that I'm with child."

"Good God!" The dreamily romantic mood vanished as he caught her shoulders and held her away from him so he could look into her face. A hard pulse beat in his throat. "Are you serious?"

"Serious as only a midwife can be," she assured him. "Mrs. Bancroft had told me that the beating and miscarriage I'd suffered at Branford's hands had damaged me too much to ever have a child. She would have been the first to admit that human bodies are mysterious, but I never had reason to doubt her opinion. That's why I didn't notice the signs that I was increasing." She grinned. "Like my short temper."

"Since you slept alone for all those years, her belief wasn't tested." He spread his hand over her belly in wonder, his broad palm warming her all the way through. "We shall have to take care that Benjamin doesn't feel that he comes second to any babies we may have. I want him to grow up stronger and more confident than we did."

"There is more than enough love for him." She laid her hand over his. "We must have made this baby the very first time we came together, at the inn in Grantham. I'm downright fertile."

"What you are is a miracle, milady." He scooped her up and carried her to the bed and laid her tenderly across the coverlet. Sitting next to her, he bent into a kiss, his lips clinging to her. "Mine," he murmured.

He moved lower and nuzzled open the robe so he could kiss her breasts, his tongue teasing. *"Mine."* Then he untied the sash and kissed her belly, which contained that pulse of new life. *"Mine!"*

Laughing again, she reached up to pull loose his shirt so she could stroke the smooth, taut skin of his back. "And you are mine, Alexander. Now take off these clothes so I can survey my property properly. Every scarred and beautiful inch of you."

His face lit up with matching laughter. "With pleasure, milady. All that I have, all that I am, is yours."

"As I am yours." She pulled his head down for another kiss.

Finally, now and forever, she felt married.

## Center Point Publishing

600 Brooks Road ● PO Box 1
Thorndike ME 04986-0001 USA

### (207) 568-3717

### US & Canada:
### 1 800 929-9108
www.centerpointlargeprint.com